REAL ROMANCE

and

THE SOMETIME BRIDE

Gemini Edition

By
Ginny Baird

Published by
Winter Wedding Press
Gemini Editions

Copyright 2012
Ginny Baird
Trade Paperback
ISBN 978-0-9851235-7-4

Cover by Darleen Dixon

****

REAL ROMANCE
Originally published in paperback by
Zebra Books
Kensington Publishing Corp.
Copyright 2000

THE SOMETIME BRIDE
Edited by Linda Ingmanson

About the Author

From the time that she could talk, romance author Ginny Baird was making up stories, much to the delight -- and consternation -- of her family and friends. By grade school, she'd turned that inclination into a talent, whereby her teacher allowed her to write and produce plays, rather than write boring book reports. Ginny continued writing throughout college, where she contributed articles to her literary campus weekly, then later pursued a career managing international projects with the US State Department.

Ginny's held an assortment of jobs, including school teacher, freelance fashion model, and greeting card writer, and has published more than ten works of fiction and optioned nine screenplays. She's additionally published short stories, nonfiction and poetry, and admits to being a true romantic at heart.

Ginny is the author of bestselling novels *The Sometime Bride* and *Real Romance*, and has just launched her "Girls on the Go" series, which premiered with *Santa Fe Fortune*. She's a member of Romance Writers of America (RWA), the RWA Published Authors Network (PAN), and the RWA Published Authors Special Interest Chapter (PASIC).

Ginny lives with her family in Tidewater, Virginia. When she's not writing, Ginny enjoys cooking, biking and just about any word game, including crossword puzzles and Scrabble. She loves hearing from her readers by email at GinnyBairdRomance@gmail.com and can also be found on Facebook http://www.facebook.com/GinnyBairdRomance and Twitter @GinnyBaird.

3

REAL ROMANCE

As the small group of guests mingled over cocktails, David turned away, searching for Marie.

"Looking for someone?" she asked, sneaking up behind him and almost startling him out of his socks.

"Marie," David nearly shouted, "don't... no," he said, halting abruptly, as her lips broke into a sensuous smile. "I take that back, surprise me all you want."

"Gracious," she said, stretching up on her toes and kissing him full force on the lips, "you're looking handsome tonight." And he did. Marie slightly narrowed her eyes, thinking she'd never seen him in a nice suit and tie before. And she liked it. Boy, did she like it.

Then again, she thought wickedly, she liked it best when he wore nothing at all.

David gave a nervous smile and looked around the room. Holy cow, was she forward tonight. Not that she couldn't be... But in public she was normally somewhat shy.

He studied her as her lips turned up in another naughty smile. "Had some champagne, dear?"

"Why, yes, I've had some champagne! And why not? We're celebrating here. Cel-e-brating! Yeee-ha!" she shouted, throwing her arms into the air and waving them.

"Marie," David said, clutching her to him and quickly scanning the room. "Maybe you shouldn't have any more."

"What do you mean, I shouldn't have any more? Hey sweet thing, why are you whispering?"

David held her even closer.

"Ouch! What are you—"

4

"Excuse us," David said to the very interested guests. Then he gripped Marie around the waist and carted her out of the room.

"What are you doing? I wanted to stay and enjoy the party!"

"I know you did, sweetheart," David said, bending low to grab her behind her knees. "But I've got a party of my own in mind."

"Hey, whoa!" she squealed, as he hoisted her skyward and threw her over his shoulder.

"David Lake, put me down!" she yelled, pounding his rear with her fists.

But he just pushed back the door and carried her into the night, where the December wind half froze her bare skin and sobered her up in a hurry.

"Who are you?" she asked, still hanging upside down.

"Just call me Fabio," he said, patting her bottom with a smile.

Chapter One

"So, what do you think?"

Marie McCloud opened her eyes wide and blinked. She saw bright blue eyes looking into hers, and a glacier-melting smile. What did she think, indeed.

When she'd walked into the spectacle shop nearly an hour ago, her vision had been so fuzzy she'd barely been able to make out the blue shirt and slacks the optician wore, let alone his muscular build. Now that she could focus, Marie was all too aware that the smooth-as-silk southern baritone was coming from a stunning specimen of masculinity.

She adjusted the frames on her nose and felt herself blush.

"Fine," was all she could manage to say through her clogged throat. "I'll take you. I mean, them."

Marie lifted a hand to wipe the tiny beads of sweat gathering at her hairline, thinking it was awfully hot in here for October. November. What the heck month was it, anyway?

"Well, they suit you," he said, sending the room spinning, as he leaned forward with an appraising smile.

The frames did look good with her chestnut brown hair. She was really quite attractive. Gorgeous, some would say. In an understated way, that a lesser man might think of as mousy. But David Lake knew better. He'd hooked up with more than one soft-spoken brunette in his lifetime. And every one of them had a fiery furnace burning beneath that creamy, cool exterior.

Something in her big, brown eyes told David that Marie McCloud was no different. The only question was, did she know it?

David checked his watch, then glanced back at her lovely face, trying hard not to be obvious. There was something in the delicate curve of her cheek, the long, porcelain line of her neck, the richly dark tendrils, spiraling recklessly from her pulled-back hair.

"Have any plans for lunch?" he asked, his lips racing with the thought that had barely formed in his brain.

She looked him up and down and blinked again, her color going all pink and cinnamony.

His hair was sandy and cropped short. Parted neatly on the side. He looked less like an optician and more like... a lifeguard. Marie froze momentarily at the thought of him administering mouth-to-mouth.

"I, ah..."

David glanced nervously over his shoulder to see if Caroline, his boss, had been listening. She'd have his head for certain. Socializing with the clients. Last time he'd done it, he'd nearly lost his job. Didn't help that Cindy had threatened to smash a whole wall of designer frames when he'd finally called things off.

"Can't." Marie sprang from her seat like a frightened cat. "Oh my gosh," she said, studying the clock on the wall, "twelve-thirty! Gotta be getting back."

"I'm sure they'll understand at..." David waited, hoping she'd fill in the blank.

"Books & Bistro," Marie added hastily, making her way toward the counter and digging for the checkbook in her purse. She bit into her bottom lip, realizing what she'd just done.

7

So now he knew where she worked, David thought, ringing up her purchase. And it was right around the corner.

"Well," he said, eyeing the soft curves of her body beneath her figure-hugging sweater dress. "You couldn't have overrun your lunch hour by that much. Surely, they won't throw the book at you."

Marie looked up at a smile brighter than sunlight on freshly fallen snow. His crisply pressed shirt did little to disguise his delectable shoulders and broad chest. The flat plane of his stomach that ran in a flawless line right down to...

Book! The only books Marie should have thrown at her were all those romances she wasted so much time reading. Silly escapism. Nothing like that ever happened in real life.

His hand grazed hers as he passed over a fabric-covered glasses case. "Hope you have better luck this time."

Marie laid down her checkbook and steadied herself against the counter. What was it in those clear, blue eyes that turned her knees to butter?

"With the glasses," David said, thinking he'd read her look. She'd been burned, that's what it was.

Bad luck with men, in a town like Covesville where the women outnumbered the male population ten to one, was commonplace in these parts. And David, he realized with a sense of shame, was partially to blame for those dismal statistics. He'd had plenty of opportunity with women. Plenty of opportunity, that was, to break their hearts. But why in the world was he thinking of that now?

Not that David ever tried to hurt anybody intentionally. It just appeared to be an unhappy by-product of his

8

becoming romantically involved. He couldn't seem to help it. No matter what he tried to tell himself, there was something about the notion of a woman demanding a commitment that made him want to cut and run.

"Thanks," she said, accepting the paperwork along with the receipt. "I'll try to be more careful."

Then David realized she was running out on him. He panicked and stepped in front of her, blocking her sumptuous body with his broad frame.

"Is there something I've forgotten?" she asked, looking up with doe-like eyes.

It took every ounce of his strength not to reach out and touch her. Not to find some excuse to...

David's hands were halfway to the edge of her wire frames before he realized what he was doing and stopped short.

"Just wanted to make sure the fit's okay," David said, his hands motioning in the air surrounding Marie's shoulders.

Marie smiled shyly. "Couldn't be better," she answered, her voice an inexplicable squeak.

Up close, he smelled as good as he looked. All musky and exotic, like some forbidden, sensual body oil sold in the back room of a Moroccan bazaar.

Marie shook her head, thinking she should have known better than to read the last chapter of *Arabian Lust* over a donut at her ten-thirty coffee break. There was something about this man, this tall hunk of masculinity, that made her feel very female. Maybe it was his look which seemed to strip her down, made her entertain fantasies of a long, silk veil and a privately viewed belly dance—with an audience of only one.

A short breath escaped her, and Marie brought her palms to her cheeks which she knew were flaming red.

"Well, good," he said, looking deeply in her eyes. "Just as long as we're clear on that."

"Clear?" Marie asked, feeling as if she'd missed something.

"That the fit is right."

He smiled and all reason plummeted to her stocking-clad toes.

"You know, we offer an unconditional guarantee."

"I'll keep that in mind," she said, drawing her purse in at her side and turning quickly on her heels.

What was happening? Why in the world were her palms so sweaty and her legs trembling? Marie shot for the exit before her feet could give way.

She thanked him again for his help, then pushed her way out the door to the street. She breezed past the paper turkey hanging on the front glass wall of the eye doctor's office. Eye doctor, her foot. He was more like some kind of psychic. A seer who could look right through her... and into the deepest depths of her soul.

No, that was crazy! That sort of thing never happened. She'd only just laid eyes on him, for heaven's sake. So what if he had a body to die for, and a heart-stopping lopsided grin? So what if he'd asked her to lunch, indicating both his immediate interest and availability?

She was not available—that was the important part. Marie glanced down at the meager blue stone on her left hand that served as an engagement ring. One of these days, Cecil was going to save enough cash from serving lattes to buy her a *real* diamond... That would be shortly after he finally sold his book and hell froze over, she thought with a slow, sad smile.

She knew she should have more faith in Cecil, but, after five long years, it was getting hard. If only he weren't so faithful, it would have been a cinch to look for someone else. But the trouble with all those someone else's was that *she* wasn't good enough for them. Just like Paul, they'd nail her heart, then chase anything in a skirt.

Not Cecil. Good old, reliable, thirty-eight-year-old Cecil. Though he was only six years her senior, at times Marie swore he was pushing one hundred.

Marie found herself wondering briefly about the age of the optician. Though he was probably a little older than she, there was a vibrancy in his eyes that spoke of youthful vigor. Enduring vigor. A relentless, animalistic...

She stopped herself, shocked at where her mind was going. Right down to his form-fitting jeans and dockside loafers. Then back up again—past his rock-hard torso and unforgettable smile, to his unnerving, brilliant blue eyes.

No! She wouldn't do this! As she'd learned from her disastrous affair with Paul, animal attraction only went so far... before the other partner started monkeying around.

It was better this way. Better with Cecil. Though he might not be the most exciting man Marie had ever met, he was certainly the most dependable. Five years together and he hadn't cast a roving eye at a single other woman. They got along, had some laughs. And, even though he never could interest her in that deep-thinking literary fiction that always had him so enthralled, at least they both liked to read.

He worked in the cafe, she sold books. He, after all, wrote books—even if he couldn't sell them. There was a strange logic to their arrangement. And a comfort, too. From one day to the next, Marie knew that Cecil would be there. And until today... that had been enough.

David absentmindedly twirled his pencil, then tapped its eraser against his ledger. Someday soon, his boss Caroline was going to spend her profits wisely and hire an official accountant. In the meantime, David looked at his chance to serve as both optician and bookkeeper as an opportunity. Next year, when he planned to open his own shop, the financial experience would come in handy. Then, he sighed, any rules about employee-client fraternization would be self-imposed. Or, not.

David knew it was wrong, really wrong, to hit on the women who came in here. And he almost never did. But when they handed him their cell phone numbers with a wink and a smile and a maybe-we-can-see-each-other-sometime look, it was pretty damned hard to resist. He was a red-blooded male, just like the next guy. And when they had legs like Suzanne, or breasts like Rebecca....

David rubbed his temples and glared at the column of numbers in front of him, willing the insubordinate figures to make sense. But the only figure that stood out in his mind belonged to one Marie McCloud. Not that she was as voluptuous as some of the women he'd dated. Not even that she was more beautiful. But there was something in the way she'd widened her eyes when she'd looked at him. Something in the warm flush of color on her skin.

David shook his head, thinking himself stupid for believing they'd made any kind of meaningful connection.

He turned half-heartedly and scanned through the contacts on his cell phone. Thursday afternoon, already. If he hoped for a respectable date—or even a not-so-respectable one—by the weekend, David would have to start calling soon.

But suddenly, he had the unusual notion that he'd be more happy spending his Saturday night with a book.

Marie blew into the cafe like a gust of autumn wind and settled her purse on the counter.

"Decaf, darling?" Joanne smiled, swabbing a dollop of cream off the faux marble serving bar.

Marie stared back at the older woman, somehow unable to fix her gaze. "Yes. No. I mean, I don't—"

Joanne extended a wrinkled hand in Marie's direction. "Slow down there." She had to be in her seventies, but with her batik skirt and sleek silver braid, sometimes looked more like a willowy teenager gone prematurely gray.

Joanne dropped her rag and leaned forward with a conspiratorial whisper. "What's wrong, doll? That Cecil done some—"

She fell silent as the ponytailed man materialized at her side.

"Morning, Marie." He smiled, and his even teeth shone white beneath his aquiline nose.

Marie sighed. "It's way past noon, Cecil. How long have you been here?"

He swiveled his head and glared at the clock. "Oh, since nine. Time flies when you're having fun."

Marie groaned. "Short cappuccino, Joanne. Double foam, nix the caffeine."

"Hey, Marie," Cecil said, when Joanne went to steam the milk. "About our dinner tonight..."

Marie adjusted her new frames and fumbled for an excuse. Somehow, in light of her lunchtime encounter, eating with Cecil seemed downright unappetizing.

"I have some revisions to do."

Marie smiled as his meaning dawned.

"Oh, Cecil, of course I understand. I have a little project I'm working on myself." She drew a sharp breath, wondering where on earth that had come from.

"You do?" Cecil asked, his gray eyes narrowing. At one time Marie would have called the color smoldering, like embers. But right now it looked... like smog.

She pulled two singles from her wallet as Joanne set her coffee down in front of her, puzzling at her new perspective. Surely, twenty minutes with a handsome optician wouldn't—

"A book?" Cecil pressed.

"Has to be romance," Joanne chimed in, securing the lid on the paper cup.

But Marie just turned the color of a very ripe tomato, picked up her cappuccino and left.

This time of day, right before closing, Marie normally perused the aisles to be certain everything was shelved properly. The upscale store paid its staff well to ensure a user-friendly environment for the average book buyer. But occasionally there were slip-ups, like when a new employee mistakenly placed *Growing Old Gracefully* in with New Age category books.

Marie resisted the urge to linger in the paperback romance section. Her feet ached and her back was sore from all the bending and stooping involved in reviewing the day's new arrivals. She'd arranged two author signings and helped coordinate an event for the mystery book club that was originally scheduled to meet in the cafe, but got bumped by a big-name local musician who'd agreed to play there on Monday. A real coup for Books & Bistro, but a major headache for Marie, who needed to accommodate the sure-fire crowd that live music brought, while avoiding the ire of her hard-core mystery fans. They, after all, bought more books on a regular basis than any other group—apart from romance aficionados. As a compromise, she'd offered to help sponsor a "Who Done It" wine and cheese tasting in the store's lounge area, complete with samplings from "mystery" local vineyards whose identities would be revealed at the evening's end.

Marie blew a hard breath and sent a loose lock of hair flying. And to think she'd gotten into the bookstore business because she loved to read! She rarely ever had time for it. Which is why she was so often caught red-handed over her Danish and coffee with something just as steamy as her java.

She paused mid-stride, trying to remember which way she was going. Somehow her eye had fallen on one of those gloriously embossed crimson covers, the kind boasting a manly hero with an admirable show of muscle. The title said something about a pirate and his mistress. Marie studied the male model's tawny ponytail, comparing it to Cecil's. Well, he certainly had Cecil's hair, but the body definitely belonged to...

Marie snatched her glasses off her nose and humphed into the air. Twenty minutes. Twenty minutes was all he'd had. Yet somehow it had been enough to leave his mark. She'd felt as branded by his smile as by the hottest, deepest kiss. As ravaged by his eyes, as... Marie cleared her throat and placed her glasses back squarely where they belonged. She smiled pleasantly at a passing patron who nabbed the pirate book off the shelf and openly ogled its cover. Then blushed at the thought that she had probably looked just like that only hours ago—right in the center of the spectacle shop.

Chapter Two

David made himself as comfortable as possible at the tiny cafe table. But no matter how he positioned his legs, his knees knocked against the low table top.

A ponytailed man wearing a forest green apron walked over, notepad in hand. "What will it be tonight?" he asked, his light eyes squinting.

David peered over the server's shoulders and into the book aisles. Well, he certainly couldn't order her. How much simpler life would be if you could just ask for what you really wanted. Marie McCloud, please. Single, with a dash of daring.

The waiter impatiently shuffled his feet.

"Coffee?" he asked, flipping his too-long ponytail over his shoulder.

If the man had to wear one, David decided, it would be much to his advantage to shear it an inch or two.

"Sure," David said, lowering his voice. "Say, you know any women in here?"

The waiter shot him a disgusted look.

Well, so maybe he wasn't into women. But, hey, he at least had to know who his coworkers were.

"Decaf or regular," the waiter deadpanned.

David read his name tag. "Look, Cecil."

Cecil raised one skeptical eyebrow.

"It's Cecil, right?"

"If you're in here to read, you're in the wrong section." He jutted his chin in the opposite direction. "Plenty of books over there."

17

David turned his head just in time to see the swish of a floral print skirt disappear behind the newsstand. His pulse shot up and his internal thermostat skyrocketed. The cold Virginia fall couldn't touch the current fire in his veins.

"I'll give you a minute to make up your mind," Cecil said, turning to go.

"No, wait!" David reached out a hand and the waiter recoiled. Not that it necessarily mattered to David. The only person he cared about right now stood about five foot six and had the smile of a vixen.

"Do you know that woman over there?"

Cecil raised an eyebrow. "You know, there's a ladies' night at the bar down the street..."

"Decaf is fine," David said, pushing back in his chair with a scowl.

What was this guy's problem? All David had done was ask one little innocent question. Okay, so maybe it was two.

Cecil returned quickly with a lukewarm cup of sludge that he passed off as coffee.

"Anything else?" he asked, setting down the ceramic mug.

Nothing, apparently, that this guy would help him with.

David studied the neat geometric patterns on the imitation tile floor, as Cecil tore a sheet from his pad and laid the check on the table.

"Listen..." Cecil surprised David by softening his businesslike tone. "Didn't mean to come off hard as nails earlier. It's been kind of a long day, if you know what I mean."

"Don't worry about it," David said, forcing a smile. Waiter-with-an-attitude probably wanted a tip.

Cecil pushed his pencil behind his ear in a professorial fashion and appeared to study his surly customer.

"Is it someone special? Or are you just in here shopping?"

David sighed and sipped from his cup. "I hate to shop."

"Ah, but you love to buy." Cecil folded his arms in front of him and looked smug when David didn't answer. "The direct approach always works well for me."

David gave Cecil's narrow shoulders a second look, wondering what he'd missed. A ladies' man? This guy? Well, he'd heard that some women liked the ultrasensitive, underfed type...

"Of course"—Cecil beamed—"it helps that women love artists."

"You're a painter?"

"Better yet. I write."

Better for this place, David guessed, casting a quick glance around the packed cafe. A few couples here and there. But mainly, plenty of women. Single women, David gauged, from what he knew of Covesville.

"So, then. You're into literary types, too?" David flashed Cecil his best let's-be-buds smile.

Cecil laughed. "Let's just say I've been around enough to know you can't always judge a book by its cover. And when you get between those covers..." He grinned. "You read me?" he asked with a wink. "These brainy girls"—his pale gray eyes scanned the room—"really dig a mind link. Give them an intellectual connection, and they're all yours."

"Mind link?"

"Sure, you know. Talk about Plato, or Voltaire. Meet them on their level."

The between the covers part, David understood, and Plato he'd heard of. But Voltaire sounded more like a fast car than an aphrodisiac. "So, it's books we're talking?"

"Of course, books." Cecil nabbed the bill off the table and scribbled some notes on its back. "Here are a few recommendations. And stick your nose in a *Publishers Weekly*. See what's hot."

"Cecil," David said, laying down a five-dollar tip, as Marie and an elderly woman walked by. "Thanks very much."

Marie leaned against the wall next to the water fountain in the narrow hallway and shook her head at Joanne.

"It's no use. I just can't pretend any longer."

"You're trying to tell me that all of this has happened in the last two days," Joanne said. "But my guess is, it's been building longer. I mean, look, I know you were disappointed with that puny excuse for an engagement ring."

Marie shoved her left hand deeper in the pocket of her nubby brown cardigan.

"He hasn't got it, Marie. Better you face it now than later. After, say, you've produced two or three kids together and are still waiting on that first advance check from a publisher."

"But what is *it,* Joanne? I've spent my whole life looking."

"Baby," Joanne said, patting her shoulder. "You weren't even born when I started my exploration of the great male species. The only thing I can tell you is when it's there, you know it. And when it ain't, no amount of wishful thinking will make it so."

Marie stayed still a moment, examining her friend. Though her ivory skin had wrinkled, there was an ageless quality to her features, an impish mischievousness in those coal-black eyes.

"Joanne, how is it that a hot mama like you never married?"

"Too busy being hot to cool down for the aisle, I suppose. Or maybe I just missed my chance and didn't know it."

Marie bit her lip and waited for her to finish.

"The thing is, Marie, my problem was always the opposite of yours."

"Opposite?"

"Yes, sweetie. Too into the physical aspect, that's what I was. Free love and all that. It came with the age. Age of Aquarius. I was an old maid of fifty then, and it was liberating!

"But for a spring chick like you..." Joanne clamped her hands around Marie's shoulders and stepped closer. "Honey, a nice girl like you deserves to have it all."

Marie tilted her chin toward the well-meaning older woman. "But I've had that. Don't you see? I've had all that hot-and-bothered stuff. And I ended up with a broken heart."

"And then you met Cecil, who's about as exciting as a dead fish. And you're finally starting to see that dead fish—like company—stink after three days." She grimaced. "Much less five years."

"Excuse me..."

Marie felt her skin go hot as a deep familiar voice rose over Joanne's shoulder.

"Could you ladies tell me where to find—"

Joanne stepped aside and there he was. A vision in trim white jeans and a navy sweatshirt that did nothing to conceal the raw power that lay beneath it.

"Well, what a surprise." He smiled and sent the whole room spiraling. "Marie, isn't it? Marie McCloud?" Oceans of blue crinkled slightly at their corners as the wave of his stare crashed over her.

"Umm, hmm," was all Marie could manage in the drowning silence.

Joanne whistled between her teeth and walked back into the store without saying a word.

"Friend of yours?" David asked, placing his hand up on the wall near Marie's head and inclining his body in her direction.

Speak, Marie willed herself. Say something. Anything. "You've got quite a memory for names, Mr.—"

"Actually, it's the faces I remember best," he said, dropping his chin a fraction lower. Not to mention that her body was one David couldn't forget. Somewhere beneath that fuzzy, wool sweater and modestly swishy skirt lay a very womanly form. He'd seen it at least a million times since Thursday. In his daydreams, that is.

"David," he offered with a smile. "The name is David. David Lake. The optician, remember?"

As if Marie could forget

"Although I don't think we were ever officially introduced."

She looked up at him with those big brown eyes and blinked. "Well, then, you had me at a disadvantage."

Not as much as he would have liked.

A fine wash of color was working its way across her face, but she stood her ground—burgundy suede boots planted firmly in place, daring him with her damnably intoxicating eyes.

"Sorry about that," he said. "Not many clients are really all that interested in knowing my name."

"I doubt that," she said, stunned at where that courage had come from. Flirting! She was *flirting* with the most godlike male she'd laid eyes on in a decade and her fiancé was right in the next room!

"Excuse me..." said another familiar voice.

Marie swung her head around and choked. "Cecil!" she said, coughing past the lump in her throat.

"Jeez, Marie," he said, leaning forward and giving her arm a little squeeze. "Just going to the stock room. You look like you've seen a ghost!"

He gave David a curious glance. "You be sure she gives you good service, now! If there's anyone here who can get you what you want, it's Marie." Then he slipped between them and headed for the back of the store.

Marie didn't worry about blushing in front of David anymore. She was sure, by now, that he assumed crimson was her natural color.

In light of what had just transpired, David seemed remarkably nonchalant. He just propped his hand back up on the wall in its pre-warmed spot and smiled sweetly.

"Is he always that friendly?" David asked.

No, she'd been wrong. His hand wasn't propped exactly where it had been before. It was higher now. Off center. In a way that enabled him to stand even closer than the first time. Close enough to leave Marie completely overcome by his delectable aroma. The manly scent that would intoxicate her, if he'd only stay near.

"Pardon?" she asked. Knowing, just knowing, that whatever he'd said had flown right past her. Boy, this was bad. Badder than bad. She had to find a way out of here so she could think!

"Cecil."

"Cecil? You know him?"

A rich, bubbling laughter erupted from his chest. "No, not really." David paused and cocked one eyebrow. "But he sure seemed to know you. Boyfriend?"

"No," Marie said, biting her bottom lip. "I mean, friends, yeah, sure. Good ol' Cecil is friends with the world!" Never once in the past five years had she lied about her relationship with Cecil. But since those feelings were now so unclear, was it really lying at this point?

"Yeah, I know his type," David said in a conspiratorial whisper. "Regular Don Juan."

"What?" Marie ducked her head and inched back a step so David no longer held her prisoner.

David dropped his arm to his side. She'd gone from embarrassed red to positively white. "Did I say something to upset you?"

"No. Not at all." Marie felt the heat well within her like an exploding volcano. "It's just that Cecil..." She gave a noncommittal laugh.

"Oh, I know," David said, his eyes wide with amazement. "Not what you'd expect at all. But I guess it's romantic to look like a starving artist. I've heard some people find that very exciting."

"Well, I guess some—"

"Like you, for instance?"

24

"Me? Oh, heavens..." Marie stammered. "Well, you know, I don't think I could really say."

"But he is popular with the—literary types, I mean."

Marie wrinkled up her nose. Hey, wait a minute. Wait just one minute! All this talk about *Cecil?* Oh my God, David wasn't... couldn't possibly be asking because...

"What," he asked, with utmost innocence. "What in the world are you staring at? Did I get coffee on my sweatshirt or something?"

"Are you interested in Cecil?"

David just looked at her for a long moment. A slow grin spread across his face. "Me? Holy cow, *me?*" He sputtered and began to laugh.

Marie gripped her own face in horror, realizing her terrible mistake.

"I only just met him today. Besides," he said, with a teasing grin, "he's not my type."

Marie arched both eyebrows above her turquoise wire frames.

"Females, Marie. I like females," he said, emphasizing the word by making a curving gesture with his two sturdy hands.

"Oh," she said, exhaling slowly. "I'm sorry. So sorry if I implied—"

"Well, there's a first time for everything, I suppose. Not that I'd ever—*ever* been accused of..."

She looked positively petrified.

"It was a misunderstanding," David said, steadying her shoulders in his strong grip. "Really. Let's forget all about it."

A jolt of sensation ripped through her and she felt somehow awakened by his touch, all over her body.

25

"Hey," he said, brushing the back of his hand over her burning cheek. "All's forgiven. Really."

Forgiven, maybe. Forgotten, never. Marie had the feeling she'd always remember this. No matter what, she couldn't erase the memory of his tender touch, of an attraction so real, so physical that Marie's only punishment would be in his letting go.

But this was wrong. Terribly, terribly wrong. Despite the way he looked at her, despite the way he made her feel, she'd made her pledge to another man.

"David," Marie said, her breath catching in her throat. "I'm engaged."

David blanched and crammed his hands into his jeans pockets.

"Engaged! Well, isn't that terrific! Ah, what a great coincidence that is."

"It is?" Marie asked, the blood draining from her face.

"Why, sure. You're the bookstore manager, aren't you?"

Marie nodded.

"Then who better to help me pick out a wedding planner?"

"Wedding planner? *You're* engaged?"

He gave her a humble smile that sent shivers down her—very committed, she reminded herself—spine. "Not me, my sister."

Well, it was a half truth, David told himself. Debbie had already been engaged three times. The fourth time was sure to follow.

Marie was embarrassed at the rush of relief that came at his words. The image that immediately came to mind of

David Lake looking handsome in a tuxedo and a boutonniere was enough to make her hear wedding bells.

"So, you'll help?" he asked, his blue eyes shining.

Marie swallowed hard and directed him to the entertainment and weddings section, her knees trembling ever so slightly with each new step. Really, she thought, giving herself a swift mental kick, the last thing you should have read during your dinner break was the wedding scene from *Groom To Be.*

When Marie got home later that evening, she was surprised to find a note from Cecil taped to her computer.

Great news, it said, *finally got that check from Knopf...*

Knopf? Cecil had sold a book to Alfred A. Knopf? If he'd already gotten the advance money, it had to have been weeks ago.

Diane and I...

Diane? The cappuccino girl with the body piercings?

Oh, God. Marie plopped down in her chair and tugged off her boots.

She yanked off her glasses, polished them with a tissue, then set them back on her nose, remembering something. Cecil and the lithe twenty-two-year-old Diane huddled over a back issue of *Publishers Weekly* sharing some private joke.

Yep. It was Diane, all right.

Diane and I have moved to New York. Please try to understand and please don't call. I'll come back for my stuff in a few months if you'd like to box it up.

Cecil.

Chapter Three

David held the big wedding planner in his hands and flipped through its spiral-bound pages.

"You getting hitched?" Caroline asked, her voice weighted with skepticism.

David spun in his chair to face his blond bombshell boss. Funny how he'd stopped noticing how good-looking she was the moment she'd started barking out orders. She was a tough businesswoman, but fair. And, not so incidentally, a contented wife and the mother of two children. Definitely off limits. Caroline chided him about settling down, in a tolerant big-sisterly way. Not that she was that much older, but her superior professional status brought out the mother hen in her. David suspected he was about to get pecked on.

"Can't a man do a little leisure reading on his lunch hour?" David asked, with mock defensiveness.

"Sure, read these," she said, dropping a stack of files on his desk.

David leaned back in his chair and propped his feet up on his desk, crossing his legs comfortably at the ankles.

"You can work me like a slave driver eight hours a day, but these forty-five minutes," he said, clutching the thick planner to his chest, "are mine!"

"All right, big boy," she said, laying a hand on her hip. "What's in there? Honeymoon lingerie, perhaps?" She made a move toward the book.

"Not so fast," David said, holding her back with an extended hand.

"It's not..." Caroline's slender shoulders sagged. "Tell me it's not your sister Debbie heading down the aisle yet again."

"It's not Debbie," he said with a flawless grin.

"Okay, David," Caroline said with a giant lunge in his direction, "give it here."

She caught one end of the large book in her hand and tugged.

"Hey!" he yelped, dropping his feet to the floor, as a sheaf of papers spilled forth. "Give that back!"

"David, I swear, if there's something pornographic in—"

Caroline yanked and the planner tumbled to the floor, pages fanning out in wild disarray.

"What's this?" she asked, nabbing an unfolded brochure off the floor. "A Books & Bistro events calendar?"

"Oh my God, David," she said, furiously fanning her face with the flyer. "This is worse than I thought! You're actually reading!"

Marie crumpled up another tear-stained tissue and added it to the heap on the floor. In the three years since she'd been promoted to manager, she could count the times she'd called in sick on one hand. And today was one of them.

Cecil and Diane? How could she have been so blind? And right under her nose!

And what—if anything—did the mysterious heartthrob David Lake know about all this? *A regular Don Juan,* he'd said in reference to Cecil. Marie clutched her stomach, fearing she would throw up. How many? Just how many other women had there been, then? Five? Fifteen, twenty? Oh, God.

Marie stood and rushed to the bathroom where she vomited violently.

Thank God she wasn't pregnant, she thought, as her bare knees hit the cold tile floor. She rested her head in her hands over the porcelain john, recalling Cecil's recent suggestion that they make a baby.

"Don't you think it'd be better if we got married first?" was all she had asked.

He'd stormed out the door, and not come back for five hours—at which time he'd produced a bouquet of limp daisies and a half-hearted apology. "One commitment at a time," was what he'd said.

It had been a cruel thing to say, knowing how badly Marie wanted a child. For a while, she thought she'd never want to have her own. But, as time moved on and that old biological clock started ticking, she'd begun to change her mind.

After her parents' car accident, she'd practically raised her four younger brothers and sisters. Her mother had died instantly, and her father had become permanently disabled. At age sixteen, Marie had been thrust into the role of running the household, scrounging together nutritious meals on the meager checks from her dad's disability payments.

Those had been some dreadful days. Coming of age as a woman and yearning for her mother, all the while having to hide that fact because "mother" was precisely what she had to be.

Marie stood and splashed cold water on her face, feeling better.

Now, each of her siblings was on his own. Her two sisters married, Johnny engaged, and Mark just enrolled in graduate school. She'd done a good job with them, she supposed. But then again, so had her father. He'd been a rock for the family until he'd died last spring. Always keeping his chin up, despite his paralysis. Never too tired or preoccupied to listen.

Marie knew her sometimes unruly brothers wouldn't have turned out nearly as well without their father's patient wisdom to guide them. At times, they'd driven Marie so crazy with their teenage antics, that her only refuge had been to escape to her room with a book.

Reading had seen her through the difficult times. No matter what was going on outside her bedroom door, she could curl up under the covers and imagine that someday a handsome prince would come along to take her away from all of it.

But all the handsome princes in Marie's high school class went off to college while she had to stay home and help support the family.

Her first job in a bookstore was heaven. She felt a comfort in the unending rows of books, a special camaraderie with the host of unexplored fictional characters—just waiting for her touch to reveal their secret worlds.

Marie walked to the kitchen and poured herself a glass of water, wondering what she would do with herself today. It had been at least a year since she'd had a Sunday off. She was out of books and out of money, and the local library was closed. Oh well, she thought, flipping on the coffeemaker. There was always a walk in the park. Maybe the fresh air would do her good.

David pulled back as Jupiter strained at the leash.
"Whoa there, boy! Hang on!"
But it was David who was hanging on for dear life as the black Lab fixated on the squirrel with a whine, and then another... *yank!*
David stumbled forward as the big dog broke free and bolted into the trees.
He rubbed his sweaty palms on his pants and looked frantically in all directions. Now what was he going to do? Caroline would kill him if he lost her stupid dog.
"Jupiter! Here, fella!" he called in his biggest, booming voice.
Nothing.
He forcefully clapped his hands together and tried again.
There was a slight rustling in the bushes behind the park fountain.
"Jupiter!"
The movement stopped.
David had an idea. He placed two fingers between his teeth, spun around and whistled—hard.
"Most people just say hello."
David jerked his head sideways.
There stood Marie McCloud in a knee-length overcoat, hands fitted tightly over both ears. Her cheeks were flushed with morning cold, her lips the prettiest shade of pink.
For a moment David forgot all about the dog.
"Marie!"

"What," she asked, giving the park a suspicious sweep of her eyes, "exactly are you doing?"

"Oh," he said, letting out a full breath that clouded the air, "looking for Jupiter."

Marie's eyebrows shot up. "Hate to tell you this, but I think you'd have better luck at night."

David looked blank. Blank, but incredibly handsome, she decided. Even in his ratty gray sweats, and sky-blue parka. Didn't hurt that the color of his coat matched his gorgeous eyes.

"Oh!" he smiled, his whole face lighting up. Then he laughed in that rich, rumbling baritone Marie liked so much.

"Not the planet," he said patiently. "Jupiter is Caroline's dog."

Oh, Marie thought, as disappointment hit her hard. So he *was* taken. She felt her temper begin to simmer. Taken, and yet he'd still invited her to lunch?

Marie stared down at the leash dangling in David's hand. "Well, I'm sure Caroline won't be any more upset about you losing her dog than you hitting on your clientele."

"Client..." David's voice fell off, as his face turned a hue akin to purple.

"One question, David," Marie asked, her anger growing. "Do you always make passes at girls who wear glasses? Or, was I special?"

"I, uh..."

His neck was crimson, and his ears so vivid they looked like they were about to fall off.

At that moment, a frisky black Lab bounded out of the bushes and made a beeline for her knees.

"Hey there, big guy," she said, bending to scratch the salivating animal behind its ears.

Marie stuck out a hand and snatched the leash, instantly clamping it on to Jupiter's collar in one deft move.

"Go home to Caroline, David," she said, standing and handing over the lead.

"Home?"

Marie turned and began walking out of the park.

"Wait!" David said, racing to meet her, Jupiter galloping at his side. "Caroline's not at home!"

Marie cast him a sideways glance through heir glasses. "Sorry, David. I'm not into that. You'll have to do your two-timing with someone else."

She picked up her pace and kept going.

"No, you don't under—"

Jupiter collapsed in a heap and rolled sideways.

"Get up!" David pulled on the leash, but Jupiter just lowered his head to the pavement, tongue lolling out.

David looked up at Marie's curvy figure disappearing through the morning fog.

"Wait! Don't go! You've got it all..."

But it was too late. She'd already melted into the mist.

David put down the book and rubbed his temples. Holy cow, this was going to be even harder than he thought. What was the deal with this stuff, anyway? The dialogue wasn't even in quotation marks, for God's sake. So how in heaven's name was he supposed to know who was saying what? Much less thinking it?

David massaged his aching knees in frustration and stood to grab a beer.

He walked to the refrigerator, picked up a bottle and popped the top. Was she really worth it? David had never done anything like this before. Gone completely overboard for some woman. Some women who was *engaged,* for crying out loud. And she disapproved of him anyway, because she thought he had a woman named Caroline at home.

Marie was neatly tied up in a relationship that meant matrimony eventually. But then again, maybe it didn't. That was the hope David clung to. He knew from his sister Debbie's experiences that engaged women didn't necessarily walk down the aisle every time. Heck, for some women, it seemed to be a whole lot like shopping. Don't like the man after a while, return him. Nonetheless, David wanted to believe that once Marie committed to him, her shopping around would be over.

David froze as an ice-cold swig sliced down his throat.

Of course, that meant that his shopping around would be over as well... No more late nights with Candy, the aerobics instructor, or Lizbeth, his sexy new mechanic.

David took another swig of beer, letting the panic pass.

He was getting way ahead of himself here. Thinking about happily-ever-after! Holy cow. That wasn't what he wanted...

Was it?

He wanted Marie's attention, sure. But the exasperating woman didn't seem to want to give him a second look.

At first, there'd been a gleam in her eyes. That telling sparkle that told David he had half a chance...

But after the park, she'd acted like she could barely stand the sight of him. Even when he went into her store to buy some of Cecil's recommendations.

He'd approached her directly, but she'd claimed she was busy setting up some kind of wine tasting and assigned a flunky to help him.

Give him a break! Did Marie really expect David to believe they'd be serving wine in a bookstore? They couldn't possibly have a liquor license. Unless, of course, the brother of the guy who owned the place, who just happened to be the sheriff, had called in some favors at City Hall.

David set his beer on the counter, and began to imagine himself and Marie running down the steps of City Hall, hand in hand, smiling and happy. Her dark, wavy hair was piled high and studded with wildflowers, sweet curls breaking free to frame her glowing face.

David coughed loudly and shook his head. Next he would be seeing babies!

Better get back to his reading, he thought, carrying his brew to the armchair. All this fantasizing was getting him nowhere. And David Lake wasn't made for dreams. He was built for action.

Now, if he could just finish this blasted book, then maybe he'd be able to convince Marie his actions spoke louder than words.

Chapter Four

Marie surrendered the floor to a round of applause.

"Thanks, Chad," she said, walking over and taking the sheriff's hand.

"No problem, hon." He smiled as his silver hair caught the light. "I like a good who-done-it just as much as the next guy." He leaned forward and winked. "Just as long as the bad guy winds up behind bars."

"Didn't know you had the time for reading, Sheriff."

Chad let out a laugh. "Well, I'll tell you a secret if you keep it quiet..." He brought his head to hers and whispered in her ear, "The life of crime is dead in Covesville."

Marie laughed and patted Chad on the arm. "Since you've got to be here anyway, pull up a chair and join us."

"Think I'll do that," Chad said. "To tell you the truth, Marie, it's been kind of hard to fill the hours since my Emily passed away."

She caught a glimpse of Joanne, bending low to shelve books at the far end of the aisle.

"I know it's been a rough couple of years," she said, smiling warmly at the older gentlemen. "You sit. Plenty here to take your mind off that extra time you've got on your hands."

Then she walked down the aisle and asked Joanne to take Chad a complimentary glass of Chablis.

"Mind if I join you?"

Marie raised her eyes from *Destiny's Desire* just in time to see David break into a broad grin.

37

"Looks good," he said, surveying the flesh-revealing cover.

She settled her book next to her cup of cold coffee and checked her watch. "Not working today?"

"Boss gave me the day off."

"Look, David," Marie said, stopping him from pulling out a chair, "I'm really not interested."

"Of course, it helped that I took such good care of her dog."

He must have showered just for the occasion and put on an extra splash of cologne, because he smelled even sexier than the last time he'd been this close. The time he'd laid his strong, masculine hands on her yielding flesh...

Wait a minute! That was *Destiny* talking. Destiny, the heroine from her steamy historical novel who had the hots for a man named Cane. A man she'd sworn was sweeter than sugar.

David picked another chair at the table and sat down, undaunted.

"Hey, that Jupiter was a real handful."

"Jupiter?" she asked, stifling her surprise.

"Sure, you've met him. Big, black hairy beast with a penchant for civil disobedience."

If she'd been outdoors, Marie was certain her glasses would have fogged with embarrassment.

"Are you telling me that Jupiter, the dog you were with, belongs to your boss—Caroline?"

David nodded. "Caroline Richards, a real taskmaster."

"So why take care of her dog?"

"Oh, well, she needed a favor. Besides," he said, leaning over with a whisper, "I have a soft spot for the physically challenged."

38

"Oh, poor woman," Marie said, thinking of her father. "What's she got?"

"Two kids and a husband," David answered.

"What's so challenging..." Marie thought of her brothers and stopped herself. "Was that supposed to be funny?" she asked David, who had begun toying with her book.

She slapped her hand down hard upon its cover to prevent him from picking it up.

David coolly withdrew his hand and settled it under his square jaw. He gazed into her eyes, seeming to search for something.

She was even more gorgeous than he remembered. Tastefully dressed in a black turtleneck sweater that made the most of her curves. If only he could figure a way to get her fiancé out of the way... Out of the way of those beautiful brown eyes.

"Has anyone ever told you how pretty you are?"

Marie stood abruptly from her chair, knocking the tabletop with her knees and sending her coffee dregs sloshing.

David sprung to his feet and piled napkins on the mess. "Whoa! Hey! Where are you going?"

"Coffee break's over, David. My boss didn't give me the day off."

Unbelievable, Marie thought, leaving him there with coffee dribbling on his shoes. Utterly unbelievable!

"Well, I really don't see what the harm was in a cup of coffee," Joanne said, as she closed down her register.

"It wasn't the coffee, Joanne, but the sugar that went with it."

Joanne smiled understandingly and shook out her hair. It wasn't often she wore it that way, long and straight down her back, salt and pepper streaks enlivening the gray.

"I think he's sweet on you."

Marie scanned the day's receipts, then set down her clipboard. If she didn't know better, she'd swear Joanne was humming a love song.

"Jo-anne?"

Joanne looked over with a distant smile.

"Something going on I should know about?"

"As my boss or my friend?" Joanne asked.

Marie tapped her fingers against her chin. "Why, Joanne Bright, to look at you one would almost think there was a man in your life!"

Joanne turned the most curious shade of peachy-amber.

"No need to sound so surprised, love. You're the one who turned him on to me."

"Chad?" Marie asked, trying to keep her jaw from dropping.

Sure, that had been her idea. But she'd never dreamed it would work. Chad and his late wife Emily had been together since grade school. He'd never in his life looked at another woman.

"What?" Joanne asked, setting both hands on her hips. "Did you think me incapable?"

Oh, no, Marie definitely believed Joanne was capable.

Marie felt her lips pull apart in a half laugh, half smile.

"Oh, Joanne," she said, rushing forward and taking her friend in her arms. "I'm so happy for you."

"Thanks, sweetie," Joanne said, returning the hug and patting Marie soundly on the back. "Now, it's your turn."

Marie pulled back, suddenly overcome with emotion.

"Oh," she said, tears spilling forth, "Joanne."

"Hey, hey," Joanne said, stepping forward and taking Marie in her arms again. "Everything's going to be all right."

Marie shook her head, her eyes hot, her lips trembling—grateful that, at this hour, no one else was left in the store.

"You just don't understand, Jo. I've had my chances. Two of them. And I blew them both."

"You, angel, didn't blow anything. It was those devils disguised as men who did the damage."

"They're all devils," Marie said, more tears bursting forth. "Demons... with the impulse to destroy."

"Well, maybe he's not like that."

Marie lifted her head from Joanne's shoulder and stared into her eyes with a betrayed look.

"He thinks I'm engaged, Joanne. *Engaged.* And today he had the audacity to call me pretty."

Joanne gasped and brought her free hand to her mouth. "The gall!"

Marie softened her anguished face into a semblance of a smile.

"Sweetheart," Joanne said, dabbing Marie's damp cheek with a tissue. "You shouldn't blame the poor man for being persistent. You are quite a catch, after all."

"Joanne," Marie said, holding the older woman so tightly she nearly breathed her in, "you should have been a mother."

"Well, to see that old coot Chad in action," Joanne said, with a shy grin, "I would almost swear he's working on it."

41

David scanned the groom's checklist for maybe the twelfth time in the last two hours. He closed the wedding planner wearily.

"Ridiculous," he said, sighing out loud. If all the to-dos on that list were optical prescriptions to be filled, David would be grinding glass indefinitely.

And, from what David had heard, that would only be the start of it. After the wedding, then the honey-dos would begin. "Honey, do this..." and "Honey, do that."

David caught himself smiling and realized with surprise that he'd actually enjoy Marie ordering him around. He stretched back in his chair indulging in a fantasy about just what she might order him to do. But his fun was interrupted by his ringing cell.

"David, this is Caroline. Look, I have to wait at the doctor's office with Sally. Hope you can hold down the fort the rest of the afternoon."

David swung his feet to the floor and cleared his throat.

"Sure thing, Caroline. Been working like a madman, but another hour or two alone won't kill me."

"Thanks, David, I really owe you."

"No problem, boss. Say, how is your little girl anyway? That fever of hers any better?"

"Not really." Caroline huffed into the phone. "The nurse thinks she might have chicken pox."

"Chicken pox? Holy cow."

"Yeah, right, say a prayer. Please. I can't have chicken pox right now. The nurse says she'll have to stay out of daycare for at least two weeks. I knew I should have gotten her that vaccine, but Jim insisted..." Her voice dropped off and David could tell she was covering her cell while she talked to someone else. "...Oh. Oh, okay, just another minute," she was saying.

"David? You still there?"

David slid the wedding planner in his desk drawer and shut it.

"You bet. Hey, I'm awfully sorry about Sally."

"You and me both! Well, anyway, the receptionist says I have to get off the phone. I really appreciate your filling in."

"This afternoon's no problem, Caroline. Don't you worry."

"This afternoon? David, I'm talking about possibly the next two weeks."

Two weeks with no supervision and the whole place to himself? David grinned wickedly, because he knew she couldn't see it.

"You can count on me to keep things humming."

Marie stretched out her neck and rolled her head on her shoulders. She'd been having trouble getting into the swing of things all day, and now this. Her children's storyteller called in sick. Something about a chicken pox epidemic, and guess whose kids had it?

She shrugged and tried to work out the tension in her shoulders but it was useless. In less than twenty minutes, she'd have to put on her most sunshiny face and go greet the mini-masses.

Oh well, she thought, studying the shelves for something appropriate, that's what being a manager meant. When someone didn't show, you stepped in. The show must go on, and all that. Particularly with the sales the children's department had been racking up since Marie had initiated story hour.

Marie sat on the cushioned stool and watched as the kids filed in, grown-ups in tow. Mothers, mostly. But there were one or two dads. And, oh yes, how sweet—a set of grandparents.

"Well, boys and girls," she began, after checking the wall clock. "Does anybody know what month this is?"

"Novemberary!" somebody shouted.

Marie smiled warmly at the little boy in oversized britches. "Very good... You're Tommy, right?"

Tommy ran a hand through his curly red hair and beamed from ear to ear.

She'd thought she'd recognized him from last week when he'd come by to search for birthday books with his mother.

"Right! November! And who here in this very intelligent crowd can tell me what holiday comes in November?"

David followed the turkey noises to the back of the store. The older lady at the front desk—-Joanne, he thought, she said her name was—told him that Marie was doing story hour. David hadn't been exactly sure what that meant until he came upon Marie and the group of children following her.

David half hid himself behind a cardboard book display and watched in amazement as Marie led a line of unruly "turkeys" around the children's book department. Amazingly, it looked like even a couple of grandparents had joined in!

Marie stopped and pulled the glasses off her nose, laughing as a giggling band of children thrust themselves at her legs. She was enchanting, David realized. Absolutely charming...

And, he remembered, as someone rudely nudged past him, engaged to someone else.

David was just regaining his balance, when a second person pushed by him, completely upsetting his footing. David cast one desperate glance in Marie's direction and saw her meet his eyes with a horrified look, as he grabbed the softcover book display and carried it with him as he crashed to the floor.

For what seemed like endless seconds, David kept his nose buried in a mound of tumbled paperbacks, praying he'd awaken from this nightmare.

And then he felt her hand on his shoulder.

"David?"

It was Marie's voice. Marie's beautiful, soft voice. David swallowed hard and looked up.

"Oh my God, David! What happened? Are you okay?"

Well, at least he didn't look damaged. Only embarrassed, as well he should be. Pulling her latest merchandise to the floor. Really. What was it about this man that was just so...

Hunky, Marie thought, as he brought himself up on all fours and stared into her eyes. Heavens, he looked like a panther in that pose. And his smell...

Marie's eyes flashed at the suggestion, but then she shut them tight, recalling where she was.

"Here," she said, extending a hand, "let me help you up."

"Marie," he said, dusting off his jeans. "I'm so sorry. I'll pay for the damage. And help pick up. Whatever you want me to do."

She tried not to let herself think too hard about that, and picked up a couple of books to examine their spines.

"I think they'll live," she said, trying to sound flip while struggling to control the butterflies in her stomach.

"I ruined your story hour," David said, his face sagging as scattered hordes of children made their departure.

Marie tugged at the neck of her dress that suddenly seemed too tight.

"Oh, no. Really. Story hour was just winding down."

David righted the cardboard display and started restocking it with books, his muscular buttocks tensing under denim with each swinging movement of his arm.

Marie found herself unwilling to leave him there all alone, what with the buxom brunette in the corner who seemed to be making the same study of David's anatomy.

"Say," she said, once he had neatly finished up. "You're pretty good at that. Need a job?"

"I'm not unemployed, if that's what you're thinking."

"No, but..." It was hard to keep the smile from creeping onto her lips.

"What? What is it?" David gave himself a quick once-over, as if to verify that his clothes weren't on backwards.

"I was just thinking," Marie said, "that you must be doing a doggone good job with Jupiter for Caroline to give you all this time off."

David gave her a disarming smile that made Marie wish she hadn't started this banter.

Slow down, girl, she told herself, drowning in his deep blue eyes. You 're getting in way over your head.

46

"She's given me the rest of the afternoon," David said, diving into her with his stare. "Got plans?"

Marie wanted to say yes, prepared to tell him to go take a long walk off a short pier.

But then he crinkled his eyes and his playful lips turned up in another uneven smile, and she told him she left work at six o'clock.

Chapter Five

"Where are we going?" Marie asked, as David held open the door to Books & Bistro, letting her leave first. He had a bulging green backpack slung over his shoulder and was wearing the same blue parka she remembered from the park.

"It's a surprise," he said, with a mischievous smile.

Marie wasn't so sure she should be setting herself up for surprises with this man. He'd already surprised, her enough, with the way he sent her pulse racing, and her emotions all out of kilter.

She scanned the small gravel parking area. Inside the ultra posh Books & Bistro, Marie could almost envision herself being in any cosmopolitan city in the world. But once she stepped out into the fading Virginia twilight and caught a glimpse of the Blue Ridge Mountains, she knew she was very much at home.

Covesville wasn't really much to speak of. There was this strip mall and a few downtown restaurants, plus a park, the mountain lake, and the small but distinguished women's college that sat high on a hill in the center of town.

"Where's your car?" she asked, noticing he had stopped on the curb.

"No car," he said, bending to open a padlock attached to a chain wound round a brick pillar and through the back wheel of a glistening ten-speed bicycle. "We're going by bike."

Marie gasped and brought her hands to her cheeks, staring down at her short cashmere dress.

48

"Don't worry," he said, throwing her a wink. "You'll be riding on back. I won't see a thing."

"Say," he said, shooting a glance at the bookstore. "Isn't there someone you need to call?"

"Call?" Marie asked, still wondering how she was going to modestly lift her leg over the high bar of that man's bicycle.

" Fiancé, maybe?" David said, feeling he had to ask.

Okay, he told himself, let's get this all out in the open. Acknowledge what you know. Woo her in a gentlemanly fashion. Then, after she's had a glass of wine—or two—ask her how serious she is about this guy, anyway.

"No," Marie said, giving a little cough. "No one to call."

"Now," she asked, buttoning up her lambs wool coat. "How do I mount this thing?"

David took a deep breath and strapped his backpack to a rack above the rear wheel. He wasn't altogether sure he'd be able to pedal straight with her riding his seat, her cushiony bosom pressed up against his back...

He felt his ears go tingly and knew he was reddening from the neck up.

"Here," he said, swinging his leg over the bike, "let me get on first, then I'll help you."

David steadied himself above the bar, then turned to look at her.

"Just hang on to my shoulders and hop on. The seat's all yours. I'll ride standing."

"Standing?" Marie asked, settling her rump on the hard leather seat and doing her best to tug down her creeping hemline. "Then how will I—"

But her words were lost in a rush of wind, as David lifted his lean hips and started to pedal.

49

David picked up speed and wheeled out of the parking lot, heading north.

Marie found herself clinging on for dear life to—of all things—David's rear end. She tried to center her hands on his undulating hips, but they kept slipping forward as he increased his movement with the speed of the bike. Oh my, she thought as the fingers of her right hand cupped around something hard in his jeans pocket.

She jerked her hands up to his waistline, but the bike wheels met the stones of an old dirt road and her left hand mistakenly traveled down his rock-hard thigh.

"Marie, sweetheart"—David grinned as he peered over his shoulder—"maybe we should wait until we get where we're going."

Her face burned as hot as three-alarm chili. Oh my God, he thought she was attacking him!

"Where are we going?" she yelled above the cross-winds.

Marie slipped her hands under his parka and grabbed for the waistband of his jeans, digging her thumbs under his leather belt. There, she thought, gripping his hips with splayed fingers. Now everything would stay put.

Well, well, David thought, grinning to himself. He was enjoying this ride even more than he thought he would. He'd been right about Marie. Right from the start. They had chemistry together, her fiancé be damned.

He shifted gears and brought the bike to a moderate crawl.

"Almost there," he told her, wondering why she had stopped doing what she'd been doing. Well, there'd be plenty of time for that. Plenty of time to allow those lovely fingers to explore.

David steered his bike into a clearing by a group of pines. Ahead of them, the quiet waters of Grassy Creek glimmered in the fading light, catching a purplish reflection of the distant mountains.

"A picnic?" Marie asked, as David dismounted and helped her get off the bike. Despite the fact that she'd lived here all her life, places like this were breathtaking still.

The breeze picked up and Marie huddled her arms around herself for warmth.

"Too chilly for you?" David asked, heating her with his smile.

"No, I'll be all right," she said, poking at the backpack he was carrying. "What's cooking?"

"Well," he said, looking around, then settling on a spot not too far from the water. "How do submarine sandwiches and wine sound?"

Marie heaved a sigh, grateful he hadn't decided on one of those fat-free tofu dinners Cecil had been so fond of.

"Perfect," she said, grabbing one end of the red plaid blanket and helping David stretch it flat on the ground. Maybe, just maybe, this would go well.

"Marie," David said, uncorking the bottle as she decided where to put the knees that insisted on sneaking out of her too-short-for-a-picnic length dress. "I hope you're not getting the wrong impression from all of this."

She blinked hard, thinking she couldn't have heard him correctly. This was a date, right? A romantic waterside picnic by Grassy Creek.

David placed two plastic cups on the blanket and filled each halfway before looking up. "I mean, I know you're committed to someone else and I'd never—"

"Never what, David? Ask out a woman who was engaged? Pursue her relentlessly in her place of business? Fall all over the floor of her store?"

David hoped that the elongating shadows from the pines hid his slight frown. She was supposed to be impressed by his gentlemanly reserve. Not, as was apparent, ticked off.

"I couldn't help myself," he said, handing her some wine, then holding his own in her direction.

She accepted the cup and took a long swallow without making a toast.

"Marie, you've got to listen to me," he said, desperate for the words that would bring her back to bicycle mode. "I'm not the cad you think I am. I'm a gentleman, really."

She arched both eyebrows over her turquoise wire frames and downed another sip of wine before speaking.

"Well, well," she said, her eyes showing a dangerous amount of emotion. "Prove it."

Uh-oh, this was a trap and David knew it. "Ah sure, anything. What can I do?"

"It's what you can say, David."

A trick! He knew it. Holy cow. David held his breath and counted to ten, before exhaling slowly. "All right then, so what is it you want me to say?"

Marie put down her wine and stared out at the sun that was sinking below the shadowy mountains. "What I'd like, what I'd really like, is for you to give me something no other man has."

David sat at attention, liking the sound of this.

"The truth."

It was David's turn to drink some wine. And he did, emptying his entire cup. "Okay," he began cautiously. "I'll give you the truth. What kind of truth are you looking for?"

Marie turned her deep brown eyes upon his and David could've sworn he was falling off a cliff.

"I've got to know why, David. Why me? Or is it just me—and not a whole slew of others?"

David shifted his position just slightly, feeling cornered. Of course, it was just her! She'd tortured him, turned him inside out. He'd been so far gone he was actually reading wedding planners and literary fiction, for crying out loud! Still, David couldn't deny the feminine names that took up so much space on his contact list any more than he could ignore the pounding in his chest.

"Nobody's ever done for me what you do," he said, settling on a truth that wouldn't give too much away.

"Ah, but," she said, shaking a scolding finger in his direction, "are there others out there still doing it for you?"

That seemed like a mighty personal question from a woman who was supposedly engaged.

"And what if there were?" David asked. "What precisely would it be to you?"

"Nothing," she said, her face expressionless in the near darkness.

"Nothing?" he asked, riveted to his soul.

Marie was startled by the pain she saw in his eyes. He'd wanted her to care. Wanted her to say she hoped he'd be her one and only, with eyes for no one else.

David pulled a couple of submarine sandwiches from his backpack.

"Might as well eat," he said, handing her a paper package. "Never good to drink on an empty stomach."

Marie had to agree. The one cup of wine she'd had was going to her head. She felt dizzy and depressed, and very much as if she'd made a mess of things.

David turned away and devoured his sandwich before talking again. And when he spoke, his words were bitter.

"What gives you the right to press me about my love life, when you're the one who's engaged?"

"Oh, David," Marie said, bringing her coat sleeve to her mouth and feeling as if she were going to burst into tears. "I have no fiancé. Not anymore."

David balled up his napkin and spun to face her in the moonless night.

Her eyes looked moist behind her glasses and her lower lip was trembling.

"No fiancé?" he asked, his voice a low vibrato.

She removed her glasses and shook her head.

And, with an overwhelming certainty, David knew he would have to kiss her—and kiss her as no man had before.

Chapter Six

"I think I need to go home," Marie said, getting abruptly to her feet as David leaned toward her.

"Why?" David asked, springing off the blanket, his head still spinning from the wine.

She feigned a shiver. "It's getting cold out and I..."

Cold? At the moment, David felt anything but.

"...have to be at work early."

"But Marie," David said, putting his hands on her shoulders. "We were just getting started."

Boy, didn't she know it. Getting started all over again. Getting ready to fall right into his two masculine arms.

"Here," she said, stepping away so he couldn't touch her and stooping at the edge of the blanket. "Let me help you with this."

David ran his hands through his hair, trying to think of what to do next. Picking up the blanket? No way. This was not supposed to be happening, now that he wanted to take her in his arms and tumble her to the ground.

David stood by helplessly as Marie tugged the blanket out from under his feet and folded it neatly.

"Ready?" she asked, giving him a pleasant smile he thought better suited to one of her story hour attendees.

"Ready," he said, somehow imagining that the ride going home wouldn't be nearly as exciting as the one coming out here.

David stuffed another potato chip in his mouth as Caroline leaned a hip against his cluttered desk. Her little girl did have the chicken pox. And, because she was going to be mostly at home for the next two weeks, Caroline felt the need to come in for an hour to give David all the necessary instructions.

"Don't know what I did wrong," he said, between gobbles. "I mean, I thought you women were really into that romance stuff."

"We are," Caroline said with an indulgent half smile. "But not, maybe, if you fellows come on too fast."

"Too fast? This thing has been moving so slowly I swear I can hear those wheels scrape the pavement every time I see her!"

"Come now, David. Really, what's it been? One week?"

Caroline kicked off her heels and breathed an audible sigh of relief.

David perched a handful of chips in front of his mouth and paused.

"About that, I guess. But Caroline, you know how it is. Usually the girls are all over me!"

Caroline gave a hearty laugh, inched backwards and settled her rear on his desk.

"Kind of gets to your ego, huh?" she asked, swinging her legs freely as she sat there making a study of him.

But it wasn't his ego, really. It was something more like an itch. An itch he couldn't scratch and it was driving him crazy.

"I can't take it, Caroline!" he said, heaving himself forward and pounding his fists on either side of his head as it collapsed to the desk. "I'm not that strong a man!"

"Oh now, honey," she said, running her affectionate fingers through his hair, "from where I sit, you are made of steel."

David heard a nervous cough and looked up to find a startled Marie standing in the threshold to the back room.

"I just came..." she trailed off weakly, her face turning pink. She held up a bent pair of turquoise frames, apparently almost unable to finish. "...to redeem my unconditional guarantee."

"Slow down there a minute, child," Joanne said as Marie wheezed into the ladies' room sink. "I can't understand a word you're saying."

"Don't you see? I bent my frames on purpose. On purpose, Joanne! Just because I got to thinking I'd made a big mistake..."

She burst into sobs again and honked into a tissue.

"Made of steel! I swear, I'll never forget that woman's face as long as I live."

"Honey," Joanne said, lightly rubbing her back, "Don't you think it's possible you got it all wrong?"

"Wrong?" Marly snorted. "I don't think so. She was half naked, for heavens' sake!"

Joanne narrowed her eyes.

"Well, she'd already kicked off her shoes..."

Joanne hefted her large leather purse onto the counter. "You're going to be a mess introducing that touring book author. A real mess. Here," she said, her arm disappearing into her cavernous bag. "Let me see if I've got something in here that can help you."

"Joanne," Marie said sternly, lowering her slightly crooked glasses. "If it's one of those psychedelic drugs from the sixties..."

Joanne laughed and produced a roll of hard candies.

"Lemon or cherry?" she asked with a subtle smile.

Marie popped a cherry candy in her mouth and wished that all the men in the world were as easy to deal with as Joanne. She blew her nose again, then cleared her throat.

"So, how are things going with Chad?" she asked, surveying her ghastly reflection in the mirror. She'd have to redo the blush and the lipstick for sure, she thought, fumbling through her own pocketbook.

"Oh, honey, don't you worry about me and Chad. That old gray fox and I have an understanding."

"Oh?" Marie asked, applying a dab of lipstick.

"Yeah," Joanne said, her dark eyes twinkling. "He understands what I like and vice versa."

Marie chuckled and swept on a little blush, finally feeling half human. "It's taken me a while," she said, packing away her makeup in her purse. "But I guess I can now see why you found matrimony so distasteful."

"Distasteful?" Joanne asked, puckering up her lips and examining her own image in the mirror. "Heavens, did I say that?"

Marie slapped her on the arm. "You most certainly did! At least, that's how I took it."

"Well then, love," Joanne said, fiddling with her braid and pinching color into her cheeks. "Maybe you got that wrong, too."

"Joanne!" Marie said, her eyes sparkling with disbelief. "You're not—"

"I am," Joanne said with a cryptic smile.

Marie tugged on her bedtime socks, thinking about Joanne's remarks. She was certain the other woman wasn't telling her everything that was going on between her and Chad. At least their relationship had a chance. All this fantasizing about David Lake was getting out of hand. It was wonderful to imagine that he was Prince Charming, the gallant swain that romance novels were made of. But it would only be a matter of time before cold, hard reality hit.

David was sexy, attractive—yes. But Marie needed more. A person she could talk to. Somebody with whom she could share a passionate love of life. She'd never really had that with Cecil, or—goodness knows—with sexy Paul. With Paul, it had been all smoke and fire, until the whole thing had entirely burned out and Paul had gone on to someone else.

With Cecil—well, there wasn't exactly fire, but the two of them at least could carry on a conversation, even if they didn't always totally agree. Cecil simply worked too hard at being eccentric. And, to Marie, eccentric wasn't something you became, it was something you were—like it or not. But Cecil seemed to like the image of the "starving artist" very much. Organic foods and vegetarian cuisine were his mantra, but when no one was looking he was sneaking off for fast food burgers at the edge of town. Marie knew this because she'd found a whole store of paper wrappers wadded up under the front seat of his car.

If she'd applied half the investigative skill she used in tracking missing merchandise to dissecting her relationship with Cecil, she would have seen him for who he really was sooner. As it turned out, he'd been hiding more than the burger wrappers. He'd concealed his lust for another woman and the very important fact that he'd finally sold that incomprehensible book! He'd never even let her read it. Hardly a testament to the trust between them.

Marie nabbed the romance novel off her nightstand and settled back against the headboard.

She was curious to see what direction her favorite historical novelist, B. B. Knight, had taken the noble MacMillan clan... and their ignoble forefathers. If there was anything that could take Marie's mind off her worries, it was a muscular man in a kilt.

David pushed the disconnect button on his cell phone for the third time in a row. She would kill him, that's what she'd do. He checked his watch and saw it was five past nine. Books & Bistro had just closed its doors, and Marie had been nowhere in sight.

"Went home early," Joanne had told him. And then she'd surprised him by slipping him Marie's cell number.

David wasn't sure what Marie had told Joanne about him, but from the elderly woman's encouraging reception, David suspected that she felt a whole heck of a lot better about him than Marie did at the moment.

Until he drew his final breath, David would be haunted by the total disillusionment—and shock—he'd seen in Marie's eyes. She hadn't stayed to hand over the glasses. Just turned tail and run like a frightened rabbit.

Caroline had advised him to go after her. But he'd known there was no way on earth he could have explained away what she'd seen right then. Better to give her time, he'd decided. Even though Caroline had huffed and somehow sided with Marie. Holy cow, Caroline had caused the problem! And there she'd stood, slipping her skyscraper shoes back on, telling him that he was the one making mistakes.

David inhaled deeply and tried Marie's number again. He was just about to hang up a fourth time when she answered.

"Hello?" she said, as his throat closed up. "Anybody there?"

"Marie, this is David. David Lake," he said, praying she wouldn't press *end call*.

Of course it was David Lake. How many other Davids did Marie know who sent shivers down her spine just from the sound of his voice?

"I know what you must think of me, but I wanted a chance to explain."

She wasn't speaking, so he plowed right ahead. "I know what you walked in on looked bad, but it wasn't what you thought at all. Holy cow, Caroline's my boss!"

"How convenient."

"Oh, no. It's like that," David stuttered. "She was just giving me some advice."

Marie wasn't altogether sure she wanted to hear this.

"Look, David, the picnic was nice and all, but forgive me if I say I've already figured you out."

"Think what you will, Marie, but none of it's true. I mean, yeah, maybe once..." Did he need a speech therapist or what? He couldn't seem to get words out and have them make sense. David ran a hand along the damp back of his neck. Thirty-five degrees out and he was sweating!

"Marie, a lot has changed about me that you don't know. You don't know me at all, in fact."

She knew him well enough and intended to keep it that way. More than she'd realized at first, Cecil had left her in a

61

fragile state. Now was no time to go getting mixed up with a handsome optician who left her unable to see straight.

"David," she said calmly. "It's late, I'm tired, and I'm afraid I'm all talked out."

"Well, that's too bad," David said, his scowl almost visible through the phone, "because talking's precisely what I had in mind. Fun talk. Nothing heavy. Just you and me, a cup of coffee somewhere. We could get to know each other a little better."

Marie's heart skipped a beat. Hadn't she just been thinking...? No, she told herself, violently shaking her head. She wouldn't fall for it.

"Besides, I've been reading something I think you'd really like."

"Oh?" she asked, her damnable interest piqued. If there was any way to get to a bookstore manager, it was by talking shop. "What is it?"

"Now that wouldn't be fair for me to give away all my conversation in advance, would it? Let's just say you and I might have a lot more in common than you seem to think."

Marie bit her bottom lip, telling herself not to buy it. Not to be hopeful, stupid—or both. "I don't know," she hedged.

"One hour, one cup of coffee is all I'm asking."

Well, she thought, fanning her romance book out on her chest with a sigh, what would one cup of coffee hurt? Even the fourteenth-century heroine of the book she was reading had decided to give her dastardly hero another chance.

"When and where?" she asked, sounding resigned.

The whole staff of Books & Bistro pressed their noses to the frosty glass and watched as David held his cell phone high above his head and did a celebration dance around the gravel parking lot.

And he didn't even care what they thought.

Chapter Seven

David pulled up to the small white house with the dormer windows and wicker porch swing, and smiled in reflection. Somehow it seemed just like her. All homespun and comfortable, but pretty and inviting. Its neat front walk was lined with tapered boxwoods, while the large red oak near the center of the yard filtered morning sunlight through its turning leaves. A vision of a tire swing hanging from one of the old oak's sturdy branches came to mind. But David quickly dismissed it and hurried up the steps to the house. He was ten minutes late already.

Marie checked her image in the hall mirror for what seemed like the hundredth time. If this was such a casual thing, then why did she feel like a schoolgirl about to entertain her first beau? She yanked the rubber band out of her hair, deciding the ponytail looked too perky. She was going to get better acquainted with David, not audition for the cheer-leading squad.

She adjusted the straps on her corduroy jumper, thinking maybe she'd tried too hard to look conservative. One of the sweater dresses would have been better. David had never been able to take his eyes off her when she'd been wearing one of those. Of course, David always seemed to check her out no matter what she was wearing, and in a strange way Marie found that extremely stimulating. No other man, including Paul, had seemed so totally smitten by her appeal.

The doorbell rang, nearly jolting her out of her shoes. She took a quick second look at the way her loose wavy hair fell about her shoulders, and decided it was okay. But, oh God, her glasses!

Marie lay a sweaty palm on the doorknob, knowing it was too late to do anything about those now.

"Hi!" she said, pulling back the door.

The crisp scent of autumn rushed past her, carrying his musk oil scent, and she nearly fainted.

"Hi," he said, one hand coyly tucked behind his back. He smiled and his eyes seemed as blue as the morning sky. "I brought you something."

"Oh, you shouldn't—" Marie started to protest, but when he whipped out a jumbo bag of candy-coated chocolates, she changed her mind.

"Why, thank you!" she said, hating herself for blushing. "How did you know I had a weakness?"

"All women..." David started to say, but he caught himself. Smart move, he chided himself. The playboy image is precisely what she's looking for.

He chuckled and shrugged his wide shoulders.

"Well, to hear Debbie tell it, all women love chocolate."

"Debbie?"

"My sister."

"Oh, the one who's getting married!"

"Ah, yeah. Right."

Marie smiled.

"Say," he said, motioning toward the door, "we seem to be letting an awful lot of heat out. Should we get going, or are you going to ask me in?"

Marie turned every shade of red on the spectrum, thinking he didn't know the truth in his words. Her internal combustion engine was fired up and running—right away with her reason.

"Oh, here," she said, "I'm so sorry. Yes, please come in while I get my coat."

David stepped through the threshold and into the sweetest-smelling house he'd ever been in. There was a lingering scent of cinnamon, fresh flowers, and—he swore—something that smelled just like gingerbread. For all intents and purposes, he could have stepped back in time and walked right into his grandmother's home in rural North Carolina.

"Nice place," he said, looking around. Although a bit cluttered, everything was neatly arranged. There were some nice pieces, antiques, David thought, but mainly just comfortable furniture that had seen a lot of living. "Real settled."

"Settled?" Marie asked, sticking one arm into her coat, as David walked over and hoisted the rest of it onto her shoulders.

"Yeah. Not much of a bachelorette pad, if you know what I mean. Reminds me of my grandma's house."

She pushed her glasses up on her nose and buttoned up her coat. "In a good way, I hope."

David's smile was genuine. "In a very good way, Marie," he said, his voice pleasantly husky. "I loved my grandma's house. You live here with your folks?"

"Mother died when I was young, my dad—last year," she said, taking pains to keep her eyes on her keys.

"Oh, I'm sorry."

"Well," Marie said forcing a brave smile. "Don't be too sorry for me. I've still got some pretty good memories of my mom, and my dad was a terrific father to all of us."

"All of you? How many are there?"

"Well," she said, seeming to brighten at the opportunity to show off her family. She crossed to the upright piano at the end of the living room and picked up a picture frame.

"This is Johnny. He's the oldest and has just gotten engaged to Meg. This was taken at their engagement party in July."

She pointed to a photo of another man who looked a lot like Johnny but wore a mustache. "This one's Mark. And this is my sister Jill with her husband Dan, and this one's my baby sister Teresa with her husband Jack."

Her sisters—one blond, the younger one brunette and resembling Marie—were pretty women. But, as far as David was concerned, Marie outshone them both.

"Quite an attractive bunch."

"We hold our own," she said, smiling proudly. "How about you? You have a big family?"

"Just me and Debbie." David gave her a wry smile. "She's the oldest, but you'd never know it."

"And your parents?"

"Dad's in banking down in North Carolina. Mom's made a career out of the Junior League."

"How wonderful she can volunteer."

Yeah, David thought. If only she'd spent a comparable amount of time with the only two children she had. If only his father understood that a man was worth more than the money he made—or in David's case, didn't make.

"Shall we go?" Marie asked, looking down at her watch. "I do need to be at work by noon, and it's almost ten-thirty."

"Your chariot awaits," David said, holding back the door. "Watch your step."

Which was precisely what Marie intended to do, especially since she had the sinking feeling that the rug was somehow going to get pulled right out from under her.

"Didn't know you owned a car," Marie said, sliding into his old Mazda.

He gave her a startled look and then burst out laughing. "Hey, the bicycle is mainly for work. It's close to where I live; I hate to think I'm polluting the environment just to go two blocks."

Uh-oh, Marie thought, red flag number one going up. This was Cecil talk. Not that she didn't believe in protecting the environment. It had been her, after all, who'd suggested Books & Bistro use recycled paper products. But something about the idea that David would have anything in common with Cecil Barnes made her faintly sick to her stomach.

"Glad you liked the chocolates," he said, changing the subject. "I'm a big fan myself."

Marie raised one eyebrow. A male chocoholic, now that was something. "Next you're going to tell me that you like Tater Tots, and devour potato chips by the handful."

David laughed and hung a left down the main street, leading to campus. "I am a bit of a junk food junkie," he said, looking sideways with a mischievous grin. "But please don't hold my gourmet ice cream against me."

Marie's mind painted a really naughty picture of her and a very naked David getting creative with a pint-size container on her kitchen floor.

She blinked, then leaned forward—instinctively jamming her hand under the car seat.

David pulled his car to a stop at one of the only two traffic lights in town.

"Mind telling me what you're doing?"

Marie slammed back in her seat, acutely aware of her blunder.

"Looking for rice cakes?" she said with a sheepish shrug.

David laughed so loudly that he didn't see the light change.

"Huh?"

He collapsed in hilarity again, white knuckles gripping the wheel.

"Light's green," she said, with a nudge.

"Oh, right," he said, straightening himself in his seat with another burst of laughter.

He put his car in gear, then pulled up to a nearby curb beside the *Cafe Ole Coffee Shop*.

David shut off the ignition, then turned to look at her.

"Now, why on earth would you think I'd hide rice cakes under my passenger seat?"

Marie sunk her chin below the collar of her coat.

"Wild guess?"

"That I'm a closet health nut?" David chuckled again. "No worries there, sweetheart."

"Come on," he said, scooting around the car and opening her door, "let's go in and get some coffee with plenty of white sugar. And cream."

Marie stayed, nailed to the passenger seat by his guileless eyes. What in the world had she been thinking?

That he would hide an addiction to rice cakes, just as holistic Cecil had concealed his penchant for fast food?

David gave her a crooked smile and Marie's heart beat faster.

"Coming out?" he asked, his smile broadening, "or am I going to have to come in there and get you?"

Her heart beat faster still, just imagining what that might entail.

"No, it's all right," she said, composing herself. "I can manage."

David held out his hand, but she steadied herself against the car door instead and climbed out. No way was she going to touch him now. Now that her palms were slick and her cheeks hot pink.

David took her by the elbow anyway and helped her out of the car.

"Are you always this chivalrous?" she asked, "Or is it because I remind you of your grandmother?"

Marie caught a twinkle in his eye and sensed he was thinking something that she didn't care to know.

"You bring out the gentleman in me. What I can I say?"

"Ah, so you finally admit," she teased, as they crossed the sidewalk to the cafe, "that you're not always so gentlemanly."

"Guilty," he said, with a sheepish look as he held back the heavy glass door. "But I can promise you this. I've never, ever done anything a woman hasn't wanted me to do."

Marie swallowed hard and selected a table. Something about David made her believe that a woman would actually get down on her knees and beg for his manly attention.

Not her, she decided with a shake of her head. She was getting to know him, that was all. As a friend. But Marie hadn't had a male friend in—she didn't know how long. That was exactly her problem. She'd gone from one long-term relationship to the next. What she needed now was a breather, not a man who left her breathless.

"So, what would you like?"

Marie looked up into his vibrant blue eyes. Maybe this wasn't such a good idea, after all.

"Coffee," she said, realizing the waitress had appeared at their table. "Coffee and an orange scone, please."

"Scone?" David asked, with feigned indignation. He leaned in with a gravelly whisper, "Not nearly enough sugar."

David turned and directed his attention to their server. "I'll take coffee, too, with double cream. And bring me one of those gigantic cinnamon buns with the icing dripping all over it."

The waitress nodded, and started to turn.

"No, wait! Make that two!"

The waitress's face was an open question.

"Cinnamon buns."

"David Lake, every one of those perfect teeth is going to rot and fall out."

"Marie, now you're sounding like my mother! Have you ever tried those things? They're wicked with a capital W."

No, Marie thought. Wicked with a capital W was sitting right in front of her. She didn't know how he could really eat like that. But David Lake didn't appear to have one surplus ounce on his entire body.

71

"So, David," she said, trying to get things on a more intellectual tract. "Tell me more about that book you've been reading."

But somehow, it was terribly hard to think about that boring book, with the exciting Marie McCloud sitting right across from him. She looked cute in that strappy brown jumper, pulled over a tight-fitting shirt that David wished he could see more of. Her cheeks had that gorgeous glow and her eyes fixed on him in that manner that made his head spin. David noticed her glasses sat slightly off center. Most likely thanks to that nasty dent right in the center of their bridge.

"I can still fix those glasses for you, you know."

"Huh?"

Marie brought a startled hand to the edge of her frames.

"Uh, I forgot they were... What I mean is, I can still see straight." No, that was baloney. "Fine, I mean. I can see just fine! The lenses weren't damaged at all."

"You sure about that?" he asked, reaching forward and gently lifting the glasses from her face. "Because usually when the frames get bent..."

He took the turquoise frames and turned them over and over in his hands before holding them up to the light.

"Now that *is* odd. Not a scratch on them. How did you say this happened?"

Marie blanched. "I, uh, it was the..."

"Looks almost like a child just—"

"Yes, that's it!"

She cowered, realizing her voice had risen about the buzz of the restaurant, and made an effort to speak more softly. "One of the kids at story hour—he bent my frames."

"Wow!" David said with surprise, as the waitress set down two steaming mugs. "Never realized your work was so dangerous."

Marie nervously stirred her coffee, wishing she knew what was going on behind those crystal blue eyes.

"Oh, not really so dangerous. You know kids get a little wound up at times. He didn't mean it, I'm sure."

"And the mother didn't even offer to pay to have them fixed?" David asked, dumping four packets of sugar in his cup. "I think that's awful."

"Well, what with the guarantee and all that, I figured, why make a big deal?"

David studied her as her spoon clinked repeatedly in her black cup.

"Don't you think you want to put something in there before you stir it?"

A nervous laugh caught in her throat. "I take mine black."

The waitress rescued her from further humiliation by bring their pastries.

"Well, anyway," David said, handing back her glasses, "if you want to drop by the shop later this week, I'd be happy to try to straighten those out for you—or replace them with another pair."

Marie was so flustered at the moment that all she could think of was downing her coffee and getting to work. Children's story hour? Heavens to Betsy, what had she done? Blaming some poor, innocent, imaginary little boy. When all the while it had been *her* pressing her flawless frames against the ladies' room sink counter!

"You feeling all right?" David asked, unrolling a bit of cinnamon bun and dipping it in his milky coffee.

"Fine, fine." Marie took a bite of scone, hoping she wouldn't choke. "Mmm, this is delicious."

"You sure you're okay? You look a little... hot."

Now that was the understatement of the year, David told himself. Marie McCloud always looked more than a little hot. No matter where she was, no matter what she wore, when she looked at him with those big brown eyes, she positively sizzled.

But she did look uncomfortable, sitting there going crazy with that rotating spoon. A little off balance somehow. Then she picked up her mug and drained one third of the coffee out of it before setting it back on the table.

"Well, it's true I haven't been feeling myself lately. Maybe there's something going around."

David nodded sympathetically. "Maybe you should take the day off. Grab a little R & R."

She looked over at him, and—for a brief second— seemed to be considering it.

"No, we have a staff meeting this afternoon. And I have book orders to review."

"Well, surely they'll understand if you—"

Marie stole a glance at her watch. "Oh my gosh, it's eleven-forty! David, we'd better get the check and get going."

Well, he thought, pulling out his wallet. He could never be accused of not trying.

The idea of a whole uninterrupted day with Marie McCloud tantalized David with all kinds of possibilities. He could create opportunities to get close to her and—

"Ready?" she asked, polishing off her coffee.

But, at that very moment, David feared that rising from the table would show her precisely how ready he was.

"Can you give me another minute?" he asked, stalling for time.

And then he called over the waitress and asked for a very tall, very cold glass of water.

Chapter Eight

David pulled out of the Books & Bistro parking lot, thinking things had gone exceptionally well. There had definitely been some body-talking going on between them. And, no matter how abruptly Marie had wanted to leave, David couldn't help but believe that part of the reason she'd wanted to go had to do with her growing attraction to him. He'd seen it in her eyes, sensed it in the air between them at the outdoor picnic. Even that day in the park, there'd been a spark of something mixed with an admirable ire. Boy, she was a hot one. But impossible to pin down.

No, not impossible, David told himself. Nothing was impossible right up until the point you gave up trying.

What David needed, he decided, was a new angle. That book angle he'd been working on. He was sure that's what had been holding Marie back. Idle conversation and casual picnics weren't enough for a brainy woman like her. Cecil had been absolutely right. The mind link was what David needed to establish. He knew it was a little deceptive, given his honest aversion to what he'd been reading—one of Cecil's recommendations. But, in the end, it would hardly matter. He and Marie were meant for each other. David just knew it.

The literary connection would be just the beginning. After that, he was certain they'd find other things they could talk about. Other hobbies and ideals they shared. This was just too powerful, just too earth-shaking to mean nothing but sex.

David wanted more.

Now that he'd finally finished that damned book, all he'd have to devise was a creative way to...

David signaled for a turn then let out a cry. He slammed his palm into the wheel and honked merrily at an unsuspecting passerby, as he maneuvered a quick U-turn.

Today was definitely his lucky day.

Marie closed the cover of *Too Tempted Far Words* and let out an audible sound that was half pant, half sigh. She didn't even know people had that much fun back then. But it certainly had left the heroine smiling.

"Marie?"

She looked up and realized her coffee had gone cold.

David held up one of her fleece-lined gloves.

"You left this on the seat of my car. Thought you might be wanting it later."

What Marie would be wanting later had nothing to do with putting things *on,* she realized with a jolt.

Ever since page one hundred and seventeen, every third description of this book's hero had seemed better suited to David than a sixteenth-century nobleman. Right down to his enticing... oh, never mind.

"Thanks," Marie said, biting her lip. "Didn't even realize it was gone. It must have slipped out of my pocket."

"Don't worry about it," David said, brightening the room with his smile.

All afternoon, it had been pouring, the small cafe shadowed and gloomy from the rain outdoors. But suddenly, it was all warmth and sunshine in here and Marie regretted that her coffee break had ended and it was time to get back to work.

"I'm sorry, David," she said, standing. "But I've got a staff meeting in five minutes."

"And afterwards?"

"And afterwards, I've got inventory. Cash register receipts. A chance to review the coming week's schedule—"

"Excuse me," David said, clearing his throat. "And just where does the fun get penciled in?"

"Fun?" Marie asked, clutching her book to her chest as if he could see right through its very cover and know exactly what she'd been reading.

"Oh David, I don't have time for..."

But the way that he looked at her told her that she did.

"We never did get to discuss that book," he persisted.

"Oh right, the book!" she said, relieved to be on a safe subject. Nobody could shake Marie McCloud when it came to books. Now there was an area in which she felt confident.

"I could bring it by, if you want."

"By where?"

"By your house, of course. I've already finished the whole thing." And was that ever an accomplishment in his mind. "And I was thinking it would be great if you read it, too. Then we could discuss it."

Well, that was an intriguing proposition. As long as Marie could keep her mind on whatever he brought and her hands off the delivery man.

She tried to sound nonchalant. "I won't be home until after nine."

"Is ten o'clock too late, then?"

"Ten is fine," she said, feeling her whole world careen out of focus.

David showed up at ten sharp with—of all things—
Silence In The Trees.

"A literary thriller?" Marie asked, trying hard not to remember that the author's previous work had been Cecil's favorite, and that this one featured a philosophical serial killer who was forever quoting Nietzsche.

"Why yes. Have you read it?"

"Not yet," she answered, an unexpected queasiness in her stomach.

"Well, great," he said, standing under the dim porch light, night sounds echoing all around him.

Marie had planned to ask him in, had straightened the house and whipped up a batch of store-mix brownies. But... *Silence In The Trees?* Her stomach clenched.

Marie knew she was supposed to be impartial. And she was, when it came to book store management. She studied demographics, knew her market, purchased what would sell in this little town. But when it came to her personal taste, Marie much preferred works with dialogue in quotation marks and no Nietzsche.

"Thanks, David," she said, feeling very much like she wanted to be alone.

"No problem." He smiled and backed into the darkness. "I'll be looking for you at my shop. Stop by and left me know what you think of the book. Oh, and I'll fix those frames."

Marie tossed *Silence In The Trees* onto the coffee table and sunk into the sofa, removing her glasses. Red flag number two, she thought, massaging her throbbing temples.

David just might be a self-proclaimed environmentalist with a pretentious literary bent.

This was what she had feared was coming. The one-two punch at the end of her long day. The stark reality of life in the not-so-fast lane.

Well, who had she been fooling anyway? To think there'd be someone out there just like her had been ridiculous. Impossible. And in Covesville, impossible things weren't happening every day.

Marie waited a respectable two days, then decided to return *Silence In The Trees* to David. She'd read some of it—but she couldn't stand to have the book taking up space in her house one day longer.

If this was what David was into, he had far more in common with Cecil Barnes than Marie had ever dreamed of. The writer was a whiz at description—including painstakingly graphic portrayals of gruesome serial murders—but didn't care at all about romance. There was potential there. Such great potential, for something heated to develop between lead investigator Mona Malcom and the falsely accused Brad Billingsly. But nothing doing. Each protagonist seemed much too self-absorbed to attempt to peel the clothes off someone else. For heaven's sake! Was this considered entertainment?

Not in Marie's favorite stories, where good always triumphed over evil and love conquered all. Hey, if she wanted the bad news, she'd read the newspapers. Fiction was supposed to be about feeling better, about *forgetting*.

Well, forgetting was exactly what she intended to do. Forget all about those idealistic notions that made her want to believe David was more than a small town stud in tight-fitting jeans. That he—heaven forbid—might actually be the one! The one for what, for goodness sake?

Just because he pushed her buttons as no other man had, that didn't mean he was the right one for her. The right man, when he came along, would have a whole heck of a lot more going for him than a mesmerizing smile, melting blue eyes and a body to yearn for.

No! She was doing it again... remembering all the wrong things instead of focusing on the differences between them.

Despite his protests to the contrary, David was most certainly a ladies' man, one who'd never be contented with a bookworm like her. At least, not for the long term. She knew his game. It was the challenge that was driving him, that was all, but she wouldn't give in.

And if he actually liked that awful book... well, that was just more proof that David's vision of the world was one hundred and eighty degrees different from hers. Of course, that figured. After all, he'd made a point of mentioning that he came from a wealthy family where his mother had been able to stay home and dedicate herself to charity causes.

Marie's background had been the complete opposite. Hers had been an upbringing filled with blood, sweat and tears. And yet, despite the hardships, she wouldn't trade her experiences for anything. What she'd gone through had made her strong, capable of standing on her own. And, despite her girlhood fantasies, Marie knew she really didn't need a man to sweep her off her feet. Even though, at times... it still sounded awfully good.

No, but that was crazy. David Lake was not the sort who thought of ever after. He was more the here-and-now kind of animal. And she'd just have to keep him at bay.

Marie pushed through the door to the optician's shop, ready to fight. She'd just gotten off work and wanted to get this over with as quickly as possible, so she could go home, order a pizza and enjoy her juicy new novel in peace.

David's eyes sparkled when he caught sight of her. "Well, well, Miss McCloud!" he said, with a jovial smile. "Good afternoon! Be with you in just a second."

He seemed to be busy helping some college coed select a glasses case. Although to look at the young woman, practically panting at him, Marie could have sworn her interest was more in David's potential rigidity than in whether her case should be soft or hard.

Marie watched the girl giggle and tighten her arms to her chest so that her cleavage would be more visible. Although Marie wasn't sure just how much more visible it could get. The woman's breasts were practically falling out of her low-cut lycra leotard.

Her nylon shorts were cut high on her thighs, which Marie was sure David had noticed were much more shapely than hers. Though Marie didn't think she had a bad figure, it certainly looked nothing like *that.* Poor child must have to sweat through an aerobics class at least three times a day to maintain a body that perfect.

She leaned forward, her loose blond hair swinging above her ample breasts, and blew David a kiss.

"Ciao, sweetie," she said, doing her best to sound sensual. "Don't forget to call when you're ready for that workout."

82

Marie stepped forward and dropped her books onto the counter with an attention-getting thud.

Cat-like green eyes turned in her direction. "Here to get your glasses fixed?" the young woman asked with a purr.

"Actually," Marie said, removing her glasses and leaning over so she could grip David by the elbow. "I came in to see my very good friend, David Lake."

Holy cow, what was this? David looked from Marie to the customer and then back again. The threat of competition? He wished he'd thought of that earlier.

"If you don't mind," Marie said, turning her steely gaze on Candy. "David and I have something to discuss..."

"Whatever," Candy said with a tug at her low neckline and a careless shrug of her shoulders.

"You got my number, babe," she said to David, as she turned and began a hip-swiveling promenade out the door.

Marie had the strangest look on her face. And until she grinned, David didn't realize she was about to burst out laughing.

"David!" Marie said, catching her breath. "Don't tell me you find that kind of blatant sexuality attractive!"

"No," David said, looking deep in her eyes. "I like the more understated kind."

She inhaled and lifted his book off the counter, forcing herself to remember her mission. "I brought back *Silence In The Trees,*" she said, striving to ignore her feeling of embarrassment. "Although I hate to admit—"

"Marie," David broke in, setting both hands down in front of her, "I hope you didn't think that Candy—"

"Candy?"

83

"The girl who was just in here." David actually blushed. "I just wanted you to know... I mean, she's an aerobics instructor at the gym where I work out. That's all there is to it, I swear."

Marie lowered her glasses. "I'm not so sure she knows that."

"No, but she will. Trust me," David said, lifting his hands and coming out from behind the counter.

She pivoted to hold his gaze and backed right into a display case.

"And just how are you planning on breaking the news?"

"I'm planning," David said, closing the distance between them in two long strides, "on telling her I'm involved with someone else."

Marie's heart raced and her skin went all damp and clammy. This was *not* why she'd come in here.

"Well, now that you have the book..." she said, trying to inch away.

But David stepped forward and pinned her to the counter with two strong arms.

"Marie," he said, looking into her eyes, his heated breath warming her skin. "I've got something to tell you."

Oh, no you don't, she wanted to say. Hoping to find some way, any way to stop the sweet words she feared would come, melting her more than the desire in his eyes.

Marie knew she should turn. Knew she should run. But instead, all she could do was stand up on tiptoes and stop his confession with a kiss.

David nearly toppled backwards when the blissful cotton candy of her mouth melted against his lips. She was kissing him! And didn't it feel good...

He responded with all the erotic skill he had, lightly parting her lips with his. It only made him want to beg for more.

Marie nearly swooned in his arms, grateful that his strength would support her. His kisses were hot and sensual. And persuasive. Oh, how she wanted to go where his touch promised he would lead.

David's hand slid under the front of her coat, found her breast, and stroked it.

Oh God, she was going to die of pleasure right then and there. And then he held her closer and she knew she wanted to live long enough to taste his heaven.

There was the light tinkling of a bell, and Marie tried to pull back from his desperate kiss.

"David," she said, as he brought her closer still, "I hear bells."

"Mmm, sweetheart," he said, nuzzling her neck. "Me too, me too."

Suddenly the bell sounded again. Only louder this time, and David broke contact.

"Is this any way to run a business?" Caroline asked, her hands on her hips.

"Of course not," David answered, taking Marie by the hand. "But now that you're here, Marie and I are going to take this business home."

Chapter Nine

"You're going to lose your job!" Marie yelped, as David pulled her down the sidewalk.

"Yeah," David said, sweeping her into his arms. "And what a way to go!"

His hot mouth fell upon hers as his muscular arms pressed into her back, holding her so close she swore they were melting together. Particularly since she was wearing this heavy coat!

"David," Marie said, pushing back on his shoulders, "people are staring."

A group of college students with backpacks were waiting at the crosswalk and turned to gape, wide-eyed at the spectacle they were making of themselves.

David shouted at them with a frisky wave of his arm.

"Hey! You kids need glasses—there's an optician's shop right there!"

Marie burst into a giggle and buried her head in his shoulder.

"You," she said, whacking him on his backside, "are impossible."

"Spank me again," he said with a naughty grin, "I liked it."

Liked it? Oh my, she had liked it too. She was enjoying the sexual playfulness between them, without a trace of her usual inhibition.

"Come on," he said, securing an arm around her waist. "My car's over there."

"Car?" Marie asked, a little disappointed she wouldn't be treated to another bicycle ride. "But I thought you biked in. Good for the environment and all that."

David grimaced. Well, hey, it had sounded good at the time. Very Cecil-like. And Cecil, it was apparent, knew all about women like Marie. When David had gone back to Books & Bistro to thank him for his reading suggestions, he'd been told that Cecil had run off to New York with some girl writer half his age. The man had probably established that mind link he'd been talking about. David guessed that when it came to intelligent women, Cecil definitely knew his stuff.

"Ah yeah, right," David said, sliding his key into the passenger door. "Environment's definitely a top priority. Greenspace and all that."

"Greenpeace?" Marie asked, looking up as she adjusted her seat belt.

David smiled and shut the door. Boy, he'd have to watch what he said with her. She clearly knew more about all this than he did.

A frigid burst of wind reddened David's face as he scooted around the car.

"David," Marie said, as he climbed in and started the engine. "Your teeth are chattering. You really shouldn't have gone out without a coat."

Maybe not. But in his hurry to rush past Caroline, picking up his belongings had been the last thing on his mind.

"I'll be all right," he said, flipping on the heater. "At least until my boss catches up with me."

"What about your boss?" Marie asked, as they pulled away from the curb and headed towards campus. "Do you think she'll really let you go?"

"I doubt it." David eyed the digital car clock. "Look, it's almost six anyway. Caroline can just as easily close the shop as I can."

"Yeah, but how do you know that—after today—she won't change the locks?"

David chuckled. "Well, you can be sure she'll be mad at first. Caroline has a temper. But after a while, and especially after she's talked to Jim, she'll calm down and forgive me."

"Jim?" Marie asked, relieved to at last be able to unbutton her sweltering coat.

"Caroline's husband. A true romantic."

"Really?"

"Sure. He's a screenwriter."

"No kidding?" She wriggled her arms out of her coat one at a time. "What does he write?"

"Romantic comedy, of course." David flashed a big smile. "We could sure give him a few pointers."

Marie adjusted her glasses, hoping he was joking.

"Hey," David said, patting her arm. "Don't look so worried. I'm only kidding!"

She let out a soft breath, then sat bolt upright.

"Oh my gosh, David," she said, bringing her hands to her face, "I left my book in there."

"Silence In The Trees? Hey, don't worry about it. I'll just pick it up tomorrow."

"Not your book, mine!"

"Well, what's the big deal? I can bring it to you."

The big deal, the very big deal, was that the book Marie'd left at the optician's shop was *Check It Out,* a romance about a small town librarian who, thanks to the local physician, happily finds the cure for all her libidinal ills.

"Besides," David said, laying a firm hand on her thigh. "Something tells me that—this evening—neither of us is going to have much time for reading."

"David," Marie said, as he stood fumbling with his key at the door to his upstairs apartment. "I think we might be taking this a little fast."

Fast? Oh, no. David could practically hear the mental brakes grinding to a halt.

"We can take it at any speed you want," he said, his key finally engaging in the lock. He looked at her reassuringly.

"Listen, Marie, I'm not the kind who's going to pressure you into anything, if that's what you're afraid of."

She shivered a little. David pressuring her was not the trouble. It was the way that she couldn't seem to keep her hands off of *him* that had her worried.

Against her better judgment, Marie nodded and stepped into the lion's lair. A quick image of him on all fours on the floor of Books & Bistro burned through her mind, and she shivered again.

"Nice place," she said, looking around at the living area, sparsely furnished with odds and ends. It was all one room, with a galley kitchen at the far end. Marie looked at the large platform bed in the corner, then looked quickly back to David.

"Not much furniture. Mostly Grandma's attic, if you know what I mean. But I make do."

He grinned and she felt all hot and cold at the same time.

"Here," he said, lifting the coat she had lightly draped over her shoulders when she'd exited the car, "let me hang this up for you."

David reached over and hooked her coat on a rack by the front door, then took her by the arm.

"Come on," he said, his voice as smooth as whiskey, "let me show you around."

"There's more?" she asked, catching her breath as his hand slid down her sweatered arm and felt for her palm.

Marie tugged at the front of her dress, suffocating in its ribbed tightness.

"If you're getting too warm..." David said, looking down at her in a way that seemed to stop time.

She counted the heartbeats drumming loudly in her ear. When she got to three, David reached up and brought his free hand to her face.

Her heart raced past four, and, before she knew it, she was pressing seven. If she got to ten, something told her, she would not be able to stop whatever it was they were about to be doing.

"Marie," he whispered, as she counted eight... then nine....

David leaned in for a kiss.

"Oh!" Marie shouted, stepping backwards and dropping his hand.

"What is it? What's wrong?"

He looked earnestly into her eyes and placed both hands on her trembling shoulders.

She squeezed her eyes shut—hard. But in her imagination, it wasn't David that she saw. Only Cecil. Cecil and Paul, the two of them throwing their heads back in hilarity at how easy she was.

"You think," she asked softly, as her eyes blinked open, "we could open a window?"

"A window?" David stood upright and scratched the back of his head. "Sure, sweetheart, anything you want."

"Do you call all your women sweetheart?" Marie asked, nabbing a magazine off a cluttered end table and fanning her face.

"Beg pardon?"

"Sweetheart."

"Yes, dear—" he said, drawing closer, the fire in his eyes seeming to reignite.

"No, no," Marie said, pushing him back. "Answer the question."

David frowned. "Now, what would that be?"

"Do you," she asked, blowing out a hard breath and tugging at her dress again, "call all your women sweetheart?"

David stopped for a moment, as if to think, then walked to the window and threw it open wide.

"First," he said, as he slipped back behind her and linked his arms under her chest, "let's get this straight."

Marie bit her lip, as his hand brushed her hair and his heated breath tickled her nape.

"There *are* no other women. There have been no other women—ever since I first laid eyes on you."

He lowered his lips to her neck and trailed kisses to her ear.

"David—" Marie said, wishing he would stop and then wishing he wouldn't.

She let out a cry of half surprise, half pleasure as he turned her around slowly. His hungry mouth fell upon hers and ravished her lips, moving down swiftly to the soft, vulnerable spot at the base of her neck.

"David—" she groaned, as the magazine she'd been holding fell to the floor.

David pulled back, his hair disheveled, passion in his eyes.

"Oh, Marie. Baby. Sweetheart. You make me crazy. So totally crazy. But I promised... I know I did. If you want me to stop, tell me now." He sighed. "Because another minute or two of this and I don't think..."

Marie ran her sweating palms through her long, loose hair, knowing exactly what he meant. She had no business being here, putting herself in such a compromising position with a man who...

Her eyes dropped to the floor.

... reads *Publishers Weekly!*

"What's this?" she asked, swooping down like a raven and pulling the magazine off the carpet.

David swaggered back a step and straightened his shirt collar.

"Oh, it's just one of those book-biz magazines I subscribe to."

Marie flipped the *Publishers Weekly* over in her hand, but saw no address label.

David snatched back the magazine and smiled between his teeth.

"Not that I actually subscribe to this one. Gotta cut costs somewhere. Bought this issue at the newsstand."

She lifted one eyebrow. He was acting very suspicious. *Publishers Weekly* cost twice as much at the newsstand.

But, why oh why, should that surprise her? It appeared that all the men who read that rag had something to hide.

Red flag number three—or was it four, by now?—went up the pole.

Marie paled. Seeing red, she realized, made even the most mentally challenged of animals want to run.

Without another word, Marie walked over and grabbed her coat off the rack.

A befuddled David raced toward her. "Wait! What happened? What did I do?"

"I don't even know," she said, opening the door. "Guess that's the point." She walked out.

David stood there in utter disbelief, his tiny apartment still resonating from the sound of the slamming door.

"Thanks a lot Cecil," he said, chucking the *Publishers Weekly* into the trash.

And then he bolted out the door and sprinted after her.

Marie was crying so hard she couldn't see two feet in front of her. This was it. Absolutely it. With the exception of her romance heroes, from this point forward all men were off limits.

After all she had done to build a life, these—cavemen came along and scattered it to stones. Loving Paul was an innocent mistake, her first wide-eyed romance, so she hardly blamed herself—even at this point—for falling for him.

By the time she'd met Cecil, she should have known better. At twenty-seven, she wasn't exactly an innocent anymore. But, for all her savvy, she might as well have been Little Red Riding Hood.

And now, here was David—the man with the irresistible eyes who told such nice lies. First there was that little story about the bike. Environmental awareness—hah! She was sure now it had been a ploy to get her close to his admittedly perfect body.

And then, all that nonsense about literary fiction and the obviously unread copy of *Publishers Weekly*.

For all Marie knew, David probably didn't read anything without a centerfold.

She pulled herself to a stop at the corner near the familiar display of lights. Books & Bistro's elegant awning stood out among the group of shops that lined the outdoor mall.

David raced through the darkness, wondering where on earth she'd gone. He ran to the corner and frantically called left and right, before deciding to head back to the mall. If she'd gone anywhere, it had to be the bookstore. Her car would be there, at least.

David crossed the street and picked up speed, his toned thighs swinging into motion.

What had she been thinking, he asked himself, his head pounding as he ran.

He maintained his speed, crossing the second street, which, fortunately, was free of traffic. His panic-stricken eyes continued to search side streets.

What if she'd wandered off? What if she'd gotten lost? In Covesville?

David stopped at the crosswalk, acknowledging the absurdity of the notion. He was gasping for air, leaning forward to catch his breath, when he looked up and saw her disappearing into her car.

Oh, hell, no!

David ignored the Don't Walk sign and bolted into traffic, dodging angry drivers as several cars nearly collided, screeching to a halt in the middle of the busy intersection.

But by the time he got to the parking lot, all that remained of Marie were her tail lights fading in the night.

Chapter Ten

David kicked open the door and entered the optician's shop, scowling.

"Good morning to you, too," Caroline said from behind the counter. "Good thing my husband Jim likes the same ball teams you do, or you'd be out on your rear."

David motioned her away and stormed toward the coffeepot.

"I mean it, David! What if I hadn't been here to lock up last night? Would you have done the wild thing right in the center of the floor with a million"—she gestured to the mirrored walls of frames—"eyes on you?"

"Don't be cute, Caroline," he said, filling his mug.

"Oh, so I get it," she said, stepping around the counter and walking over with her own mug. "She blew you off, did she? Got you all hot and bothered, then—"

"You know," he said, bringing his coffee to his lips, "sometimes you just don't know where to stop."

"No, David," Caroline said, slamming her mug onto the table. "You don't know where to stop! Has it ever occurred to you that this is a business? That maybe one of our clients could have walked in here with a five-year-old child when you were in the middle of your amorous romp?"

David dropped his head, knowing she was right. It had been reckless of him, foolish. Different, if he'd had the foresight to draw the blinds and lock the doors...

"All this talk about Marie!" Caroline shouted walking back into her office and then returning with a book. "Marie,

Marie, Marie. But you can't seem to figure out what she wants."

David brought a hand to his aching head and massaged his brow with his fingers.

"Here," Caroline said, thumping something hard into his chest. "Sally's better now, so take the day off. Do some serious reading."

"What's this?" he asked, staring down at the maroon cover.

David took the paperback in his hand and read the blurb before flipping it back over. For an inane little romance about a small-town librarian with the hots for the local doc, *Check It Out* displayed some pretty steamy artwork.

"Don't know who left it here," Caroline continued, "but it's good. I've read it. Maybe you should, too."

As David fanned through the pages, hoping for more suggestive artwork, a receipt fluttered loose and butterflied to the floor.

"Books & Bistro?" Caroline asked, snatching it off the carpet before David could even bend at the waist.

Caroline shook her head with a wry smile. "Now, I wonder who on earth this belongs to?"

Marie collapsed on the sofa and lifted the ice pack to her swollen eyes. If the puffiness didn't go down soon, she'd have to go in to work anyway. It was bad enough she'd called to say she'd be late. With Thanksgiving next week, Books & Bistro was under the gun to prepare for the pre-Christmas purchasing frenzy. And, with so many of her employees taking leave for next week's holiday, that meant that this Friday was the deadline she'd decided to go by. If she could get everything done and organized as she'd planned, then maybe even she would get a chance to enjoy some turkey and sweet potato casserole in peace.

It was draining enough for Marie to host the meal for her sisters and their husbands, plus her brothers Johnny and Mark and their significant others. Last thing she needed on top of that was work stress to face the next day.

Of course, when Marie was being honest, she didn't really mind having everyone over as much as she pretended. There was something comforting in having the flock gather and knowing she was still—in some small way—in charge of the fold. She had been the one left with the family homestead, after all. So it was up to Marie, as the eldest, to uphold family tradition.

The only part of the tradition she didn't savor was her brothers' good-natured ribbing about her single status. She was sure to get an earful this year, now that Cecil had blown right out of her life like an autumn leaf caught up in a gale.

High winds pounded her front door screen and sent it rattling in its frame. The gustiness of central Virginia's fall was upon them, and it'd soon be time to bring in the porch swing, lest it get carried off somewhere far over the mountain one night while she was sleeping. The weatherman had predicted snow on the heels of the frigid front that was blowing in from Canada. Just as long as it held off until Friday, Marie thought, it could snow all it wanted. Wasn't often they got a white Christmas in these parts, and white Thanksgivings were rarer still. Snow here in November would be the talk of the town, and that would suit her just fine. One less reason for her brothers to focus on talking turkey about the obvious lack of a man in her life.

David ordered a decaffeinated coffee and carried his book to the high bar running the length of the long glass wall that separated Books & Bistro's interior cafe from the wrought-iron tables on the sidewalk outside.

Not a soul was out there. It was no wonder, David thought, as the wind gusted and blew two metal chairs to the ground.

The cold was coming, and David was glad. He was a winter sports fan, and because he had grown up in Asheville, quite an accomplished skier. There was something about a mountain lodge with a roaring fireplace after a long day on the slopes. Of course, it helped if you had someone to share it with. And, this time, he wasn't thinking about Bitsy, the chair lift attendant.

David sighed and cracked open the book. He was curious to see why Marie had been so upset about leaving it behind. Doubly interested because the style of the cover looked strikingly similar to the book he'd caught her reading over coffee just last week. Maybe Cecil had recommended the wrong approach. In fact, maybe Marie got enough of intellectual literature and grim best-sellers working here. She probably read books like this to relax. Nothing wrong with that.

David dove right into the prologue, his eyebrows shooting skyward.

Holy cow, he thought, marking his place and pausing to remove his pullover sweater. He had a feeling he'd be able to get into this.

Marie was just dropping her keys into her purse and stepping up onto the curb at Books & Bistro, when she came to an abrupt halt. Her eyes had to be playing tricks on her.

She removed her glasses and wiped them on her coat lapel before putting them back on again.

Oh, my. She just stood there, her feet rooted to the ground, her cheeks turning pink from the icy air.

There at the counter of the cafe sat David Lake in all his glory, reading... *reading...* her book!

Marie blinked twice as David lowered his hand to the counter, nabbed a paper napkin, then wadded it up against his brow.

He was so engrossed in the book he didn't even see her walk in, and right up to the stool where he sat.

"Were you planning on reading it first, and then giving it back?"

David raised his eyes, then nearly fell off the stool.

"Hey! Whoa—Marie!" he said, standing and slamming shut the book. "What a surprise!"

"A surprise, David? I work here." She looked him up and down, trying not to remember how good he'd felt pressed up against her. "What's your excuse?"

"I, ah, was returning your book," he said, thrusting *Check It Out* in her direction.

"It looks used," she said, taking the book but keeping her eyes on his.

David racked his brain, trying to recall the very careful plan he'd concocted on the way over here, but his mind swirled with visions of adventuresome librarian Judith Just enjoying her first complete examination by the probing Dr. Robert Right.

"Well?" Marie asked, tapping one beautiful foot on the floor. He studied that beautiful foot and her delicate ankle, and then his gaze moved up that long sweep of leg—which went on and on and didn't stop until it hit that hint of hemline just above her knees.

"I... uh." David cleared his throat.

"I think you already said that."

"Yes, well..."

He choked on air as she unbuttoned her coat. He noticed she was wearing another one of those sweater dresses that showed off her curves so well.

"I was waiting." David clenched his fists and dug his fingernails into his palms. "Waiting for you to get here."

He smiled through gritted teeth, and looked for all the world like a naughty boy who'd been caught with his hand in the cookie jar.

"Well, here I am," she said, unable to keep her gaze off the warm gleam in his eyes, the broad musculature of his chest... the snug fit of his faded denim jeans.

"Well, there you are," he said, motioning to the book he'd already placed in her hands.

He shuffled his feet and glanced out the window. "I hope you're not still mad about last night. Because if you are—"

"David," she stopped him. "It wasn't you, necessarily."

He inhaled deeply and his chest swelled, the taut muscles rippling beneath cotton.

Marie blinked and continued. "I mean, in some ways it was. But look," she said, trying hard not to. Why, oh why, did her eyes keep roving over him? "What I mean is, there's been so much going on in my life, and if you can't be honest with me—"

"Honest?" He folded his arms in front of his broad chest and knitted his brow. "Just what is it you think I've done to deceive you?"

"You tell me," she said, clutching her book to her bodice.

David looked positively stupefied.

"Does this have something to do with *Publishers Weekly?*"

She stood motionless, a hard look in her eyes beneath those charmingly tilted frames.

"Well, look, Marie," he said, giving a little laugh. "If that's all it is, I can explain. Not that I really understand why a simple little magazine would cause such a reaction..."

"It's just that it all started when Cecil—"

"Cecil?!"

"Sure, yes. Cecil, you know—"

"I know damn well who Cecil is, but I thought you said you didn't."

"Didn't I? I mean, no, I don't. Just a little—"

"Are you and Cecil in this together somehow?" she asked, eyebrows arching.

"Together? Wait. Whoa. I don't think you're getting-"

"Oh, I'm getting everything just fine. I might not be from your sophisticated background, David. But I didn't just fall off the turnip truck. You and Cecil devised some kind of plan, didn't you?"

Plan? Holy cow, what was happening here? This whole thing was spinning way out of control. He'd never seen her so furious.

"You hit on me, get me out of the way, so he can run off to New York with Diane."

102

"Diane? No—"

"Good job, David. Bravo," she said, a cold dismissal in her eyes."What with your talent, maybe you should join Cecil in New York. Hear they're in need of actors there."

"Marie, please."

She turned, and he placed a hand on her shoulder.

She looked back and narrowed her flaming eyes. "You lay one more hand on me, David Lake, I'll call security. Now, I've got a life to lead," she said, striding away. "I'm sure you've got one waiting for your somewhere, too."

Chapter Eleven

Mark looked over his shoulder and called back into the house. "Hey, Marie! There's some turkey with a bird on your doorstep!" She didn't answer.

"Just kidding, pal," Mark said, giving David a slap on the arm. "Come on in."

"Oh!" Meg, John's fiancée, rushed over. "You must be the guy! Marie told us last month she was getting married, but we all knew—-just knew—it couldn't be to that old boring Cecil!"

Despite her willowy frame, Meg looked pixie-like with her bridge of freckles and short red hair. "Johnny," she called, leaning back into the living room. "Oh, John-boy, come here!"

A tall, muscular man with jet-black hair appeared from around the corner, his dark eyes widening with surprise. "Well, hey there! You must be David."

"How did you know his name?" Meg questioned, swatting her fiancé on the rump.

"Talked to him on the phone."

David shifted the heavy turkey pan uncomfortably in his hands.

"Here, let me take that." A pretty ponytailed blonde with apple-dumpling cheeks appeared and lifted the roasting pan out of David's hands. "Honey," she said, talking to the lanky fellow behind her, "this is David, Marie's fiancé."

"No, wait!" David held out his hand.

But a dark-haired woman about an inch shorter than Marie walked over and used the opportunity to slip off one arm of his coat. "Your true love's here," she sang back into the kitchen in a lilting voice, before yanking the other arm free, then carrying his coat to the closet.

"What in the world is all the..." Marie strode into the front hall and froze, as an extremely tall brown-haired guy materialized at her back.

"You must be Jack. Jack Wagner," David said, stepping around Marie and stretching his hand out toward Teresa's husband. "Carolina basketball, right? ACC Championship year."

Jack gave a modest grin and nodded his big, square jaw.

David knew he'd recognized the face.

"Would somebody—*anybody*—mind tell me what's going on here? And just who let *him* in?" Marie shouted, as a flushed David turned to face her.

Mark quietly backed away, as the others appeared to decide whether or not they wanted to be discreet, or stay and watch the action.

"Well, I think," Meg said, tugging on Johnny's arm, "that we should all go and see what's cooking in the kitchen, and leave these two lovebirds alone."

"Good plan, sweetie," Johnny said, leaning over and planting an affectionate kiss on her cheek. "Especially since," he whispered in her ear, but not quite softly enough, "I'm the one who asked him to bring the turkey!"

Marie gave her brother an accusatory glare, but he just took Meg's arm and ignored her as he exited the room.

"Wow," David said, bringing his hands together in a clap, "what a great family you have."

Marie blinked behind her perfectly straight frames. "All right David, the truth. Just what are you doing here, and just how did you finagle a dinner invitation from my unsuspecting little brother?"

She looked so beautiful standing there, wonderfully domestic with flour dusting her bright red cheeks, her sensuous curves hugged ever so tightly by a full-length, green print apron. Those mesmerizing brown eyes and spectacular lashes flashing behind... wait!

"You got them fixed!" David blurted out. The surprise waned to disappointment when he realized that meant she'd taken them to someone else.

"Don't look so crestfallen," Marie said with a little shake of her head. "Though you may not be my type where romance is concerned, I didn't toss you over for another optician."

David instinctively stepped one inch closer, but she inched back.

"Caroline replaced the frames for me. No charge."

"Caroline?" David asked, startled. "But she didn't say a word." And, blast it all, she knew first-hand all the agony David had gone through since last week when Marie had shut him out of her life.

"Of course not," Marie huffed. "Caroline apparently has a deeper sense of loyalty than my traitor brother!"

Johnny, who had stuck his head into the foyer and was about to come get something, suddenly changed his mind and disappeared down the back hall.

"Oh, don't be too hard on Johnny. He just happened to pick up the land line. And, after all the times you'd slammed it down in my ear—"

106

"Now, don't you go defending my brother!" Marie said, taking one big step in his direction.

"No, I wouldn't dream—"

"And don't," she said, coming closer and thumping him on the chest, "go sharing your dreams—or fantasies, as they may be—about us being engaged with my family!"

David looked into her eyes, all fire and ice, and swore he felt his adam's apple melt.

"I didn't," he squeaked, then cleared his throat.

"So, is this the way it's going to be, then?" she asked, stepping up to him so her hairline was level with his shoulders. "More dyed-in-the-wool, bald-faced lies?"

She tilted her chin upward, set both hands on his shoulders, and gave him a rude push backwards. "Get out of my house!"

"Now, Marie," her sister Jill burst in. "Is that any way to treat the man you've pledged yourself to for eternity?"

Marie gritted her teeth and made some kind of snarling sound David couldn't identify. "For the last time—"

Jill laid a soothing hand on David's arm and a peace-making arm around Marie's shoulder. "Come on now, kids," she said, forcing a brilliant smile. "It's Thanksgiving. Let's all try being a little grateful for what we've got, huh?" She gave Marie a light squeeze, patted David affectionately, then walked into the arms of Dan, who'd been watching from the sidelines.

"Hello!" Marie screamed. "Hello, I know you're out there!"

David watched in amazement as heads popped out from around door frames and the rest of her siblings emerged from their hiding places with guilty looks.

"Really, guys," Marie scolded, "I thought you all had outgrown that nonsense by the time I was seventeen."

"Not quite," Mark said with a grin. "And, boy, did we see some good stuff! What was that fellow's name? Big guy you took to the prom?"

To Marie's relief, Johnny walked over and popped Mark on the head with a rolled-up newspaper. Just like Mark to make trouble. It was the first Thanksgiving in years that he hadn't brought home a girl, and his boredom was showing already.

"Soup's on!" Meg called, approaching from the kitchen. David had thought one was missing when he'd counted eavesdropping heads. No, two. David looked around. Where was Jack?

As if in answer to the question, Jack came out of the dining room. "Where shall we seat our guest?" he asked tactfully.

It annoyed Marie no end that she apparently had no say in whether or not David was staying for dinner, even though she was hosting it.

Not only that, but then everybody squabbled over where he would sit. Jack wanted to talk basketball, while Teresa wanted a detailed story about how Marie and David met. Mark wanted to discuss all the best ski resorts. Meg had grown up in North Carolina, and Johnny, the surgeon, was suddenly eager to hear all about some new lens-making procedure from David.

Marie sighed and cleared the salad plates, relieved that David had been seated at the opposite end of the table, but still not entirely sure she liked him occupying her father's chair. She walked to the kitchen, as a round of laughter exploded at her back, and the thought occurred to her that she might as well not be here at all.

She deposited the plates in the sink, then felt the rush of revelation. Of course! It was so obvious, she hadn't even seen it. As much as she loathed him being here, as desperately as she'd been trying not to meet his gaze, David was actually rescuing her.

For once in the past eight years, Marie was going to be able to enjoy a Thanksgiving dinner in peace. No probing questions, no ribbing. Done. It was settled. She was engaged! And now the spotlight was on David, not her.

Marie released a deep breath and let go of a lot of tension with it. If David was happy to play along, as he seemed content to do, then why not her? Get through this annual holiday. Get back to work, then move on. All she needed was a little more cooperation from David, and then after a couple more weeks she'd tell her siblings the engagement was off. With her track record, they'd certainly believe that.

Marie squared her shoulders and walked to the swinging door that led to the dining room. "Oh, David," she said, peeping through the door, her voice all sugar-sweetness. "Honey, could you come in here and help me with the turkey?"

"Carve it, you mean?" he asked, feeling his blood rush to his feet. David knew what that would require: long, sharp knives—or at least one. And one was all it would take, with a woman as riled as Marie. She'd hardly spoken to him all evening. Had barely turned her eyes upon his. And, when she had, he'd seen nothing more there than utter disregard.

109

David excused himself from the table and walked toward the kitchen, believing, at least, there was safety in numbers. Her whole family seemed to like him. And, boy, what a nice bunch they were. His family's dinners in Ashville had never been like this. No, instead of warm exchanges and laughter, they'd been filled with financial figures and boredom. He and his sister Debbie had never gotten a word in edgewise, and were always dismissed the moment they had finished their dinners.

"You called?" he asked, as the swinging door closed at his back.

"David," Marie said, holding up a long, gleaming knife. "I have a proposition."

David swallowed past the lump in his throat. "Oh, yeah?" he asked, his voice suddenly squeaky as a thirteen-year-old's.

"You and I are engaged," she said, digging the knife into the breast of the turkey and slicing off a chunk.

"Okay," he said, making no effort to move from where he was.

"Come over here, will you?" she said, motioning with the knife. "I don't want to shout it, for heaven's sake."

David steeled himself and took a few steps forward.

"What's wrong with you, anyway?" Marie asked. "One minute you're the loving fiancé, the next you act as if you're afraid..." She looked down at the knife which she'd thrust back into the turkey carcass.

"Oh, no!" She burst out laughing. "No, no, no..." Marie snorted. "You couldn't possibly have thought—ha!" She dropped the knife to the carving board.

"Hey!" Mark shouted from the dining room. "Are we going to get any dinner in here, or should we all just depart and leave you two alone?"

"David," Marie said, bringing herself under control and standing to grip him by the elbows. "I'm not going to hurt you, I swear. "She found herself giggling uncontrollably. Her? A menace? Hooo.

"David," she said again, blinking hard and straightening her quivering lips. "Here's the deal."

He looked at her without flinching, his crystal blue eyes calm.

"You and I are engaged."

"Okay."

She narrowed her eyes and resisted another giggle. "You started it, I didn't."

"Okay."

"Therefore, you are mine until the night is through."

David's heart did cartwheels, but he didn't say a word.

"What I mean is, we can play this game for a few hours, just to get my family off my back. But when the clock strikes midnight..."

Holding his tongue seemed to be working so far, so why wreck it now, David reasoned.

"Then you go home."

"Got it," he said, bowing backwards as she dismissed him with a wave of her knife.

And then he darted through the swinging door and gave Johnny a high-five before Marie could rejoin them.

"More wine?" Johnny asked, passing the carafe in Marie's direction.

She'd already had two glassfuls and was thinking she should stop. But then she looked over at David holding court at the other end of the table and motioned for Johnny to fill her glass halfway.

Maybe it was the wine, or maybe it was the lateness of the hour. Or maybe, it was because she was so full of sweet potato casserole and pecan pie she couldn't think straight. But the truth of the matter was that David looked *good* sitting there in her father's chair.

He seemed so at ease with her family. And, for a man who had never met them before, it had certainly been a baptism by fire. Yet, none of it appeared to faze David at all.

"Sweetheart," he asked, looking in her direction as he stretched back and patted his belly. "Can I help you with the dishes?"

"See there," Meg said, nudging Johnny. "This man isn't domestically impaired. He's offering to help in the kitchen."

Johnny flushed and drained his wineglass. "Oh now, honey, you know I'm helpless when it comes to you ordering me around."

David knew just how Johnny felt. He got to his feet, the room turning a bit at an odd angle. Just how much wine had he had? Though he hadn't been counting, the carafe had seemed to make quite a few trips to his end of the table.

"Come on, hon," Marie said, coming over and rubbing the back of his waist.

Wow. The room came into focus then, along with all sorts of electrifying images in David's mind.

He pulled a stunned Marie into his arms. "Baby," he said, his voice husky from the wine, "you should know better than to touch me like that in public."

112

Someone at the table let out an amused giggle. But all Marie could see was the fire in David's eyes. It was all too clear what was on his mind.

"Maybe we should get going," Jill said, tugging on Dan's sleeve and rising from the table.

"No," Marie said, trying to break the lock of David's arms but failing miserably, "stay."

David nodded slowly as a sexy grin worked its way across his kissable lips.

Gracious! Marie thought, feeling a little sweat trickle down her cleavage beneath her too-warm dress.

"Ah, yeah," Mark said, slapping the table loudly and springing to his feet. "Time's a-wasting. We'd best all get on the road before that big storm hits."

"Storm?" Marie asked, finally wriggling free of David's embrace and practically running to the opposite end of the room.

"Yes," Meg said, as Johnny went to collect their coats from the hall closet. "Haven't you heard? They've predicted a lot of snow tonight."

"Say," Jill said, as Marie wondered what on earth she was going to do once she was left alone with David in the house, "You sure you don't want us to stay and help with the dishes? We've made quite a mess."

But David just smiled and muttered something about helping the little woman all she wanted.

Little woman, her foot! If Marie had had darts to throw, she would have aimed them straight at David.

What was wrong with her anyway? This entire fiancé thing had already gotten out of hand. There she'd sat all through the meal, envisioning David as a permanent fixture in her father's chair. And rather than her siblings, all the other seats around the table had been occupied by imaginary children—her and David's, to be exact. Six of them altogether.

She shook off an unwanted chill as David's warm hands settled on her upper arms.

"Sweetheart," he said, leaning over and kissing her fondly on the forehead, "don't you want to go and say good-bye to your brothers and sisters?"

"Of course," she said, her face the temperature—and the color, she just knew it—of stewed tomatoes.

Marie stood on the front porch and said her goodbyes, each sisterly and brotherly hug punctuated by some whispered comment about what a catch David was.

When she turned to go back in the house, David was standing in the doorway.

"How much of that did you hear?" she asked, feeling her breath stick in her throat.

"None of it..." David began.

But before Marie could get out her sigh of relief, he finished, "Except for all the good parts about what a great catch I am."

She tried to think of something witty to say, some snappy comeback that would break the heated tension of the moment. But instead her boot heel caught on a floorboard and she stumbled forward into David's arms.

"Hey," he said, shoring her up by the elbows and then tugging her in close. "I think that you're quite a catch, too."

"David," Marie said, as he pulled her to him, her soft breasts pressing his pounding chest. "I think we're letting heat out."

Didn't he know it. David swooped in for a kiss, oblivious to the fact that his backside still propped open the door.

"David!" she said, stopping him in mid-approach. "My electric bill!"

David turned and looked into the house, then gave her a thousand-watt smile. "You're right, my sweet fiancée, we're burning way too many lights in there. Where do you keep the candles?"

Chapter Twelve

Marie struck another match, wondering what on earth she was doing. But then David came up and nuzzled the back of her neck with his five o'clock stubble, and she knew exactly.

"Oh, David," she said, as little tingly kisses worked their way around the side of her neck, "you just... you just—"

"I know," he said, hungrily looking in her eyes. "You do it for me, too."

He laid his hands on either side of her glasses frames and gently tugged the turquoise wires from behind her ears.

"David," she said, her breath straining with the word. For heaven's sake, she couldn't even say his name without a million shivers racing down her spine. "I can't see a thing without those."

"Give me your hands," he said, whispering a kiss first onto one eyebrow, and then another.

Marie tightened her grip around his back.

"No," he commanded, with a fierce nibble to her neck. He raised his head and looked down into her eyes.

Even through her hazy vision, she could see him wanting her, needing her. She released her grasp and willingly surrendered her hands to his.

"What you can't see," he said, lowering her hands to the front of his jeans. "You can feel..."

Marie held her breath, as her heartbeat became a gallop.

He brought her hands around to his lean hips and held them there. "And, you can certainly hear..."

He paused and then put his mouth over hers and completely devoured her in a passionate kiss.

"Marie," he said, pulling back for a moment. "I have something very important to tell you."

And, this time, she wouldn't stop him. Because nothing in her entire life had felt so right, as she stood there holding him, unabashedly enjoying the feel of his muscular body.

"I'm glad I didn't tell you earlier, that you didn't let me," David said, his voice a low tremble. "Because then, it was only something I thought was coming..."

He pulled back his brow and swept loose strands of her hair behind her ears.

"Marie," he said, taking her chin in his hands, wanting so badly to kiss her, to dive into her sensuous fire once again—but knowing he needed to finish. "I've fallen in love with you."

She felt her knees buckle, but he lowered his strong arms and caught her around the waist, just in time.

"You look like you need to lie down," he whispered, giving her the softest kiss. "Which way is the bedroom?"

Marie didn't know what had happened to her voice, but it was gone. Or, maybe he'd scared it out of her with his sinful-as-sex, wet kisses.

He loved her? *Loved* her?

Her heart thumped loudly in response. No, it couldn't be. Not so soon after...

But then again, this felt nothing like Cecil, or Paul, or even eager Eddie, her very amorous date for the high school prom.

But, she ached in her very soul to believe this was love.

Fortunately, his safe supporting arms were still around her. "Ah... I do need to lie down."

He bent low to scoop her trembling knees into his left arm, but she stopped him with a hand on his shoulder.

"David," she said, as he straightened to look in her misty eyes. "I don't know how, I don't know why... but I've fallen in love with you, too."

Through the mist, she saw him flash a smile, and then, quicker than she could blink, she was quite literally swept off her feet and carried down the hall.

David dropped Marie onto the cushiony goosedown duvet, then straightened to loosen his belt. Though she couldn't see the details of his features, she'd captured it all picture-perfect in her mind. His ocean blue eyes, his divinely lopsided grin, his gloriously golden, manly-smelling skin...

Marie reached up and caught the front of his jeans by the waistband.

"What's this?" he asked, as she tugged him forward.

"David Lake," she said, her voice taking on a sultry quality he'd never heard. "I'm ready."

David sucked in a breath as Marie unbuttoned his pants and yanked down his fly.

"Come here, David," she said, sliding her hands down into his jeans and under the band of his briefs. "I want to see you."

David exhaled and dropped his jeans to the floor, not sure his own knees would hold up during all this excitement.

"Wow!" he said, kicking off his shoes and the rest of his jeans and springing onto the bed. "Keep talking!"

"Oh, honey," she said, purring kisses into his chest as she unbuttoned his shirt. "You haven't heard anything yet."

David fell back on the bed in wonder. Ecstasy. Excitement, as she trailed kisses down his chest, stopping at his navel to tease it a little with her tongue.

Marie didn't know what was happening, or what had overcome her. All she knew was that she wanted him, and wanted him in the worst way.

She caressed his broad chest once more, exploring the muscles there, then trailed her fingers softly, slowly down the line of his belly.

"Marie, Marie," David moaned softly. "Oh... don't stop."

He sounded positively... out of control.

She was liking this a lot. Then she straddled him and slid one hand over his hard arousal, rubbing it gently through the soft cotton of his briefs. Taking the initiative again, she pulled them off, leaving him. naked except for his open shirt.

David sat up and pressed her lightly on the shoulders. "You have me at a disadvantage," he said, kissing the top of her head.

Marie looked down at her sweater dress, wadded up around her thighs, and knew he was right. She reached for his hands and brought them to her hemline, encouraging him to help her.

In one quick move, David had lifted the dress over her head and reached for the clasp at the back of her black lace bra, as her hair cascaded down around him in waves.

"Help me," he pleaded, unable to work the clasp to his hurried satisfaction.

She reached back behind her and undid her bra, shaking it loose so her ample breasts fell freely into David's waiting hands.

"Baby," he moaned, leaning forward to lick and nibble, caress and suckle, until her panties felt damp and she knew she'd have to remove them.

Marie climbed off of him and sat on the side of the bed to remove her pantyhose and high-cut underpants.

"Come," he said, quickly shucking his shirt. He pressed her down onto the bed, "it's my turn."

She lay back on the pillows as he crouched over her in that panther-like pose she now loved so well.

"Marie," he said, lowering sensual kisses to her neck, her lips, her breasts. "I do love you, I do."

He brushed his length against her, and she felt her insides clench with a desperate yearning to know more of him.

David lowered his hips to hers, supported himself on one elbow, then used his free hand to caress her breasts once more. He lightly pinched her erect nipples and rolled them until she cried out with pleasure. Then he brought his full warm mouth down upon each, in its turn, to arouse her even more.

"David," she said, shifting her hips, "I don't think I can wait..."

That was all the encouragement he needed to lower his hands to her hips, stroke her thighs, then slip a hand in between her legs. He inserted one finger and tested the wetness there with a tender skill.

"Oh," Marie cried out, feeling her body convulse. "Oh, oh..."

David slowly withdrew his touch, and parted her thighs, positioning himself to enter her.

She gripped her hands around his naked backside and pulled him into her—hard.

He began to move in a powerfully erotic rhythm and her whole world started to dissolve.

Marie arched her hips as David caressed her breast with one hand and cupped her bottom in the other. Then he began to ride her hard and fast.

"More!" she cried out, as he tightened his grip and lowered his mouth to hers.

Their tongues tangled, their teeth nipped, and he thrust harder, over and over again, sending her to one peak after another. Marie bit his shoulder, his neck, lost in passion... until they each cried out, a deep primitive sound that united them both and sent them spiraling into bliss.

David wrapped his arms around the sex goddess snuggled against his chest. He had suspected from the start there was more to Marie than met the eye, but he'd had no way of knowing she'd respond so ardently.

"Well. That was heaven on earth. What next?"

"Dunno," she murmured. "Let's do it again."

"You're insatiable."

"If you've got a better idea, I'd like to hear it," she said sleepily.

He ruffled her already tousled hair. "You're only half awake. How about a bedtime story?"

"Hmm. Just so long as it's not *Silence In The Trees.*"

"Hell, no."

121

Something in his tone made Marie sit up partway, and study him for a long moment. "Wait a minute. Are you telling me you didn't like that book?"

David yanked up the sheet and buried his chin in the covers. "Guilty," he said, barely visible from his eyebrows up.

He lowered the blankets and gave a tentative smile. "Do you hate me?"

"Hate you? Oh, David! You nut," she said, giving him a playful shove. *"Silence In The Trees* was without question one of the most boring books I've ever read. But"—she stretched one long leg over his marvelously hairy calves, and snuggled closer—"I thought you liked it!"

"Well, honestly," he said, lightly caressing her arm. "It was a strain making it past Chapter Two."

"But you said—"

"No, I didn't," he said, shaking his head. "I said I thought *you'd* like it. Hey, wait a minute!"

He tilted sideways and tried to meet her eyes. "Next, you're going to tell me you don't like reading *Publishers Weekly* either."

"I don't," she said, sounding indignant. "Except, of course, when business calls for it. I'm a bookstore manager, what do you think? I read all the journals, but that doesn't have to mean they're my idea of fun."

David swatted her on the bottom through the thick layer of bedclothes. "That's my girl! I knew you had better sense than that."

He cocked one eyebrow. "You prefer that steamy stuff—"

"Romance, David. It's called romance."

"Oh, right. I really liked the part where that buxom librarian and her friendly doc were getting, uh, romantic."

Marie grabbed him by the chin and looked up. "Admit it, big boy, you liked that book, didn't you?"

"Wellll..." He drew the word out, stalling for time.

"David Lake!" she said, releasing his chin and popping his shoulder. "You were really into it... I saw you. Anyway, what *do* you like to read?"

"Well, I've got another confession," he said, ducking back under the blankets. "And this one, I don't think you're going to like as much."

He couldn't see her troubled look.

"I don't read much," his muffled voice said through the covers. "Not really." He peeped out into the darkness, expecting a verbal assault. "That is, unless you count the sports section of the newspaper."

He was sure that she'd be angry, that she'd discount him as a worthless fraud. But instead, she burst out laughing.

"Oh, David, I'm so glad."

"Glad? That I'm not well-read or—"

"David," she said, patting his chest, "I like you just the way you are." The fact that he wasn't into pretentious modern literature made him even more attractive than she'd found him to begin with. And to think, at one time she'd compared him to that unmentionable man now in New York.

David sighed and hugged her tighter. "Well, I'm glad that little mix-up with Cecil didn't do any lasting damage."

Marie wriggled out of his grasp and sat bolt upright in bed, clutching the blankets to her chest. "What mix-up? What are you talking about?"

"Well, I might as well tell you," he said, reaching over to massage her arm. "Now that we have an understanding."

She scooted over on the bed and withdrew from his reach.

"Hey," he said, his hand suspended in the darkness.

"David, tell me the truth. The whole truth, this time, about you and Cecil."

"Huh?"

"David," she said sternly, as if she were scolding a child.

"It's nothing," he said quickly. "Nothing, I swear. I didn't know the guy from Adam when I walked into the cafe looking for you. And then we got to making conversation. He, oh, brought me my coffee. I asked if he knew you, but he... what I mean is, he told me he had a way... that literary types liked him."

Marie humphed, but he continued. "Then he offered—I swear, I didn't ask—some recommendations on things I could read, an approach I could take to get a women like you interested."

"Like me, specifically?" she asked, crossing her arms in front of her.

"Holy cow... I mean, oh, boy. I mean, no, absolutely not."

She narrowed her eyes and wished she had her glasses.

"You don't think," he said, "I would have actually mentioned you by name? That I was interested, I mean? But I was. Boy, oh, boy, was I. From the moment you walked into my—"

"David," she said, unfolding her arms and crawling back over to him, "you can stop babbling now. I forgive you."

He lay there, feeling a little stunned, as she perched like a lioness and clambered on top of him.

"But I—" he said, as she began to tug down the sheet, "I just wanted a chance to explain."

"Don't worry," she said, stripping him naked on the bed. "I understand. It was natural. You figured since he was my boyfriend he'd—"

David reached up and put his hands on her shoulders. "Boyfriend?"

Marie settled her bare derriere on his thighs. "Didn't you know?" she asked innocently.

"I—uh—boyfriend? No way! When I asked you..."

"Guilty," she said, feeling anything but. "I guess we've both told our fair share of little white lies."

She looked down and spread her hands on his beautifully solid chest. He was without a doubt the handsomest man she'd known.

"Forgive me?" she asked, wriggling sensually.

"Oh, God, Marie," he said, grabbing her hips, "anything. Anything at all."

Chapter Thirteen

Marie found her glasses in the living room and stumbled to the kitchen, tracking the appetizing scent of frying bacon. She walked to the threshold, set her glasses on her nose and paused.

Mmm. A blond Adonis was standing shirtless at her kitchen stove cooking up a breakfast that smelled divine.

He turned and smiled in her direction.

"Morning, wild thing. I was starting to wonder when you'd stumble out of bed."

She felt a warm sweep of color suffuse her face.

"Was I really that... wild?" she asked, tightening her robe and sidestepping to the coffeepot.

"Oh, baby," David said, coming over and drawing her into a bear hug. "Yes." He gave her a mischievous grin. "So," he said, leaning forward and giving her a hard smack on the lips, "what's your pleasure?"

"Why, David Lake," she said, looking up into his beautiful blue eyes and feeling as if she were drowning all over again, "I believe you know the answer to that."

"Yes, darling," he said, reaching behind her and playfully squeezing heir rump. "But what would you like for breakfast?"

"I... uh, coffee first," she said, still feeling foggy. Next time—and to look at him now there would certainly be a next time—she wanted to be as clear as day.

David motioned for her to sit at the breakfast table and brought her a cup of coffee. Black, just how she liked it.

"How did you know?"

"Manly intuition."

"No, I mean about the coffee," she said, hiding her blush behind her mug.

"I remembered from our coffee date."

Marie raised her brow.

"The endlessly clanking spoon."

"Oh," she said, with a giggle. She felt unnervingly silly. Like some wayward teenager who'd gotten away with doing something naughty in her parents' bed. She laughed out loud, realizing that was precisely what she'd done.

David walked over and set a plate of bacon, scrambled eggs, and toasted English muffins in front of her.

Marie brought her hands to her brilliant cheeks.

"Oh my, I don't think I've ever been cooked for before."

"Sweetheart," David said, leaning over and kissing her forehead. "Get used to it."

"But, wait! Oh my goodness..." Marie jumped to her feet, nearly upsetting the table.

"David! What time is it? I can't believe it, but I almost forgot I have to go to work!"

What couldn't she believe, Marie asked herself? That the most unforgettable man in her life had made her forget all about things like mundane responsibilities?

"Slow down there, honey," he said, pushing her back down into her chair. "Enjoy your meal. You won't be going to work or anywhere else today. Or so says local radio station WCVX."

She dropped back into her seat with a questioning look.

"Snow, Marie. The most beautiful snowfall I've seen in years. While we were heating things up last night—"

She didn't wait to hear the rest, dropping her napkin and running to the front door.

"Gracious," she said, throwing it wide. "A winter wonderland!"

A blanket of white covered the ground and delicate icicles hung from the trees, catching the color of the morning sky.

"Wanna play?" David asked, stealing up behind her and nuzzling her neck.

After breakfast they put on their coats and headed outside, and fortunately, David was the right size for Mark's old snow gear. They threw snowballs, raced circles around the big oak tree, and made snow angels on the ground when they were too tired to run anymore.

"My!" Marie said, panting as she ran back into the house. "Next time I face off against Mark and Johnny in a snowball fight, remind me to put you on my team."

"You got it," David said, laughing and peeling off his wet outer clothing. "Where shall I put these?"

"Here"—she took them—"in the dryer."

"Hmm, "David said, sneaking up behind her as she bent over the lint trap. "I've got some other parts that need warming up too."

"David Lake! Are you always this bad?" she asked without turning.

David reached forward and cupped her breasts in his hands. "Only with you."

Marie forgot all about loading the dryer and chased him back into the bedroom, where they stripped in record time and engaged in another hour-long sexual romp.

"Well!" she said, throwing herself belly down on the bed. "Now, what do we do for the rest of the afternoon?"

"How about Monopoly?" he asked, running a trailing finger down her back.

"Monopoly?" she asked with a giggle. "Are you serious?"

"Well, I like it, don't you? Sometimes when Deb and I were snowbound in Asheville, it was the only way we had to entertain ourselves."

Actually, when Marie thought about it, she and her brothers and sisters had spent an awful lot of time playing that game during the dreary winters.

"I get to be the banker!" Marie screeched, springing off the mattress and grabbing for her robe.

Hours later, they settled back in front of a blazing fire and sipped their hot cocoa.

"Today's been like a dream," Marie said.

"Yes," David answered. "Too bad the snow's melting."

She sighed heavily and rested her head against his arm. "Well, I suppose for both of us, duty calls. Your shop will be open tomorrow and so will mine."

"Uh-oh," David said, setting down his mug. "Are we getting to the part where you tell me it's time to go home?"

"Not on your life," she said, tightening her hand around his arm.

In fact, Marie realized with stunning clarity, she never wanted David to go home. Though it had been only twenty-four hours since the fiancé charade began, she was starting to realize that she didn't want to give it up. Not just the fabulous sexual attraction between them, but the other ways they related as well. David was easy to talk to, and fun-loving in a way that reminded her of her younger brothers. She'd never laughed so much with Paul, or—heaven knows—Cecil. With those two, she'd always felt as if they were observing her, just waiting somehow for the inevitable moment when she would slip up.

David, on the other hand, didn't seem to have a judgmental bone in his body. He took her for who she was and seemed to love every bit of it. What, oh what, had she done to deserve him?

"You're being awfully quiet," David said, bringing his feathery breath to her cheek.

"I was just thinking," she said into the firelight. "That other than our both hating *Silence In The Trees...*"

David chuckled.

"You and I seem to have a lot in common."

"Yeah," he said, lightly kissing her hair. "And who knows? It's only the beginning."

A beginning without an end, Marie found herself hoping.

"For example, I bet you like oldies... classic rock. Seventies and eighties, mostly."

Her eyes widened behind her glasses. "Amazing! David, how did you—"

He threw his head back with a laugh. "Studied your CD collection earlier," he said with a stealthy grin. "While you were sleeping."

She shook her head and sipped from her cocoa.

"My point is," David continued. "I like that music, too. You and I must have twenty duplicate CDs."

"Really?"

David stopped talking and seemed to scrutinize her for a moment.

"What? What's wrong?" she asked, feeling suddenly self-conscious.

"You have the cutest little mustache."

"Mustache?" She touched a finger to her upper lip.

"Made out of cocoa, right—there."

He leaned over and gave her a sweeping kiss.

"David," she said, pressing back on his chest, "if you start that all over again, I'll never get you to leave."

"That's precisely what I'm counting on." And he kissed her again.

"So, how was your extended holiday?" Caroline asked, as David bounced into the shop the next morning.

"Dandy," he said, sweeping her into his arms and swirling her across the floor. "Just dandy!"

"Uh-oh," Caroline said, breaking free and shaking out her hemline. "Something tells me that you saw Marie. And that you two shared more than turkey."

"Yeah!" David said, catching an unsuspecting Caroline off guard with an exuberant high-five.

"So, what does this mean?" Caroline asked, steadying a hand on her hip. "Is today going to be one of those wedding planner days?"

David gave a hearty laugh as Caroline blew out an exasperated breath.

"Look, with the holiday rush upon us, I can't afford to give you any more time off."

"Not even," David asked, giving her a pleading smile, "for my honeymoon?"

Marie was dreamily thumbing through a bridal magazine in the employee lounge when Joanne walked over and tapped her on the shoulder.

"If you're looking for me," she said, "I think I'm a little old—*and experienced,* "she added with a whisper, "—to be wearing white."

She looked up in surprise and then her eyes darted to Joanne's finger.

The elderly woman proudly stuck out her left hand to display a glittering solitaire.

"Oh, Joanne!" Marie said, springing to her feet and wrapping the other woman in her arms. "I can hardly believe it! After all this time... Chad?" she asked.

Joanne's cheeks turned a dusty rose.

"Took me home to meet his children. His children, Marie! Over Thanksgiving. It turned out that his grandson and I both like the Grateful Dead. I think that clinched the deal."

Marie laughed loudly and sat back in her chair.

"Sit," she said, tugging warmly at Joanne's hands. "I want to hear every thrilling detail."

Chapter Fourteen

"Oh, David!" Marie said, racing into the optician's shop. "I'm so excited about the wedding I can't stand it!"

"Wedding?" David was going to get that little snitch. He'd wanted so badly for it to be a surprise, and Caroline had sworn she wouldn't say a word.

"Yes, it's so hard to believe after all this time!"

"Well," he said, looking over at a customer who was inspecting a display case of frames and trying to sound nonchalant. "You know what they say, when it's right, it's right."

Marie glanced quickly around the shop.

"Oh, my gosh, David," she said, bringing her hands to her flaming cheeks. "You're working! I'm so sorry. I'll come back later."

She spun and swirled for the exit.

David had never seen her move this fast. It was making him dizzy.

"Oh, honey," she said, gleefully passing through the door. "It's so exciting. So very exciting! I've got so much to do!"

David watched as Marie disappeared down the icy sidewalk, her coat caught up in a gust of wind.

The gentleman selected a pair of frames and set them loudly on the counter, his eyes traveling to the woman outdoors.

"My fiancée," David said with a tight smile and a shrug.

Since Caroline had taken the afternoon off to meet with a supplier, David used his lunch hour as an opportunity to lock up the shop and go hunt for Marie. He was sorely disappointed that Caroline had let the cat out of the bag. For once in his life, David had wanted to do it up right: wine, dinner, the romantic proposal.

Oh well, he thought, shaking off the chill that sliced through him with the wind, at least she was happy. Ecstatic, in fact. He'd never seen Marie so positively glowing. Well, almost never, he thought, with a lustful grin.

But just because she somehow knew, didn't mean they wouldn't have to talk about it. They'd have to set a date, make some plans, and—David acknowledged—no matter what she thought she knew—he'd still have to ask her officially. Get down on his knees and all that.

Besides, as the groom, David had certain responsibilities. It was his job to take care of certain details... plan the honeymoon, for example. It was right there on page three of the groom's checklist. He'd read it with his own eyes, at least a dozen times.

David strode purposefully into Books & Bistro and searched the aisles until he found her, systematically turning books cover out on the shelves so that their authors' names would be prominently displayed.

"I'm so glad I found you," he said, rushing over and giving her a tight hug.

She glanced down the aisle as if she hoped no one was looking. Well, he thought, so now it was her turn to be embarrassed.

"David! What a surprise!"

"Surprise, sweetheart?" he asked, grabbing for her once again, but she stepped backwards and bumped into a shelf. "Thought for sure you'd be expecting me."

"Well, I..." Marie brushed some imaginary crumbs off the front of her dress. "What are you doing here?" she asked, lowering her voice along with her glasses, peering at him.

"I came to discuss plans."

"Plans? Oh, David, how sweet. Joanne will be so touched."

"Joanne? I didn't know you two were that close."

"Oh, yes," Marie said. "She's like a mother to me."

"Well, then by all means—"

A customer walked over and interrupted Marie with a question. When she'd finished directing him to the New Parenting section, she turned back to David.

"So, anyway... Here's what I was thinking. It's too cold to have it outdoors. But the ceremony really shouldn't involve much fuss."

"No fuss?"

"Well, come on, now, David. Once you get to a certain age, white lace and frills do seem a little ridiculous."

She sounded like she was already putting them out to pasture. David didn't feel *that* old.

"Besides," she said, her lashes fluttering lightly behind her frames. "I think our focus should be on the part that come afterwards."

"Right," he said, stepping forward eagerly.

"David!" Marie said, halting his advance with a hand to his chest. "What's gotten into you? I'm talking about the reception."

135

David wiggled his eyebrows. "And I was talking about the honeymoon."

"Honeymoon?" Marie looked a little baffled. "Well, I don't think you and I need to worry about that!"

David cleared his throat. She might be walking all over him where the other arrangements were concerned, but she was not going to take the reins away from him on this. "You just go ahead and worry about everything else. I'll take care of the honeymoon."

"You? But David, you barely even know Chad and Joanne. I mean, offering to help with the wedding is one thing—"

"Chad and Joanne?"

"Of course, Chad and Joanne. Who in the world did you think we've been talking about this whole time?"

David searched his brain for a quick answer.

"Oh, I knew who we were talking about, all right," he said with a modest laugh. "It's just that I was so surprised that old Chad hadn't planned anything, I thought I might suggest—"

"Now don't go offering unsolicited advice like Cecil," she said, squaring her shoulders and closing in. "You've already seen where that sort of thing can lead."

David stepped forward and drew his arms around her waist. "Oh, I don't think things have turned out too badly in the end."

"David!" Marie said, pounding his shoulders. "I'm working!"

"Working when it comes to me, but not when it comes to planning Joanne's wedding?"

"She's a coworker, silly! For heaven's sake, it's practically company business."

136

David still didn't let go.

"Wait a minute," she said, finally breaking free of his grasp, "you're not wriggling out of your offer to help, are you?"

"To help with Joanne's wedding? Of course not, I meant every word I said."

"Good, because it's going to be sort of crazy between my helping with hers, and Johnny and Meg's ceremony coming up next month."

"And when will *you* get a chance to take a break?"

"Oh, I don't know," she said, running her fingers through her hair. "Unless Fabio sneaks in and steals me away to Jamaica, I'll probably be stuck here till New Year's."

Well, he wasn't exactly Fabio, but... David smiled brightly and gave her a whopping kiss on the lips. She'd just given him the most brilliant idea.

Marie tried hard not to get too concerned that she hadn't heard from David in a couple of days. After all, he'd warned her that Caroline was planning to take inventory for the rest of the week, so he'd be working long hours.

It was probably for the best anyhow. Because, as much as David had expressed his interest in helping, Marie had her hands full planning Joanne's reception. When she thought about it, she realized he would just be in the way.

The bookstore had been incredibly busy ever since it had reopened after Thanksgiving. At peak hours, the aisles were so crammed Marie often had trouble simply maneuvering to do her regular duties. The business was good for the store, as well as its employees, who would all be getting healthy bonuses this year. But the extra paperwork high-volume sales produced made additional demands on her already limited time.

Although Johnny seemed to be heading for his upcoming nuptials with a certain degree of nonchalance, his fiancée Meg was positively frantic. With only two brothers and a misguided, twice-divorced socialite mother to help her, she'd been phoning Marie almost daily for support. With the wedding less than four weeks away, the caterer had canceled, the music director had been jailed for bootlegging CDs, and the bridesmaids' dresses—all seven of them—had arrived in the wrong color!

Marie hung up the phone and collapsed in a heap on her living room sofa. Weddings were an unbelievable amount of trouble. There was so much work involved—and planning. Just look at poor Meg. She was supposed to be preparing for the most memorable day of her life, but instead she'd been biting her fingernails to the quick in nervous anticipation of what disaster would befall her next.

Somehow it seemed to Marie that the more time and planning that went into a wedding, the greater the opportunities for things to go wrong.

When she'd been little, she'd envisioned all the same things Meg had. A candlelit ceremony, followed by a sit-down dinner and dancing in a castle courtyard to an elegant string quartet.

The main problem with that picture was that Marie wasn't a princess with a courtyard, or a fortune to afford that kind of soiree. In fact, up until very recently, she didn't really imagine she'd ever find a prince.

Her sisters Jill and Teresa had found their princes early, but instead of crumpets in the castle halls, they'd been treated to tea and cake in the big reception hall of their

Methodist church. To see the smiles on their faces, though, it hadn't mattered to either, not one bit.

Marie kicked off her shoes and propped her aching feet on the coffee table. What with all the circles they had to run around in prior to the big day, it was a wonder brides could dance at their own weddings at all.

No, this was too much. Too much altogether. By the time Meg and Johnny tied the knot on December twenty-eighth, Marie would have assisted with the planning of *four* weddings—Joanne's included.

She tugged the scrunchie out of her hair and shook it out as it fell to her shoulders. Gracious, she thought, straightening her curls with her fingers, maybe she'd missed her calling as a wedding coordinator.

No, scratch that. She truly enjoyed what she did for a living. What she'd enjoy even better, Marie thought, sinking low in the sofa and burying her head in her arms, would be for someone else to do everything for her when her time finally came along.

Joanne leaned in to the mirror and pinched her cheeks.

"Well, what do you think?" she asked, turning her head coyly from side to side and studying her reflection. "Not too bad for an old bird?"

"Oh, Joanne," Marie said, hugging her shoulders. "You look marvelous. Beautiful!"

It was true. One look at the glow on her face and the shine in her eyes, and anyone would swear Joanne was twenty years younger. Her hair was done in a loose upsweep with little sprigs of flowers tucked in all around. Lilac, to match her flowing, floor-length dress.

"You were so sweet to close the store, love. All on my account."

Marie chuckled. "Well, Joanne, I think it helped that your brother-in-law-to-be owns the place! But you're welcome just the same. It does seem like the perfect place for the ceremony."

"Perfect," Joanne said, smiling back at her reflection. "The scene of the crime, as Chad calls it. You know if it hadn't been for you, young lady—"

"Oh now, Joanne," Marie said, patting her affectionately on the arm. "Don't you go giving me too much credit. To look at the two of you now, there's no doubt in my mind that you and Chad would have found each other sooner or later."

Joanne turned quickly and looked at Marie. "Well, now, who on earth are you, and what have you done with my skeptical friend?"

Marie grinned and lowered her glasses. "She fell in love."

"You?" Joanne bounced on her heels like a five-year-old. "But you never said a word... How serious is it?"

"One blushing bride at a time, please," Marie said, spinning her back toward the mirror. "Now, let's be sure all those pins are in place. You wouldn't want to prick Chad when he gives you that 'I do' kiss!"

David sat nervously on the sidelines, acutely aware of what all this meant.

The back of the bookstore had been decorated to look like a wedding chapel, complete with an improvised canopy and lots of crepe paper decorations and fresh flowers. Marie had done a good job at making things look

140

special. But then again, everything she touched seemed to have a hint of magic in it.

David hoped he was doing the right thing, and wasn't making some big blunder. But the entire family had assured him his take on the matter was perfect.

With Marie's father being gone, Johnny had been the logical one to approach. But after speaking with him, Johnny had indicated that Mark might feel a little left out unless David also talked to him. Of course, Mark then pointed out that Jill and Teresa were Marie's sisters after all, and if—after speaking to Mark and Johnny—David somehow omitted them in the process, they'd be awfully hurt.

After all that, David had decided to sit down and have a chat with Dan and Jack as well. Oh, and he'd called Meg, in North Carolina, just to be sure his idea wouldn't upset her wedding plans in any way.

David sat at attention, as the wedding march started to play on Chad's grandson's boom box.

Marie walked in first, looking lovely in a low-cut, black sheath dress, and holding a bouquet of roses.

Then he smiled in wonder at the elegant old lady gliding down the aisle. Love, at any age, he decided, was stunning.

And he knew with a clarity beyond reason, that he and Marie would still share its glow—far past the day when their own hair turned gray.

David discreetly raised a hand to wipe away a tear as the minister stepped forward to begin the ceremony. For this would not only be a day that Chad and Joanne would remember for eternity, he was hoping... oh, how he was hoping... it'd be a landmark day for him and Marie, as well.

As the small group of guests mingled over cocktails, David turned away, searching for Marie.

"Looking for someone?" she asked, sneaking up behind him and almost startling him out of his socks.

"Marie," David nearly shouted, "don't... no," he said, halting abruptly, as her lips broke into a sensuous smile. "I take that back, surprise me all you want."

"Gracious," she said, stretching up on her toes and kissing him full force on the lips, "you're looking handsome tonight." And he did. Marie slightly narrowed her eyes, thinking she'd never seen him in a nice suit and tie before. And she liked it. Boy, did she like it.

Then again, she thought wickedly, she liked it best when he wore nothing at all.

David gave a nervous smile and looked around the room. Holy cow, was she forward tonight. Not that she couldn't be... But in public she was normally somewhat shy.

He studied her as her lips turned up in another naughty smile. "Had some champagne, dear?"

"Why, yes, I've had some champagne! And why not? We're celebrating here. Cel-e-brating! Yeee-ha!" she shouted, throwing her arms into the air and waving them.

"Marie," David said, clutching her to him and quickly scanning the room. "Maybe you shouldn't have any more."

"What do you mean, I shouldn't have any more? Hey sweet thing, why are you whispering?"

David held her even closer.

"Ouch! What are you—"

142

"Excuse us," David said to the very interested guests. Then he gripped Marie around the waist and carted her out of the room.

"What are you doing? I wanted to stay and enjoy the party!"

"I know you did, sweetheart," David said, bending low to grab her behind her knees. "But I've got a party of my own in mind."

"Hey, whoa!" she squealed, as he hoisted her skyward and threw her over his shoulder.

"David Lake, put me down!" she yelled, pounding his rear with her fists.

But he just pushed back the door and carried her into the night, where the December wind half froze her bare skin and sobered her up in a hurry.

"Who *are* you?" she asked, still hanging upside down.

"Just call me Fabio," he said, patting her bottom with a smile.

Chapter Fifteen

Marie adjusted the heater vent in her direction, then folded her arms across her chest.

"I'm going to give you exactly five seconds to explain yourself, or else..."

David raised his eyebrows.

"Or else I'm calling the police."

"You mean Chad?" David tried to hold back a chuckle, but didn't quite succeed.

She huffed and looked out the window.

"Great to see you think making a spectacle of yourself is so funny."

David widened his eyes and thumbed his chest.

"Hey, wait a minute, *sweet thing*. That is what you called me in there? *Sweet*—"

"Okay, David, I get the point. So I had a little too much champagne. Well, it's been a long week. I've been working late, haven't slept much. And then with all the wedding—"

"Marie," he said, with one of those deep blue looks that made her completely lose sight of her point. "You don't have to explain yourself to me."

"Oh, good," she said, blinking, and glad—so glad— that she remembered what she'd wanted to say. "But maybe you have to explain yourself to me. I mean, what was that caveman act back there?"

David merely shrugged. "You mean you didn't like it?"

"Well, I..." The truth was, she *had* liked it. Liked it very much, darn it. It had made her feel all feminine and submissive—like a romance heroine being swept away by the masterful hero of her dreams.

"I still insist on knowing why you did that."

"I wanted to take you to dinner."

"Have you ever thought of just asking, or is that approach too ordinary?"

David smiled and lightly thumped her nose."I guess you bring out the beast in me."

"You know," he said, resting his very warm hand on the side of her neck, "I used to be a fine, upstanding citizen. But now," he said, slipping his palm around her nape and leaning his face in toward hers, "I'm just an—animal."

Marie's eyes flashed as he drew closer. What was it that this man did to her? She tingled all over whenever he was near.

"Marie," he said, so close she could almost taste him, "the truth..."

Her nipples went hard and her body arched as all her senses recalled what David's physical truths felt like.

"Do I bring out the beast in you?"

He nibbled lightly at the base of her neck, on her earlobe... at the very tip of her chin.

"Grrr..." she said, latching on to his ears and pulling his mouth down on hers.

Marie pushed back in her seat and latched her seat belt.

"Are we really going to dinner," she asked, "or was that just a ploy to get me in the car and feel me up?"

David laughed and turned the ignition. The caveman routine had worked like a charm.

"No, sweetheart, no ploy. We have reservations at ten."

"Ten? Isn't that a little late for dinner?"

145

"As late as they'd take at the Italian Chef, but I had a hunch it might take us a while to get there."

Italian Chef? Marie's mouth watered at the thought of a rich pasta alfredo coupled with a strong Chianti... followed by a sensual night in bed with her favorite man.

"I do appreciate being taken to dinner, even if the invitation was a little heavy-handed." Her stomach growled loudly as if to accentuate her point, and they both laughed. "I haven't eaten all day."

"Marie, sweetheart," he said, lowering his voice, "you really need to take better care of yourself. Or maybe what you need"—he cast her a meaningful look but she looked away—"is someone to do the job for you."

She gripped the door handle, telling herself not to read too much between the lines.

"From where I sit," she said, trying to make light of it, "I've got plenty of people to run my life. There's Johnny and Mark—"

David started to say something, but stopped.

"What's wrong?"

"Holy cow," David said, wiping his brow with the back of his sleeve. "Talk about running things, I just zipped right through that red light!"

Marie bit her bottom lip, wondering why she'd been thinking he was such a wild man. "Wouldn't worry about it too much, David. All the police in this town are at Books & Bistro drinking champagne."

"Right," David said, sinking back in his seat with a sigh. Man, he'd have to be more careful. He needed all his wits about him tonight.

They sat face to face at the small corner table.

"I've always liked this place," Marie said, raising her glass in David's direction. "But none of my other dates," she said, her face brightening in the candle's glow, "could ever afford to bring me here."

"I'm not a rich man, Marie," David said, clinking his glass to hers. "In fact, my parents have disowned me. But I pledge to do my best to keep you in style."

Marie set down her glass.

"What do you mean, disowned you?"

"I wanted to be my own man, start my own business someday," David said. "An optician's shop. That wasn't good enough for them."

She straightened her glasses on her nose and pushed back a few locks of hair from her forehead, waiting for him to continue.

"Dad wanted me to go into the family business."

"Banking?"

"Avariciousness was more like it."

"But I thought they were well off. Didn't you say something about your mother and all her charities?"

"Oh, they were generous, in their own way. But you better believe they always knew exactly how generous they were. And everybody else did, too. Down to the last cent."

Marie reached out and laid a hand on the arm of his suit coat.

"Oh, David, I'm sorry. I didn't know it was like that—with you and your folks. Don't you even... keep in touch?"

"Sure," he said, with a wry smile, "we get together every time Debbie plans a wedding."

"Oh," Marie said, dabbing her lips with her napkin and seeming to change her mind. "Guess it's not something you want to talk about."

David brought his other hand to the table top and linked it in hers. "No, go on. I want to hear what you have to say."

"It's really not my place."

"If it were your place," he said gently, "and I asked you, would you tell me?"

"Of course," she said, unable to look away.

"Then tell me, Marie. Whatever it is that's on your mind."

"It's silly, maybe. Because I don't know Debbie at all. I mean, I'm sure that—if I did—I'd like her."

"She'd like you too," he said with a tender smile, "very much."

"Well, anyway, if your family really doesn't get along and you don't see each other much... don't you think it's possible Debbie keeps getting engaged as a way of bringing all of you together?"

David blinked and looked down at the table. It was scary, positively alarming the way she'd looked right into the situation and seen it so clearly for what it was. Of course, she had to be right. Right about his sister, right about his family.

Right on the money when it came to him.

David reached his other hand toward her, and they sat holding hands for the longest while, neither one speaking.

"I used to get sort of frustrated with the service in here," David said, slowly looking up, "but tonight I'm sort of glad for the lull. I don't know how you do it, Marie," he said, his crystal blue eyes starting to blur, "but you have a way of looking right through me, of seeing"—he brought one hand to his chest and pressed her palm to his heart—"what's in here."

Her lower lip began to tremble. He couldn't possibly be—

"Alfredo?" the waiter asked, handing over her plate.

They continued to talk throughout the delicious meal about every subject under the sun, but somehow they always came back to tonight's topic: weddings. David was regaling her with anecdotes from all the ones he'd attended and Marie listened raptly.

"Well, anyway," he went on, laughing, "until tonight, of course, that was the last wedding I went to. And after seeing the way those other groomsmen tossed poor Blake into the pool, I said never again."

"Never again, that you'd go to a wedding or be part of one?"

Marie smiled politely at the waiter as he cleared their dishes.

"Participate—as a groomsman, I mean. Hey, I was minding my own business at the bar. I had nothing to do with that let's-throw-Blake-in-the-pool-and-spray-shaving-cream-on-his-new-car business. But he was seeing double from the chlorine. To this day he holds me culpable. You try to be a nice guy..."

"And look where it gets you," she finished for him.

Yeah, he was looking. Looking right past those turquoise frames and into a soul he knew sparked with desire. She was beautiful tonight. More beautiful than ever: her upswept hair surrounding her lovely face with curls, her sleek, long neck begging for his kisses, her tastefully low-cut dress tempting him to touch...

"Well, if it matters to you," she said, bringing him back to earth with her smile. "I'm completely in your corner. I've sworn off weddings, too."

His heart sank. "Huh?" he asked, none too eloquently, reaching for his water glass with a gasp and downing it completely.

She eyed him curiously, but kept talking.

"Weddings. They're for the birds. You know, the ones who eat the rice. Such a headache, too...."

David looked around desperately for the waiter, but when he couldn't find him reached for Marie's water glass instead.

"Help yourself," she said, wrinkling up her nose. My, he was acting strange all of a sudden.

"You mean," David asked, his voice still a bit froggy, "you don't want to get married? Ever?"

Marie grabbed back her water glass and took a long sip, before setting it back down at her place.

"Who's asking?"

"I, uh..."

David turned red from the neck up.

"I am," he said, loudly clearing his throat.

She gasped at him, momentarily tongue-tied. His eyes were earnest and opened wide, his upper lip quivering.

"Marie," he said, shocking her by pushing back his chair and falling to his knees beside her. "Marry me."

Her first reaction was joy. Sheer, overwhelming joy. The man of her dreams had actually...

But then she thought of Johnny. Johnny and Meg with their own wedding three and a half weeks away.

And of all the time she'd already taken to help Joanne.

She wanted to say yes, but not right now. Find a way to keep him holding on for just a couple of more months.

But then he reached his hand into his coat pocket and pulled out an envelope.

"What's this?" she asked, as he set it down on the table before her.

"Open it," David urged. "Don't say yes or no. Just open it."

David watched her studying the envelope and held his breath. It took all his restraint not to lean over and rip it open for her.

He tried to take a mental picture to capture the moment in his mind. He'd proposed! Gone and done it! Taken the plunge headlong, and now the rest was entirely up to her.

David began a silent prayer, looking skyward.

And then, as if in answer, she fitted her nail under the seal and popped it open.

"Airline tickets?" she exclaimed, astonished. "Oh, David, that's so sweet, but—"

"Read them," he said, leveling her a look from his kneeling position.

Marie looked back down at the round-trip tickets in her hand.

"Jamaica?"

"There's something else in there," he said, still on the floor.

She narrowed her lovely eyes, then peeked into the envelope again.

"Oh, David," she gasped, pulling out a gorgeous solitaire.

David took the diamond from her hand and gently slid it onto her left ring finger.

"Marie McCloud," he said, his voice now stronger, braver, than he ever could have imagined. "Will you do me the honor of becoming my wife?" He took a very deep breath. "Let me carry you away to Jamaica where we can

151

say our vows on a sandy beach, without the worries, the headaches..."

He gave a shaky smile as a tear broke free from the corner of his eye.

"Hey, I'll go if she won't!" someone shouted from the back of the restaurant.

"Oh, David," Marie said, leaping to her feet and pulling him up from the floor. "You make it awfully hard to say no. I do want to marry you, I do. And I love you," she said, looking deep in his eyes.

"I love you, too," he whispered back, bringing his arms around her waist and pulling her up against him.

She hardly knew whether to laugh or cry. "But I can't go to Jamaica. I can't..."

David quelled her emotion with a kiss.

"You can," he commanded firmly. "I've already arranged your vacation with your employer. We'll be back in plenty of time for your brother Johnny's wedding."

"David," she said, breathless, her helpless knees giving way. "I have obligations to meet. Deadlines... You can't just sweep in here and carry me away!"

"Watch me," he said.

And then, to a round of applause from the restaurant patrons, David swooped down and threw her over his shoulder.

The End

THE SOMETIME BRIDE

Carrie swirled the ladle nervously around the near-empty punch bowl. The shower had gone off without a hitch. She and Mike—uh, Wilson—had even gotten some lovely gifts. A blender, cooking utensils. Towels. All the nice little odds and ends that help make a newlywed house a home. This wasn't such a good idea, after all. In fact, it was terrible. So many people had gone to so much time, trouble, and expense. Even Nellie's place cards were beautiful. A keepsake for the happy couple. Carrie frowned at her murky reflection centered in the twirling ice ring.

And to make matters worse, Mike had been an absolute champ. Everybody adored him implicitly. He'd been warm, witty, and charming the whole afternoon through. His act as her fiancé had almost even seemed real; at least his hugs and affectionate glances had seemed authentic enough. And those few unexpected kisses, though innocent enough in their placement—one at her temple, one on the back of her hand, the one at her neckline... Well, all right, maybe the one at her neck hadn't seemed quite so innocent in intent as the others. But still, no matter where his kisses had landed, each time Mike had surprised her with the warm contact of his lips, her world had caved in and her heart had let go. Let go of any notion that this thing between them was little more than make-believe. Because, though words could deceive, feelings seldom lied, and when Mike brought his flesh to hers... Carrie dropped the ladle into the punch bowl as goose bumps tore down her spine.

Carrie felt the hair swept from her nape. "Ready to leave?" Mike whispered, bringing his mouth close to her ear.

Carrie turned in surprise and found herself directly in his arms, her backside pinned against the table that held the punch bowl. "Never," she said, bringing her arms up and around his neck and pulling him in close as their lips melded in the final consummation of what they'd both been desiring all afternoon.

"Why don't you kids run on home?" Grandma Russell asked, blinking the dining room chandelier on and off above them.

Mike pulled back in a damp sweat. "Let's!" he said, giving Carrie a firm, virgin peck on the lips.

Chapter One

Carrie St. John strode to the edge of the pool and tugged the ring from her finger. One year, six months, and four days exactly. *Yank.* The dang thing was stuck.

Carrie looked down in frustration at the glittering diamond offset by tiny emeralds. Beautiful, yes. But— *yank,* the ring worked free of her knuckle and glided off her narrow upper finger—only a poor reminder of a relationship gone sour.

Carrie clutched her hand around the meager gems, wondering if Wilson had paid more for them, he'd have been more reluctant to leave. Hogwash, she thought, tossing back her arm and prepping for a long throw. Wilson would have left regardless. And if it hadn't been for Teresa, it would have been for someone else.

But of all the rotten things to do! Take Carrie to a scenic country inn, then drop the bomb. More like a blazing comet, Carrie thought, feeling the raw burn in her heart as she lobbed the ring forward over the water. The engagement ring pitched in a perfect arch toward the water, then plopped beneath the surface with a deafening calm.

Mike Davis ran a flat palm along the bumpy bottom surface of the pool. It had to be down here somewhere, darn it! Four months of hard-earned commission down the chlorinated drain!

If Mike had had any inkling how callous Alexia could be, he would have never gone to the trouble. Not to mention the biting expense. Now if he couldn't find the darned ring, he'd be set back financially for nothing!

Already was set back financially for nothing, Mike reminded himself, feeling his lungs drain of air. This was his third dive under and still nothing doing.

Hey, wait a minute…

Mike fishtailed over to the center of the pool where something glistened against its bottom. Yep, that was it! Had to be…

Mike swept toward the gemstone like an alligator on the prowl, then plucked the tiny ring off the pool bottom, examining it through the blurry haze caused by pool lights and chemicals. No way. But it was. Somebody else's ring entirely. The ring Mike had presented to Alexia had been a solitaire.

Despite years of high school swim-team accomplishments, Mike felt his wind quickly abating. He'd been down here too long, he realized, angling toward the surface and pressing his heels off the bottom.

Mike rocketed skyward, another woman's engagement ring clutched in his hand. Another woman who was likely just as heartless as his Alexia. When Adam gave his rib to Eve, Mike thought, breaking into the chill of the evening, the poor schmuck hadn't realized the woman had plans to barbeque it!

Carrie let out a shriek as water barreled forth and a man emerged from the center of the pool.

He shook out his honey-blond head, then paddled over to the side where Carrie stood.

"Lose something?" he asked as Carrie backed up a step.

Carrie raised a hand to her cheek and stroked back hot tears. "Where on earth did you come from?" she demanded of this Poseidon-like god, whose eyes, she noticed, were as green as the Caribbean Sea. Though she didn't know why she'd noticed, or—more importantly—why she particularly cared.

"I came from the bottom of the pool," he said, his tone not the least bit friendly. "Where I ran into a little something that might just be yours."

With that, he pulled his right hand out of the water and gingerly steadied Carrie's engagement ring between his thumb and forefinger.

Despite his hostile tone, Carrie grudgingly admitted that this swim god was actually quite attractive. Alarmingly attractive, in a way that would make most women swoon. But not Carrie, she told herself, backing up another step. Attractive meant trouble, and, in the last four hours, Carrie St. John had endured enough trouble to last a lifetime.

"I'm sorry," she said, shaking her head, "you've got the wrong girl."

Well, that was one way to look at it, Mike thought, shifting his gaze between the ring pinched in his fingers and the enigmatic woman on the pool deck.

She was dressed in a summer sundress, wavy brown hair flowing to her shoulders. Her eyes, he thought, were just as dark. Although from this angle it was pretty hard to tell.

Mike braced himself on his arms as he rose from the water.

"Don't think so," he told her, lightly shaking off and extending his hand, palm up, in her direction.

"Excuse me?" she asked, trying her best to look indignant. There was a little pout to her mouth that looked almost appealing. Almost, Mike reminded himself, not quite. Brunettes, in general, meant trouble. And Alexia had taught him that trouble not only hurt like the dickens, it was darned expensive too.

"Your ring," Mike said, stepping forward.

"You have a lot of nerve…" she said, setting her chin. Yep, Mike told himself, they were definitely brown. Chocolate-brown eyes that could probably look enticingly warm were they not so heated with vehemence. "…intruding on my private moment!"

Mike laughed. "Intruding? But I was here first!"

She shuffled sandaled feet beneath the low hemline of her dress. Feet that were attached, Mike couldn't help but notice, to two very well-formed feminine ankles. "Well, if you were, I certainly didn't see…"

Mike arched his eyebrows, and she stopped. By the way her appreciative eyes had traveled from his damp pecs to his navel, sure as heck looked to Mike like she'd been seeing something.

"What I meant to say was—"

Mike walked forward and lifted a balled-up fist from the woman's side. "Here," he said, prying her fingers loose as she looked on with incredulity.

Mike pressed the ring into her palm. "Someone spent hard-earned money for that. Don't think it's very good of you to go throwing it away."

Carrie glared at the insolent man, wondering how he'd known exactly what she'd been doing. More puzzled still at how he dared intrude on her life. "Don't think it's very good of you to go telling a complete stranger how to run her affairs!"

"Oh, so it was only an affair, was it?" he asked, with a cool sheen to his evergreen eyes. Eyes that Carrie was quite certain could look enticing under different circumstances. "Somehow I imagined it was a heck of a lot more serious than that."

"Well, maybe," she said, flipping over his wrist and cramming the ring back into his hand. "You ought to think of something better to do with your overactive imagination than torment women you don't even know."

Carrie turned her back on him and started toward the inn. Of all the indignities. To be trounced upon by one man during dinner, then have a hunky dish like this one serve up insults for dessert.

"Hang on!" he called, hurrying to catch up with her. "Your ring!"

"Finders, keepers," she said, picking up her pace. But what Carrie most desperately didn't want to find herself doing was falling for another man. Especially one who looked like that in a pair of swim trunks—all six foot something of virile man, dripping wet... Criminy! Carrie scurried up the cold stone steps to the main building's front door. The flame was barely extinguished on her relationship with Wilson and here she was already playing with matches!

Carrie struggled against the notion of turning back toward her predator but knew he stood silently watching her at the bottom of those stairs. Silently—rugged, handsome, yes, darn it, handsome. And wet. Carrie's throat went dry at that last thought.

"What?" she asked, spinning abruptly on her heels. "What in the world are you staring at?"

But Mike, who truthfully didn't know, just stood there dumbfounded with this beautiful stranger's ring in his hand. Beautiful, indeed. There was a fine sweep of color that just dusted her cheekbones, and somehow—given all the crying she'd apparently been doing—Mike didn't imagine it was the magic of makeup. No, there was something much more powerful going on here. Something that made absolutely zero sense. And, for a lunatic instant, Mike found himself wishing he hadn't wasted his heartfelt offering on Alexia but had given it to this goddess instead. Lunatic was right. Mike gazed up at the powdery quarter moon threading stardust through the trees, deciding he'd been out in the night air too long.

But whether he was crazy or not, Mike knew one thing and one thing only. Before she disappeared into the inn, and perhaps for eternity, he had to get her name.

"I was just wondering," he began tentatively, feeling the heat expand from his temples to the tops of his ears. "What your name is." Holy Christ. He was insane! Alexia's ring was still at the bottom of the pool, and here he was…what? Making eyes at another woman who'd just now broken some Romeo's heart?

"Why?" she asked, holding court at the top of the stairs but not looking half as menacing as she apparently intended.

"Just in case the law comes after me for stealing your ring," Mike raced in, thinking quickly. He gave her his best smile but found it impossible to tell whether she was charmed by it or not.

"Very funny."

He guessed not. "Seriously, I—"

"Name's Carrie, if you must know. Carrie St. John, and you can rest assured, uh…"

"Mike," he filled in with a grin.

"Mike," she said, clearing her throat and averting her eyes from his naked upper torso, which he'd noticed her perusing just the same. "You can rest assured I won't be calling the police on you anytime soon."

"Ah, so you do admit the ring was yours, after all."

Her eyes flashed as she turned and headed through the door.

Conniving male! They were all the same, every last one of them. And what, pray tell, did this dripping hunk of flesh plan to do with that information? Blackmail her? As if the entire world wouldn't find out soon enough. With Carrie's luck, it would make the morning edition.

Carrie let herself into her room and fell in a heap of emotion onto the bed. Her life couldn't possibly get any worse! First, Wilson brought her all the way here, to this gorgeous historic home—to tell her he's fallen in love with another woman. Then he left her, more like deserted her, in this love nest built for two, and had the gall to tell her to enjoy the rest of the weekend. His treat.

Carrie pressed her palms to her forehead to ward off her ensuing headache. But knew that it would come regardless. This was stress with a capital "S"! She'd been such a fool, had already invited six women to be her bridesmaids! And now she'd have to call each one and confess her misfortune.

And what was worse, what would truly be the worst part of all would be in facing her matchmaking grandmother. The grandmother Carrie had finally managed to convince she'd found a dashing bachelor to make "an honest woman" of her.

Carrie rolled over on the bed and clutched her pillow to her streaming cheeks. One time. Okay. But this was the second disaster she'd endured at the near-altar. What was it about her, Carrie wondered, that made men want to cut and run? Or worse still, rush straight into another woman's arms? Carrie had actually seen Teresa, knew exactly who the woman was. And though as a fellow stockbroker of Wilson's she certainly shared Wilson's business savvy, Carrie truthfully didn't find Teresa that much to look at.

And that made matters all the worse, Carrie admitted to herself, as her throat swelled tight and tears blazed trails down her cheeks. She couldn't blame Wilson's leaving her on something as base as hormones, or his sheer physical attraction to another woman. No, what had caused Wilson to leave ran deeper than that. When he'd looked beneath the surface of his relationship with both Teresa and Carrie, Teresa had won hands down.

Mike took another dive below the surface and cursed himself once again for his inability to find Alexia's ring. If she wasn't going to use it, she could have at least had the good grace to return it, not toss it in the pool.

What was it with all the women in this place? Had they made a silent pact to simultaneously ditch their men in this affronting fashion? Maybe that was what this vacation locale was all about. Some sort of fantasy dumping ground for all disenchanted females. Bring your man to the Sawyers House and be rid of him for good! Elegant starlight pool, suitable for ring-tossing!

Mike was just about to call it a night when he saw something shimmer at the far corner of the pool bottom. Aha! It was his ring all right. One perfect solitaire that obviously hadn't been enough to do the job. *"Marry you?"* Alexia had scoffed. *"You can't be serious?"* Only as serious as a heart attack, a heart attack Mike had sorely wished he'd had rather than face the blistering look in Alexia's cool blue eyes. *"But, sweetheart,"* she'd told him, *"everything's been so good so far. Why would you want to go and ruin it now?"*

Gee, call him a fool, but somehow Mike hadn't seen wanting to spend the rest of his life with someone as "ruining" things. What an idiot he'd been, believing that someone like Alexia could possibly care. Even in refusing his ring, she'd been the quintessential ice woman. Couldn't she even have pretended to have been impressed by the half-carat diamond?

Instead, when their server had arrived with dessert, she'd pushed the small velvet box aside and urged Mike to be "mature" about things. She certainly wasn't ready for that kind of commitment—and he could keep the ring.

Mike had shoved the box back in front of her, saying she could hang on to it until she felt ready. She'd given him a thin smile and said, *"Fine."* It was only because he'd followed her when she'd excused herself to the ladies' room that he'd witnessed her break the delicate ring free from its velvet prison and lob it into the pool before climbing into her black Jaguar and driving out of his life.

Just like that.

Alexia hadn't even planned to say good-bye.

Mike sat on the end of a lounge chair and studied the two rings in his hand. One glistening solitaire, the other an elegant arrangement of emeralds and diamonds. For all Mike knew, he thought, casting a tired gaze over the pool surface, there were others like these down there. Dozens, maybe. Heck, if he looked long enough, he might even find thousands.

He could start his own business: Ring Finders Unlimited. He'd make a fortune on broken hearts…

Mike blinked back the heat in his eyes and stared up at the star-speckled night, realizing just how cynical he'd become.

It was really too late to drive back to the city, and his room for the night was bought and paid for. Plus, he still had mystery woman's ring in the palm of his hand. Mike didn't know how, but some way before he left here tomorrow, he was going to get that woman to take back her ring. Then maybe she could return it properly to whoever had given it to her in the first place.

Not that it was Mike's normal style to go inserting himself in other people's relationships, but someone had to wise the female species up to the damage it was doing out there. And, since he had nothing left to lose, Mike thought, tightening his grip around his solitaire, it might as well be him.

****

Chapter Two

Carrie sat at the small breakfast table, absentmindedly stirring her coffee.

"Good morning," a deep baritone echoed from above her.

Carrie looked up at the dapper man in chinos and a button-down shirt. "Mike! I almost didn't recognize you with your clothes on!"

A couple at the next table set down their grapefruit spoons and stared.

"I mean," Carrie backpedaled, perspiration sweeping her hairline, "dry." Oh, Criminy. Carrie picked up her cup, but Mike just grinned and pulled out a chair.

"Mind if I join you?" he asked.

Now that was a loaded question for eight o'clock in the morning. Carrie picked up the Style Section of the newspaper and rapidly fanned her face. "Sure, why not?" Anything, she thought. Anything to get this Greek Adonis to sit—and her to stop babbling like an idiot in this public place.

"Listen," he said, squaring his chair in with the table. "I think we got off on the wrong foot last night."

"Look, Mike," Carrie said, reaching a hand across the table to touch his arm, then instantly regretting it. It had to be over eighty degrees inside, with the air-conditioning in this antiquated building malfunctioning, and yet, still, the contact sent shivers up her spine. "As far as I'm concerned, the two of us aren't even going anywhere. So, wrong foot or no, it's all water under the bridge."

165

"Or, into the pool," he said with a smile that pinned her in place even though a very big part of her longed to spring from her chair and race from the room. What was it with her? What in the world was she afraid of? Mike...? And if it was terror she felt, then why did every inch of her skin vibrate with electric fire each time his sea-green eyes settled on hers?

Carrie took a very long, deliberate sip of water, then set down her glass. "You know, I never got your last name," she said with a smile she hoped looked pleasantly interested, not recklessly giddy.

"Davis," he said as a server sauntered over. "No," he told her as she tilted the silver coffee carafe, "I'm not staying."

"You're not?" Carrie asked before she could stop herself.

Mike arched one eyebrow, and the slightest tingle took hold of Carrie's tailbone. Damn it, she thought, shaking off the confusion. She was not attracted to this man, not attracted one iota. And she was going to prove it. To him— and the rest of the world, as well.

"Please," Carrie said in her most gracious Southern tone. "Do stay. It's the least I can do for..."

Their waitress colored slightly as Carrie's words fell off.

Mike accepted a cup of coffee then met Carrie's eyes with a sly smile. "You know," he whispered as their server departer. "I think you almost embarrassed that woman."

"Truth be told," Carrie admitted, taking a sip of coffee that had grown lukewarm, "I almost embarrassed myself."

Mike tore open a sugar packet and dumped the contents into his cup. "Do tell."

But Carrie didn't want to tell—tell this man any more than she had to. For, in a very big way, she already feared she'd told him way too much. Maybe not in so many words but certainly with her eyes. Guy who looked like that was bound to be experienced. Would certainly know when a woman was…what? Ogling him? Impossible. Carrie St. John was a business professional, a seasoned woman of the world. She did not ogle. She appraised. And every one of Mike's assets, darn it, were starting to add up.

"I never kiss and tell," Carrie said, realizing afterwards just how flirtatious that sounded.

Carrie flagged down the waitress and asked for another glass of water, wondering if she wouldn't be better off having the waitress dump the whole pitcher in her lap.

Mike stirred his coffee, then set aside the spoon. "Okay by me," he assured her with earnest green eyes. "Believe me, I won't be pressing you for details."

Carrie shifted in her chair, wondering why his gentlemanly assertion made her heart drop down to her belly. It wasn't that she wanted him pressing her—for details.

Criminy! She was a mess!

Carrie gratefully grabbed her refilled water and downed half the glass in one long swallow. "Won't be here for too much longer anyhow," she said, searching for a reasonable-sounding way out of the corner she'd painted herself into. "Least ways, not long enough to engage in long-winded conversation."

"I see," Mike said, studying her white-knuckled grip on her water glass. "So, then, where will you be going back to?"

"Mill Creek," she told him, feeling the room lightly spin around her. As ridiculous as it seemed, there was something about him that made her want to forget about going home altogether. Maybe it was in the heart-stopping way he looked at her, even when he pretended to be making normal conversation. Or maybe it was in the way he looked when he was half undressed…

Carrie bit into her bottom lip as Mike fell back in his chair with surprise.

"No kidding? I'm right next door in Redfields!"

"So what are you doing up here?" she asked, trying to keep her thoughts on the straight and narrow. Straight and narrow? Holy cow! Totally wrong image! What on earth was wrong with her? Never in her life had her mind been so carnally occupied!

His eyes fell to his coffee cup. "Maybe it's best if I don't kiss and tell either."

"You mean," Carrie asked with surprise, "you were here with a woman?"

He looked up, little wrinkles creasing his brow. "You find that so amazing?"

Actually, what Carrie found amazing was that any woman in her right mind who'd come here with Mike in the first place wouldn't still be here with him now. "What happened?" Carrie asked, softening her voice in concern. "I mean, certainly you don't have to tell me, but—"

"She dumped me," Mike said, bright eyes darkening. "Sayonara. Just like that. Didn't even have the courtesy to say good-bye. Simply walked out at dinner and never came back."

"No…" Carrie said, catching her breath on the unbelievable. That actually sounded worse than what had happened to her!

"Wish I could say it wasn't so," Mike said with a shake of his head, "particularly after all the… Well, never mind," he told her, fingering the rings through his pants pocket. "None of that matters much now."

Mike reached into his chinos and pulled out the pair of rings. "Not quite a matching set," he said, laying them on the table. But quite an attractive pair just the same."

Carrie blanched and looked up. "Are you telling me that… Now, wait a minute—"

Mike nodded. "Uncanny as it seems, my ring got tossed in the pool as well. Maybe it's some sort of unwritten bylaw to staying in this place."

"Only when the guys involved are first-class jerks," Carrie said with a hard edge to her voice.

A rosy band of color swept across the bridge of her nose. "Oh, sorry… Didn't mean it to—"

"So, you're assuming it was somehow my fault?" Mike asked.

"Well, it's only natural. If she felt strongly enough to throw your ring in—"

And here he'd actually been feeling sorry for her. Had been entertaining these ridiculous thoughts. Ideas that he and this fellow lovelorn soul might actually have something in common. Or maybe he'd just been deluding himself to keep his mind off his raging heartache.

Mike pushed back abruptly from the table. "Enjoy the rest of your stay," he said, dabbing his mouth with his napkin.

"Wait!" Carrie said, leaning forward across the table and attempting to grab his arm. But it was too late. He'd already laid a ten dollar bill on the table and walked away.

Carrie tipped the waitress, then hurriedly made her way out the front door. Bright sunlight spun gold through lilac bushes lining the cobblestone walk in front of her. Overhead, morning birds called out in song as the fragrance of early summer laced the air.

This was absurd! Carrie didn't even know where in the inn he'd been staying, much less what kind of car he drove. For all she knew, he'd already gone!

Carrie looked down in a cold sweat at the two rings nestled in her damp palm. She hadn't even wanted one, and now she'd been saddled with two of them! One from a man she thought she'd known but actually didn't know at all. The other from a virtual stranger!

Carrie raced down the path, then halted where it met the gravel drive. Off to the left and down at the bottom of the grassy hill, lay the gazebo—and the swimming area.

Of course, she thought, squaring her shoulders and taking off in that direction.

Mike sat at the end of the chaise lounge, knowing it was more than just Alexia. His failings at romance had an awful lot to do with himself. Hadn't he just proven that back at the inn ten minutes ago? Fifteen minutes with a woman who didn't know him from Adam and she'd already pitched him straight into that flaming barbeque pit.

Well, fine, maybe monogamy wasn't all it was cracked up to be anyway. Just because he'd always thought he'd wanted a wife and family didn't necessarily mean that was in his cards. And every good poker player knew when to hold 'em and when to fold 'em. Maybe, at thirty-eight, it was time Mike cashed in his chips. He'd always yearned to do something different. Move to the Caymans, maybe, and open up that dive shop he'd always dreamed about.

Before, with gold-digging Alexia, he'd been reluctant to leave his "stable" job in real estate and pursue something more daring. Now, he had nothing in the world to stop him.

"Thought I'd find you down here."

Mike looked up in surprise to find Carrie standing radiant in the sunlight.

"I believe I have something of yours," she said, walking toward him and turning over his solitaire in her hand.

Mike stood. "That was awfully nice of you. But you didn't have to. Particularly after the way I—"

She gave him the soft smile he'd always known her capable of. "Didn't mean to offend you—or imply that you, personally, were any kind of jerk. That's just…uh, been my own unfortunate experience."

"Yeah, well, unfortunately, my experience with women hasn't run much better."

A cool morning breeze lifted off the water and fanned Carrie's long skirt around her legs. "We're a real pair, aren't we?" she asked, bending down to smooth out the clingy material that Mike kind of wished she'd left in place. It had been doing a spectacular job at emphasizing the curves of her luscious legs.

"A couple of losers, you mean?" he asked, wrinkling his brow. "Now, I don't think I'd go as far to say that."

171

"Losers, absolutely not," Carrie said, coming over and sitting in a nearby chair. "Just down on our luck a bit at the moment."

"I'll say," Mike said, pulling up another chair and sitting beside her. "Worked a good long time to buy that ring. That last house, especially, was a bear to sell. But I knew if I didn't have the commission—"

"You're in real estate?" she asked, looking amused.

"What's so surprising about that?"

"Oh nothing, really," she said, pursing her lips and looking toward the pool. "Just somehow I envisioned you in a line of work a little more—physical."

Mike spurted a laugh. "Lifeguard, you mean?" He pondered the notion of giving her mouth-to-mouth as she turned her very kissable lips toward his. Lips that had no business looking so damn inviting on such a downright disastrous morning.

Carrie shrugged two silky white shoulders that peeked out from beneath her halter-style dress. "Well, sure. That— or a rock climber. Firefighter. Policeman..."

Carrie bit her tongue, realizing how very much she sounded as if she were exercising her fantasies. And if she put her mind to it, Carrie was quite certain she could come up with one or two of those involving the well-built man beside her—clothed or not.

It was probably getting close to checkout and time for Carrie to get back to her room. Her first order of business was calling her grandmother to tell her tomorrow afternoon's bridal shower was off. It would be a sorrowful disappointment to her grandmother and all of her grandmother's old friends who'd worked so hard in the planning. Not only that, they'd all been expecting to meet

172

the groom! And here Carrie was having to show up empty-handed.

Carrie cast a sideways glance at the man beside her, a totally absurd notion popping into her brain. No, he wouldn't. She wouldn't even dare to ask!

"You know the worst part about all of this?" Mike asked, still studying the water. But Carrie truly couldn't imagine anything worse than the look on her grandmother's face when Carrie confessed she'd let another eligible bachelor slip right through her ineffectual fingers. "It's my reunion."

"Reunion?" Carrie asked.

Mike grimaced. "High school. And for once, I thought I'd finally have a fighting chance to prove them wrong."

Carrie heaved a deep sigh, grateful that her own twentieth was still a good, safe five years away. Other than business success, she'd had nothing to show for herself at her tenth, so hadn't gone. By her twentieth, she'd been certain she'd have a dashing man—perhaps even a baby or two—on her arm. Now, she wasn't so certain.

"Which one is it?" Carrie asked, thinking she knew but feeling it only polite to ask.

"Twentieth," Mike reported with a frown. A frown that didn't much become him, Carrie decided. His was an open, expressive face meant for love and laughter. Carrie blinked hard at the thought, wondering where that love part had come from. "And the sad thing is—after all these years—I'm only going to prove those fellows right."

"Which fellows?" Carrie asked.

"The ones who voted me 'Most Likely to Remain a Bachelor'."

"Hmm."

Mike turned to look at her, his eyes catching a glint of sunshine bouncing off the spreading oaks that surrounded the pool area. They were deep-green eyes and swimming like the ocean, a deep, lulling current Carrie was quite sure she could get lost in if she wasn't very, very careful. "That's not why I proposed to Alexia, if that's what you're thinking."

"Alexia?" Carrie pondered. "Sounds very— sophisticated."

"That's a polite way to put it."

Carrie laughed. "Well, I'm sure not the most objective one to pass judgment at the moment."

"And you and yours?" Mike asked. "Mr. So-Wonderfully-Terrific you felt compelled to chuck his ring into the pool?"

"Well, I doubt I could be very objective about him either," Carrie admitted, sheepishly studying her toes through the straps of her sandals. "But then again, men like Wilson Haywood don't deserve much objectivity."

Mike cracked a grin. "Wilson, huh? Sounds very— sophisticated.

Carrie's lips pulled into a smile.

"Say," Mike began, his eyes lighting with mischief. "I've got it! How about we get your Wilson together with my—"

"Afraid it wouldn't work," Carrie said, shaking her head. "Wilson's already taken."

"That fast? That's gotta be some kind of… Oh," Mike said, his smile fading in understanding. "No wonder you chucked his ring! So tell me, what was it with this guy? Deaf, blind, or stupid? Or possibly all three?"

174

Carrie let loose a belly laugh, delighted with the turn this conversation had taken. "All three, I guess," she said, giggling into her hand. "And your girl? Alexis?"

"Alexia," Mike corrected.

Carrie shrugged.

"You're right," Mike agreed. "Really doesn't matter anymore now, does it? I mean, you give a gal the perfect ring…"

Carrie suddenly realized she still had Mike's ring clutched in her hand with the other. "Oh my goodness," she said, attempting to pass it over. "Here! I almost forgot!"

Mike shook his head. "Finders, keepers."

"Now, wait a minute! You left this on the table by accident!"

Mike gave her a sly wink. A wink that did terrific things for the tingles that had been lying dormant in her spine. "You quite sure of that?"

"Of course, I'm sure. You went to all the trouble to dig it out of the pool, didn't you? The ring obviously still means something to you, even if the woman you intended to wear it doesn't."

Yeah, Mike thought, that ring still meant a lot. Like about three thousand dollars, an amount he honestly couldn't afford to throw away, not with his renewed plans to move to the Caymans. If he was to make that long-lost dream a reality, he'd have to start counting every dime.

Mike stretched a reluctant hand in Carrie's direction and took back the ring.

"Quite a game of ring toss we're playing here, eh, Mike?" Carrie asked with the most compelling smile he'd seen on her face yet. Boy, wouldn't his old high school buddies just die if Mike showed up with someone like that

175

on his arm. Classy but genuine, with an unguarded warmth that seemed to be getting hotter by the minute.

Mike wiped an arm across his moistened brow. "Got that right," he said, giving her a smile. "And it's getting a little warm out for ring toss…" Her dark eyes widened, expecting who knew what kind of proposition. "But perfect for a swim," he finished as he watched the color rush back into her face.

Yessiree, she was quite a looker. Would knock every one of that high school gang out cold! If only Mike could think up a way to take her.

"Oh no," Carrie said, scrambling to her feet. "I'm not much for swimming."

"No?" Mike asked, standing beside her. "But why in heaven's name not? It's hot as blazes out—"

Yes, damn it, Carrie could quite appropriately feel the heat. It was sticking to every inch of her with gummy fingers that prickled her skin with perspiration and sent a cascade of droplets sliding down her cleavage. But no way in Hades was she going to let a man as perfectly formed as Mike Davis see her practically naked in a swimsuit—even her modest, one-piece kind. Carrie wore her dresses ankle-length for a reason, a reason that centered mostly around her buttocks and thighs.

"Besides," Carrie added hastily, "I've got some packing to do."

"Packing?" Mike asked, looking crestfallen. "But I thought for sure you were staying. Isn't there some sort of two-night weekend minimum at this place?"

"Why yes, but—"

"Well, then, what's your hurry?"

And why, Carrie wondered, scrunching up her lips, was he trying so hard to convince her to stay? "I've got things to do," she informed him. "Arrangements to—cancel."

"And tomorrow will be too late?"

"Might be," she told him, meaning it absolutely. Too late for a lot of things. Particularly her heart. This man, Mike Davis, had an unsettling effect on her. His whole wounded-puppy-dog ploy had worked wonders at disarming her emotion. Emotion she'd sworn only last night, as she stood weeping by this same pool, she would indefinitely keep under wraps.

"Aw, come on," he coaxed with a crooked grin. "I'll bet your room's already paid for."

She looked at him and blinked. The fact was, Wilson had already footed the bill.

"Hey, I'm not proposing anything indecent here." For some reason, that admission did not make Carrie happy. "Only a little attempt at sweet revenge."

Carrie eyed him suspiciously. "Revenge how?"

"Revenge in our not letting them ruin our weekend."

Big, fat chance of that one, Carrie thought. More than her weekend had been ruined. How about her life? "Listen, Mike, it's a sweet idea, your wanting to keep me company and all…"

Now that was putting it mildly, Mike thought, feeling the rising sun beat down through his stuffy cotton shirt. Disturbingly, he was finding himself wanting to more than "keep her company." He wanted the opportunity to not even let her out of his sight—for the next twenty-four hours, at least.

The guy who'd tossed Carrie away just as cavalierly as Alexia had thrown his ring in the pool had been a total imbecile. The sweat dribbled down Mike's open shirt collar and pooled, damn it, somewhere near his navel. Without even trying, the woman set him virtually on fire. And here she was saying she was about to leave?

Carrie tapped her toe against the pool deck and considered his disappointingly not-so-indecent proposal. Forgetting the drop-dead gorgeous part, he did appear to be a very nice guy. Maybe even nice enough to be her friend. Which would be a definite first for Carrie St. John, as she'd never befriended any man for longer than thirty-six hours without things between them becoming intimate. But, of course, as her track record consisted only of two serious beaus, maybe she was being a bit hasty in making a sweeping assessment.

Besides, friendship was good. Perhaps even what she most needed at the moment. And having a friend who looked and carried himself like the athletically inclined Mike Davis, could quite possibly come in handy. Maybe even in the very near future.

"All right, I'll stay," Carrie said, "but under one condition."

"Any condition's fine with me," Mike said, knowing that as long as whatever it was involved his taking off his boiling clothes, it would be A-OK with him. Particularly if it involved Carrie St. John stripping down as well.

"You understand this thing between us is about camaraderie. Two down-and-outs on the same flip side of the coin. Compadres."

Mike gave her a tight smile, damning every inner instinct he had and telling his licentious libido to behave.

"Sure thing, Carrie," he said, reaching out an arm to shake her hand. "We'll play it any way you want."

****

Chapter Three

Carrie sat in the narrow oaken stairwell, finally getting a cell signal. The remoteness of the inn made service unpredictable. Carrie hadn't been able to pick up more than two bars anywhere but here.

She nervously twirled a lock of chestnut hair, rehearsing what she would tell her grandmother. *I'm sorry, Grandmother, but things just didn't work out…* No, Carrie had already been there and done that one. Besides, her second strike would make her look like a total washout, not the "together" young woman her adoring Grandma Russell took her to be.

Grandmother, there's been a last-minute change in plans…

Nope, that would only make her look inconsiderate. Horribly inconsiderate, given the wedding shower was scheduled for tomorrow.

Carrie sighed and hit autodial, trusting something brilliant would come to mind the instant she heard her grandmother's voice.

"Hello?"

"Grandmother, it's Carrie—"

"Oh, sweetheart," her grandma began in her endless prattle, "so lovely to hear your voice. Amelia and I were just discussing china patterns, and we really think the one you—"

"Grandmother…"

"Oh, lands sakes, child. I know, I know! Really none of my business. But, to tell you the truth, the everyday

180

pattern you picked is ever so much more attractive and could really double for formal ware if push came to shove, and—"

Carrie blew a hard breath. This was going to be even harder than she'd imagined. "Grandmother!"

"Well, okay, okay, dear. You are absolutely right about that! Who needs to fret over china patterns when you've got a perfectly gorgeous man on your arm!"

"Grandma Russell!" Carrie shouted into the phone.

"Well, gracious me, child, you don't need to yell. Ma Bell's improved quite a bit since the days I courted your grandpa." She chuckled. "Lands sakes, child. Meant that one the other way around—quite the other way…"

Carrie sighed and slumped back against the wall behind her.

"Now, sweetheart," her grandmother finally asked, "what was it you wanted to tell me?"

Carrie racked her brain for a creative intro. "Well, it's about seating arrangements, actually."

"Tomorrow, sweetie? Your great-aunties and I've got that all worked out. No need for you to fret one bit. Nellie even hand-stitched the place cards."

The bottom dropped out of Carrie's stomach. "Aunt Nellie crocheted those beautiful lace place cards? But, I thought… That was supposed to be part of her wedding gift! I thought she was making those for the…wedding."

"Couldn't wait to see your face, she said. And you'll have to really butter her up on this one too, sweetness. She did a divine job. Absolutely divine! You would think the royal family was coming to tea, and not just your wedding party."

Carrie swallowed hard and tried to summon her courage. "Grandma…?"

"Yes, dearie?"

"What time is the shower again?"

"Land sakes, child, you are a nervous bride, aren't you? Four o'clock, same as it was last time you asked. But don't worry if you're not here right on the button. Just don't make us old gals wait too long. You know how it is with us geriatrics. We tend to nod off after a while when nothing's happening!"

"Don't worry, Grandma," Carrie said. "I promise not to put anybody to sleep."

Grandma Russell chuckled. "From what you've told me, you and that handsome groom of yours will be sure to wake up any crowd!"

"Right," Carrie agreed, feeling the fire of deceit spread from her temples to her collarbone.

"Can't wait to see what he looks like, dearie," Grandma Russell crooned into the phone. "Me and the girls have been speculating all day."

"That makes two of us," Carrie said quietly, ending the call.

"What's that?" Mike asked from the landing.

Carrie looked up, startled. "Oh, Mike, I didn't hear you come in."

"No?" he asked. "Could have sworn you said something about the two of—"

"Oh no," Carrie said with a blush. "That was my grandmother. Just got off the phone with her about…"

"Some of those plans that needed canceling?" Mike ventured.

Carrie gave him a shaky smile. "More or less."

"Say, you all right?" he asked, taking the steps two at a time and coming up to where she sat trembling at the bend in the stairs. "Because to tell you the truth, Carrie, you don't look so hot."

"Bet you say that to all the girls," she said, twisting her lips into the best imitation of a smile she could muster.

"Actually," he told her, "it's just the opposite."

"Now I see why you're not married."

Mike crossed his arms over his chest and leaned a shoulder against the wall. "This has something to do with Wilson, doesn't it?"

Carrie vehemently shook her head as moisture brimmed in her eyes.

Mike cocked his chin and scrutinized her.

"Okay," she admitted, making an inch-wide motion with her thumb and forefinger. "Maybe a little…"

Mike shook his head and held his ground.

"All right already! More than a little bit, okay? What is it exactly you want me to say?" she asked as coal-hot tears streamed down her cheeks. "That my life is a total mess? That everyone in my hometown is expecting me to show up for a bridal shower tomorrow—with my groom-to-be—and my groom-to-be has dumped me for a woman with a better financial portfolio?"

Mike dropped down on the step beside her and draped a steadying arm around her trembling shoulders.

"You don't have to be nice to me," she asserted, trying her damndest to set her jaw but failing miserably.

"I know," Mike said, reaching over and raising her chin. "But I want to be."

"But why?" Carrie asked with a sniff. "What could possibly be in it for you? I've already told you I want nothing more than…"

"Carrie, I have a question," Mike said, searching her bleary eyes.

"About what?"

"The people at this shower. Do they know…? I mean, have any of them actually met Wilson?"

"Well, only Paulette. But that was over a year ago."

"So then, she might not notice if Wilson has changed a bit? Lost some weight? Shaved his beard?"

"Lost some weight? What in the world are you talking about? Wilson was—and always will be—the ultimate bean pole! And he never had a beard!"

Carrie stared in amazement as Mike's lips curved into a devilish smile. Though, in truth, the thought had crossed her own mind once or twice—she'd never envisioned the absurd notion becoming a reality.

"Wait a minute! You couldn't possibly be thinking… That you—"

Mike nodded. "Darling, I've waited forever to meet your family."

Carrie straightened under the weight of his arm. "Very funny."

"I wasn't joking."

Carrie looked him square in the eye. "But you can't be serious! Why ever on earth would you do that for me?"

"To buy you some time?" he said, giving her shoulders a light squeeze. "Hey, I know firsthand how disorienting this type of situation can be. The last thing a nice girl like you needs is having to face her family with the abysmal news—when you alone haven't even adjusted to it yourself."

Carrie wriggled out from under his arm and set aside the cell phone. "Who says I haven't adjusted?"

Mike raised his brow and trailed a finger down her tearstained cheek. "Wild guess?"

Carrie dropped her head. "I would never accept an offer like that from a stranger." Even one who sent her stomach all aflutter like him, Carrie told herself. "Particularly not knowing you well enough to really know what you expect in return."

"No problem. I can tell you that."

Carrie looked up and arched both eyebrows.

"Class of Ninety-two."

****

Chapter Four

"The plan is impossible," Carrie said, stabbing into her salad with her fork.

"Improbable, maybe," Mike said, biting into his burger. "Nothing is impossible."

"But you're talking about walking into a big group of my relatives and friends and convincing them we've been an item for—what?—a year and a half now? They'll see through it in an instant."

"Not if we're convincing," Mike said, shaking his head. He set down his burger and picked up his bottle of imported beer. "Besides, how much do these people really know about Wilson Haywood anyway? You said the two of you met in New York."

"We did."

"That your relationship was mainly on weekends."

"It was."

"Sometimes there, sometimes here—right in quaint little Mill Creek."

"What, precisely, is your point?" Carrie asked, sipping her iced tea.

"My point," Mike said, taking a swig of beer, "is that your relationship with Wilson wasn't exactly...normal."

"Oh, and you're such an expert on normal relationships," she pointed out with a broad sweep of her knife.

Mike bolted backward in his chair. "Watch it with that thing! Don't slay the messenger. I'm just telling it like it is. People don't see you all touchy-feely with your fiancé, they might figure, well, that's just a product of how things developed."

Carrie took exception to what he was suggesting. On the one hand, he might just be trying to save her some trouble by playing things cool like she wanted. On the other, he might very well be insinuating that Carrie was a cold fish. Which she certainly was not. And clearly wouldn't be with a man like Mike Davis standing beside her.

"And if things were 'touchy-feely,' as you put it, between me and Wilson?"

"Were they?" Mike asked, little crinkles tugging at the corners of his sea-green eyes.

Carrie put down her knife and thought about that. The truth was, no. Wilson had been very businesslike in a number of things, including in his relationship with her. She'd even sworn he'd timed their lovemaking so as to be less disruptive of the professional calls he'd always placed before—and afterward.

"Well?" Mike pressed, his honey complexion taking on a deeper hue that perfectly complemented his rugged appeal. It was hard to picture him in real estate, when the word outdoorsman was written all over his chiseled face. Not to mention his hard-toned body.

"Well, if you must know," Carrie began, feeling the slightest bit naughty but not the least bit ashamed of her duplicity. "Wilson was quite an affectionate man."

Mike choked on his pickle. "That so?"

"Oh yes," Carrie said, putting on her most confidential face. "It was somewhat embarrassing actually. PDA to the max! Sometimes, I practically had to beat him off with a stick!"

"A stick?" Mike gave up on his pickle and took a long drag of beer. "That doesn't mean you'll be hurting me, does it?"

"Not in the least," Carrie assured him, feeling a familiar ache wend its way all the way down to her bones. An ache that told her she was going to enjoy this little party a lot more than she'd originally suspected.

"Ah darn," Mike said with a Cheshire-cat grin. "But, no worries. We can work around that."

"You just remember your mission," Carrie cautioned him sternly, again with the knife.

"Anything you say, oh knife-wielding one."

Carrie laughed and looked down at her hand. "No cracking jokes at the shower. Got it? Especially none that would give the two of us away."

"Your wish is my command."

Carrie wondered about that. Wondered, especially, if she'd been just a tad bit rash in insisting this thing between her and Mike remain simply "friends."

"You're awfully quiet," Mike said, cocking one eyebrow. "Thinking up those three wishes?"

But, honestly, Carrie only found herself thinking of one. About how nice it would have been if Wilson had been a bit more like Mike. More relaxed and easy to get along with.

"It's funny, really," she admitted over the rim of her tinkling glass, "but I was thinking about how different you are from Wilson."

Mike settled back in his chair. "And that—at this precise moment in time—would be a compliment?"

Carrie smiled and set down her glass. "You're a nice man, Mike Davis."

"Ah-ah," he said, shaking his head. "Please don't tell me that!"

"That you're nice? Why ever on earth not?"

Mike coughed and picked up his beer. "Let's just say that the only woman who's ever called me nice and is still talking to me is my second-grade teacher, Mrs. Rich."

"Let me guess," Carrie said, narrowing her eyes. "Alexia said you were too nice for her."

"Bingo," Mike said, setting down his empty beer. "Ditto that, Carol. And Marianne, and Barbara…"

"My, my," Carrie said, pursing her lips. "You do have quite a reputation, don't you?"

"As the perpetual bachelor, yes," he said with a frown.

"But that's a reputation most men would savor."

"Well, if you haven't noticed, I'm not most men."

Oh, she'd noticed all right. Noticed in a heartbeat. "So what exactly is it that you're after, nice-guy Mike Davis?" she asked with a teasing smile. "If it's not your personal freedom, like most men."

"I've had my personal freedom," he assured her. "So much of it, I'm practically drowning in it. But to answer your question—"

"Honestly," she said, laying her napkin on the table, "all kidding aside."

"Honestly? Don't you think it's a bit risky to be asking honesty of a man you met less than a day ago?"

"No more risky than taking him home to meet my grandmother."

Mike gave her a broad, sweeping smile that settled into an affectionate grin. "Ah Carrie, you're really very sweet."

"Now, don't go calling me sweet—"

189

Mike chortled. "Let me guess? Something like my Mr. Nice Guy?"

Carrie felt the heat envelope her at the thought of being read so easily. But he could read her easily, this man she scarcely knew. Or perhaps it was simply because the two of them were in the same boat that he happened to know exactly what she was feeling, precisely when she was feeling it.

"Okay," Mike continued, "to answer your question—honestly. What I'm after is probably not so different from what you are. A stable relationship, a home. Kids, maybe."

"A white picket fence?" she asked, feeling the renewed heat in her cheeks.

"Sure, why not? If you can get one of those in the Caymans," he added with a grin.

Carrie's heart fell a million miles. What on earth had she been thinking? Kidding herself about a potential relationship with someone she'd met in such a haphazard manner? Hoping against hope that taking him home as the man of her dreams would somehow convert him to that before her very eyes? *Come on, now, Carrie, wake up—and join the twenty-first century!*

Besides, the man was already making plans to move to the Caymans. More than a stone's throw from Virginia. This little charade between them involving her shower and his reunion next weekend was all she had. And Carrie St. John and her woebegone heart would do very well to remember that.

Mike took a running dive into the crystal clear waters of the pool, thinking that things weren't going quite as swimmingly with Carrie St. John as he'd planned. He was

glad she'd agreed to go to his reunion. More than glad—
ecstatic, actually—that a stunning woman like her would
help him save face with his friends. And he didn't mind
stepping into Wilson's shoes for her bridal shower one bit.
What bothered him was the make-believe element to their
whole affair. It was definitely a screwy way to begin a
relationship. Non-relationship, he reminded himself, as per
Carrie's instructions.

For anybody else, it would have been the perfect setup.
He'd make out like a bandit at his high school reunion—no
strings attached. But, for Mike, who felt an inexplicable
yearning to stay by Carrie's side in a much more than
fraternal fashion, the whole picture rotted—big-time.

Plus, it really seemed like an unfair trade. Carrie's
shower, after all, was only a mere couple of hours out of
one afternoon. His reunion, on the other hand, was an entire
weekend-long extravaganza. Of course, he hadn't quite told
her that—yet. But he would. Just not until after she'd been
sufficiently impressed with the way he'd wowed her family
and friends. Then, she'd feel beholden—at least in some
small way—and would still agree to come to his rescue.
Even if it involved a fancy dinner and a Sunday afternoon
picnic.

Yeesh! This was where having gone to a private school
most definitely paid. Nothing that Ashton Academy did
was anything less than first-class. And Carrie St. John was
definitely a first-class kind of girl. Mike would be the envy
of every man in that room, he thought with a smile as he
stroked his way across the pool. Heck, if only it weren't
such a big illusion, he'd even be the envy of his own
former self!

Carrie turned in the mirror and studied the cellulite on her thighs. What had she been thinking? Telling Mike she might possibly join him for a swim? These thunder thighs weren't going anywhere except for maybe into a pair of shorts. A pair of very long, very modestly proportioned shorts, Carrie thought, rifling through her suitcase.

But if Mike was supposedly nothing more than a friend, what was she all hellfire worried about? Friends didn't dump friends over a pair of weighty thighs. Friendship was based on other things, like mutual respect. Common interests and goals…

Carrie sat heavily on the bed. She certainly hadn't known Mike long enough to get a handle on the interests part, but she and the "swim god" definitely shared common goals. Though she hadn't dared tell him so, the ideal he was after wasn't really so far from her own. Except for the Cayman Islands part. The Caymans! Ironically enough, an investor's heaven. One of her business associates in New York had been pressing Carrie to open up a bank there for almost a decade. But Carrie had always preferred to channel her funds into more personal ventures. It was helping out entrepreneurs that gave her the most satisfaction. Small businesses, start-up operations like this country inn here.

Then again, the Caymans did hold possibilities… Not the least of which stood about six foot two and had the perfect smattering of dark blond hair on its chest.

Carrie walked to the bathroom and threw some cold water on her face. She was losing her mind! Losing it completely! Actually considering the notion…

Now, for a vacation, maybe.

Carrie smiled into the mirror at visions of her and a very oiled-up Mike Davis stretched out on a white-sand beach.

But that idea was ludicrous too! She and Mike didn't stand a prayer of a chance starting out the way they had. Besides, the two of them had made a pact. And, despite his occasional flirtation which Carrie assumed was second nature to a man like him, he truthfully didn't seem interested in being more than just friends. All Mike was after was a way to impress his old high school buddies. But returning to the full-length mirror and studying her silhouette once again, Carrie was uncertain why he imagined she could do the trick. Though Carrie considered herself reasonably attractive, she was well aware she had what the magazines called "figure flaws." Flaws that Wilson had occasionally been unkind enough to point out—in his own teasing way. A way which Carrie hadn't found the least bit amusing.

Maybe she'd just slip on the denim shorts and stroll on down to the pool. It would look odd if she failed to show completely. And she certainly didn't want Mike thinking she was nervous about facing him. Though she was. Utterly nervous. Mostly because, when she saw the man half-nude, her thoughts ran wild. Straight into the "Mike, Tarzan; Carrie, Jane" jungle! And now that she figured him to be a nice guy on top of the way he looked... Well, Carrie wasn't quite sure she could trust her own reaction.

She'd heard of people on the rebound. The rampant bed-hopping that sometimes went on when one wounded partner was getting over the other. But Carrie had never figured herself to be the bed-hopping type. In fact, before Wilson, there'd really only been one other man. The first one she'd thought she would marry and, soon after their break-up, had started referring to as "old what's-his-name."

But even "old what's-his-name," her first lover ever, hadn't stirred her half as much as Mike Davis. But maybe that was what she got for comparing twenty-two-year-old apples to thirty-something-year-old oranges. Very ripe, very succulent oranges. Criminy!

Carrie sighed and hunted for a belt that would do her waistline justice—meaning suck it in just a tad more than its natural state. Though, of course, a friend wouldn't notice her waistline one way or another, she told herself, sweeping her hair into a ponytail and arranging her tresses in the mirror. Friends didn't care what friends looked like, just as long as they kept their word.

Mike's eyes popped open when he heard the clack of sandal heels on the pavement. Carrie St. John headed down the path in strappy black sandals, a formfitting tee and cuffed denim shorts. She certainly was revealing a lot more flesh than she had been earlier, but not nearly enough for Mike's satisfaction, he thought, sitting up to disguise his reaction that would have been otherwise quite evident through his swim shorts.

"You're not swimming?"

"Can't," she said with a congenial smile. "Still got lots of telephone calls."

A buzz of panic shot to Mike's brain. "But I thought we—"

"Oh yes… I mean, no." She blew a soft breath that sent a loose tendril spiraling. "I'm not backing out of our deal or anything like that."

Mike sat back against the lounge chair, relieved. He'd actually been looking forward to playing Carrie's fiancé. Especially, he thought, eying her well-formed bosom through her unforgiving cotton top, once he'd learned about that touchy-feely part.

"It's just that I've still got a lot of calls to make, and I want to try to catch the businesses while they're still open."

Mike raised his eyebrows.

"Flower shops, the caterer… You would not believe all that goes into a wedding!"

"No." Mike gave her a melancholy smile. "Guess I've never gotten that far."

"Oh, sorry," Carrie said, bringing her hands to her flaming cheeks. "Didn't mean to make you feel bad."

Actually, Mike thought, Carrie did a pretty fine job of making him feel terrific. "It's all right," he assured her. "But I thought you weren't going to cancel those things until after the shower?"

"The sooner, the better," she told him. "Unless I want to get stuck footing the bill for a wedding that doesn't happen.

"You're really sweet to agree to be my fiancé tomorrow. Really very sweet. You were absolutely right; I needed to buy myself some time. Once I've taken care of canceling the other arrangements and smoothing out all the wrinkles, breaking the news to my family won't be as hard."

"Glad I could help," Mike said, feeling as if he should stand but still not exactly trusting what his body was doing. Carrie St. John had an unusual effect on him. Though she was certainly not the most beautiful woman he'd ever seen, she was definitely one of the most womanly. There was something very sensual about the way her feminine curves suited her just right. Curves he found himself itching to get his hands around.

"Gonna cool off," Mike said, startling Carrie by bolting to his feet and diving in a split-second lunge into the pool.

"Fine!" Carrie called after him as he popped his head above the water. "I'll be back at the inn. Maybe we can meet for dinner and plan out tomorrow?"

"Absolutely!" Mike called after her before dunking his steaming head back under the surface.

****

Chapter Five

Carrie dropped down on all fours and searched the oriental carpet for the back of her earring. This was ridiculous. Really! Five minutes until dinner and Carrie was quaking in her sandals like a nervous teenager. You would think this was her first date and not a mere business arrangement with a friend.

And that's strictly what it is, she thought, finally locating the jewelry piece and standing to insert her earring in the mirror. Strictly business. She and Mike Davis had made a deal, a pact to help each other out in this uncanny time of distress for the two of them. He would butter up her family, and she, in turn, would schmooze with his prep school cronies. Next weekend would be over before she knew it, and her loosely knotted affiliation with Mike Davis would be over altogether.

Carrie frowned at her reflection, wondering what would have become of her and Mike Davis if Mike had truly occupied Wilson's slot all this while. Of course, she wouldn't have met Mike in New York, but then, as he lived closer, perhaps their relationship would have been better maintained than her and Wilson's weekend-style affair.

Carrie watched herself color at the thought of maintaining any kind of affair with the hunky Mike Davis. Criminy. Blushing like a schoolgirl, and he wasn't even in the room!

Mike tossed his Polo shirt onto the bed, thinking it was really too damn preppy. Not only that, he reminded himself, at this sort of place, one had to wear a tie.

Mike walked over and thumbed through the hanging clothes in the mirrored armoire that served as his closet. A sports coat and light starch button-down would work. That and his conservative yellow—no, too Wall Street, he told himself. He certainly couldn't have Carrie thinking stockbrokers on a night like this.

Although it was true Mike was out to impersonate Wilson, he was just as determined to prove to Carrie just how different from Wilson he actually was. Because, like it or not, in less than a day, the voluptuous Carrie St. John had gotten right under Mike Davis's skin. He didn't know how it'd happened. Or even how in the world she'd done it. Particularly since—from the get-go—she'd seemed so determined to keep this arrangement between them strictly friends.

Oh, Mike could get friendly with Carrie, all right. More than friendly. Downright carnal, in fact. But the puzzling thing was, Mike's growing attraction to Carrie involved more than just hormones. There was something about her. Something very earthy and real that set her miles apart from plastic, poised women like Alexia.

Carrie was pretty, all right. No one could argue that point. But what made her truly beautiful was that—unlike Alexia, who'd been attractive in a more Seventh Avenue way—she didn't appear to know it. Yet, there was something very womanly about her. Something so soft and feminine it made Mike ache to be all man. Christ, he thought, looking down at his boxers. Only three minutes till eight, and he'd have to take another cold shower.

Carrie sat alone at the romantic outdoor cafe table. All around her, other couples dined, trading secrets in hushed whispers, many of them linking hands.

This inn was the perfect lovers' retreat…assuming the lovers were still together, she sighed. Well, maybe her grandmother was right. Ever since she'd been a little girl, Grandma Russell, who had raised her, had insisted that things always turned out for the best. And maybe finding out Wilson was a two-timing jerk was best done now—and not after the wedding.

The maître d' appeared and offered to pour her wine, but she told him she'd wait. Carrie checked her watch and saw it was ten after eight. Terror flashed through her. What if Mike had deserted her too? What if, despite her initial impression, he turned out to be just as gutless as Wilson and had—at the last minute—ridden off into the sunset, leaving her to face her grandmother, great-aunts, and friends all on her own?

Carrie noticed a dignified older gentleman standing near the door that led to the inn's kitchen engaged in conversation with the maître d'. The silver-haired man, whom Carrie guessed to be in his late sixties, stroked his goatee, then sent Carrie a warming smile across the nest of tables that separated them.

He must be the innkeeper, she thought, taking a sip of water. But before she could set down her glass, he approached and extended his hand. "Ms. St. John," he said with a genuine smile, "Charles Gilpatrick. I wanted to tell you what a pleasure it is to have you at our inn. I would have spoken with you yesterday evening but have just now returned from an innkeepers' conference in Roanoke."

Carrie gave his hand a firm squeeze and smiled back at him. "I'm so glad you came over to say hello. You've done a remarkable job with the inn. It's beautiful."

"And suited to your taste, I trust?" he asked, releasing his grip. "We can't have our chief financier unhappy with the accommodations."

Carrie felt her cheeks warm at the compliment but held a single finger to her lips. "Let's just keep that our little secret," she said with a wink. "I don't get away on vacation that often, and when I do—"

"Yes, of course. I realize how difficult it must be for you not to be bothered. You are probably one of the more successful investors of our time."

"You do go on!" she said with a laugh.

"Well, any woman who makes the cover of *Forbes* by age twenty-six…"

Carrie shushed him with a shake of her head. "When I'm in Virginia, Mr. Gilpatrick—"

"Please, call me Charles."

Carrie smiled up at the ingratiating older man. "Charles. While in investment circles I may be known for my financial acumen…" A modest, self-deprecating laugh. "In Virginia, I prefer to simply be known as Carrie."

"But of course," Charles said, extending his grip to seal their agreement. "The girl next door. Not a problem, Ms. St John."

"Carrie," she corrected, graciously accepting his lingering handshake. "And I thank you for your discretion."

Charles lifted her hand lightly to his lips and gave the back of it a deft kiss.

"Will your fiancé be joining you for dinner?" Charles asked, straightening. "I understand his name was on the register."

"He'll be here any minute," Carrie said in an effort to reassure herself just as much as the innkeeper. Where on earth could he possibly be? Women were supposed to be the tardy ones. And clearly that was understandable, what with all the primping and trouble that went into sliding on control-top panty hose without running them silly. But Mike Davis was strictly wash-and-wear. Carrie was certain he'd look just as good stepping out of a shower as he had coming out of the pool. What was keeping that infuriating man?

Mike froze in his tracks, unable to believe what he was seeing. Who was that old goat sending his roving eyes all over Carrie's plunging neckline? And why was she laughing and tossing back her head in that coquettish fashion that said whatever he was telling her really floated her boat?

Mike blew a hard breath and ran his fingers through his hair, thinking he was probably blowing things all out of proportion. That couldn't be Wilson, could it? Come back to claim his bride? The man was old enough to be her father!

Carrie turned her head in Mike's direction, and he ducked back behind the fanning leaves of a potted fern. Mike needed to really think this thing out. Maybe if he asked one of the waiters…

Mike jumped a mile high when he felt the feminine touch at his forearm.

"Not going to find me in there," Carrie said, motioning to the spreading fern.

"No, of course not," Mike said. "I just dropped a…" Well, as he wasn't wearing a tux, he certainly couldn't say cufflink.

"An engagement ring?" Carrie questioned with a teasing smile.

"Why, no. No… A pen."

"Right," Carrie deadpanned.

Mike's brow shot up. "Pen? Ha-ha! I said pen, didn't I? No, I actually meant—"

Carrie twisted her lips and studied the color sweeping up his neckline. Mike hadn't dropped a darn thing into that planter. He'd been spying on her!

"Well, look, if it isn't the Hope Diamond you've dropped in that dirt, how about you forget about it for now and come on over to the table. There's someone there I'd like you to meet."

Mike looked her up and down and swallowed hard. God, was she gorgeous in that long black dress. It was simple but elegant, just like her. "Oh?" Mike asked, clearing his throat. "Friend of yours? Old…friend?"

Carrie held back a laugh at his curious expression. She couldn't decide if his color was more eggplant or pomegranate. But why? Over Charles Gilpatrick?

"Why, yes. I suppose you could say that. At least you've got it half right."

Darn it. Mike knew it! Half right meaning he'd been correct about the old part. Clearly Wilson would no longer be Carrie's friend. But why, then, had she been carrying on in such a flirtatious fashion? Encouraging the geezer, who was, holy cow, old enough to be her father! When he'd agreed to pose as Carrie's fiancé, she hadn't told him he'd have to dust his head with baby powder!

"Listen, Carrie, I don't know if now is the time…"

But she'd already latched on to his arm and was dragging him toward her table. "No time like the present."

The white-haired gentleman stuck out his arm. "Wilson Haywood, I presume."

Mike firmly gripped his hand, slam-dunked by the realisation. Hey, whoa! It took every ounce of restraint Mike had not to thumb his chest like an idiot and say, *"Who, me?"*

He shot a quick glance at Carrie, who slipped him a sly wink. Oh, so it was showtime, was it? A little practicing up for his big debut? Yeesh! The least Carrie could have done was warn him. Well, now, maybe it was her turn to be caught off guard.

Mike gave the older man's hand a firm squeeze. "Indeed it is. And, you…?"

"Sweetheart," Carrie said, beaming a bit too radiantly, in Mike's opinion. "This is Charles Gilpatrick, the innkeeper here."

Mike's chest wall relaxed a notch. Of course he was the innkeeper. Who on earth else could he have been?

"I trust," Mr. Gilpatrick said, directing his question at Mike, "you and Ms. St. John are enjoying your stay here?"

Mike stepped over and drew a tight arm around Carrie's shoulders. "Delightful place. You should be very proud of what you've done with it. You've only been in business for about a year now, isn't that right?"

Gilpatrick's gray eyes warmed in appreciation. "I see Carrie's not the only one with an aptitude for doing her homework."

Mike pulled Carrie in a little tighter, her side heating his skin, even through his clothing. "She's quite the student, my Carrie," Mike said, caressing her shoulder.

Carrie squirmed in his grip as his fire spiked through her. It started at his fingertips, where they lightly massaged and caressed her bare shoulder, ricocheted to her breastbone, then sank low in her belly. Boy, was she done for, Carrie thought, realizing she'd missed something in the conversation and that both Charles and Mike now had their expectant gazes turned on her.

"Honey?" Mike asked, leaning over, his whiskey whisper tickling her ear.

Carrie blanched, suddenly light-headed. "Yeah, sure. That's fine," she responded, sinking into her chair beneath the two men's congenial laughter.

"The Merlot will be fine, Charles," Mike said. "Thanks so much for the offer and coming over to introduce yourself."

"The pleasure's all mine," Charles said, departing with a nod of his head.

Carrie picked up her water glass and drained most of it while Mike sat across from her. "What was so funny?" she asked, knowing she'd embarrass herself by asking but fearing it would be worse for her still if she never even knew.

Mike's smile broadened over his own water glass. "Charles had offered a complimentary bottle of Virginia wine, or in your case, since you're such a special guest— his entire wine cellar, to which you—"

204

Carrie rested her near-empty water glass against the side of her flaming cheek. "Indicated I'd take the whole wine cellar."

"More or less," Mike replied with a grin. "But, no worries, I saved our new friend from bankruptcy by agreeing to take him up on his earlier offer of a Merlot instead."

"I see," said Carrie, setting down her glass.

A wine steward appeared and displayed a Norton Vineyard label before Mike. "Excellent year," Mike said. "Believe that one was an award winner, wasn't it?"

Their server nodded solemnly and uncorked the bottle with white-gloved hands. After a brief wine-tasting interlude, the beverage was poured and Mike and Carrie left alone to once again confront each other in peace.

"Mind telling me why we are considered such special guests in this place?" Mike asked, lifting his glass.

"Mind telling me how you know so much about Virginia wines?"

Mike swirled his glass and surveyed the softly shadowed face of the woman in front of him. Elegant, sophisticated, and, if she was getting special treatment from innkeepers, most likely rich. In light of all that, Mike somehow didn't think telling Carrie he'd spent his high school summers working the vineyards would sound all that impressive.

"Let's just say," Mike said, lightly clinking her glass, "I'm a man of impeccable taste."

"To impeccable taste," Carrie said, raising her wine to her lips.

"Seriously, Carrie," Mike said, once they'd both set their glasses back on the table. "Why is it that we, or rather you, merit such special treatment here?"

Carrie looked at him innocently and shrugged, picking up her menu.

Mike reached out and lowered the laminated page so he could look in her eyes. "Are you...? You're not...?"

"What?" she asked, her eyes lighting with amusement. "Somebody famous?"

Mike leaned in just a tiny bit more. "We-ell?" he asked, drawing out the word in a blood-pounding way as sea-green eyes washed all over her.

Carrie laid down her menu and gripped the table edge to get her bearings. "Nope. Nobody famous, if you must know. Just your regular old girl from Virginia. Hope that doesn't disappoint too much."

Uh-uh. Carrie St. John had done nothing to disappointment him yet, and she wasn't going to start now. Her eyes were fanning wide, half playful, half daring. The deepest chocolate brown, even darker by candlelight than they'd appeared in the light of day. And everything about her seemed to be drawing Mike closer. Even as he willed himself to remain stoic in his chair.

But instead of staying put, Mike found himself reaching across the table. Wrapping her satiny shoulders in his trembling grip, leaning his mouth in toward hers as the moonlight and the table and the milling voices of others all melted away.

Carrie tilted her chin in expectation and didn't break away. Rather than pause, she seemed susceptible to the same raging pull that had engulfed Mike's senses. Her eyes lingered tantalizingly on his own—beckoning, promising. She let out a little gasp, lightly moistening her lips.

"Ready to order?" the maître d' inquired, slicing the air between them.

"Not on your life," Mike said, slamming down his napkin.

****

Chapter Six

"Excuse me," Carrie said, abruptly pushing back her chair. "I'm going to powder my nose."

Thank God, Carrie could hear herself thinking. Thank God, thank God, thank God! If that maître d' hadn't interrupted just in the nick of time, who knew what would have happened?

Carrie knew exactly.

She pushed her way into the ladies room and made a beeline for the faucet, where she ran the water cold.

Get a grip, Carrie, she warned herself sternly, dousing some paper towels and dabbing them at her neckline and brow. Water streamed from her neck to cleavage, reminding her of the effect Mike Davis had inspired at the pool. What was it with this man and water! Every time Carrie thought of him…

Carrie looked up into the mirror and found her face a heated flush

And this was supposed to make things all better? Getting tangled up with someone new when her heart hadn't even had half a chance to heal was going to somehow alleviate the ache in her life?

Carrie shook her head at the woman in the mirror. Plain old girl from Virginia was right. To look at her now, no one would ever suspect her worldly sophistication. They'd liken her, in fact, to some high school hayseed, fallen right off the turnip truck.

Mike sat at the table, dumbfounded. This had to be the longest nose-powdering in history, he thought, staring down at his and Carrie's lukewarm entrees.

She'd agreed to let him place the orders, but then had bolted like a minnow in the path of a manta ray.

Mike racked his brain for something—anything—he could have done wrong, but all he came up with was that "almost" kiss. Now, if he had kissed her and botched it miserably, he would have understood her wanting to take flight. But he hadn't even gotten his chance. And, no matter what excuses she planned to offer to the contrary—and Mike was quite certain that was what she was doing at the moment, concocting excuses—there'd been that unmistakable look in her eye that said she'd wanted him to take it.

Mike had been with plenty of women, enough of them to know when one wanted kissing and wanted it badly. Was it really possible all his years of training could fail him now?

Mike stood from the table, thinking he should go check on her. As far as he knew, Carrie didn't own a black Jaguar to escape in, but Mike supposed it was possible that Carrie could decide to run out on him just as Alexia had.

Mike was just rounding the corner where trellised vines climbed heavenward when he ran smack into Carrie.

"I was just coming to check on you," he said when she halted in surprise.

"Sorry," she said with a trembling smile. "I had to collect myself."

"You doing all right?" Mike asked with concern.

Carrie looked at him, then pursed her lips to keep them steady.

"Carrie?"

Her eyes fell to the ground as she slowly shook her head. "It's no use, Mike," she said, her voice cracking up. "This whole charade is—"

"Who says it's all a charade?" Mike asked, stepping forward and taking her by the elbows.

"Mike," she said, looking up and trying her damndest to look tough. Be in control. But Mike could see Carrie St. John was no more in control of her own racing heart than he was of his. "This thing, this arrangement, simply isn't going to work."

"Says who?" he asked, stepping closer as a couple of departing diners scooted around them on the pathway. "Did you find that on some literature in the ladies'?"

Carrie heaved a sigh without smiling, but he could tell she was loosening up.

"Or perhaps," he said, sliding his arms around her waist and tugging her into his rock-solid frame, "you found something disparaging written about me on the bathroom walls?"

Carrie looked up at the impossible man and shook her head, trying to deflect the comfort of his humor, trying to make herself believe that nothing Mike Davis could say could possibly make things seem any better.

Mike reached out and tilted her chin. "None of it's true, Carrie," he said, his mouth closing in. "Except for maybe the part about me being a good time…"

Carrie's knees went weak at that thought, as his overpoweringly male scent washed over her in ocean waves.

Trying to fight her natural attraction to Mike Davis, she decided, was a losing battle.

And when he claimed her mouth with his, she knew it wasn't only battles they were talking. They were playing for the highest stakes. Every ounce of her hurting interior was at war with what her body was doing. Reveling in, encouraging, his bittersweet, luxurious kisses. Carrie wasn't even sure it was legal to kiss that well. Especially in the state of Virginia. Where exactly was that turnip truck, anyway? Carrie wondered, feeling herself spiral further and further away into the magic of Mike's embrace.

"Carrie," Mike said, pulling back, "maybe we ought to find someplace more private…"

A fanning burn in her throat prevented her from answering. She was hot and tipsy, his raging fire still tearing through her like the strongest scotch whiskey. And this was a drink she wanted straight up. No ice.

Mike bucked as the icy chill raced through his sports coat and centered in on his spine.

"Oh! Oh, my goodness!" the befuddled voice called behind him as a hard metallic clank echoed from somewhere near his feet. Cold water sloshed forward, followed by a parade of ice cubes. Mike whirled to find the red-faced young woman who'd just poured her champagne bucket down his back.

"Oh, gracious!" she continued to babble, kneeling to scoop the miraculously intact bottle of champagne of the brick walk. "I'm so sorry! Must have run straight into—"

From just over his shoulder, a woman erupted in raucous laughter.

Mike spun to find Carrie cupping a hand over her mouth as her whole upper body quaked with mirth.

If only he'd known what she'd been thinking! What was it about Mike Davis, Carrie wondered, that always

211

seemed to attract him to water? Or vice versa, Carrie thought, exploding once again in giggles.

Mike ignored the woman at his feet, busily scooping ice cubes back into her silver bucket, and kept a watchful eye on Carrie as he stealthily removed his dripping sports coat and shook it out at arm's length.

"Feeling all better, I see," he said, cocking one eyebrow and looking— what? Carrie wondered—amused at her amusement?

"Sir, I—"

"Don't worry about it," Mike said, nearly deaf to the stranger's apologies as he stooped to gather ice cubes and toss the cleaner ones back into the bucket. "Accidents happen." But what had happened between him and Carrie just now hadn't been an accident at all. For the briefest moment, she'd been all his. And it had been wonderful. So wonderful he'd been itching to continue things on an even more intimate level back in his room. And now—this.

Finally, their embarrassed interloper straightened and made off with her champagne. Carrie, Mike noticed, still looked as if she was going to burst into hysterics at any moment.

"I—" She sputtered a laugh, then stopped and collected herself. "I am feeling much better, thank you. But you're— all wet…"

"Nothing that I haven't been before," he assured her, holding up his jacket to examine it in the moonlight. "I'm sure my clothing and I will survive."

To her embarrassment, Carrie's stomach growled loudly.

"Still hungry?" Mike asked, feeling for the ice cube that had wedged itself between his belt and waistband at the small of his back and plucking it free.

Carrie giggled again as he offered it as further proof of his ordeal.

Carrie lifted the ice cube from his palm and hurled it into the darkness. "Starved. But how about you? Don't you think you'd better, uh…change?"

"Change?" Mike grinned. "Thought you were starting to like me just the way I am."

Carrie felt herself color from head to toe. "You, Mike Davis, are—"

He cocked one eyebrow and waited.

"—a very nice man," she finished, feeling renewed heat in her cheeks.

Mike chuckled and brought a tender hand to her face. "Ah, Carrie. Yes. And you, my dear, are very—sweet."

Mike leaned forward and kissed her lightly on the forehead, something akin to affection sparkling in his eyes. No man had ever looked at Carrie like that before. With hunger, anticipation, yes. But this was a different sort of appreciation altogether, and it warmed her through and through.

"Want to see if dinner's still on the table?" he asked, taking her hand.

"Great idea," Carrie said, wondering what on earth was happening to her. This wasn't love. At least, not like she'd ever known it. Carrie St. John was falling "in like" with a man who looked like a god, and neither her heart nor her head knew precisely what to make of that.

213

Chapter Seven

Mike draped his still-damp clothing over the wooden hangers he'd suspended from the shower bar. All in all, things hadn't gone badly. Even if he had taken a bath, in a manner of speaking, the look on Carrie's face had been worth every ounce of icy discomfort. Somehow, Mike suspected, Carrie didn't get the opportunity for laughs often. Though laughter suited her beautifully. So well, in fact, Mike was going to make it his personal ambition to ensure she wore it more often.

Mike puzzled at his instant attraction to the woman he'd met a day ago. Yet, somehow, when he looked in her deep-brown eyes, he had the notion he'd known her a lifetime.

Now he was getting sappy, Mike thought, sitting down on the bed to tug off his socks. Thinking that things between him and Carrie had, in some way, been preordained. Just who did he think he was kidding? Mike's judgment in the past regarding women had left much to be desired. And yet, what he desired more than anything was a chance to prove—to himself and Carrie—that perhaps this time his instincts were dead-on.

There was something about her that got to him on more than just a physical level. He liked Carrie. Honestly enjoyed spending time with her. And, looking back, Mike wasn't sure he could make that unequivocal statement about any of the previous women in his life. Up until now, Mike had always looked at romance as a love/hate proposition. The woman you loved was supposed to drive you mad, wasn't she? Feminine wiles were supposed to be mysterious, impossible to understand. And, up until now, Mike hadn't given one iota whether he'd understood them or not. Wooing women was something Mike had experience in. Plenty. But befriending them? That was a totally new concept altogether. And a woman who could prove both a lover and a friend...?

Mike fell back on the bed and pulled a fluffy pillow over his head. Maybe once he got down to the Caymans, he wouldn't have to deal with such bubbleheaded notions. A woman as a friend! Hoo! Who in Hades did he think he was fooling?

Carrie fluffed the pillow and repositioned it beneath her elbow, making believe she was reading the magazine. But truth be known, she'd been staring down at the same article on backyard decorating for the past twenty minutes and hadn't absorbed a thing.

The rest of the evening had gone like a charm. The two of them swapping humorous stories over their second bottle of complimentary Merlot. Though he'd had nothing to do with it personally, the innkeeper had been quite embarrassed by Mike's earlier run-in with the champagne bucket and had insisted on more wine as an apology.

Mike had accepted graciously, asking if it would be too much trouble to sample a different vintage, a sweet Virginia red perhaps, as they'd already moved on to dessert.

It still struck Carrie as odd that a realtor knew so much about wine. Not that he didn't have a right to be a connoisseur if he wanted. It was just that Carrie couldn't help the niggling sensation that something about Mike didn't add up.

He seemed so out of character as a realtor. And yet, if he professed that was what he did, what gave her reason to doubt him? Perhaps it was merely her own guilt seeping through. Guilt over not being completely honest with him about who she was or what she did. Though she'd informed him of the generalities, she'd very purposely ignored the particulars.

Mike seemed to like her so much, just as she was—the homespun girl from Virginia. And she, Carrie admitted truthfully, laying a palm over her fluttering heart, had been very much enjoying his down-to-earth, manly attentions. Finding out her net worth would surely change how he looked at her. And, at thirty-three, Carrie St. John had tired of being looked at as nothing more than a financial opportunity. Both of her boyfriends thus far, even the younger one in college, had seemed to sense she was going places and had wanted to latch on to her coattails. At least temporarily.

And that, probably, was why the romance had never lasted. No man had ever truly been attracted to who she was inside. No matter what her bank account said now, on the inside, Carrie was still the same simple girl who had sewn her dress from scratch in order to afford the prom.

But understanding her humble roots was not something even a nice man like Mike Davis could likely relate to. He, after all, had grown up in the lap of privilege himself. Ashton Academy cost more per year than Carrie's full university scholarship had provided per annum.

Carrie snapped off the light and sank back into the mattress, wondering just who she thought she was fooling.

Mike was simply a nice man who had taken pity on her
present circumstances. And no matter how badly her heart
ached to be near him, it was high time Carrie started
listening to her head. They were far too different from one
another—she and Mike—to ever form anything long-
lasting. She might as well just lie back and enjoy the
temporary ride of having him in her life as her fiancé. From
the looks of her life, it was as close to the real thing as
Carrie would ever get.

"Ready to go?" Mike asked, standing in her open
doorway. After a quick, cordial breakfast together, they'd
each headed to their separate rooms to pack up.

He looked even better this morning than Carrie'd
remembered, his well-tailored slacks and sports coat over
open-collared shirt accentuating his exceptionally fit form.
Carrie heaved a sigh, grateful, at least, for the dynamite
impression he was going to make. But in some ways,
having him wow her family was going to make it that much
harder to disillusion them in the end. Somehow, she'd
never considered that angle. Although it was definitely far
too late to go having second thoughts now.

"Having second thoughts?" Mike asked, leaning
forward and picking up her suitcase.

"Not at all," Carrie reported, fighting the fire in her
cheeks. "Let's get started."

Mike took a cursory scan around the gravel parking
area. "Your car or mine?"

Carrie cast a sideways glance at her shiny teal-blue
BMW convertible. "Yours would be better, I think. Mine—
needs work…"

217

"Oh?" Mike asked. "Maybe I can take a look at it. I'm pretty handy with cars, you know."

As far as Carrie was concerned, Mike seemed pretty handy with just about everything. "Uh, no. Thanks, I'll just take it to the shop when I get back."

"Seriously," Mike said, dropping the bags dangling at his sides to the ground. "Might be something really simple. I'd hate to think of you spending the—"

"Maybe when we get back," Carrie said, tugging at his elbow. "We really can't be late. My Grandma Russell would have a fit."

"Okay. Let me just put your suitcase in your car, then."

Carrie blew a hard breath and nervously latched on to a loose strand of hair. In all her boardroom negotiations, she'd never come across anything like this. Still, a very large part of her success had come from thinking on her feet.

"Actually," she said, motioning to her bag, "I've got some gifts in there for my aunts and grandmother. Too cumbersome to get it all out now."

Mike shrugged, seeming to buy that easily. "Oh, all right. I'll just toss it in my trunk, then."

Mike strode over to a late-model Mustang. Ancient but meticulously restored. Candy-apple red.

"Love the car," Carrie said, appreciatively patting the hood as Mike laid the bags in the trunk. "She's a real…" Carrie stopped short of saying "investment goldmine." "…beaut. You've done a great job with her."

"Thanks," Mike said, smiling as he came around to unlock Carrie's door. "I guess I do pretty well at taking care of the things that are important to me."

218

Carrie swallowed hard and stepped into the car without uttering a word. Did his words really carry the weight she thought he'd intended them to? No, Carrie, she admonished herself, don't be stupid. Get through this day, that's all. One day at a time. She'd think about the coming weekend, and Mike's reunion, and her miserable life afterward— tomorrow.

****

Chapter Eight

Paulette Pierce held out her narrow grip. "My, my, how time improves," she said, unabashedly looking Mike up and down. The moment they'd arrived, Carrie had been lost to a swirl of old ladies in pastel brocade, and Mike hadn't seen her since.

"Why thanks, Paulette," Mike said, shifting on his feet and taking her hand. The woman was birdlike and gaunt, probably Carrie's age, though her thinness made her appear much older. "I take that as a compliment."

Paulette enclosed his hand in her viselike flesh and leaned forward. "A compliment meant for you, not Wilson Haywood," she said in a hushed tone.

Mike fought the urge to wince in her talons and forced a tight smile.

Paulette kept hold of his hand and took a step forward, straight honey-colored hair swinging over her shoulders. "That stuffy old suit, Wilson," she continued in a whisper. "I can barely remember. But you, sweetheart, a gal's not likely to forget."

She leaned in and brought her mouth very close to his ear. "Is it serious?" she asked, just as Mike felt a hand on his shoulder.

"Paulette," Carrie said, stepping between the two of them. "How nice to see you getting reacquainted with Wilson." Carrie slipped an arm through one of Mike's and linked him in tight. "Isn't he even better than you remembered?"

"Quite," Paulette said, eyes narrowing. "In fact, if I didn't know better, I'd say—"

"Of course, the plastic surgery helped a lot."

Paulette's jaw dropped open. "Wait a minute. You're not saying—"

Mike raised his free hand and massaged his rugged jaw. "A little here, a little there. Filling in the face, that is. Worked wonders. Maybe you ought to try it."

Paulette huffed, but Carrie just bit into her bottom lip and raised her eyebrows.

"And the gym helped too, of course," Mike continued, finding himself getting more and more carried away. "But I said to myself, I said, nothing's too good for my Carrie. She wants a certain type of man, she's going to get it..."

Carrie held her breath and watched Paulette's eyes widened.

"I mean, why not?" Mike asked. "You women do it all the time, reinvent yourselves for your men. Breast augmentation—"

Paulette went positively white and glanced down at her own flat chest.

"Come on, Wilson," Carrie said, nudging him soundly with her elbow. "Time you talked to a few more of our guests..."

"And not," she whispered sternly in his ear, when they'd left the mortified Paulette behind them, "about breast implants." In spite of her admonition, Carrie found herself fighting the urge to giggle. From the time she'd been fourteen, Carrie's first cousin Paulette had made it her personal goal to steal every man in Carrie's life right out from under her. Well, not this time, Carrie thought, glowing brightly as the man on her arm looked down into her eyes with a naughty grin.

"She deserved it," he whispered back. "Not only did she suspect the truth, she was coming on to me besides."

Carrie looked back over her shoulder at Paulette, who was downing a fast cup from the punch bowl, then broke into a chuckle. "Oh Mike," she said, patting his arm. "You're absolutely right. Busybody Paulette got just what she deserved. But do you think she'll tell?"

Mike looked straight over the top of Carrie's head. "I think she's leaving. Hope she wasn't your maid of honor or anything important like that."

Carrie spun around to see the back-porch door swinging shut at Paulette's back. "Holy cow!" Carrie exclaimed, stretching up on her toes and giving Mike's cheek a firm peck. "How on earth did you do that? I've been trying to get Paulette to keep her nose completely out of my business for nearly twenty years and never even came close to succeeding until now."

Mike's cheek tingled where Carrie's warm lips left their mark, reminding him ever-so-pleasantly of the type of fiancé he was expected to be. Touchy-feely. Amen, Mike thought, winding his arm around Carrie's shoulders like a prayer. She was truly radiant today. Looking very bride-like in her white linen dress, its clean lines unintentionally outlining every curve. Even its scooped neckline, which professed its innocence by camouflaging itself with a hint of lace, looked positively villainous in its enviable position right next to Carrie's bosom.

"What? What is it?" Carrie asked, bringing a hand to shield her briefest hint of cleavage. "There something wrong with my dress?"

Mike gave her shoulders a reassuring squeeze and planted a light nibble on her tantalizing neck. "Nope, nothing at all. I was just thinking about how great you look in white."

Carrie slapped a palm into the side of Mike's head. "Behave yourself! Grandma Russell's coming!"

"Just playing the part," Mike said, drawing her into an affectionate hug and kissing her lightly at her temple. "Of the loving fiancé."

Carrie blinked as her world went cold and hot. Hot and cold. No, wait! Her palms were sweating, but her belly was a pit of ice.

"Carrie, darling!" An elderly lady with more salt than pepper in her short curly hair scuttled over and wrapped frail arms around the two of them.

"Wilson," she proclaimed, beaming up at Mike and whacking him soundly on the shoulder. "I do declare, you *are* a hunk!"

Somewhere in the heat of the moment, Carrie found her tongue. Which was, dammit, stuck to the roof of her mouth.

"Grandmother!" Mike exclaimed, lifting the 110-pound woman into the air with his bear-hug embrace. "It's so good to finally meet you."

Well, now, Carrie thought, Mike was carrying things a little far. Paulette was one thing, but…

Mike set Grandma Russell down as she reached up and pinched his cheek. "He is a doll, Carrie! An absolute doll! Just somehow I never pictured him as a blond. You should have told me he looked like Robert Redford but green-eyed, young, and sexy."

223

Mike laughed out loud but felt his ears tinge hot just the same. Though he was used to compliments from women, up until now, most of those offering their rabid appreciation had been under fifty.

"Come on, darling," Grandma Russell said to Mike. "Let me show you off…" She gave a little chuckle. "Show you around, that is. Carrie's aunties are all dying to meet you."

Carrie swirled the ladle nervously around the near-empty punch bowl. The shower had gone off without a hitch. She and Mike—uh, Wilson—had even gotten some lovely gifts. A blender, cooking utensils. Towels. All the nice little odds and ends that help make a newlywed house a home. This wasn't such a good idea, after all. In fact, it was terrible. So many people had gone to so much time, trouble, and expense. Even Nellie's place cards were beautiful. A keepsake for the happy couple. Carrie frowned at her murky reflection centered in the twirling ice ring.

And to make matters worse, Mike had been an absolute champ. Everybody adored him implicitly. He'd been warm, witty, and charming the whole afternoon through. His act as her fiancé had almost even seemed real; at least his hugs and affectionate glances had seemed authentic enough. And those few unexpected kisses, though innocent enough in their placement—one at her temple, one on the back of her hand, the one at her neckline… Well, all right, maybe the one at her neck hadn't seemed quite so innocent in intent as the others. But still, no matter where his kisses had landed, each time Mike had surprised her with the warm contact of his lips, her world had caved in and her heart had let go. Let go of any notion that this thing between them was little more than make-believe. Because, though words could deceive, feelings seldom lied, and when Mike brought his flesh to hers... Carrie dropped the ladle into the punch bowl as goose bumps tore down her spine.

Carrie felt the hair swept from her nape. "Ready to leave?" Mike whispered, bringing his mouth close to her ear.

Carrie turned in surprise and found herself directly in his arms, her backside pinned against the table that held the punch bowl. "Never," she said, bringing her arms up and around his neck and pulling him in close as their lips melded in the final consummation of what they'd both been desiring all afternoon.

"Why don't you kids run on home?" Grandma Russell asked, blinking the dining room chandelier on and off above them.

Mike pulled back in a damp sweat. "Let's!" he said, giving Carrie a firm, virgin peck on the lips.

Carrie sat in Mike's car, anxiously fiddling with his radio and waiting for his return from the grocery store. Though he'd said he'd only be a minute, she could only guess at what he'd buy. Champagne? Wine and roses? Were things between them really moving that fast?

And where on earth would they go? She wasn't sure she was ready for Mike to see her place. Besides, she was totally unprepared for company, and her cottage was a total wreck. Though the setting, at the western edge of the county, was gorgeous, the inside of her home looked like it had been hit by a black tornado. If there was one thing Carrie didn't do well, it was clean. Well, in truth, her laundry skills weren't so hot either. All the whites always seemed to come out a weird shade of neon pink. Even after all this time, Carrie couldn't figure out which of her red sweater tops had been doing all that running.

The driver's door popped open, startling Carrie from her reverie.

"Miss me?" Mike asked with an earnest grin.

"Absolutely," Carrie said, hoping her face didn't look nearly as hot as it felt. "What you got there in the bag?"

"Uh-uh," Mike said, scrunching the paper roll at the top of the bag a bit tighter and slipping it into the backseat. "It's a surprise."

The only problem was, Mike still hadn't settled on the perfect place to share it. Not at his place, for sure. His apartment was a pigsty. Not that it was usually that bad… Mike slumped back against his bucket seat at the inner half-truth. The fact was, compared to its usual state, his apartment looked good. Which wasn't saying a whole heck of a lot.

Mike could tell from meeting her family and seeing the tidy home she'd grown up in that, though she hadn't been raised rich, she'd definitely inherited class and style. A style that would be severely undone by the sight of his dirty boxers strewn all across the backs of his chairs. And those beers cans… Mike scratched the back of his head, trying to remember if he'd put that last batch of trash out to recycle. Better not chance it, he decided, heading the car west of the city.

"Where to?" Carrie asked, a fine sweep of color caressing her cheeks, but only half as tenderly as Mike wanted to at this moment.

"Someplace special," he said, lowering his window just a crack to let in a refreshing breath of cool evening air.

But deep inside, Carrie knew that it scarcely mattered. Someplace special seemed to be right here with him.

****

Chapter Nine

Mike hoisted Carrie down from the top of the split-rail fence and led her into the vineyard.

"Well, what do you think?" he asked, clutching his mystery paper bag to his chest.

Carrie inhaled deeply, absorbing the scent of summer hills and lilac. For acres before them, rows upon rows of trellised vines bloomed in lush splendor, their endless trails spilling toward the tumbling Blue Ridge. Mountain upon haze-tipped mountain fell backward in smoky array, blending infinitely with the settling twilight.

"It's gorgeous, just gorgeous," Carrie said, talking not only of the scenery around them. For in this afternoon alone, she'd seen something altogether different in Mike. Not the tempting bachelor, nor the friend with a penchant for making her smile. But a regular family man. Carrie was certain now he hadn't been fabricating his desires for that white picket fence. Mike was good in a crowd, great with people—young and old alike. And playful to boot. Carrie was sure he'd make an excellent father.

"Care to sit?"

Carrie looked down, realizing Mike had removed his jacket and laid it as a cushion on the ground for her to protect her clothing.

"You know," she said, taking a seat and arranging her dress on the jacket to defend it from the spreading clay-dotted grass around them. "Alexia was really a very stupid woman."

Mike grinned in surprise and scooted in beside her on the splotchy earth. "Kind of you to say so."

"I mean it," Carrie assured him. "But she was smart in one regard."

Mike raised his brow in expectation.

"Picking you out in the first place."

Mike sputtered a laugh. "Alexia always was a good shopper."

Carrie tried to keep her eyes focused ahead of her, but it was impossible not to be drawn to the man beside her. Never in her life—nowhere in the world—had Carrie St. John come across the likes of Mike Davis. He was handsome and charming, absolutely. But much more importantly, he was genuine.

"You know the thing about Alexia—"

Carrie reached out and latched on to his rugged chin. "Mike."

He stopped midsentence and questioned with his eyes. Beautiful, earth-moving, sea-green eyes.

Carrie settled her other hand at the side of his face. "Shut up and kiss me."

"Thought you'd never ask," he hummed, closing in.

After they'd necked like teenagers for nearly twenty minutes, Carrie felt something moist and clammy seeping onto her outer thigh.

"Oh my God!" Mike said, looking down in horror at the leaking paper bag pressed up against Carrie's leg. "Your beautiful dress!"

Carrie puzzled at the mysterious green stain on her leg. She wiped a hand against the sticky mess, then brought a palm to her nose. "Mint?"

"Mint chocolate chip," Mike said, sheepishly unrolling the bag. "Ice cream sandwiches."

Carrie threw back her head with a belly laugh. "Ice cream sandwiches! And there I thought you'd gotten us another elegant vintage of wine."

"Carrie," he said, pulling a clean handkerchief from his pocket and dabbing the side of her clothing. "I'm so sorry about your dress. I forgot all about—"

"That's all right," she said, giving his chin an affectionate nuzzle. "I did too. And no worries. The dress will wash." And if it didn't, she could always get another. But Carrie was as certain it wouldn't be so easy to replace Mike Davis. "Think they're still any good?"

"Of course! A little soggy, maybe," he said, pulling the soppy package from its dripping bag. "But edible, nonetheless. How about it?"

"I'd love one." Carrie smiled. "Mint chocolate is my absolute favorite. How on earth did you know?"

"Wild guess," Mike said, grinning naughtily. "And your Grandma Russell told me."

"Cheater!" Carrie said, swatting him playfully across the chest. "You just wait till I corner some of those old high school chums of yours and get the dirt on you!"

"So, you're not disappointed, then?"

Carrie warned herself to proceed with caution. "In...?"

"The ice cream. I mean, it may not be the rare vintage you were—"

"I love the ice cream. I don't think any man has surprised me with ice cream before." Much less spread it on my thigh, she heard herself thinking but thank God didn't say. All of a sudden, Carrie was developing lots of innovative ideas about what she and Mike could do with ice

230

cream. But not here, not now, not in the middle of somebody else's vineyard.

"What is this place?" Carrie asked, taking a bite out of her dripping sandwich and delighting in its fresh minty taste. Nightfall was almost upon them, shadows stretching long over the vineyard. The top third of the mountains had already faded to black. If they didn't head back soon, they might have difficulty finding the car in the darkness.

"Just a place I stumbled on long ago."

"It's yours?" Carrie asked, surprise and delight firing her eyes. "I should have known you were a vintner! Now, it all makes perfect—"

"Carrie," Mike answered, crestfallen. "It's not mine." He couldn't bring himself to tell her that he'd only worked here as a hired hand during his high school summers. That his background was much more modest that hers ever was. He and his dad never had a nice home—of any size—to call their own. They had rented and lived out of trailers. His graduation from Ashton had been thanks to a full athletic scholarship.

"Maybe you should buy it, then?" she continued, seeming happily excited by the notion. "It would make a wonderful investment!"

"Investment?" Mike had never been able to invest in anything beyond his next month's rent.

Carrie appeared to pick up on his mood and halted. "Oh, I'm sorry," she said, wadding up her ice cream sandwich wrapper and balling it in her fist. "It wasn't my place at all to suggest that."

And why, indeed, would she suggest it? Just as breezily as if wishing could make it so. Did Carrie St. John actually have that sort of money herself? "Would you

231

invest in it, Carrie?" Mike pressed, wanting to know if his hunch was accurate.

Criminy. Carrie had really painted herself into a corner this time. Here she'd been all this time not wanting to let on she had money, and then she went and said a stupid, unthinking thing like that. "Why, no. No." Carrie felt herself growing warm in the chill of the evening. "Just making conversation, that's all," she lied, scrambling to her feet. "You know, it's getting late…"

"I know," Mike said, looking deep in her eyes as if trying to discern something.

"Think you could drive me back to the inn so I can collect my car and get on home? I have to work tomorrow and I'm sure—"

"No problem," Mike said, scooping their litter off the ground and trying to discern what she was hiding. Mike weighed the dichotomy of her simple, small-town roots against the exceedingly preferential treatment Carrie had been afforded by Charles Gilpatrick back at the inn. Was Carrie St. John filthy rich, someone famous to be reckoned with?

"Who are you, Carrie St. John?" Mike asked as the breath of night threaded silken silence between them.

"Just a simple old girl from Virginia," she said, needing him desperately to believe it.

****

Chapter Ten

Carrie made the forty-five minute drive from the country inn to her country bungalow with her top down. The nippy evening air lit up her senses and helped her focus her attention on the issues at hand, as weaving wind whipped fingers through her long, loose hair. At least she'd had her wits about her when Mike had dropped her back at the parking area and had been able to concoct that missing earring story that had allowed her to duck back inside. She'd watched out the window of the inn until a few minutes after Mike had driven away. Though here he'd been insistent about staying and seeing her to her car, she'd fabricated an excuse about also having to settle some business arrangements with Mr. Gilpatrick that might take a while.

While in looking at his watch, he'd seemed dubious, Mike had finally acquiesced and settled for a formal good-bye on the steps of the inn. The same stone steps where Carrie had first beheld him in his dripping-wet, near-naked glory on that fated night they'd met.

Carrie's throat went dry at the recollection as she sailed through the yellow light. Carrie quickly checked her rearview mirror, but saw, with relief, that even the cops in this sleepy berg were already in bed tonight. Carrie felt the spreading heat at her collarbone and inhaled deeply, fighting off the thought of anything that put Mike Davis and beds together in her mind. She was falling for him. Falling badly. And there didn't appear to be a darn thing she could do about it except for trying to keep this silly illusion from blowing up smack in her face.

How long did Carrie really believe she could go on like this? A week, a month? In the outstanding event their relationship endured beyond Mike's reunion, sooner or later he was bound to start asking questions. Already had started asking questions, Carrie reminded herself.

Criminy.

Carrie ran a hand along the back of her stiff neck as she wheeled her car onto the exit ramp that led to the isolated country route that would take her home.

Oh what a tangled web we weave…

Carrie slowly shook her head.

All she'd really wanted was for Mike to like her for herself. But now she wondered precisely what that was. A liar? A manipulator? Someone with just as little integrity as Mike's old fiancée Alexia?

Carrie blinked hard as hot tears pressed with biting force from her bleary eyes. It was no wonder she'd never found a man. There, without even trying, she'd gone and done it again. Screwed her love life all to heck and back. Love life, ha! she thought, laughing bitterly into the wind. As if she'd ever truly known the meaning of the phrase.

Mike scurried around his apartment, tossing empty aluminum cans into the recycle bin. Holy cow! He didn't know why he had so much nervous energy. But whatever the reason, he might as well put it to good use.

Mike paused in the threshold to his bedroom, mentally trying to calculate when he'd last changed the sheets. Well, if he couldn't remember, then the likelihood was they needed changing again.

Mike tugged back the fitted sheet, trying to recall the last time he'd actually had a woman in the place. Alexia, neatnik that she was, had always insisted he come to hers. Alexia had always insisted on a lot of things, like her pleasure first, for example. Not that Mike minded giving a woman pleasure. That aspect, in fact, excited him. But when it was that woman's pleasure to the exclusion of everything else in the world, including the presence of her partner...

Mike shook his head and carried the pile of sheets to the washer. He was quite certain Carrie wouldn't be like that. Carrie was a warm and sensuous woman. Inviting yet giving all at once. It was there in the way she kissed, the way she teased and beckoned with her eyes. The way her tantalizingly womanly curves ached for a masculine touch...all...over...her body...

Christ.

Mike looked down at his boxers, realizing he was going to need another cold shower. His second since he'd dropped Carrie off at the inn and come home. And, for crying out loud, their parting kiss had been nothing if not chaste.

Maybe that was what it was. She was driving him to distraction by holding back. Though, when he was being honest, Mike had to admit that Carrie wasn't the only one who seemed adept at putting the brakes on their relationship. While their mutual attraction was too strong to deny, there was something else holding each of them back. Mike couldn't put his finger on it exactly. But his gut told him it had to do with more than just the faux-fiancé game going on between them.

Mike heaved a heavy sigh and flipped on the cold water. What was it about Carrie St. John that always left him all wet?

Carrie rolled over in bed and lazily lifted her cell. "Hello?"

"A dillar, a dollar…"

"Grandma Russell?" Carrie asked, her head pounding. She squinted against the bright light streaming in through the tilted Venetian blinds.

"Lands sakes, child, did I wake you? I thought you investment types were up catching worms well before dawn!"

Carrie reached out her free hand and angled her clock radio toward her so she could read the time. Ten thirty. She'd missed her nine-thirty appointment. Carrie's head fell back against her pillow with a thunk.

"No, Grandma." She held aside the receiver and yawned. "Been up for hours."

"Well, sweetheart, you're not really sounding too chipper."

"Just a stress headache," Carrie said, massaging her throbbing temple. "It will get better." Already, Carrie was making a mental list of all the conference calls she'd have to rearrange. Mondays! What a mess!

She must have been exhausted. Totally wiped out from her weekend experiences. And it was all Mike Davis's fault.

"Well, maybe my cheery bit of news will leave you feeling better… That fiancé of yours—"

Carrie sat bolt upright in bed, not knowing quite what to expect.

"—is such a doll. You'll never believe what that Wilson did!"

"No, I probably wouldn't," Carrie said, meaning it absolutely.

"He sent the sweetest note—with the flowers."

"Flowers?"

"Yes, indeed, perfectly gorgeous arrangement. Must have cost the man a fortune, but, of course, like you've told us, the man is dirty rich, so it really is the thought that counts."

Carrie's temples constricted and pounded anew. "Filthy, Grandma. The term is fil—"

"Well, now, sweetie, you may call the man a dirty rascal if you want to for outfoxing you with this sweet surprise, but I wouldn't go as far as to insult his personal hygiene. In fact, he looked exceptionally well-groomed to me!"

Carrie's head thumped back against the headboard, ramrodding the base of her skull with another lightning bolt of pain. Flowers? He'd sent flowers? How in the world would she ever explain breaking off an engagement to a wonderfully thoughtful man like him now! Her grandmother was totally smitten! "It was a very sweet gesture, but I'd caution you against taking anything he said too much to heart."

"To heart?" Grandmother Russell shot back. "The man has a heart the size of Nebraska! Looking forward to being a part of your beautiful family was what he said. Brought tears to Nellie's eyes it did. Real tears, not just the ones she sometimes puts on during confession."

Carrie sighed and squeezed shut her eyes, wondering how on earth she was going to get out of this mess, while her grandmother continued to wax poetic on "Wilson's" attributes.

"Wasn't that just the most eloquent…"

Carrie could practically feel the steam blowing out of her ears. Nice job, Mike Davis! Playing the perfect gentleman and leaving poor Carrie holding the bag. The time for beating herself up over her own duplicity had ended. Now Mike was the one with the answering to do. And Carrie was going to see to it personally he did some talking.

Mike was just going out to get his mail when Carrie roared into his apartment's parking lot like a storm cloud on the wings of—holy cow—a new-model BMW convertible. She did have money. And lots of it.

That wasn't the only thing, Mike saw, backing up a step as she leapt from her car and made for him like a thunderbolt. "You!"

Mike inched back toward the mailbox. He'd never seen a woman so positively incensed. Not even any of the several who'd dumped him.

"Hi, Carrie," he offered lamely, as she walked right up to his chin, then poked him in the chest.

"Thanks…one…whole…heck…of a…lot!" she said, emphasizing each word with the pressure of her pointy finger. "You, Mike Davis, have single-handedly ruined my existence!"

"Hey, whoa…" He tried to lay a steadying hand on her shoulder but backed off when the look in her eye told him she just might bite it off.

"What right," she asked, again with the pointy finger that—dammit—was starting to hurt, "do you have…sending flowers…to my grandmother?"

Mike gripped his hand around the offending digit and held it in place.

"Let me go!" Carrie charged.

"Only if you promise to stop poking."

Carrie glared at him and pulled back her hand, massaging its aching joints. Poking into his chest had been painful for her as well, though she didn't dare let him know it. It had taken her over three hours to find him. She'd gone through six other Michael Davises in Redfields before she'd finally happened upon this place here. And now he owed her some answers.

"Like some iced tea?" Mike asked, pinned to the mailbox, his eyes darting furiously between Carrie's still-idling car and the woman in front of him.

Carrie ran a frustrated hand through her tangled hair. "Well, for heaven's sake," she said, her shoulders sagging just a tad so their positioning didn't look quite so combative. "I'm not a bee that's going to sting you."

"Tea?" Mike repeated, his voice coming out an octave higher than intended. Okay, Mike, he told himself, now would be a good time to think up the reason you did that. She obviously wants an explanation. But do you understand it first?

All he knew was that when he'd awakened that morning feeling sunny, sending flowers seemed the perfect thing to do. Gracious. Thoughtful. And the truth was, he adored Carrie's grandmother—along with the rest of her extended family.

Carrie set a hand on her hip and shook her head. "All right, I'll come in for tea, but under one condition. You promise to be completely honest with me."

"That cuts two ways, Carrie," Mike called as she walked back to her car and yanked her keys from the ignition.

Criminy. She hadn't even considered that.

Carrie sat across from Mike at his kitchen table in his tiny but tidy efficiency apartment. Carrie looked around, somehow finding all the cleanliness disheartening. More undeniable proof of just how highly unsuited to each other the two of them were. What had she been thinking?

"Well," Carrie asked, setting down her glass. "I'm waiting."

Mike was waiting too. Waiting for something brilliant to occur to him. But all he could come up with was the very embarrassing truth: he'd wanted to impress Carrie's family.

"It wasn't meant in malice, Carrie," he began tentatively, pushing aside his tea glass.

"Well, of course, I know that!"

"Well, then...?" he asked, gently pacing his words, lest her iced-tea glass wind up on his head. "Why are you so darned mad?"

"I'm mad because... Because..." Carrie faltered. She was so furious she could barely form her words. But what, in truth, drove her anger was even beyond her comprehension. All she knew was it had something to do with Mike inserting himself deeper in her life than he had a right to go.

"We made a deal, you and I."

"That was ages ago."

"Three days," she corrected without blinking.

"Well, it seems like ages, Carrie. It seems impossible I've only known you that long. The two of us, we…"

"What?" she demanded, looking him square in the eye.

"You can't tell me you don't feel it too?"

Carrie pushed back from the table and stood. "No way. No way, Mike, are you turning the tables back on me. We are not here to discuss my feelings!"

"Okay," Mike said, taking a lingering sip of tea. "Shall we discuss mine, then?"

Panic gripped Carrie by the throat. What was happening here? No! She was here to confront him. She was furious! And there he was looking—what? Humble? Self-effacing? Forgivable?

Carrie bit into her bottom lip and dropped back down into her chair. "What do you mean by that?"

"What I mean," he said, looking right through her with earnest green eyes, "is that you said you wanted honesty. I'm prepared to fess up, if you are."

Carrie gulped and grabbed her tea glass, which was empty.

"Refill?" she asked weakly.

"In a moment," he said, reaching across the table and encircling the hand that gripped her glass with both of his. "First, we talk flowers."

Carrie tried to steady her resolve, remind herself of just how infuriated she was. But when she looked at him, really looked at him, Carrie knew in her heart Mike was telling the truth. He hadn't sent those flowers to upset her. Or anybody else, for that matter.

"So why?" she asked, the still air settling around them as Mike released his grip on her hands and laid his palms on the table.

"I can't tell you what it felt like. Being there in that room of people—with your family. I felt so included. Really a part of things. I didn't mean to make anything harder on you. Truly, I didn't. I just wanted to say thank you."

The gratitude part she could buy. He seemed sincere enough in his emotion, but... "The note?"

Mike wrinkled up his brow. "Guess I crossed the line on that one. My apologies. I sometimes get so swept up in things, I act before I think."

Carrie held her tongue, knowing very much what that felt like. Okay, so maybe he had acted on impulse. And maybe out of good intention. But what a viper she was going to look like now when she announced her relationship with Mike had ended.

"How about your family?" she asked after a long pause. "Don't they make you feel—included?"

Mike gave a slow, sad smile and studied the tabletop. "Well, I guess family's a pretty subjective word, isn't it? Mine isn't all that big, really. Just me and my dad."

"Oh, I'm sorry." But Mike didn't offer any more. He just sat there being very quiet. Abnormally quiet.

Carrie studied the man with the gorgeous green eyes and shoulders broad enough to take on anybody's troubles. It wasn't only his trick with the flowers that was going to make ending this charade difficult.

After what seemed like eons, Carrie reached across the table and laid a hand on his arm. "Mike?"

"My dad's sick, Carrie," Mike said, looking up with moisture-tinged eyes. "Very sick. For the past two years, almost all of my income has gone to his care."

Carrie felt the raw burn in her throat. She'd never known her parents. They'd died in a house fire when she'd been barely a year old. By a twist of fate, she'd been staying with her grandmother as her parents were planning on going away together for their second anniversary trip. They'd never made it, and Carrie, thanks to the luck of the draw, had survived to be raised by her Grandmother Russell and doting great-aunts.

Still, she couldn't imagine what it would feel like to lose someone who'd looked after you, somebody you'd equally loved and cared for. Carrie bit back the sting in her own eyes, realizing her Grandma Russell's time probably wasn't that far away.

"I'm so sorry," she said. "I had no idea."

"Well," Mike said with a shaky smile, "Dad's had a good life. A good hard life, lived the way he wanted to live. I can't fault him for that."

"What's he got?"

"It's more like what hasn't he got? His liver's going, he's got heart trouble. But, you know, the great thing is he's still out there kicking. Tough old coot..." Mike's voice faltered. "My dad. Still got that great sense of humor. In fact, just to look at him, you'd never..."

"Oh, Mike." Carrie stood from the table and walked to where he sat, putting her arms around him. Her heart went out to this man. This man who always tried to put on a good face, who had worked so hard to make her laugh... Who had sent her grandmother flowers. Who could kiss like nobody she'd ever known.

243

"Now, don't go feeling sorry for me," Mike cautioned, looking up and returning her hug.

"What I feel for you," Carrie said, for the first time admitting it to herself, "goes way beyond sorry…"

Oh great, Mike thought, she pities me. That's even worse.

"And the love I see in your eyes for your father only reconfirms it. I've seen somebody very different here today. And yesterday, at the shower also. It's not just that you're a warm, caring person. Not just that you can make me laugh…" Not just that he looked like sin, she told herself.

Mike drank her in with his eyes, beholding a million new possibilities. Then stood to cradle her in his arms.

She was going out on a limb here, and she knew it. But the words that were welling within her were so fierce, so true, she was losing all power to hold them back.

"Mike, I think that I'm falling in love."

Mike nestled her closer and brought his forehead to hers, kissing her sweetly on the lips. "Only think?" he asked with a twinkle in his eye.

"Oh Mike." She brought soft hands to his cheeks and looked at him deeply. "More than think. I know it's brazen of me to say so. That it will probably take a while for you to feel the same way. I don't understand what has happened to me. How all of this has happened so fast. I never really thought…"

Mike hushed her by tracing the tender line of her lips with one finger. "You don't know how long I've waited to hear you say that."

"But Mike!" she said, splaying her hands against his chest. "We've only known each other three days."

244

But three minutes was all it had taken for Mike to know. The moment he'd seen her holding court at the top of those stairs at the inn, Mike had ached inside at the feeling someone like her could never be his. And now, every ounce of his being ached at the possibility that she could.

Mike couldn't believe that any woman as warm, as wonderful, as completely genuine as Carrie, could be standing here professing her love. But she was. And not just with her words—with her eyes. Eyes that searched his soul and begged answers to so many questions.

"Carrie," he said, kissing her at first lightly and then feverishly before pulling back. "I want to make love to you. With you. For as long as you can possibly stand."

Carrie grinned as the smallest—daintiest—tingle took hold of her tailbone, then spread like rapid fire. "That's the best offer I've had all day," she said with a kiss.

****

Chapter Eleven

Mike took Carrie's hand and led her back into the sparsely lit bedroom. At the height of the afternoon, it was unmistakably the brightest room Carrie had ever had occasion to make love in. She'd always required it dark and comfortable. For her, that was, and her multitude of figure flaws. But here, in the light of day, with nothing but Mike's king-size bed before them, there was nowhere to hide.

Carrie thought of asking Mike to close the blinds but then saw the single shade was already drawn.

"Come here," Mike said, pulling her down onto the bed beside him. "Let me look at you."

She was as beautiful as ever, a patterned sarong skirt wrapping around her curvaceous hips. Her knit sweater top highlighted every curve.

"I think," Mike said, reaching up to touch her face as they lay sideways on the bed, "that I've died and gone to heaven."

"You're not dead yet," she assured him with a kiss.

"Then why do I feel like I'm floating?" he asked, running a stroking hand up and down her bare arm.

Carrie's skin ignited at his touch as his caress wandered lower, strumming over her hip, wending around to her bottom, where he gave her tush a playful squeeze.

Carrie colored in spite of herself.

"You're not inexperienced, are you?" Mike asked, bringing his nose to hers and nesting a hand in her hair.

"Heavens no," she said, coloring again. And feeling all the while like a liar. She'd never experienced anything quite like him. Her heart was beating so furiously she was certain it would break free from her chest cavity at any moment and make a mess of the bed.

But Mike assured her with his heated kiss they'd find others ways to dirty the linens entirely.

"I knew from the moment I saw you," Mike said, rolling her onto her back and straddling her legs with his own, "that something would develop between us."

"You knew this?" Carrie asked doubtfully, tugging lightly at his derriere and situating him comfortably on top of her. Boy, he felt like heaven. All six foot two of manly heaven. And, positioned just right.

"Well, I hoped it actually. You looked so pretty standing there. So defenseless—"

"Defenseless?" she challenged, lifting her head from the pillow.

Mike chuckled and kissed her sweetly. "No, my love…"

Carrie's heart fluttered at the sound of that.

"You are absolutely right. You are many, many things, but defenseless is not among them."

"Mike," Carrie said, wrapping her arms around his shoulders, "it's getting hot in here."

"Baby," he replied, bringing his mouth to hers. "You don't know the half of it."

With that, he clambered off her, taking her elastic-waist skirt along with him in one swift, tugging motion.

Carrie brought her hands self-consciously to her outer thighs, but Mike reached out and held her wrists captive.

"You, Carrie St. John, are the most exquisite woman I've ever seen. Please, don't hide from me."

With that, he released his grasp and gripped the hem of her knitted top, yanking it deftly up and over her head in one smooth move. Carrie willed herself not to dwell on his apparent ease at clothing removal but to focus instead on the calming lull of his eyes. Eyes that seemed to be looking down and into her. Steadying, reassuring that nothing—and no one—else on this earth mattered.

"Carrie," Mike said, bringing his lips to her cleavage, just above her bra, his hands cupping both breasts. "You're beautiful."

Carrie sighed, leaning back against the mattress, sure she must be dreaming. Savoring the sensation of his touch as she reached out and explored the leanness of his hips, the tautness of his derriere.

Carrie felt for his belt buckle and unhitched his pants as he kissed her with the desperation of a dry man in the desert seeking water.

"Carrie," he said, cradling her head in the muted light of the room. "I've waited a lifetime for you."

Though all reason argued against it, her heart dared to believe as she reached for his shorts and slid them down toward his knees.

Mike briefly righted himself and did away with his clothing. All of it.

Carrie marveled at his size, at his rigidity, longing to make him all hers.

"Here," she said, pushing down her panties and urging him to help her.

He stripped away those and the last barrier of her bra with skilled ease.

"Mike, don't you think—"

But he was already miles ahead of her and unrolling a condom onto his ready form.

And Carrie was ready too. Oh so ready, like she'd never been in her lifetime.

Mike reached up and gently gripped her breasts in his hands, then rocked slowly onto her, carefully aligning their bodies until their lips and every other inch of them met exactly where they were meant to.

"Ready?" he asked, sliding his hands up her rib cage, alongside her shoulders, up her neckline and into her hair.

"As ready as I'll ever be."

"Then I," Mike assured her, filling her slowly, single-mindedly, with his manly need. "Am going to show you just what loving is…"

He gave her a tender smile. "Until you cry uncle," he said, bringing the furnace of his mouth down on her own.

"Uncle!" Carrie cried, several hours later.

Mike raised a moist chin from between her legs.

"Uncle, uncle, uncle!" she yelped, slapping him on the shoulder. "My God, are you trying to kill me?"

Mike grinned and fell down on the mattress beside her. "Just trying to take you to heaven, angel."

"Been there and back. There and back. And then some," she assured him breathlessly, tugging at his arms.

"Good, then that means you liked it?" Mike asked, sweetly stroking her knees. The sensation of his touch—lingering, strong, tender—sent shivers racing to her core.

"Liked it?" Carrie exclaimed, raising herself up on her elbows. "Gracious. Now that I've, uh, tasted it, I fear I'll never be able to live without it!"

Mike fell down on the mattress beside her and pulled her tightly into his arms. "Precisely what I wanted to hear."

"I've really got to go," Carrie said, trying halfheartedly to escape once again.

Mike linked his arms around her naked torso and nibbled the small of her back. "Uh-huh."

"Don't you have a job?" Carrie asked in exhaustion. Already it was Tuesday. Heaven only knew where the past eighteen hours had gone.

All Carrie knew was that she was hungry—and late for work.

"Probably not anymore," Mike answered. "But real estate was never really my calling anyhow."

"No," Carrie said, turning on the bed and kissing the man behind her fully on the lips. "Your talents run much deeper than that."

Mike hooted and sprang from the bed. "I've got it! How about we go to breakfast!"

"Breakfast?" Carrie asked, sitting up and clutching the comforter to her chest. "But I have to get to work! I never even reported in yesterday."

"Great," Mike said, coming around the bed and kissing her on the top of her head. "Then you've set a precedent."

Carrie's eyes traveled the nude expanse of his body, thinking over all the precedents the two of them had set within the last several hours. There was no denying it. Mike Davis had positively swept her away. "Well, I suppose I could phone my secretary…"

Mike shot her a triumphant grin. "Get showered," he said, striding to the bathroom and returning with a towel, which he lobbed in her direction. "I'll make the coffee."

"Like that?" Carrie asked, observing his stunning form.

"What's a matter?" he teased, "too sexy for you?"

"Goodness, no," she answered. "Just sexy enough. Just don't count on getting to breakfast anytime soon," she said with a growl as she leapt from the bed and tackled him to the carpet.

Mike bit into his bagel with gusto. Apparently, he'd been just as starved as she was. "You know, Carrie," he said between mouthfuls, "I don't think this reunion thing is going to be very hard to pull off."

Carrie laughed affectionately and ran a tender hand down his face. "No," she answered, "I think we've got that touchy-feely part down pretty well."

In between their hours of lovemaking, they'd also done some soul-spilling. Among other things, they'd both revealed how much each one had been itching to get physically close to the other. Carrie had confessed that the whole "touchy-feely" pose regarding Wilson had been a total sham, and Mike had admitted how he'd eagerly planned to take advantage of that idea.

Well, she supposed they both were satisfied now. Carrie blushed at the thought as the waiter refilled her coffee.

They were in a small diner a few miles from the hometown university. The place, it turned out, where both Carrie and Mike had secured their undergraduate degrees and Carrie had later gone on to graduate school in pursuit of her MBA.

Mike still didn't know about the money. And Carrie still wasn't sure if she was willing to tell him. There she was, a hopeless, helpless mess. Totally in love with a man she'd known for less than a week but who'd seemed in tune with her soul for a lifetime. Could she really risk messing it all up now? They hadn't even made it past the hurdle of the reunion and her hidden mission of impressing his friends.

Not to mention the very pointed fact that, in spite of all of his words of love, despite the way he looked at her and made her feel, Mike still hadn't said *"I love you."*

"Penny for your thoughts," Mike said, clinking his coffee cup to hers. "Feeling tired this morning?"

Carrie lifted her coffee cup to her lips and smiled naughtily over its rim. "Not as tired as I could be."

Mike laughed in surprise. "Why, Carrie St. John," he returned with a sly wink. "You are insatiable."

Only with you, she replied in her heart. Only with you.

"Okay, here's the plan," Mike informed her as he stood kissing her good-bye at her car. "First of all, you and I phone in to be sure we still have our jobs."

Carrie laughed and mussed his hair. Tuesday had somehow melted into Wednesday, and then Thursday had come along straight out of nowhere. In between it all, they'd gone out to restaurants, called in to their respective offices occasionally with "no show" excuses, and done plenty of dirtying of Mike's sheets.

"You probably ought to do the laundry while I'm gone," she teased with a poke at his chest that had now become a silent joke between them. At one point during their hours of lovemaking, Mike had maintained she'd merely given him her rigid finger as a phallic encouragement. Carrie swore to herself with a grin, she'd never give anyone but Mike Davis that sort of finger again.

"Hey, baby," he said, leaning in close and nibbling her neck. "You trying to tell me something with that finger…?"

"Mike!" she said, swatting him on the backside. "You don't watch yourself, the two of us will not only be out of jobs, we'll entirely miss your reunion."

"And what a tragedy that would be," he said, enfolding her in his arms.

"Okay," she said, reaching behind her and popping open the driver's door. "I'm going this time. Really, really going."

Mike raised one sexy eyebrow. "Well, personally, I like it better—"

"Don't you even say it, you beast!" she said, climbing into her car. "Heavens, I've become involved with an animal."

"Aw, come on now, Carrie," he said, leaning in over her door, "you know you love it."

The truth was she did. But for now, she decided, the satisfaction of that knowledge would be hers and hers alone.

****

Chapter Twelve

Carrie unfolded the tissue and heartily blew her nose. "Oh, Grandma Russell," she sobbed. "It's no use. There isn't going to be any wedding!" She'd decided it was time. Time to tell the truth about the whole sordid affair. Now that she'd fallen in love with Mike, she couldn't have her grandmother go on thinking he was Wilson. And—with Wilson out of the picture—there was that little matter of a wedding to cancel. Something that she'd been putting off and putting off, and finding excuses not to do.

"Now, now, honey," her grandmother said, reassuringly patting her hand. "Don't go blowing things all out of proportion like you sometimes do. I swear, you must get that from your Aunt Nellie."

Grandma Russell leaned forward and lifted her china teacup off the low tabletop in front of them. "Drink your chamomile, dear. It will make you feel better."

Carrie wrung her tissue in exasperation. Her grandmother apparently hadn't heard a word she'd said. She'd come here first to confess and secondly to beg moral support. Possibly even to seek approval—and forgiveness—for her new choice. But all she'd received thus far had been tea and crumpets with some prattle on pre-wedding-day jitters.

"You don't understand," Carrie sniffed. "Tonight's the big night."

"The reunion. Very sweet." Grandma Russell smiled as if in fond remembrance. "Dear Wilson told us all about it. He was so very proud at the prospect of having you on his arm. Never knew that New York man of yours had such local roots." She shrugged with a thoughtful smile. "Well, I suppose that does explain the accent."

Carrie set down her teacup and rummaged through her purse for her aspirin.

"If you ask me," her grandmother offered, unsolicited, "you keep popping those things, you're gonna get a hole in your stomach."

Carrie ignored that bit of advice and downed two tablets with her, by now, room-temperature tea. "It's not just the reunion, Grandmother. It's looking serious. He's taking me to meet his father!"

"Wonderful!" Grandma Russell said, clapping her hands together. She paused a moment, looking puzzled. "Are you saying you've not yet met him? And what do you mean by serious. Of course it's serious. You're getting married, aren't you?"

"No," Carrie said, dropping her eyes to the sofa and wishing with all her might she could sink right between its cushions. "No, Grandmother, I'm so sorry. There isn't going to be any wedding."

Grandma Russell set her cup down so firmly on its saucer the two pieces rattled. "Nonsense, Carrie girl! That's just pre—"

"Grandma," Carrie said, looking up through streaming eyes. "No. I'm sorry. Really, really sorry I waited until now to tell you. But I…"

Her lower lip began a violent tremble that prevented her from finishing.

Grandma Russell turned sideways and swept her into her arms. "There, there, child. Everything's going to be all right. I promise it will. Nothing at all that Wilson could have done could merit all this. There is always a way—"

"He left me, Grandmother," Carrie said, finally finding her voice. "Just like that. No warning at all. And," she said, her voice taking on a renewed tremble. "For another woman."

Grandma Russell stiffened in shock. "That letch! I never in a million years would have believed that charming man capable of—"

"Not that charming man," Carrie corrected with a shake of her head. "Wilson."

Grandma Russell's ebony eyes went wide as saucers. "Wilson? What are you saying, child? That the man you brought home—"

"An imposter," Carrie admitted, hanging her head.

Grandma Russell straightened her spine. "Well, he looked real enough to me."

"No," Carrie said, forcing herself to press ahead. "It was all a ruse. We met at the Sawyers House."

"That local inn you financed?"

Carrie nodded and kept going, lest she lose her nerve. "It was really kind of funny, in fact. When I met Mike—his name is Mike, by the way."

"Good, solid, masculine name," Grandma Russell interjected.

Carrie gave her grandmother a twisted smile. No matter what the rest of Carrie's story, Grandma Russell had quite obviously made up her mind.

"Mike Davis. Guess you like the Davis part too?"

Grandma Russell smiled warmly. "It does have a certain ring to it. Listen, sweetheart, you can fill me in on the particulars you'd like to. But it really isn't necessary. Like the television commercials say, life happens.

"So Wilson was a creep and left you. Good riddance to that one, I say! And this Mike—Mike Davis, the man who not only can't keep his eyes off you in a crowded room but also wowed your family, just happened to be at the right place at the right time. I think it's beautiful. It's fate. And he's a hunk. You're three for three on this one. Looks, tenderness, compassion... What on earth are you staring at, child? Did I forget to wax my mustache?"

"Do you really think so?" Carrie asked, studying her grandmother's face for wisdom. "Believe Mike and I met for a reason? That in spite of our odd beginnings, it was somehow meant to be?"

"Certainly, I think so! Didn't I ever tell you how your grandpa and I met?"

Carrie shook her head. She'd thought she'd heard all of Grandma Russell's stories by now, but this, apparently, was a new one.

"It was back in the days of panty raids..." her Grandma began sheepishly.

Carrie chortled. "They still do those, Grandmother."

"Do they now? Well, how prehistoric! At any rate, as I was saying, it was back... Well, whatever! I'll just cut to the chase and tell you. The October of my Freshman year at the Women's College, there was a panty raid on my dorm one night. And your old grandpa just happened to be below my window in the marauding crowd."

"You threw your panties at Grandpa?" Carrie gasped. From the little she remembered of her grandfather, he'd always seemed such a straight arrow.

"Not my panties, heavens no. Needed those. Tossed something much more enticing…"

Carrie waited patiently as her grandmother drew out the moment for suspense.

"Myself!"

"Yourself? You threw yourself out the window?"

"Well, not intentionally or anything like that. But I was young, you see. A brand-new student. And it was all so exciting and hedonistic. The very idea of panty raids."

Carrie giggled, trying to envision her white-haired grandparents in the picture Grandma Russell was painting.

"Well, anyhow," her grandmother continued. "I was leaning out the window just a bit, trying to get a better look at the boys down below. One was quite handsome. Tall, redheaded, sure of himself. Looked to me like a Scot."

"Grandpa," Carrie guessed.

Grandma Russell smiled, then chuckled at the faraway memory. "Indeed, it was your grandfather. And a very striking young man, at that. Well, I happened to catch his eye, you see. I could tell because there he was at the bottom of the window looking straight up at me. Not chanting or carrying on like the other boys. Just very stoically standing there, looking up with the most curious smile. And then it happened. Somebody moved behind me, and I lost my balance and fell. Tumbled right out the window and over the sill—straight into your grandfather's arms!"

"He caught you?" Carrie gasped.

"More or less." Grandma Russell grinned and turned a curious shade of plum Carrie didn't think she'd ever seen on her grandmother. "But the important thing is, even the parts he didn't catch survived the fall. It was only half a story, with the back of our building constructed into a hill.

But still, from that time on, your old grandfather and I had a lot of fun joking about that fateful day I 'fell' for him."

Carrie studied her grandmother, trying to discern whether what she'd just shared was honest-to-goodness family lore or a simple cock-and-bull story. Either way, Carrie knew and appreciated exactly what her grandmother was trying to do.

"So, then," Carrie said, balling up her tissue and tucking it into her purse. "There's something to this fate business after all."

"Not a doubt in the world."

Carrie's face fell. "But we'll still have to cancel the wedding, Grandmother. I've been avoiding making all the calls. Every time I've picked up that telephone, something inside just wouldn't let me do it."

"Well." Her grandmother smiled. "Maybe that something inside knows there is going to be a wedding after all."

Mike stared into his closet and frowned. Less than two hours to showtime and not a thing to wear.

He scratched his head, thumbing through the several designer suits Alexia had given him. It was no wonder he didn't like his wardrobe. It was all a patent reminder of not-so-pleasant times gone by. Well, all right, maybe not all of it.

Mike pulled out a charcoal gray suit, one of the few he had purchased on his own. The others, he realized, would have to go. Not to mention that glaring ring on his dresser.

Why Mike had waited so long to return Alexia's ring, he really couldn't say. For sure, he needed the money. And the Caymans…

Mike laid out his suit on the bed, recalling the long, lazy, and often playful afternoons most recently spent with Carrie. Was chasing his dive-shop dream really all it was cracked up to be? If that was still what he so desperately wanted, why hadn't he already cashed in that ring—or called the jewelers, at least, to make arrangements.

Mike walked to the mirror hanging above his dresser, realizing the startling truth. There were simply far too many things holding him to Virginia. His dad, of course, was currently on his own. But eventually, he'd need more personal looking after. Mike had already done some investigating. Private-care arrangements were expensive. No way could Mike realistically budget for those and still be able to sink money into starting a new business.

And then there was Carrie to think of. Carrie St. John, the woman who'd admitted with a full heart that she loved him and whom his own raging insides told him he loved back. And yet Mike hadn't been able to find the words to tell her. Perhaps because he was still coming to terms with the concept himself. Or maybe, more critically, because he believed on a superstitious level that, by admitting his feelings, he would somehow jinx what was happening between them.

In spite of his track record, Mike had never told any woman he loved her. Not even, surprisingly, Alexia. Adore, yes. Worship, on occasion. But love? Those three little words had never slipped from his mouth. And the reason for this was crystal clear, Mike saw, looking in the mirror.

The day he finally uttered those words would be the day he was prepared to ask a woman to be his wife—and really mean it. None of this marriage of convenience BS or racing to beat any sort of artificial time clock. Just a true, honest desire to share the here and now, and forever after, with the woman of his dreams.

Mike's eyes dropped to Alexia's ring, glistening on the dresser top. Maybe returning it wasn't what he needed to do after all. Perhaps that was what the hesitancy in his gut about taking back the ring had been trying to tell him all along.

Mike walked to his nightstand and picked up the telephone to call the jewelers—with one very important question.

Carrie reached behind her and zipped the back of her red-sequined dress. She straightened and studied her reflection in the mirror, hoping she wasn't going overboard. The plunging neckline, though not untasteful, still might be a little much.

Carrie held a couple of dangling earrings up to her lobes and considered the picture. A little too uptown? Licentious, even? The lady in red…

Carrie walked to her closet on her tiptoes, carefully lifting the hem of her dress off the polished oak floor. With heels on, the length was perfect. And the height difference between her and Mike certainly allowed for any size heel Carrie desired.

With Wilson standing five foot ten, only two inches above her own five eight, she'd always had to be more careful.

Carrie stopped considering the two pairs of shoes in her hands and realized for the first time she hadn't thought of Wilson in days. Of course, she'd mentioned him in her conversation with her grandmother. But, in truth, even in speaking his name then, she'd thought more of his imitator

Mike than Wilson himself. In fact, it appeared Wilson had been replaced entirely by Mike Davis.

Oh dear. Carrie made her shoe choice, then gripped her hem and tiptoed back over to the bed, wondering if this was good. She'd warned herself sternly about the rebound thing. But surely this wasn't what this was. It was fate, a preordained opportunity—just like Grandma Russell had said. And if she ever thought of Wilson Haywood again, she conceded, it would have to be in gratitude. For had he not dumped her on precisely that day at precisely that time, she wouldn't have wandered down to that pool.

Carrie sighed, recalling her startling introduction to her "swim god." Not nearly as dramatic as what had happened to her grandmother but certainly unforgettable in its own special way. Carrie would never forget how Mike had taken her breath away when he rose from the water, dripping wet, insinuating moisture racing down every trail of his muscular body.

Carrie swallowed and sat to slip on her shoes. Well, maybe the dress was a little showy. But she'd clearly seen enough of Mike that he deserved reciprocation.

Carrie blushed at the notion that he found her beautiful. That he found her body enticing, alluring…feminine. Not only had he failed to mention her "figure flaws," he, in his manly appreciation, appeared totally unaware they existed.

Carrie slid in the earrings, then stood to examine the total effect. The dress was exquisite, the shoes and jewelry the perfect complement. But what shone out among it all was the light in her eyes. The fresh color in her cheeks. The first dewdrops of love everlasting.

If Mike could do this to her now, Carrie realized, she'd be a real stunner by the time she reached Grandma Russell's age.

****

Chapter Thirteen

Mike took the winding country road that snaked through the open tract of undeveloped land. As per Carrie's instructions, he started counting mailboxes when he got to the top of the hill. When he hit number four, he made a hard right and steered down the gravel drive that led through a covering of trees. And then his passage through the cluster of woods spilled out into open pasture. A huge purple-blue sky draped with lazy clouds danced high above the nearby mountains. The scenery took his breath away.

Mike spotted the small white-stucco house nestled back against the edge of the property. And, as he drew closer, he spied its immaculate gardens forming a meticulous border around the cottage's outside. Boxwoods and azaleas, tastefully interspersed by wild flowers, lavender, and zinnias. And nearer the railing of the small wraparound porch, towering sunflowers strained skyward to catch their last glimpse of the fading day.

Up on the porch there was a swing, patently built for two. Mike sighed, taking in the idyllic picture, thinking the only thing that would make it complete would be a passel of kids playing in the grassy yard that butted up against the neighboring orchard.

Mike suddenly looked down at his watch, realizing he'd been sitting there daydreaming. Daydreaming about a home and a houseful of kids. His kids, he realized with vibrant shock. His and Carrie's.

Mike scrambled from the car, warning himself to take things slow. Follow through with his premeditated plan.

For all of his previous slipups, this was one thing he was going to get right.

Mike stepped up onto the porch, straightened his tie, then rang the doorbell. When nothing sounded inside, he tried waiting a few moments, then knocking instead.

A few seconds later, Carrie pulled back the door. "Oh, I'm sorry, did you try knocking? I've been meaning—"

But Mike stopped her with a deep, rumbling, "Wow! Carrie, you look like a million bucks."

Another point she'd made plans to discuss with him, Carrie reminded herself, making space for him to scoot by her into the room. "Thanks, you look terrific too." And, boy, did he ever. Very stylish in his charcoal gray with muted pinstripes.

Carrie shut the door behind them and looked down at her dress. "You sure this isn't too much for tonight? I mean, I didn't really know how formal the dinner-dance was going to be."

"You look perfect," he assured her, a panther-like look in his eyes. "Absolutely perfect. In fact," he said, pulling her into his arms, "if I hadn't already promised you dinner…"

"Mike!" she protested, pushing back on his shoulders, "you'll muss my hair!"

"That won't be all," he said, kissing her sweetly but then pulling back when she exploded in laughter.

"Have my skills deteriorated that badly?" he asked, offended.

"Oh no," she said, laughing as she reached for a tissue from the entrance table and dabbed his lips. "It's just that you're wearing my Magenta Rose." She chuckled again.

"And, I'm not so sure that's the impression you wanted to give at this reunion."

"Ah," Mike said, smiling and kissing the tissue in understanding. "Better now?"

"Don't know." Carrie brought a hand to her chin. "Maybe we ought to try it again, just to be sure?"

Mike gave her a teasing wink. "Why, Carrie St. John, if you keep threatening me with kisses…"

"No, no," she said, lifting her purse off the table. "You promised your dad we'd be there at six and it's already half past. If we're going to have any opportunity for a visit before the dance, we'd best get going."

"Only if you promise we can play that little lipstick game later on."

"All you want," she said, beaming up at him as he held back the door.

Mike pulled open the screen door of the trailer, letting Carrie inside.

Jack Davis stood from his chair at the kitchen table with a cat-calling whistle.

"Dad!" Mike admonished, standing beside Carrie just inside the door.

Carrie's cheeks lit with color, but she remained composed as she crossed the small room and extended a warm hand in the older man's direction. "Mr. Davis—"

"Nope," he broke in, taking her hand and surprising her by pulling her into a bear hug. "You, young lady, can call me Jack."

Carrie returned his firm squeeze.

"Jack," she said, patting his back. "Mighty glad to meet you."

Jack pulled back and gave her a broad, welcoming grin. "She's even prettier than you let on, boy," he directed at his son. "Might just think about keeping this one for myself."

Mike walked over and whisked Carrie out of his father's arms. "Sorry about that, old man. But I got to her first, and you know what they say—"

"Finders, keepers," Mike and Carrie parroted together.

Jack's eyes sparkled. "Quite a handsome pair the two of you make. So, when's the big day?"

Mike swallowed hard.

"June 23rd," Carrie raced in. "The church has been reserved for months."

Jack shot Mike a quizzical look. "That so? I was under the impression the two of you had only recently met."

"Yeah, but I'd been hoping," Carrie said, giving Mike a megawatt smile.

June 23rd? What on earth...? Oh, okay, Mike got it. Maybe this was all a little part of the rehearsal for Carrie's big performance at the reunion. Well, fine, he could play along with that. For now. Assuming Carrie accepted his authentic proposal—and that was still a big "if," his dad certainly wouldn't mind a change in dates later on. Jack wasn't, and never had been, a stickler for details.

"It's a really long story," Mike said, reaching down and taking Carrie's hand. "The important thing is, we've already set some of those...uh, wheels in motion."

Mike didn't know the half of it, Carrie thought, giving his hand a squeeze. Not only did they have a church and a reception hall reserved but also a caterer and a three-hundred-dollar wedding cake. Mint chocolate, through a little creative rearranging, on Carrie's part, she thought, feeling rather proud of herself. The only thing standing in their way was the minor detail of the formal marriage proposal. And that little nuance of Mike's admitting he loved her, which, by now, she was quite certain he did. He'd brought her home to meet his father, hadn't he? Even Alexia, as it turned out, hadn't gotten that far.

"Yes," Carrie said, taking the chair at the table Jack had offered. Mike pulled out another and sat beside her. "But we can get to all those details later. We still have plenty of time."

Jack shook his head with an eye on his wall calendar. "Looks more like two weeks, by my calculation. Now I don't know much about women stuff, planning weddings and all that, but it really seems to me the two of you might be cutting things a bit tight here."

Carrie and Mike looked at each other.

"Not that I'd want to do anything to discourage ya!" Jack said, whacking Mike across the shoulder in a sign of approval. "You just tell me what I'll need to do from my end."

"Not a thing, Dad. Not a thing."

"You could walk me down the aisle," Carrie raced in impetuously. She bit her lip in hesitation as Mike dropped his jaw and stared. "I mean," she continued tentatively, "I never knew my father, and Grandpa's been gone for years…"

"I'd be honored," Jack said, a barely perceptible moisture gathering in the corner of one eye.

Holy cow! Was she nuts! How could she even do this to him? Why would she even do this do him? Nothing like this was in his presupposed plan. Though he'd hoped to ask that big, big question. He was still smack dab in the middle of finessing the hows and whens. Now, if he didn't act soon, he'd be lunch meat in his father's eyes. Just look at him! Less than ten minutes flat, and his dad was already eating right out of Carrie's hand!

"Uh, Carrie, sweetheart," Mike said, laying a hand on her forearm resting on the table. "Don't you think that invitation is a little—premature?"

"Premature? Heavens no!" she said, wriggling her arm out from under his grasp and glowing at Jack. "Like your dad said, our wedding is only two weeks away."

Our wedding. It was the first time Mike had actually heard her say it. And it sent simultaneous shivers of delight and terror straight through him. This was really going to happen. He and Carrie. All pretending aside. Holy cow.

Mike withdrew a hanky from his breast pocket and dabbed his dampened brow.

"I agree," Jack said. "Two weeks is no time at all. Besides," he said, looking very pointedly at Mike, "she asked me, not you, young man. So, stay out of it!"

Jack returned his affectionate gaze to Carrie. Though his hair had gone completely gray, Carrie could definitely see where Mike had gotten the gorgeous green eyes from. "So, young lady, tell me a bit about yourself. You from these parts?"

"Yes, sir, grew up in Mill Creek, right around the bend. And Mike and I, as it turns out, both went to the university."

"Not together, I would guess? You seem a good bit younger than Mike."

Carrie grinned. "Only a few years, sir. But, you're right, we're far enough apart that we weren't in school at the same time."

269

"Ships passing in the night," Jack commented with a rather melancholy smile.

"More like swimmers," Mike mumbled under his breath.

"What's that?" Jack asked when Carrie burst out laughing.

"He's just being silly," Carrie said, kicking Mike under the table.

"Won't be the first time," Jack said. "Well, at least it's good to see his taste in women has improved. Are you working in the area?" he asked Carrie.

"Yes, I'm an investor."

Jack whistled. "Big money in that, hear tell."

"Dad…" Mike cautioned in a low vibrato.

Not here, not now, Carrie told herself. "Uh, yes, sir. Yes, sir, there is."

Carrie glanced down at her styled gold watch, the one she reserved just for evening wear. "Oh my gosh, will you look at that! Seven fifteen. How far a drive did you say it was?" she asked, turning to Mike.

"Hey, yeah, we'd better get going," he said, standing from his chair. "Dad," he said, giving his father's shoulder a pat. "You take care, now. And no more flirting with those nurses. If I get one more call from Dr. Shafer's office about your hitting on the staff…"

Carrie laughed all the way to the car.

"Does your dad really hit on the nurses?" Carrie asked once she'd adjusted her seat belt.

"Only the pretty ones."

Carrie smiled and shook her head as Mike started the ignition. "Now I definitely see where you get it from." But what Carrie secretly found herself wondering was if any of her and Mike's children would be half as bad.

****

Chapter Fourteen

The parade of oaks leading up to Ashton Hall was magnificent. Though Carrie had heard of the all-boys boarding school, she'd never once been there. Likely because the high school circles she'd run with didn't exactly involve a "moneyed" crowd.

Carrie had plans to discuss her financial "predicament," meaning the fact that she was exceedingly wealthy, with Mike tonight. The time for pretense was over. He'd proven well enough, in a million different ways, that the woman he cared for had nothing to do with her bank account. Of course, he'd seen her car and knew she worked in finance. What he didn't know was that her title in New York was Venture Capitalist and that her account balance registered in the seven digits.

Carrie prayed inwardly that it wouldn't make too much difference. Mike certainly didn't strike her as the sort of man who would feel emasculated by a wife who made more money. The impression he'd given her was that Alexia had been well-off, and that, in and of itself, apparently hadn't fazed him in the least. "Thank you for doing this," Mike said, shutting off the engine and pulling his keys from the ignition. "You don't know what it means to me to have you on my arm tonight."

Oh yes, she did. Because whether or not he suspected it, it meant just as much to her. And not simply because she planned to pose as his fiancée for the night. But, more importantly, because she hoped to soon make that role a legitimate position.

Mike walked around the car and opened her door. "You ready to be my bride-to-be?" he asked with a grin that sent her stomach all aflutter.

More than he knew. But she just said, "Yes."

Ashton Hall was an impressive two-hundred-year-old red-brick building, elegant, high white columns flanking the tall main entrance. The striking Georgian architecture reminded Carrie of parts of the college campus where she and Mike had both studied.

"Wow," Carrie said as Mike ushered her in the door.

The domed central ceiling, in and of itself, must have reached over forty feet. Elegant crystal chandeliers dripped light like sparkling teardrops onto the well-placed circular tables that dotted the perimeter of the room.

White linen tablecloths lapped hand-sewn oriental carpets. And above the clatter of clinking glasses and conversation, a band played jazzy eighties tunes from a stage set up far against a back wall.

The mood was all genteel opulence. They'd been standing there scarcely five seconds when a server strode briskly over, offering up a tray of champagne.

"Carrie?" Mike asked, lifting a single flute off the tray and extending it in her direction.

From the trailer park to this. All at once, the disparity hit her. "Thank you," Carrie said, accepting the champagne.

Mike picked up a glass of his own, and the white-gloved server made himself scarce.

Carrie took another look around the room. "I said it before, but it bears repeating. Wow."

"I know it must seem odd," Mike said. "I mean, after seeing the place I grew up."

Carrie heated at the notion that he'd read her thoughts. How embarrassing. He probably assumed her to be judging him. "No, actually—"

"It's all right. Really. Though I may have been somewhat ashamed of my humble roots as a teenager…"

"You should never have felt ashamed of your father, Mike. He's a wonderful man."

"Easy for me to accept now," he told her as they made their way into the busy room. "Not so easy for a boy in high school. I landed at Ashton Academy like a total fish out of water."

"Scholarship?" Carrie guessed.

"Swimming."

She might have known. "Well, I think it's fantastic you had the opportunity. When I was a teenager, I didn't even know places like this existed."

An attractive couple wandered over. A pretty blonde and a stocky brunet about Mike's age. The husky fellow set his glass on a nearby table and took up Mike's free hand with great gusto. "Mike the Spike!" he said, cheerily pumping Mike's arm. "Great to see you, buddy!

Mike's eyes lit up. "Figaro? Oh, my… How are you?" he asked with unfeigned delight. "Uh, oh, forgive me. Carrie St. John, this is Fig."

"Fig's not his real name," the blonde interjected. "It's Paul. Paul Westinghouse III."

Mike chuckled and turned his eyes on the woman. "Why, hello. Are you the lucky missus?"

"Am at that." She smiled. "My name's Wendy. And you, officially, are…?"

"Mike Davis," Carrie supplied, easily following the protocol where the women spoke for the men. She could get used to that. "But I want to know where that 'spike' part came from," she said, playfully poking Mike in the chest.

Mike looked down at her rigid finger and chuckled at their private joke. "Now, don't go getting any dirty ideas," he whispered in her ear. He turned and winked at Paul. "Spike comes from the way I used to dive."

"Straight out like this," Paul said, striking a pose by extending his arms arrow-straight over his head. The group broke out laughing.

"And Fig?" Carrie asked with a grin. "I can't fathom that one."

"That's because he swam like a song," Wendy reported. "You know, *Figaro, Figaro, Figaro…*"

"Yeah, a swan's song," Mike chimed in.

More companionable laughter.

"So, you two were on the swim team together?" Carrie asked.

"Yes, ma'am," Paul answered, "though it looks like your husband's keeping much more fit than I am. Congratulations, by the way," he said, turning to Mike and once more pumping his hand. "Somebody made an honest man of you after all."

"Well, not quite," Mike began.

"Yeah," Carrie said. "He's still as dishonest as they come."

Paul and Wendy roared.

"Know what you mean," Wendy added. "Once incorrigible, always incorrigible. Wedding band or no."

Wait a minute! What was happening here? He was assumed to be married? Mike shifted and dug his left hand into his pocket.

"Well, buddy," Paul said, lifting his glass in Mike and Carrie's direction. "Guess you had us all fooled. Heartiest congratulations on your excellent taste."

When Paul and Wendy had made their polite good-byes and departed to mill with other guests, Mike turned to Carrie. "Holy cow, those guys thought we were married!"

"Imagine that," Carrie said with a curious poker face. "Well," she said after a brief silence, "stop staring. It's what you wanted, isn't it? To be known as the man who beat his perpetual bachelor status?"

"Well, yes, but—"

"Look," Carrie interrupted. "People are getting seated. We'd better find our places before they start serving."

Mike and Carrie were lucky enough to find their place cards at the same table with Paul and Wendy and a few more of Mike's old swim-team cronies. Mike looked around the room, seeing that many of the other groups that hung together in high school had also been placed together at their respective tables. Whoever had been in charge of the seating chart had done an excellent job.

The various courses flowed by with good conversation and wine, both of which seemed in endless supply. Everyone at their table was duly impressed with Carrie, both her financial acumen and her personal style. Mike could tell by the body postures of his former fellow athletes who seemed intent on angling close to Carrie to absorb her every informed word on the financial markets. Either that or to catch a whiff of her heather perfume, which made Mike more than just a little bit jealous. Though he didn't know why. She was doing exactly as he'd hoped she would, knocking the socks off every one of his buddies. If only they didn't look like they'd be happy to also have Carrie knock their boxers off…

"You've been quiet," Carrie whispered in his ear. "Getting tired?"

"Just tired of the conversation," Mike whispered back.

"Ah," she replied, her tone still hushed, "finance bores you."

"No," Mike said, his voice coming out louder than intended. "Men putting the moves on my 'wife' bore me."

The two couples seated across the table from them stopped conversing and stared.

Oh Jesus. Mike pushed back his chair and stood. "Excuse me, I'm going to get some air."

"Then I'm coming with you!" Carrie said, scrambling to her feet and hurrying after him.

Carrie followed Mike out a large glass door that led to a sweeping veranda, then settled beside him on a carved marble bench. She couldn't believe it. He was jealous! All rationale told her that was a bad sign. The books, the magazines all told you that jealousy meant possessiveness. But way deep inside, Carrie's heart was doing a jig, shouting *yes, yes, yes!*

He loved her; she knew he did. All she had to do was get him to say it.

"If any of those men were flirting," Carrie lied, "I certainly didn't know it."

"Flirting? Carrie, Billy Smith looked like he was ready to up and carry you away! That, with his wife Elizabeth sitting next to him!"

277

"Mike," Carrie said, scooting in toward him. "Only one man in this crowd could carry me away. And I think you know exactly who that is."

Oh, if only, Mike thought, looking up at the big, bold moon. But what if when he really asked, she said no? Mike had nothing to offer her. Nothing but what was in his heart. And Carrie already had it all. He knew from talking to her grandmother. Feeling it only right, he'd gone by this afternoon to discuss his intentions. Grandma Russell had assured him that the money business didn't really matter one way or another. And, at the time, feeling hopeful, he'd believed it.

Now he just didn't know. Mike had seen the way Carrie's jaw had dropped when she'd walked in here. Though she came from more humble roots like he had, this was the sort of world she was meant for. That ambition was what had taken her to New York. And to see the way she had meshed with his Wall Street buddies at the table, he guessed that was where she belonged. Certainly not stuck permanently in Central Virginia with the likes of him, much less down in the far-off Caymans. Mike heaved a sigh, his heart heavy with the moment.

"Penny for your thoughts?" she said, lightly touching his arm.

"Carrie," he began, "there are some things I need to tell you."

"No," she said, laying a hand on his thigh. "Me first."

Mike looked up into her beautiful dark eyes sparkling with starlight.

"I think," she began, then stopped. *Come on, Carrie, don't lose your nerve.* But what if he couldn't love her for who she really was, a woman with money? What if he said they were too different, that their lives were worlds apart?

"What do you think?"

"Mike, I have something personal to tell you. I mean, personal about my job. Of course, normally, it's nobody's business, so I don't discuss it at all. But with a man I... What I meant to say was... Criminy!"

"Criminy?" Mike asked, leaning in and raising her chin.

"Oh gosh, it's an expression I picked up from my grandmother."

"Speaking of your Grandma Russell..."

"No, Mike," she said, lightly brushing aside his hand. "Let me finish. It's very important to me I get this out— before I lose my nerve."

Mike set his palms on his thighs and waited.

"Mike, I'm—"

"Dirty rich," he said, turning his eyes on hers.

Carrie gasped. "Have you been talking to my grandmother?"

"Carrie, beautiful Carrie," he said, cupping his hands over her satiny shoulders. "Did you for one minute think that wealth would be a hindrance?"

Carrie nodded but saw nothing besides her own confusion mirrored in his eyes.

"Honey, the only one setting up roadblocks here with his miserable life is me. You, Carrie St. John, have everything any woman could ask for. You're intelligent, attractive, accomplished at your job—and rich. I, on the other hand—"

"Oh," she said, scooting back and out of his grip. "So you are holding my bank account against me."

"That's not what I said."

"Well, it's certainly what you implied by telling me I already had it all. For your 411, I don't. At least not what I most want in here." She stopped and thumped her chest. "And in case you haven't heard, money can't buy you love."

"Oh, I know that for certain," Mike assured her. "And for your information, though I had suspicions you had money, my falling in love with you had nothing to do with your bank account!"

"Your what?" she asked, her voice softening in disbelief.

Holy cow! He'd gone and done it. And for crying out loud, right smack in the middle of the closest thing they'd had to an argument yet.

Carrie reached up and pinned his face between her hands. "Repeat what you just said."

Do it better this time, Mike warned himself. Much better.

"I, uh…" Mike swallowed hard past the lump in his throat. "Carrie, it's true. I know I was a jackass at dinner…" Oh great, he was doing just wonderfully. Curse words and all. "I mean, I know I overreacted. But, in truth, it drove me crazy seeing those other guys vying for your attention. And it made me think about… Realize just what a danger it would be to have you on the open market." Nice, Mike. Real smooth, you unromantic doofus! Well, at least she wasn't laughing.

It was all Carrie could do to stifle a chuckle. He was trying so hard it almost hurt her to watch. For all his experience with women, it was overwhelmingly obvious

Mike Davis was, at this moment, mapping uncharted territory.

"Carrie St. John," he said, the words erupting from his throat like red-hot lava. "I love you."

Carrie wasn't sure whether he looked more amorous or petrified, but whatever it was, she understood that Mike had just put his heart on the line.

"And I love you back," she said, bringing the cushion of her mouth up to his.

"Now," she said after their long, languorous kiss, "let's go dance while the two of us still seem to be agreeing on something."

"I don't like to dance," Mike protested.

"Oh yes, you do," Carrie answered with a mysterious grin. "I'll prove it."

Carrie was right about the dancing part, Mike thought, reveling in the comfort of her curvaceous body snuggled up against his own. The song playing was a band arrangement of Led Zeppelin's "Stairway to Heaven." It had been the only song in high school, Mike recalled, shutting his eyes, that even the nerdiest guys could get a dance for. Though he wasn't prepared to tell Carrie just yet, in his day, the swim-team fellows weren't the most sought after of the jocks. Mike's early successes with women came later, in college. But now, thinking back to his Ashton days and gently swaying to the music with Carrie, he was glad for every forgotten dance. Every pigtailed, pug-nosed girl who'd ever rejected him. And yes, even snooty Alexia. For if it hadn't been for any of them, he would have had no way of knowing exactly what he held in his arms now.

The music slowed to a stall and polite applause, and Mike feared the band leader would pick up his tempo. But instead he sent a smile over Carrie's shoulder and gave Mike a knowing wink as he began a slow, jazzy rendition of "Lady in Red."

Carrie didn't know if the music was still playing, or if it was merely the pulse of her heart that was lending rhythm to her feet. All she knew was that she felt protected, sheltered, and loved. Wholly and unconditionally drawn straight into Mike's warmth. They couldn't have been more connected had they been in bed together. Or maybe they were, and she was dreaming.

Mike reached up and stroked her hair, causing her to melt into him another inch. He'd never peel her off now. Carrie couldn't even say where Mike ended and she began. The only thing she knew for certain was that she never wanted this feeling to stop.

"I'm sorry, folks," the band leader said, lightly tapping Mike's shoulder. "But we're closing up."

Carrie opened her eyes in astonishment to find the room had cleared. Only a few staff persons remained, busily bussing tables and stacking up chairs.

"Holy cow," Mike said, squinting into the brightness of the lights that were now turned way, way up.

"Holy cow is right," Carrie said, bolting back into foggy reality and sweeping a hand through her hair. "We've shut the place down!"

****

Chapter Fifteen

A few hours later, Carrie stroked a hand down Mike's naked chest and snuggled deeper into the crook of his arm. "You know," she said as moonlight threaded through the spreading oak outside and danced with the sheers at the open window, "I really loved being your wife tonight."

Mike tightened his arm around her and kissed the top of her head. "And I really loved the honeymoon," he said with a growl.

"Mike!" she said, swatting his biceps.

Her hand relaxed against his skin and began to massage. He was all solid muscle but with just enough give. Rock hard, with a covering of bristly masculinity. Carrie shivered as she felt a renewed stirring in her loins. It was true. She was insatiable with Mike. But then what woman in her right mind wouldn't be? No woman who would ever get the chance to find out again, Carrie told herself securely.

"You know," Mike said, trailing a finger down her back to the point where it met the sheet. "You were right about that dancing part. I sound like a sappy movie, but I could have danced all night."

"Hmm," Carrie said, laying a light kiss on his shoulder. "But I'm awfully glad we came back to tango here."

Mike chuckled and patted her backside. "I could get used to this."

Carrie's heart stilled.

"Carrie?" Mike asked, as the wind rattled the window panes. "How would you feel about making things more permanent?"

Carrie's insides did cartwheels, but somehow she'd gone mute.

"I mean, I'm not asking—yet."

"What?" she asked, finding her voice.

"You'll have to trust me on this. I really want things to be perfect. You deserve perfect."

Carrie didn't understand. Nor could she imagine anything more perfect than this. "This—"

Mike rolled sideways and shushed her with a kiss. "You'll have to trust me, okay? Just swear you won't go running off with any of my old swim-team buddies within the next couple of days."

"Not a chance," Carrie said, her heart thundering as he threaded his fingers in her hair and brought his mouth to hers.

"So?" Grandma Russell asked. "Tell all, sweetness! Details, details! You haven't been answering the phone all morning."

Carrie walked to the kitchen with her portable phone and poured her coffee. "I'm answering now, aren't I?"

"Yes. But that only proves he's finally gone."

Carrie smiled into her coffee mug, feeling wicked. For some reason, Grandma Russell's accurate suspicion that Mike had stayed over didn't embarrass her. She was a grown woman, after all. And her grandmother, for one, didn't sound the least bit offended. "Why, Grandma Russell!" Carrie said, feigning shock.

"Goodness, child," her grandmother retorted, "I wasn't born yesterday. So, tell me. I'm all ears. Did he pop the question?"

Carrie frowned. "No."

"No?" her grandmother said with surprise. "Well, that's a man for you. Probably waiting till the time is right."

Now it was Carrie's turn to be surprised. "Grandma Russell, you are one cagey old bird, aren't you? How ever did you know?"

"Tweet, tweet," her grandma said with a chuckle. "Oh darling, just because my hair's gone mostly gray doesn't mean I've forgotten entirely how the male species operates. You can chase them back all you'd like during the courting stage, but when it comes to asking the 'big one,' most men still want to feel like it's their idea. Even if it generally isn't."

Carrie took a sip of her coffee and sat in the big easy chair that afforded her a view of the mountains. "Men!" she said, but her mood was lighthearted. He'd said he loved her. Loved her! And then that talk about making things permanent.

"Indeed," Grandma Russell answered. "But who, honestly, wants to live without them?"

Carrie knew that she didn't, not any longer than she possibly had to.

"So," her grandma asked. "We still on for the 23rd? The caterer phoned this morning, wanting the second half of her money."

Carrie hesitated. Talk about risky investments... But now was not the time to push Mike with a timetable. Her grandmother was right. At this point, it was important for him to take things on his own terms. To go at his own pace. Carrie thumped the table nervously with her free hand. "Sure," she said, biting into her bottom lip. "Why not? It's only money."

Grandma Russell laughed. "You, child, are probably the only person I know who could say that and really mean it."

Mike got down on one knee and looked up at his father. "Okay, Dad, tell me how this sounds…"

"What you got your elbows all sticking out for? You trying to imitate a chicken?"

Mike pursed his lips and stood. "Are you going to cooperate or aren't you? I thought you liked her."

"Love her, son. She's a regular doll. And, not so incidentally, probably way too good for you. But I can't for the life of me understand what you're all so hellfire worried over. You never practiced up for any of the others."

Mike blew a hard breath and ran his fingers through his hair. "Well, maybe the other times weren't nearly as important."

His dad laughed and shook his head. "You, boy, are the only man I know who asks women to marry him just as easily as most ask girls out for burgers."

"You aiming to insult me?" Mike asked, setting his hands on his hips.

"Nope. Just wondering. Does Carrie know about the long line of others before her?"

"She knows about Alexia."

"And what about Marianne? The one with the big…" Jack made a curvy motion in the air with his hands.

"You really do have a one-track mind, you know that?

Jack twisted his lips in scrutiny. "You're really going to do it this time, aren't you? What about that island thing? You always said if you found the right girl to share your dream…"

Mike felt the sweat form at his brow. "Carrie doesn't even know about that island thing. Besides," he said, unable to keep his face from falling just a bit, "like you're so fond of saying, Dad, you can't have it all. At least, not if you come from the same side of the tracks we do."

Jack raised his eyebrows and studied his son. "If you'll recall, boy, another thing that I'm fond of saying is, it never hurts to ask. Have you even talked with her about it?"

"Ridiculous," Mike said, shaking his head. "The whole notion is pie-in-the-sky at this point. Besides, if she says yes to my proposal, I'm going to have to find a way to up my income here. Not go tossing pennies in a far-off well. I've been thinking that maybe I could talk my broker, Colleen, into making me a partner. My sales have been really high lately, after all."

"I thought Carrie was well-off."

"Exceptionally well-off. Precisely why I can't let her think I won't carry my weight. Maybe it's old-fashioned of me, but I inherited my values from you."

His dad gave him a proud smile.

"Now," Mike said, dropping back down on his knees. "You going to help me with this or not?"

Jack held out a leathered hand. "Yes, dear," he said, in a high falsetto. "You were saying that I hung the moon…?"

Carrie walked into her office and dropped some files on her secretary's desk. "Mary?" Carrie said, looking down at the trim young woman. "Didn't expect to find you here on a Sunday."

Mary pushed her gold wire-rim glasses up a bit higher on the bridge of her nose. "Yes, ma'am. Well, it seems that we've fallen a bit...uh, behind this week."

Carrie flushed, knowing that was because of her series of unexcused absences.

"Just here catching up."

"Great," Carrie smiled. "Me too." Since she and Mike had slept in, they'd completely missed the opportunity for the Ashton Academy reunion picnic. Yet somehow that thought hadn't mattered to either of them.

Carrie walked back to her desk, dismayed to find the pink message notes practically spilling off it. She really had been gone awhile. And now, she thought, looking down at her watch, since it was Sunday there wasn't much she could do about the phone calls. Well, there was computer work to do. And, she could check up on the stock reports, compose some letters.

Carrie plopped down in her chair, the brilliance of an idea hitting her. He hadn't mentioned it in days. But then again, in spite of her deepest desires, Carrie hadn't exactly been spouting picket fences either. Mike was just the sort of man to give up his dream for the woman he loved. But what he still didn't know was that in love, all things were possible.

"Mary," she said, calling out to her secretary. "Do we still have that old file on the Caymans?"

"Acquisition proposal?" Mary called back.

"That's the one." The thick one that contained all that research Mary'd done on property availability and Mom-and-Pop investment opportunities.

"Yes, ma'am. Got it around here somewhere. Though some of that information is bound to be dated."

"How long will it take you to correct that?"

"About twenty-four hours," Mary said, carting the heavy file over to Carrie's desk with a smile.

****

Chapter Sixteen

Mike strode purposefully into his broker's office, a broad smile on his face. "Colleen," he announced. "I'm getting married."

Colleen raised her eyebrows above the listings she was perusing but didn't look up. "That's nice." She laid down the papers and pulled a pen from her desk drawer. "Mike," she said, circling a few of the real-estate offerings detailed before her. "These are the ones I want you to call on first."

Mike stepped forward and snatched the stack off her desk. "Colleen! Didn't you hear me? I said—"

Colleen cocked her head to the side and called out in a big, bellowing tone that attracted the attention of two agents working at the copier, "Call a news conference! Send out the releases! Mike Davis is getting married…"

He glared at her.

"Again," she finished more quietly.

The other agents, a man and a woman, both junior colleagues of Mike's, went back to work with respective shrugs.

"Listen, Mike," Colleen said, clearing her throat and looking combative. Her eyes were an icy blue that matched the color of the glasses' chain around her neck. Glasses, Mike had noticed, she never seemed to wear but often seemed to look for. "Your little absences last week put us in quite a pinch here. You owe Megan and Kurt over there, and owe them big-time for picking up your slack."

Mike sank down in the chair opposite her desk, figuring now might not be the best time to ask for a raise.

"You don't watch yourself, young man, you're going to be out of a job."

Oh no. That would be even worse than failing to secure a promotion. Mike gave a pleading smile and strove to look humble. "I'm so sorry, Colleen. Really, I am. But the thing that came up last week was—unavoidable."

"Unavoidable for five days running?"

"No, I came in on Friday."

Colleen squinted.

"For half a day," Mike said, hanging his head.

She sat there waiting like a Mother Confessor.

"Listen, Colleen. Haven't you ever been in love? I mean, really in love?"

"Yes," she answered flatly. "But apparently not as many times as you have."

Mike leaned forward and accepted the real-estate listings she was extending in his direction.

"The top ones first," she said. "They need screening for an out-of-town client. And since not all of them came with pictures—"

"No problem," Mike said, standing. "I'll get on it right away."

Carrie had tossed and turned all night, excited at the prospect of her new project. But was she really doing the right thing? What if Mike hated the idea or resented her getting involved in his professional life? Unasked, no less.

Carrie looked in the mirror and tugged at her cheeks, dismayed to see the puffy bags under her eyes didn't dissipate. Maybe she should just ask him. Flat out.

But no. That would completely ruin the surprise. Carrie had seen the way his eyes had sparkled at the mention of moving to the Caymans. Once, she was certain, that had been his goal. But now, with her in the picture, could it be he was planning to put it aside? He hadn't even mentioned it since that early conversation back at the inn. Maybe he thought the idea wouldn't appeal to her.

Carrie considered how awful it would be to have something, or even somebody, unwittingly discourage your dream. Since the time she'd entered college and worked her way through, Carrie had pursued everything that was important to her. Nobody had ever told her that she couldn't. And her Grandma Russell, bless her, had always said that all she had to do was try.

Having been employed by a large New York investment firm right out of grad school, Carrie had been lucky in business. It wasn't long before she was making good money, and, because she honestly didn't have a lot of places to spend it, the money had amassed quickly. Before long, people were coming to her for favors, or opportunities for helping people just seemed to land at her feet. There was her favorite hot-dog vendor with his dream of opening up his own deli, her coworker whose aunt's independent bookstore was on the brink of foreclosure and badly needed refinancing, her apartment manager who was quite sure, if he had the funds, he could turn his dilapidated building into some of the finest condominiums on New York's Upper East side.

All of those dreams had become realities thanks to Carrie's personal investment in each of these ventures. The results had given her more than satisfaction; they had given her purpose. Within a year, she'd become incorporated and established her own independent investment firm. Two years later, she made the cover of *Forbes*. But in spite of the increasingly lucrative opportunities that poured her way, Carrie stayed true to her initial calling of helping the small businessman. Though she'd never been precisely poor, her background had been modest. And she'd seen from her own experience that a "rags to riches" existence was possible. All so many people needed was just a chance to get them started. And if the man she loved needed that same kind of chance, she would move heaven and earth to make it happen.

Carrie scooped the morning paper off her front porch and sat down to browse the financial section over coffee. She had figured Mike for some sort of real-estate venture. High-end sales, perhaps combined with property management of some of Grand Cayman's larger estates.

Carrie laid down her paper, a surprising thought taking hold. What if Mike hadn't planned to work in real estate at all in the Caymans?

But what else was there? Certainly not early retirement for a man as clever and energetic as Mike. He still seemed way too ambitious, not to mention physically…

Physical! But of course, Carrie thought with a grin. Her "swim god" wanted to go to the Caymans to capitalize on his native expertise. And Carrie wasn't talking about lovemaking… Though she was certainly hoping there'd be plenty of that.

The moment Mike stepped from the car, it hit him with a one-two punch. This was it, he thought, looking around. This was home.

The white Cape Cod was nestled in a quiet grove just west of the city. It was zoned for the best school system,

one of his client's priorities, and had enough bedrooms—
four—to accommodate a houseful of children.

Mike stood on the front circular drive looking up at the
dormer windows protruding from the second story. Those
would give plenty of light, and most likely have window
seats, to the children's rooms.

When Mike stepped inside and walked through the
foyer and directly to the back of the house, he was not
disappointed. The high stone hearth made the open family
room connecting to the kitchen look cozy. Mike's trained
eye swept over the kitchen appliances, which all looked to
be less than five years old. A good sign for a house that had
been built in the 1940s. It was an indication the owners had
routinely kept it up and not just bandaged things at the last
minute for the sale.

At the back of the kitchen area sat a large bay window
looking out onto immaculately tended gardens. One hosting
several rows of summer vegetables, another sporting
colorful flowers surrounding a sparkling pond.

Mike's heartbeat picked up a notch as he circled back
through the formal living area and dining rooms, both of
which needed painting but boasted gorgeous ceiling and
chair-rail moldings.

Though it was his job, Mike felt surprisingly like
Goldilocks as he took the stairs two at a time and hurried
upstairs into the bedrooms. He went to the front of the
house first, where he found, as he'd suspected, a couple of
cheerfully decorated children's rooms complete with sun-
dappled dormer windows.

The master bedroom was good-sized but not so large a
couple could get lost in it. And the fourth bedroom, which

was currently used as an office, and two upstairs baths were inviting and well maintained.

Mike felt he was bursting at the seams as he took it all in. He'd always heard buying real estate was an emotional experience. Had witnessed that enamored expression on the faces of many of his clients. But never in a million years did he dream that besotted feeling would happen to him.

Carrie would love it. He just knew it. Though her current place was charming, it was nowhere near big enough to accommodate a large family. And this house here, situated at the crest of a sleepy knoll, was not only roomy enough for plenty of children, all the rug rats Mike secretly hoped he and Carrie would make—it also afforded the same stunning view of the mountains.

Mike went downstairs and walked out onto the back patio, eyeing the one accoutrement that had cinched the deal from the moment he'd hit the property line. Fanning the border of the house's perimeter was a neat arrangement of flowers and shrubs. And behind those—gleaming in the sunlight—stood a freshly painted white picket fence.

****

Chapter Seventeen

Carrie picked up her office phone and dialed. Though she quite obviously sometimes gambled with her heart, when it came to business dealings, Carrie was exceedingly cautious. Before she went and did anything involving money, she needed to make certain her hunch was accurate.

"Hello?" Jack Davis answered.

"Jack, good morning. This is Carrie, Carrie St. John."

"Why, Carrie!" he said, sounding genuinely pleased to hear her voice. "How are you? That son of mine behaving himself? 'Cause if he's not, I'm still available, you know."

Carrie chuckled. "Oh Jack, you are bad."

"Thank you, my dear. So, what can I do for you this morning? Time to start practicing our wedding march already?"

Carrie blanched before remembering she'd impetuously invited Jack to walk her down the aisle. An act she still wasn't sorry for. Mike's dad was adorable. "Oh no, not that. But I'll certainly let you know.

"Actually, I was calling with a question—about Mike."

"Mike?" Jack exclaimed. "Well, I can't completely promise you I've figured that boy out. But go ahead and shoot, if you'd like. I'll do the best that I can."

Carrie hoped she wouldn't disillusion her prospective father-in-law by seeming too forward. But, in for a penny, in for a pound, she told herself. "It's about the British West Indies. The Cayman Islands, specifically."

Jack seemed to be waiting on the other end of the line. Not commenting, just waiting for Carrie to finish. She wasn't sure if this was good but decided to press on ahead.

"Anyhow, I realize Mike has an interest in the Caymans—"

"That so?" Jack butted in. "Didn't know he'd discussed it with you."

Ah, Carrie thought, then there was something to discuss, and something to her gut feeling after all. "Well, he mentioned it somewhat. Some time ago, actually. But I could tell, even at the time, how very important it was to him."

"I think Mike's just recently found what's most important to him."

Carrie colored at the compliment, despite the fact Jack couldn't see her. "I appreciate that, really I do. And Mike is very special to me. Extra special. I hope to marry him."

Jack was quiet for a moment before speaking. "That's wonderful! He's asked you, then?"

"Well, uh…not exactly. But let's just say I see it coming."

"Then I say, your vision's twenty-twenty, my girl."

That extra bit of reassurance warmed Carrie through and through. "But because I love him, Jack, I'd hate to think of Mike giving up any long-term dreams on my account."

"Oh, now, fluff," Jack said, huffing into the phone. "Don't you go worrying your pretty little head over that. I never really believed the boy was going to open that dive shop anyway."

Carrie hung up the phone after thanking him and promising Jack she'd let him know just as soon as they'd scheduled the wedding rehearsal. Wedding rehearsal? They still hadn't invited half the guests. The ones who would fill in the slots Wilson's missing family would have occupied. Oh well, Carrie decided, she could think of that tomorrow. Today, she had some phone-calling to do.

"Mary," she called into the next room. "Do you have a moment to come in and make some notes?"

"Yes, ma'am," Mary said, appearing at the threshold.

"Great," Carrie said, her grin as wide as the big outdoors, "because we're slightly revising our project. Ready to dive in?"

"You sure about this?" Colleen said, staring up at Mike in disbelief. "A four-bedroom house is a big investment for a bachelor."

Mike patiently shook his head. This afternoon, not even Colleen was going to sour his mood. "Already told you, Colleen, not going to be a bachelor that much longer."

Colleen dropped into her chair in shock. "You're dead serious about this, aren't you?" For the first time for as long as he could remember, Colleen lifted the dangling bifocals from her neck and shoved them up on her nose. "Shut the door, Mike."

Mike walked to the back of Colleen's office and closed the door, giving the two of them privacy.

"Have a seat," she instructed when he returned.

"Now," Colleen said once he was seated. "Tell me honestly, what kind of trouble are you in?"

"Trouble?"

"Is the girl pregnant? Because, if she is—"

"Pregnant? Holy cow! Pregnant, Colleen?"

Colleen motioned downward with her outstretched palms. "Just calm down there, Mike. You won't be the first one on my staff who's gotten himself into a bit of a, uh...personal pickle."

"Colleen, I'm not asking you for money! I have enough for the down payment in my account. I've been saving it up for a while now for...for... Well, never mind. It's not important anymore. What is important is that I'm not asking you for any special favors here. Only the standard cut on the price based on reduced commission since someone in this office is buying it. I don't see the big deal. It's accepted protocol. I've seen you authorize such sales at least a dozen times."

"So she's not pregnant?" Colleen asked, as if she hadn't heard a word.

"Give us a couple of months," Mike said, settling back in his chair.

"How much is the house?" Colleen asked, sighing and eyeing him quizzically.

"Two-forty."

Colleen raised her eyebrows. "Joint mortgage?"

"Absolutely not," Mike told her. "This one has to be all mine." His to own and his to give away—with a full heart, Mike thought with a deep inner peace that spread from his heart to his belly.

Carrie couldn't believe her luck. There was a small store for sale just at the edge of trendy Seven Mile Beach. With all the major resort hotels nearby, the location couldn't have been more perfect. The shop, just outside of George Town, was even guaranteed docking privileges. It couldn't have been more perfect. Of course, as the store had formerly served as a knickknack-and-jewelry shop, they'd have some remodeling to do. Probably plenty of remodeling to do, given the bargain-basement price of the property, Carrie decided.

Still, if the appraiser she'd contacted at the Grand Cayman bank came back with the report Carrie expected, the place was a steal. An investment waiting to happen. Carrie's palms moistened at the possibilities. She couldn't wait to see the look on Mike's face.

And yet, she'd have to proceed cautiously. Make certain he didn't mistake this for some kind of handout and become offended. But Carrie had never planned to give him the money, only loan it—on a long-term repayment, low-interest basis like she had for each of her other clients. It could give him the chance he needed, if he wasn't too darn proud to accept it.

Carrie paused at that last thought, considering. What if he became furious at her intrusion? What if he accused her of trying to run his life? What if he truly couldn't see that this was no sort of manipulation; it was a gift from the heart?

Carrie slouched back against her high-backed leather chair and spun to face the window. She supposed it all depended on timing. First, they had to get beyond that proposal part, so Mike wouldn't think she was trying to buy his affections. But when, oh when, was that proposal part ever going to waltz along?

Mike had said to trust him. But for how long?

She wondered if he'd even considered the wedding angle, or if he'd find using her premade arrangements tacky. To Carrie, it just seemed a terrible waste to let all that planning and expense go, just to reinvent the wheel.

Well, they would sort all of that out soon enough. First things first. She'd found the ideal property for Mike's dive shop, and if she didn't move on it quickly, somebody else would, she knew. The location was just too hot.

And, if after all her trouble, Mike hated the idea? Had completely changed his mind, and no longer wanted to move to the Caymans? Well, then, she'd just have to cross that bridge when she came to it. The shop would be a surprise, a wedding gift. And if he didn't care for it, Carrie would just have to find someone else, another entrepreneur, to take advantage of the opportunity. But that wouldn't happen. She was sure of it. Once Mike was advised of all the particulars, he was going to be over the moon.

Mike sat at his desk mooning over a picture of the house he was about to purchase and wondering how soon it would be available for occupancy. Colleen had already phoned the owners with his offer and would be letting him know that detail along with their counteroffer, when it came.

Now, if he could preoccupy—and be in within a month—that would be even better. He'd asked Colleen to inquire about the possibility. Mike couldn't wait to get started on a life with Carrie. Real stroke of luck she already had the wedding arranged. Though they hadn't talked it over officially, he guessed since he hadn't proposed "officially," Mike assumed that was what they would do. Go ahead and use the facilities and services Carrie had already arranged. She'd never canceled them, as she'd threatened to do earlier. Grandma Russell had told him so.

It made his heart spring-dive just to think she'd forgone canceling those arrangements because she'd held out hope for a future with him. With him! And, holy cow, it was happening.

The house he'd found was perfect, so perfect that…

Mike stopped congratulating himself as his blood ran cold. Oh my goodness. What if he'd done the wrong thing? What if Carrie became incensed at him making such a major decision for the two of them? Without even consulting her first?

What if she didn't even want to live in Virginia but had someplace else in mind entirely? They hadn't even had a chance to discuss those kinds of future plans. Mike had just seen the house, the white picket fence and—whammy! He'd gone and done something huge, something impetuous, something nearly irrevocable. Holy cow. Mike blew a hard breath and sat back against his chair as fear settled into his belly.

Surely, Carrie wouldn't fault him for a wedding gift? Yes, that was what he'd call it. And, if she didn't like it…? Well, though they couldn't exactly return it, they could surely work something out. Find renters, resell after a while. But Mike didn't want to resell. He absolutely loved the place. And Carrie would too. He just knew it.

****

Chapter Eighteen

Carrie nervously bit into her bottom lip, smearing her lipstick against her teeth. Darn it! She'd have to start all over again. Ever since Mike had called this afternoon, she'd suspected something was up. There was an urgent expectation to his voice. No, it couldn't be tomorrow; it had to be tonight. Even though Carrie had loads to do at the office and was expected to work late, she'd come home early, showered, and put on a fresh sundress. And he wasn't even expected until seven thirty! Seven thirty. What was Carrie going to do with herself for the next forty-five minutes while waiting for him to come?

Her stomach rumbled, reminding her she should probably eat something. No, she was going to throw up. Carrie raced to the toilet, thinking she was going to lose her lunch. But after a few moments of staying still, the clench in her belly eased.

Criminy! She was a wreck. Didn't even know for certain tonight was the tonight.

Like hell she didn't, Carrie thought, racing back to the bathroom.

The telephone rang, and she limped into the bedroom to pick it up, all the while clutching her midsection.

"Darling?"

"Oh, Grandma Russell, thank goodness! I am such a wreck. Such a *wreck*. Mike called and said—"

"Hold on there, child. Slow down. Can't make out a word you're saying."

"I'm, um…" Carrie sat down on the bed and started to cry. "Oh Grandma, I've never wanted anything more in my life."

"Calm down. Just take a deep, deep breath."

Carrie inhaled.

"Now let it out."

She did.

"Go on, a few more times. In and out. I'm not going anywhere; I can wait."

Carrie wiped the moisture from her cheeks and sat up a little straighter.

"Now, you still with me?" her grandmother asked. "Or should I call the rescue squad?"

Carrie let out a laugh that released more tears. But this time, she felt more in control. "Thanks, Grandma," she said, taking another deep breath. "You're the best."

"What's all this about wanting? You mean the dang hunk hasn't proposed by now?"

"Not yet, but it's coming," Carrie said, holding out her trembling left hand and examining the bare ring finger. "I can feel it. Just like that musky heat right before a rain."

"Well," Grandma Russell said, "he's been waiting for a reason. So don't you go jumping all over him with kisses and I-do's before he can get two words out. First, give the rascal a chance to say his piece."

"Jumping…? Why, Grandma Russell, what do you take me for, an impatient woman?"

Her grandma chuckled. "Just a woman who knows what she wants. And I can't say I blame you. He is a dish, that Mike Davis, he is."

"Grandmother! It's not all about the way he looks, and you know it!"

"Yes, I know. But I also know enough to know looks don't hurt. Especially when the man in question looks just like a young Robert—"

"There you go with that movie-star thing again. I swear, that's not helping."

Grandma Russell hooted. "I can't wait for the big day. It will be so nice feeling like you are finally anchored in Virginia, Carrie love. I just know with that man of yours at home, those week-long trips to New York won't seem nearly as enticing."

Carrie thought about telling her but decided against it. Why spoil her grandmother's jovial mood? Besides, Carrie was finally feeling better herself. Perhaps if she had some yogurt and a bit of soda. She definitely needed something in her stomach, and the soda would help her queasies.

"I think I'd better go and grab something to eat before he gets here," Carrie said, standing and walking to the kitchen. "Keep those fingers crossed for me."

"Absolutely," Grandma Russell reported, "and all my lavender-painted toes."

Carrie hung up the phone, wondering if her grandmother had really painted her toenails purple or was just being funny. With Grandma Russell, one never really knew. Perhaps expressly why Grandpa Russell married her in the first place.

Okay, Mike told himself, scooping the brand-new engagement ring off his carpet for the third time. This wasn't good. Not good at all. He was all thumbs tonight. What a wonderful night to propose. Plus, it was predicted to rain. How romantic. He had planned to take Carrie to his special spot, right there in Norton Vineyards. He'd even bought a Norton Sweet Virginia Red and a whole box of mint chocolate chip ice cream sandwiches to complement the evening.

Before, when he'd acted rashly and proposed to the wrong women, he'd charted a course for disaster. Not this time. Not this time, indeed. Tonight was special. Carrie was special. And the dag-blasted ring he'd traded for Alexia's had cost only a few hundred more. A few hundred, but worth every dime.

Yet the custom setting Mike had arranged had taken time. An unsettling amount of time. On a couple of occasions, in fact, Mike had actually feared Carrie was going to propose to him instead, if he didn't hurry it up.

Well, now all that was neither here nor there because he had the ring, he thought, wedging it back in its box and shoving it down in his pocket. He walked to the kitchen counter, completing his mental checklist. He had the wine. Check. He felt his other pocket for the Swiss Army knife with the corkscrew. Check. And the ice cream... He opened the freezer to find it bare.

Mike whirled on his heels toward the center of the kitchen where a soggy brown-paper bag wilted against the table. Holy cow! Not again. But it was, in fact. Even worse than the first time.

Carrie fiddled with her watch and paced the living room. She picked up the remote and switched on the television. News and game shows. She switched it off again.

She checked the mantel clock. Seven forty-five. All right, Carrie, she told herself, fifteen minutes late does not a disaster make. He could be running a bit behind, could have stopped for gas.

Carrie felt like she was getting a sick headache. No, not tonight, she prayed. Not tonight of all nights. She went to the kitchen and poured some water from the tap, preparing to take two aspirin, when a firm knock sounded at the front door.

Carrie's stomach revolted.

She raced to the door and tugged it open, just before making a beeline for the bathroom. Carrie slammed the door at her back and fell to her knees.

Mike trailed Carrie to the bathroom, only to have the door slammed in his face. Poor thing, she looked positively awful. White as a sheet. Holy cow. What was happening here?

Mike tapped lightly at the door. "Carrie? Honey, you all right?"

"Fine, fine," she muttered through running water. But she sounded less than perfect.

Mike looked down at the two bags clutched in his hands, thinking that neither the new ice cream he'd just picked up nor the wine would look too appealing to Carrie at the moment.

After a few minutes of silence, he tried knocking again. "Carrie?"

Finally, she pulled back the door, looking ghostly.

"Oh sweetie," Mike said, "come over here and sit down. You don't look so hot."

She gave him a twisted smile, remembering the first time he'd said that. "Bet you say that to all the girls."

"No," he said, depositing his bags on the coffee table and sitting beside her on the sofa. "Actually, it's just the opposite…" He reached out and took her hands in his. "Is it the flu? Did it hit suddenly?"

"You could say that," she answered, smiling past her queasiness.

"Stay put," he said, releasing her hands and giving her knee a light pat. "I'll go and get you some ginger ale."

"What did you bring me?" she asked when he returned from the kitchen and handed her the glass.

Mike followed her gaze to the two paper grocery bags on the table. "Probably nothing you'd feel much like having now. How about I tuck them in the fridge?"

Carrie nodded and took a very slow, small sip from her glass.

Mike shook his head as he stored the wine and ice cream in the refrigerator. Sick? She was sick? After everything he had planned—rehearsed—to make this night perfect? Holy cow.

Just when he thought things couldn't possibly get any worse, Mike heard the hard rhythm of rain beating against the kitchen window.

Carrie wanted to curl up into a ball and die. Whatever he'd planned… All the trouble he'd gone to, and now she couldn't even lift herself off the sofa. This was not the way she'd envisioned things at all. Maybe she was jinxed, or perhaps she'd already gotten her fair share of uneventful proposals. Whatever the reason, she was damned upset it was happening to her now.

Carrie glanced up toward the ceiling, hearing a sound smacking the red-slate roof. Perfect, it was raining.

"Penny for your thoughts?" Mike said, coming back over to the sofa and sitting beside her.

"Oh Mike," she said, her voice breaking up, "I'm so sorry…"

"Hush," he said, bringing a hand to her lips and gently stroking her chin. "You can't help any more that you're sick than I can the color of my eyes."

Oh, she wished she could believe it. But no, she felt responsible. As if the whole disastrous evening, one that could have been the most memorable ever for the two of them, was all her fault. If only she hadn't worked herself into such a tizzy. If only she'd had a regular dinner. If only…

"Carrie," Mike said, laying a hand on her forearm. "How do you think the air would do you?"

"Air?" she asked, not understanding.

"I was thinking of the porch swing."

Carrie agreed that it was a fine idea and that being outdoors might actually help her. So she accepted Mike's assistance and leaned on him heavily as he helped her outside and onto the porch swing, all the while thinking that this was how life would be. The two of them leaning on each other, growing old together. Each one forever supporting the other.

Carrie felt the moisture on her cheek and raised a casual hand to her eye, hoping Mike hadn't seen. He already thought she was falling apart. Why give him further proof?

"Need a blanket?" he asked as a heavy gust of wind dusted a spray of rain in their direction.

"Just your arm," she said, smiling up at him.

Mike sat and wrapped his arm around her, scooting in close. Carefully, slowly, when he felt her capable of tolerating the motion, Mike sent the swing into a gentle rock.

Far away, the mountains dripped and bled color in the evening rain. And, closer at hand, an occasional whistling wind across fresh flowers sent lazy summer fragrances wafting onto the porch. Mike held her and stroked her shivering arm until it steadied in his warmth.

Brushstrokes of light streaked into blackness in the darkening sky as her head dropped against his shoulder in easy comfort and they continued to rock. And when she grew heavy and still, Mike knew that she'd fallen asleep.

It was just like the dancing. And he wanted it to go on and on and on… Yes, he was sorry about the evening and his lost opportunity for fulfilling plans. But he was doubly grateful for the chance just to hold her now, with nothing but the scent of the rain between them. If this snapshot was an indication of the next sixty years, Mike was awfully glad he'd seen the big picture early.

Carrie awoke with a start to see the sun peering over the purple mountains. It was only when she heard the low rumble that she realized Mike was sitting and snoring beside her.

"Mike?" she said, raising a hand to his face. "Mike?"

"I'd like to counter that offer," he said, snapping to attention.

"What offer?" she asked, laughing in surprise. "Were you dreaming about real estate?"

Mike opened his eyes wide, then blinked at his surroundings. "Yeah, I guess that I was," he said, rubbing the sore back of his neck. "Did we sleep here all night?"

"Unless little trolls carried us to my bed, then replaced us on the swing before sunup."

Mike pulled her into his arms and nuzzled her neck. "You know," he said, "that's the first time I've ever done that. Pulled an all-nighter with a woman on a swing."

Carrie smiled, enjoying his warmth, enjoying the new day. Savoring the implausibility of the moment. And thinking that she'd happily wake up with Mike Davis anywhere.

"You stick with me, and you'll get lots more opportunities for firsts," she said, feeling playful. And, thank goodness, so much better.

"You're looking brighter this morning," he said, stroking her cheek. "I was so sorry to see you so ill."

"Thanks for staying with me. Being with you really helped."

Mike turned to the woman beside him. All night on the porch after an evening of illness, and Carrie St. John was without a doubt the most beautiful women he'd ever seen. The only woman with whom he could envision sharing a lifetime.

"Think you could get used to it?" Mike asked, moving his hands to her shoulders and looking deep in her eyes.

Carrie nodded but didn't say a word. Because her heart was on fire. She knew, unmistakably, what was coming next. But this time, Carrie wasn't anxious or afraid. Every nerve ending was ready.

Mike slipped out of the rocker and got down on one knee.

311

"Carrie," he said, taking her left hand in both of his. "I have something very important to ask you. And just so you know, I want to tell you I already did the proper thing and talked with your grandmother."

"Yes!" Carrie said, springing off the porch swing and into his arms as he stood in surprise to catch her. "Yes, yes, oh Mike, yes," she said between vibrant kisses that ran from his mouth to his cheek to his neck to his forehead.

"Carrie—" he said, stopping her when she was almost to his mouth again. "You didn't even let me finish asking."

"Oh," she said, consumed by a groundswell of heat. "Sorry." Carrie primly smoothed out her hair and sat back down on the swing. "Continue," she said, looking up, a million constellations in her eyes.

Mike smiled to beat all get-out and pulled a ring box from his pocket. "Before I say what I have to say," he told her while her heart beat fiercely with anticipation, "I want you to promise me you'll keep that level of enthusiasm for the next say, oh…fifty to sixty years."

"It's a deal," she said with a sexy grin that almost made him drop the box and cart her straight inside.

"Carrie St. John," Mike said, dropping back down on one knee, half wondering if he might get tackled. He pulled back the velvet lid, revealing a beautiful blue diamond surrounded by six perfect rubies.

"Oh Mike…"

"I'm sorry it took a while, but this ring was sort of a symbolic gift. I wanted to get it just right."

Carrie wrinkled her brow as Mike plucked the ring from its box.

"The diamond… Well, of course, you know what the diamond means, love everlasting and all that." He grinned, and she shot him a look with her eyes that dazzled.

"And the rubies?" Carrie asked. She counted. "Six of them?"

"Well, these first two," Mike said, pointing to the stones set at the top. "These are you and me."

Carrie's eyes watered.

"Because, well…" He looked at her and smiled. "I figured out some time ago that you and I are—two of a kind. Destined for each other. Meant to be."

Carrie swallowed hard past the lump in her throat. "And the others?"

He gave her a hopeful smile, green eyes glistening. "Jack, Amanda, little Carrie, and Mike Junior," he said, touching the stones one by one with his right index finger.

Salty tears streamed from Carrie's eyes. Amanda was her Grandma Russell's name, though how Mike had known, she couldn't fathom.

"Of course, if you don't like those names, we could choose others," he said, reaching up and wiping her cheeks.

"I love those names. But…four?" she said, her voice warbling.

"For starters, anyway," Mike said with a Cheshire-cat grin as he slipped the ring on her finger. "Carrie St. John," he said, looking into her deep-brown eyes, "will you be mine, to have, to hold, and to cherish from this day forward…?"

Carrie nodded and kissed his hands still holding her own. "Oh, I will. I will, I will, I will!" She smiled, giving the morning sun a run for its money. "But…Mike, I kind of think you're supposed to save those words for the wedding."

"The wedding?" Mike asked, pulling her up and into his arms. Right where she belonged. Torso to torso, heart to thundering heart.

"But that's only six days away," he said, closing in for a kiss. "Shouldn't we start practicing up?"

What, oh what, was she going to do with this man?

Keep him, she supposed.

"Absolutely," Carrie said as she kissed him back, and he swept her away.

****

Epilogue

After a private ceremony and small family reception, featuring mint-chocolate wedding cake, Mike took Carrie on a long country drive, after which he surprised her by carting her over the threshold of a darling Cape Cod with a white picket fence. After crying several million tears and drinking the sweet Virginia wine Mike had stocked in the fridge, Carrie told him about his new investment opportunity in the Caymans.

Once they'd gotten over the initial shock of just how alike they truly were, the delighted couple arrived at a happy compromise. They would rent out the new house for a year while they lived on Grand Cayman and got Mike's dive-shop business off the ground. Afterward, they would settle back in Virginia and begin fulfilling Carrie's engagement-ring promise of creating four beautiful children.

So they could keep an eye on him, Mike's father, Jack, would be invited to join them in the islands for that first year. They would rent him someplace scenic, not too far from their own home, where he could watch the saucy Caribbean sun stretching its long fingers over the morning waters—and enjoy the personal attentions of his own private nurse.

Once back in Virginia, they'd continue to vacation on Grand Cayman, and Mike would make occasional business trips, as needed, to check up on his shop. Then eventually, once Mike found the perfect piece of real estate, they'd build a breezy getaway on the island's east end and summer there on a regular basis.

And while they plotted, planned, and worked out all these intimate details, the newlyweds, Mr. and Mrs. Michael John Davis, sat on the front steps of their perfect new home and ate a whole box of ice cream sandwiches—before they melted.

The End

A Note from the Author

Thanks for reading *Real Romance and The Sometime Bride,* a Ginny Baird Gemini Edition. I hope you enjoyed it. If you did, please help other people find this book.

1. This book is lendable, so loan it to a friend who you think might like it so that she (or he) can discover me, too.

2. Help other people find this book: write a review.

3. Sign up for my newsletter so that that you can learn about the next book as soon as it's available. Write to GinnyBairdRomance@gmail.com with "newsletter" in the subject heading.

4. Come like my Facebook page: http://www.facebook.com/GinnyBairdRomance.

Look for Book One in my "Girls on the Go" series, *Santa Fe Fortune*, for sale online now, and watch for Book Two, *How to Marry a Matador*, available in July 2012.

Santa Fe Fortune and *How to Marry a Matador* coming to print soon!

Interested in seeing an extended excerpt from *Santa Fe Fortune?* Please keep reading for more.

Dear Readers,

It is with pleasure and passion that I introduce my "Girls on the Go" series with this launch book, *Santa Fe Fortune.* When I was a young college woman, I studied abroad in beautiful Seville, Spain. I was at an impressionable age to experience new things, including my first deeply felt love. And, while I developed a significant and memorable romance, the most profound discovery I made that year was the unveiling of myself. For it is often in distancing ourselves from what is most familiar that we truly come to understand ourselves.

With these thoughts in mind, I conceived this new book series, designed to showcase powerful yet evolving heroines enduring journeys of the heart while traveling far from home. So please, pack up your suitcase and join us for the adventure. I discovered Santa Fe, New Mexico last summer, and promptly fell in love. Both with the charming city, and—once again—with my wonderful husband John. *Such a lovely spot for romance,* I found myself thinking. And then, being a writer… Well, the ideas for this story started flowing.

I like Gwen a lot. She's a genuine gal, who's been through rough times and deserves real happiness. She might not be perfect, but she just might be perfect for precisely the right man. In any case, Gwen's sure to appreciate what the future heroines in this series will also learn: it's who you are on the inside that matters. Once you believe in your strengths, others will see them too.

With best wishes for happy endings,

Ginny Baird, author of "Girls on the Go"

Sometimes you have to get away to find yourself!

SANTA FE FORTUNE

"I had a really great time tonight," she said, beaming up at him and feeling very much as if it had been a date.

"Me too," he said, stepping a fraction of an inch closer. Sea-blue eyes washed over her, threatening to pull her under. And boy, did she want to get swept away. "I'm glad you agreed to see me tomorrow, even if it's just an arrangement."

Gwen sensed Dan could rearrange her heart every which way, if she wasn't careful. "I'm glad I'm seeing you too," she said, feeling the warmth in her cheeks.

"Ten o'clock work for you?" he asked, his tone growing gravelly.

"Uh-huh," she uttered, mesmerized by his gaze.

He moved nearer now, his mouth just inches away. "I'll be damned if I don't want to kiss you," he said, his voice a husky rasp.

And she'd be damned if she didn't want him to. "Dan..." she said, tilting up her chin and closing her eyes.

"But I won't," he said, snapping her back to attention, eyes open. "Not now. Not here. Not like this..."

She started to speak as he brought his fingers to her lips. "If ever I've seen a woman who deserves to be kissed well, it's you. But the timing has got to be right. You have to be sure." He cast a cursory glance at her wedding band and backed away. "I need to be sure. Something tells me we've both gone down a path neither of us wants to travel again..."

Chapter One

Gwendolyn Marsh leaned across the large oak table that served as a desk. "I'm going to be honest with you, Mr. Holbrook. I didn't fly all the way out here to get swindled."

Dan stared in disbelief at the incredibly contentious woman. *Swindled* was an awfully big accusation coming from such a small frame. She couldn't stand more than five foot five in heels, and she'd nearly tumbled off them striding into the place.

"Like I told you, Mrs. Marsh, I'm not in the position to make that decision. If two thousand a canvas is what Ms. Holstein quoted you in the email, then I'm afraid I'll need to stick by that."

Soft gold curls fell at uneven angles, framing a lovely face as deep brown eyes homed in on him. If she weren't so hard-edged, he might consider her beautiful. Dan stopped himself, realizing appraisals of the clientele weren't in his job description.

"It's *Ms.,* if you must know."

Some lucky fellow was off the hook.

"My apologies. I saw the wedding band and…"

"It's a relic, okay? I haven't gotten used to going without it."

"I'm sorry, I had no idea. I understand it takes a while."

She leveled him a look, as if he were the culprit. Hey, maybe in her eyes, all men were. Dan had met the type before and could easily read the signs: *steer clear, not for you buddy, a sexy woman's not everything…* Sexy? Did he just think *sexy?* Gwendolyn Marsh wasn't movie-star thin like most females here. Her formfitting sundress hugged every curve in just the right way. Wrong way, as far as he was concerned. This was just another sign he'd been alone too long. It wasn't like Dan didn't have his reasons. In fact, when he was being honest, Dan realized he was likely worse news for her than she was for him. All women after a while had hopes, dreams…and Dan Holbrook was just the man to dash them.

Dark eyes sparked with fierce determination. "I think I'd like to speak to Ms. Holstein myself."

"I'm afraid that won't be possible."

She arched one perfectly manicured eyebrow. "Why not?"

This was just what Dan needed, a hot-tempered, hot-bodied woman waltzing into his Santa Fe gallery on a hot July afternoon. Okay, it wasn't technically his gallery…

Dan cursed himself for his soft spot in agreeing to run the place while Nancy was away. He didn't even like being indoors.

"Ms. Holstein is in the south of France, will be until next month."

She pulled her naturally plump lips into a thin pink line. "I see." She faltered slightly, nearly losing her composure. There was sheen to her eyes that made them look moist. Dan hoped she wasn't about to break down crying. Nancy had assured him this would be easy, just a few clients flying in from out of state. Surprise negotiations and weepy women weren't in the mix. Negotiations Dan could handle. Weepy women were another story.

A bell tinkled above the door, and a couple of well-dressed patrons entered, a man in an expensive suit and a woman wearing a tailored dress and high-end cowgirl boots.

"Be right with you folks," Dan told them, surmising these were the buyers from Los Angeles.

Gwen stood, apparently taking this as a dismissal. "Well, I guess that's it, then." She tucked her clutch under one arm and thrust forward the opposite hand. "Thanks for your time."

Dan sent a furtive glance at the Californians perusing shelves of New Mexican pottery and pretending not to listen. "Ms. Marsh, I'm afraid we got off on the wrong..." She tapped a strappy sandal, sporting bright painted nails and multiple toe rings. Heat rose at Dan's nape as his gaze eased up shapely legs. "...foot."

She withdrew her hand and cocked her head sideways, waiting.

"What I mean is, please sit back down, and let's discuss this like reasonable people. I'm sure we can work something out." Dan cringed at the sound of his own voice. Groveling? Here was a word not even in his vocabulary, yet he was being just about as placating as humanly possible. Dan wasn't doing it for himself, he remembered. He was doing this for Nancy. Other than the day-to-day oversight of things, which really was no problem, she'd given him only two jobs to do. Surely a man as capable at cutting deals as he was wouldn't have trouble selling a few items to some Los Angeles industry execs and buying canvases from an easy-going North Carolina native. Dan had a notion Nancy had never met Gwendolyn Marsh face-to-face when she'd made the latter assessment.

The hardness lining her eyes eased just a little. "I suppose I could stay for a bit," she said, her voice taking on the lilt of the mid-Atlantic South. She took her seat, splaying the lap of her flowered sundress across tightly nestled knees.

The Californians tastefully removed themselves to the back of the gallery to study a photographic desert landscape series, and Dan sat as well. He plucked a hanky from his suit pocket and dabbed the back of his neck, thinking it had to be over a hundred degrees in here.

Something tender welled in Dan's throat, and he realized he wasn't just doing this for Nancy. For some inexplicable reason, he felt driven to be nice to Ms. Marsh for her own sake. Never mind that she'd practically bulldozed right over him crashing in here. After all, he'd dealt with worse in business before. The truth was Nancy had given him some leeway. If Marsh really pushed, Dan could go up as high as three thousand a pop, mostly because Nancy had faith in Marsh's work and thought it was good. Nancy also believed that Marsh could develop a Santa Fe following. Many of the buyers here came from the West Coast, and Marsh's oils capturing snippets of sea life would be a ready sell. Dan had seen the slides, and they were impressive. Borrowing more from impressionism than realism, Marsh had a way of zeroing in on the smallest, seemingly inconsequential detail, like an isolated seashell, and illuminating it in a special and grandiose way.

She opened her purse and withdrew a thin ledger. "If you'd let me show you my figures, I'm sure you'll understand why my prices have gone up."

Dan scanned the haphazardly arranged numbers, deciding she was no mathematician. He pointed to one clumsily assumed total. "I can understand where material costs have climbed, but how exactly is it that your hourly rate has doubled?"

"Hard times, Mr. Holbrook," she said without flinching. "Don't you read the papers?"

"*Wall Street Journal* and you?" he bantered without skipping a beat.

"Well, I…read, of course." With that, she awkwardly angled an elbow and sent her clutch crashing to the floor. "Oh no!"

A small cloud of makeup powder-puffed up from beneath them as a rolling lipstick assaulted Dan's loafer. To this day, he'd never understood the mysteries of a woman's bag.

"Here, let me," he began.

"No! I've got it!"

They bent simultaneously toward the mound of sprawled purse contents, nearly knocking heads. "I'm sorry!" he said, down on hands and knees to help her.

"My fault!"

A scent overtook him as cunning and fine as the most succulent desert flower. Dan looked up into bewitching brown eyes less than six inches away. Whatever was happening here, he had to put a halt to it. This was no sensible way for a man pushing forty to behave. He was reeling like a raving teenager. He hadn't been in a position this compromising with a woman in a while, and it showed. All sorts of crazy thoughts went racing through his head, like how it might feel to kiss her good and hard as she probably deserved.

"You guys okay over there?" a pair of cowgirl boots called from the corner.

"Thanks, we've got it!" Gwen replied, scooting back on her knees. She couldn't believe this mess! What had she gotten herself into? Here she was with this hunky beast of a man, trapped beneath a solid yet decorative desk.

He had a rugged face, tanned like he was used to working outdoors. His sandy hair held a hint of sunlight too. Toned muscles strained beneath his suit jacket as he posed on all fours, looking far more like a predator in the wild than a staid art collector. Gwen had an improbable instinct to flee but was powerless to run away. He'd been an impossible man above board, but down here in the shadows, he revealed something more. Instinct told Gwen that Holbrook was the sort of man who knew how to kiss a woman and kiss her right. She imagined getting swept into his powerful arms, his mouth moving down on hers...

"Are you all right?" His gaze dove into her as heat crept up her cheeks.

"Yes, fine. That's all, I think," she said, scooping the remainders into her clutch.

Gwen didn't know why his gorgeous stare had unnerved her so. It wasn't like she was attracted to him, for heaven's sake. If her take on Holbrook was correct, he had plenty of women falling all over him already. What would a sophisticated Western entrepreneur like him want with a Carolina girl like her anyway? Apart from a quick good time, probably not a lot, and Gwendolyn Marsh was quite done with being somebody's goodtime girl, thank you very much.

Little lines pulled at the corners of his mouth, and she realized suddenly they were still both on the floor. "If you've got all you need, don't you think we should..." He gave a thumbs-up, and she pushed back, standing awkwardly.

Holbrook brushed off his trousers, the slight tugs showing off powerfully muscled thighs. Clearly not just a gallery owner, she thought, cheeks flaming as he caught her staring.

A tense moment ensued as both appeared to forget where they were or what they were there for. As if to remind them, the California man loudly cleared his throat.

"Just finishing up," Dan told him. "Ms. Marsh," he began, addressing her.

"Gwen, please. I'd be happy if you called me Gwen." She smoothed the wrinkles from her dress and straightened the neckline.

"Gwen," he said, offering up his first true smile since she'd arrived, and boy, was it a winner. If a heartbreaker contest existed in all of the Southwest, Gwen would bet on Holbrook to take the prize. "I'm afraid I've already taken up too much of your time."

Gwen spied the California couple circling closer like sharks, apparently having grown tired of waiting, and panic set in. What a terrible two days she'd had. First, her flight to Atlanta was delayed. Then, she'd missed her Albuquerque connection, causing her to miss her originally scheduled gallery appointment. To top it off, when she finally got a replacement flight, she'd chipped a nail stuffing her bulging carry-on into the overhead compartment.

Making Santa Fe from the airport last night was easy. Finding the craftily concealed entity of Holbrook and Holstein on Canyon Road this morning proved more elusive. Even her GPS was miffed, telling her to make legal

U-turns wherever possible, no matter that the prospect involved going round and round in the Vegan Market parking lot.

Now, after making a wreck of this business call, she'd be leaving here having done no business at all. Not one sale to the gallery, despite her tumultuous flight and anxiety-producing encounter with Dan Holbrook.

Gwen pulled herself up a little straighter and squared her small shoulders. She couldn't leave New Mexico without getting what she came for. Too many people depended on her, and this was the one shot she had.

"Maybe we can continue this conversation later?" she asked with a hopeful twist to her lips.

"I was just about to suggest that."

"You were?" she asked with surprise.

"Ms. Marsh…" He stopped himself. "Gwen… Do you really think Holbrook and Holstein would have had you come all this way if we didn't have a genuine interest in your work?" Crinkles formed at the corners of his blue eyes, and Gwen's heart soared.

"But I thought you said the prices quoted to me in the email were…"

"Everything in life is negotiable. Well, almost everything. Tell you what, why don't you give me a few hours to put through a phone call to France, and I'll see what I can do."

In an instant, Gwen retracted every uncharitable thought she'd had about him. When she'd first walked into the swanky, upscale warehouse and spied him double-checking the pricing on a large wall weaving, she'd imagined him incredibly stuck-up. Who wouldn't be with that six-foot build and well-proportioned frame that spoke of power and unerring self-control? She'd pegged him as the rigid sort who never took no for an answer and considered his own words the final determinant. Now that he was showing a small sliver of humanity, she realized she might have misjudged him.

"I'd love to talk again," she said, meaning it sincerely. "When's best for you?"

"How about tomorrow at lunch? Will that work?"

Ms. Holstein, his business partner, Gwen presumed, had proposed that Gwen make a little vacation out of her stay in Santa Fe while she was at it. Her sister Marian had thought it was a fine idea too. *"Go for it, Gwen! Now's your chance to finally get away!"* What Marian didn't know, and Gwen hadn't been prepared to tell her, was that Gwen's coming to Santa Fe had a whole lot to do with her.

"I'm booked at the inn for ten days," she said, smiling softly. "So, lunch tomorrow is fine."

Holbrook surprised her with a smile of his own. "Awesome." He nabbed a gallery card and quickly penned something on the back. "Let's meet here. Something tells me the conversation might flow a little better between us given a couple of avocado margaritas."

"Avocado?" she retorted, half stunned, half horrified.

Holbrook gave a genuine chuckle as she accepted his card. "Nobody's forcing the hard stuff on you. I'm sure there will be tea and soda available too."

There was a twinkle in his eye that set her tailbone tingling. Slow down there, sister, Gwen told herself. This is strictly business now. Not anywhere near a date.

"What time?" she asked primly, pinning her clutch to her side.

He studied her in an amused way. "One o'clock okay?"

"One sounds fine!" she said, scurrying toward the exit before she could do or say something absurd.

"Watch the...!"

Gwen spun toward him, noting she'd nearly upset a pretty, handblown glass vase with the edge of her bag. She grimaced, slinking out the door as the gaping Californians gawked on.

Once outside and beyond sight of the gallery's windows, Gwen snatched her bag from beneath her arm and whacked herself soundly on the forehead. Stupid, stupid, stupid. She might have blown the whole thing. And not just by breaking a priceless piece of art. The way she'd started things out had been nothing short of shameless. Crafting a confrontation with the primary gallery owner. Clearly, that could lead to nothing but butting heads.

Gwen felt a warmth surge through her, recalling their close encounter of the nearly carnal kind. There was more to Dan Holbrook than met the eye. Hadn't he just proved that with his turn of kindness at the end? But the truth of the matter was that whatever sort of man he was, or wasn't, was beside the point. Gwen had come to Santa Fe on a mission, and that mission involved dollar signs. She didn't just want the money; she needed it. Twenty thousand in cash, and she wasn't leaving New Mexico without it.

Dan finished business quickly with the couple from Los Angeles after offering sincere apologies for making them wait. They'd prearranged to purchase the desert photo series, and everything, including price negotiations, thank goodness, had been settled with Nancy in advance. It was a simple matter of the pair presenting a check and Dan providing the receipt. In the morning, he'd arrange for shipping, and Nancy's gallery assistant would be in to help with the details. That would be the simple part of Dan's day. Lunchtime could prove more problematic.

Dan chided himself for suggesting Gwen meet him at La Cantina rather than here. Outwardly, he told himself that he was being charitable. Gwen had seemed so uptight at the gallery, perhaps a more comfortable venue would be less intimidating. He'd read her résumé and understood that if she sold through Holbrook and Holstein, it would be her first real sale, her official launch in the art world. But deep in the veiled recesses of his soul, Dan suspected a slight ulterior motive. He hadn't enjoyed the company of an attractive woman in ages, and this was a safe way to do it. Lunch in the middle of the day, a straightforward business deal? What could be more innocent? Raw doubts niggled at him as he warned himself against getting in too deep. The way he'd sprung the invitation on Gwen had been completely out of character. It had been a split-second decision, an act on impulse, and Dan was anything but an impulsive man.

He would never have built his empire of custom-design homes for the moneyed set if he'd operated from a basis of anything but collected cool. In those circles, Dan was known for his keen eye and level head, as well as his effectiveness in putting together a team. From the highest-level architect to the most basic yet very skilled carpenter, every one of Holbrook Designs' workers was treated with utmost respect and handsomely paid. This was particularly appreciated in the current economic climate but had always been the operational mode for Dan. Whether times were easy or hard, Dan's business remained steady. While his homes certainly weren't cheap, they were of a consistent quality the buyer could count on. Plus, Dan was a man of his word who stood by his product. People could depend on him to deliver the best and ensure they had a comfortable and stunningly beautiful place in which to live for years to come. It was an area in which Dan felt confident, competent.

This temporary gallery-running made him feel something altogether different, and Dan didn't like it one bit. While working with the California couple had gone fine, dealing with Ms. Gwendolyn Marsh had thrown him unexpectedly off-kilter. Nancy had nowhere near prepared him for that. Just because he'd helped his big sister finance this place, that didn't mean he wanted to be involved in any intimate way. Nancy was the art history major who loved the ins and outs of acquiring art. Running a gallery in Santa Fe had always been her dream, and once Dan had found himself in a position to help with that, he'd been more than happy to foot the bill. He'd never imagined that she'd repay him by listing his name as the primary gallery owner. This perpetually led to confusion, like during his exchange with Gwen today.

No matter. He'd straighten all that out tomorrow. Surely, after a good lunch and some cordial conversation, they'd arrive at a fair compromise on price. It would be a simple matter to smooth over during coffee and dessert. Then Ms. Gwendolyn Marsh could cart her sexy little tail all the way back to North Carolina, and Dan would continue counting down the days to Nancy's return, when he would once again be free to retreat to the peaceful quiet of Paradise Ranch. Life wasn't really so complicated after all, Dan decided, thinking it through. All you needed was a plan. And Dan's plans didn't include one firecracker of a Southern belle upending his world and sending his foolish heart racing. For Dan Holbrook, days like that were done. His throat ached at the memory. He swallowed hard, trying to force it back down. Dan had stepped into the fire once and had come out barbequed. No need to start poking at coals again.

Gwen sat on the patio of her airy suite, surrounded by sweeping adobe walls, potted ferns, and cactus flowers. Despite the record-high temperatures, the lack of humidity made it pleasant enough to stay outdoors in the shade. She sipped at her host's complimentary glass of chardonnay, knowing she needed to be cautious. At seven thousand feet above sea level, one glass of wine could feel like two. The inn's cocktail hour had also offered a selection of fruits, vegetables, and cheeses, and Gwen had fixed herself a small plate as a buffering against the booze. She'd have to remain mindful of herself tomorrow at lunch, particularly in light of the proposed margaritas.

Gwen couldn't help but feel a slight tingle of hopeful anticipation. For the first time in as long as she remembered, she'd be eating out with an eligible man. She knew, of course, that it was just an art deal, and she was merely passing through town. It was nonetheless hard to deny the tiniest fluttering in her tummy that sprang to life each time she recalled being face-to-face on the floor with the undeniably handsome Holbrook. Had something authentic actually passed between them, or had Gwen been so nervous and delusional as to have imagined the whole thing?

She glanced down at the simple gold band on her left ring finger. Gwen wasn't sure if it was her marriage she couldn't forget or her failure to maintain it. *"Marshes aren't quitters!"* her mom, Elizabeth, had always said. While life may have quit on Elizabeth, she wasn't about to let her daughters give up on anything. It was a mantra burned into them, her and her sister Marian both. Gwen only wished Marian had quit having babies about three children ago. Marian was expecting her sixth, and after years of verbal and physical abuse, her alcoholic husband, Tom, had finally run out on her. Gwen had truthfully considered this a blessing, as it had been clear after the first couple of years that Marian never intended to leave Tom.

Marian worked part-time as a hospital nurse and tried to get the day shift as much as possible. When she was gone, she left her oldest, the eleven-year-old, in charge. During night shifts, her elderly neighbor, Ms. Tilly, helped out. During the academic year, Marian had daycare arranged for the twins while the others were in school. She wasn't sure how she'd manage once the new baby came along, especially under the threat of losing her home. Marian's mortgage was several months overdue, and the collectors were moving in. She hadn't told Gwen that Tom stopped sending payments, or that she was in so deep, until it was almost too late. As it was, Marian barely had funds in her meager savings account to buy a few months' worth of diapers. Her checking account was essentially empty, being worn down month after month by her family's needs, including the kids' doctors' bills.

Marian had been in tears when she'd told Gwen the truth. If she lost her house, she feared her children would be taken away from her. She had nowhere else to go.

Gwen's sparse two-bedroom could scarcely hold them all, not for any length of time, at least. And their mom, having long ago been placed in the memory-care unit of a retirement home, was far from being able to help. She barely scraped by on Social Security and most days didn't recognize either of her daughters, besides.

If Marian could just hang on one more year until the twins were in school, she thought she could make it. With only the new baby to place in daycare, she'd be able to work full-time. That would give her benefits like a retirement pension and health insurance. She'd be better able to meet her kids' medical expenses as well as plan for her own future. As it stood, she had six months of back mortgage to pay and another twelve months' obligation to look forward to. She was overwhelmed and in pieces, unsure of what to do. Taking Tom to court wasn't an option. Marian didn't have the financial resources, and even if she did, it would be hard squeezing blood from a stone. Tom was on and off the bottle and in and out of work. She couldn't rely on him now any more than she had during their marriage.

It was a dire and depressing situation. Gwen had thought for weeks about what she might do to help her sister. The trouble was Gwen was in financial strife herself. Robert had been so furious at her for kicking him out, he'd run up over ten thousand dollars in credit-card debt on purpose. The pro bono women's shelter attorney Gwen consulted said there was nothing Gwen could do about Robert maxing out the account jointly held in their names. Gwen was unfortunately just as liable for half of his debts as entitled to half of his earnings. Good luck with that. Robert, a successful production assistant with a Hollywood company providing East Coast sets, had found plenty of loopholes in which to stash his cash. Gwen twisted the simple wedding band once, realizing her cheeks were damp.

She finished off her chardonnay, more determined than ever to sell those canvases and at the best possible price. She'd started small with a few local juried art shows around town, then had dared to put a modest portfolio of slides together and began sending it out. Holbrook and Holstein in Santa Fe had been her first real nibble. In effect, it had been a really big bite. Top dollar for her work, plus the cost of round-trip air tickets and accommodations to boot. Holbrook probably thought that Gwen was being greedy, trying to barter up the price for her own gain. Nothing could be further from the truth. Marian's kids needed their mama, and Gwen needed to help her baby sister. One way or another, Gwen was going to see this through. Dan Holbrook could think anything about her that he liked. She'd never see him again after tomorrow anyway.

****

Chapter Two

When Dan got to La Cantina, Gwen had already arrived. He spied her seated at a table for two in the large atrium styled like a Spanish courtyard and decorated in colorful tile. She studied the menu as he approached, a white peasant blouse sweeping her shoulders, hair pinned up in a casual way that offset her cheekbones and fair complexion. Dan had to stop walking and catch his breath. She was truly a beautiful woman, even more beautiful than he'd given her credit for yesterday at the gallery. Then again, yesterday at the gallery, she'd appeared primed to bite his head off. Today, she just looked hungry.

"Can I help you find a table, sir?" a tall waiter in a waistcoat inquired.

"Thanks, I see where I'm going," Dan said, shaking the reverie. Hearing their exchange, Gwen looked up at him and smiled. He felt a little twist in his gut and realized this was worse than he thought. Dan smiled back pleasantly, determined to pull himself together. He envisioned a large Weber grill, coals searing beneath its grate, and suddenly felt driven to thirst.

He joined Gwen at the table, exchanged pleasantries, then took a long drag of water from the glass that had been provided at his place. She eyed him curiously as he drained it all.

"It's murder out there," he said, referencing the weather.

"Certainly is hot," she agreed.

"I hope you found this place okay."

"Oh yes, just fine." Warm brown eyes sparkled enticingly.

"They've got some really great specials today. Have you taken a look?"

Gwen turned over the menu in her hands, and he wondered again about that wedding band. How long had she been divorced, and why would she continue to wear it? Dan reminded himself that delving into Gwen's personal affairs was none of his business.

She surveyed the ample list of entrees. "Any recommendations?"

"Depends on whether you like spicy."

She gave him a big, appealing grin. "I love spicy food. All kinds. But I'd love to try something particular to the region." Why did she have to look so darned likable today? She really wasn't cooperating in encouraging Dan to keep his distance.

"Would you like me to order for us?" he asked, wanting to be helpful yet not wishing to overstep his bounds.

"That would be nice. Thanks." Gwen lowered her face to her menu to disguise a faint blush.

Dan fought a swell of heat, surmising there wasn't enough air in here. "Okay, be honest with me. Yes or no to avocado margaritas?"

"You weren't kidding, were you?" she asked with surprise.

"I may be many things, but I'm not really much of a kidder."

She stared at him intently, trying to read him. Dan tried to repress a smile but felt his eyes crinkle just the same.

"That was kidding, wasn't it?" she asked, waving a scolding finger.

He let loose a belly laugh, enjoying himself. "I'm afraid it was."

Gwen released a tiny puff of air, apparently relieved. "I'll try an avocado margarita," she answered, "but just one."

A little while later, Gwen took her first taste of the tantalizing southwestern treat. Finely pureed like a smoothie, it was silky, cool, and delicious. You couldn't taste the tequila at all. Gwen was glad she'd made the advance decision to stick with one. Holbrook did too. He ordered them a delicious chicken poblano over Mexican rice, with a cold gazpacho soup to start. It was a perfect meal, and he had been right. After a couple of margaritas, their conversation flowed a lot more smoothly. For one thing, she learned that while his name was on it, he didn't actually run the gallery. He was merely filling in this month for his older sister Nancy. His real work involved home building of some kind. It was a job he seemed to enjoy and which often kept him outdoors.

"I insist that you call me Dan," he said as their plates were cleared. "Mr. Holbrook hardly seems right with me calling you Gwen. You're making me feel like an old man."

"Oh, I suspect you're not that old," she said, feeling as if she was flirting.

He colored slightly around his open collar. "Thirty-nine next month. Practically over the hill."

He was dressed casually today, in khaki slacks and an azure polo shirt that complemented his eyes. The shirt fit him nicely, stretching evenly across his broad and muscled chest. Gwen found herself wondering what it would be like to press her hands against it, feel the strength and power there. Maybe that margarita was getting to her after all.

"Well, I'm thirty-two, so not that far behind you."

He took a long, slow sip of his drink, surveying her over the rim of his glass. "Something tells me it will be some time before Ms. Gwendolyn Marsh makes it over that hill."

Now was he flirting with her? The way he studied her made Gwen think Dan had more than painting on his mind. She imagined removing his shirt and applying a deep massage oil, stroking the musculature there. Heat welled within her, sending electric currents from her fingertips to her toes. Gwen reminded herself to stay on track. Maybe the margarita was getting to him as well. Although that seemed difficult to believe, given his sturdy and scrumptious build. Oh dear, there she went again. It was a relief when Dan changed the subject by suggesting dessert. Anything to take her mind off further explorations of that come-hither chest.

"It was a wonderful lunch, but I honestly don't have room for more."

"Not even jalapeño custard pie?" Dan tempted. Gwen had the sense that Dan Holbrook could tempt even the most sensible woman into almost anything.

"Maybe next time," she said, combating a new rush of heat with a long drink of water, which, instead of hitting her lips, splashed in her lap. "Oh dear!" Gwen brought her palms to her cheeks as Dan sprang from his chair.

"Take mine," he said, pressing his cloth napkin to her skirt. Suddenly, his warmth spread through her nether regions. She gasped, and he glanced up, their eyes locking.

"I'll get it, thanks," she stammered as he pulled his napkin aside, and she took to the task with hers, promptly dropping her napkin on the floor. "My goodness."

Dan scooped low to retrieve the soggy rag. He hesitated briefly to study her dangling ankle bracelet, then righted himself slowly, his sky-blue gaze grazing hers.

Dan reddened as he handed Gwen back her napkin. "I'll call the waiter over and ask for more."

"Don't bother," she said sweetly. "I think that's got it."

Gwen couldn't believe what a klutz she'd been. What was it about this man that made her all butterfingered? Okay, the truth was Marian had sometimes accused her of being a teensy bit clumsy, but she'd never been an out-and-out wrecking ball like this. It was probably a combination of things. Her mission for money complicated by Dan's inexcusable hotness. She found herself wishing briefly that his sister Nancy had been here to meet with her instead. A split-second later, she realized that was a lie.

The hard fact was Gwen was attracted to Dan. Seriously attracted. And perhaps he'd given indications that he was the slightest bit interested in her as well. But what was wrong with that? Colleagues could enjoy a simple flirtation, for heaven's sake. Gwen was sure it happened all the time. That certainly didn't mean it had to go anywhere. Gwen hadn't come to Santa Fe to find a man. She'd come to launch her art career and help her sister. Over time, she'd also be helping herself. After a while, she could do less and less of her day job and more of what gave her pleasure and caused her spirit to soar.

"You know," Dan said as coffee arrived for the two of them. "I've gone on at length about my work, and you haven't really talked about yours. Have you been painting long?"

"I did a bit in high school, but then sort of let it go."

"How's that?" he asked.

"When I started applying to colleges, my mom encouraged me to pursue something a bit more practical." She shrugged, resigned. "She may have had a point. I'm not sure what sort of job I might have gotten as an art major. I couldn't imagine teaching something I loved so much and found so personal. I'm afraid it would have taken the passion out of it for me. So I decided to finish in music instead."

"Music?" he asked with surprise. "Are you talented?"

"Not in the least," she said with a laugh. "In fact, do you know that expression?"

Dan grinned. "Those who can, do; those who can't, teach?"

"Precisely. I can't carry a tune in a bucket, and I'm impossibly inept on the keyboard."

Dan leaned forward on his elbows. "Then how…?"

"Oh, I have a great ear for things. I mean, when someone else is doing the playing, I can pluck the mistakes right out. Not that I'm hard on my students. I'm really a very encouraging teacher." And she was too. The children appeared to love her, and their parents praised her abilities. Gwen was just thankful that none of them had borne witness to her botchery of university piano recitals. It was a blessing that she could graduate in teaching without having to prove her own exceptional skill.

Dan gave a delighted chuckle. "What grades do you teach?"

"Elementary during the school year. In the summertime, I take private piano students on, all ages up to adults."

"So you could teach me?" he asked invitingly. Uh-oh, there he went, flirting again. Gwen doubted very seriously that she could teach the dangerously capable Dan Holbrook anything. At thirty-eight, he was bound to have seen a bit of the world and more than his share of women. Gwen reminded herself not to be foolishly flattered by his probably practiced attentions.

"I'm not sure about that. Something tells me you might not be the most cooperative student."

Dan raised his brows in surprise, then released another belly laugh. "You've probably got me there. Nancy tried to teach me 'Chopsticks' once when I was ten, and I never quite got through it."

Gwen couldn't help but soften at his self-effacing honesty. If she wasn't careful, she was going to start liking the man, and that might cloud her judgment in any business dealings. She finished her coffee, realizing lunch was nearly over and they'd not yet talked turkey.

"Some people have more natural talent than others," she said kindly.

"Like you do for painting, for instance," he said, turning the conversation in what Gwen hoped would be the right direction.

"I appreciate you thinking so," she said, feeling her heart warm. "I really enjoy what I do. The thought that it might also bring happiness to someone else is just wonderful."

342

"When did you start painting again?"

"Oh, I did it off and on. Just for me, you know. Could never entirely let it go over the years. Then on my thirtieth birthday, my little sister, Marian, gave me the most beautiful gift, a completely new set of oils and brushes. I'd been getting by with old things, mostly cast-offs from the school art teacher who'd been sympathetic to my cause."

"Marian must know you very well."

"We're super close," Gwen said, feeling the burn in her throat. "The gift was extra special because oils are expensive, and Marian… Well, she…she doesn't have a lot of money."

"So that's when it really started? When you began painting more regularly?"

Gwen nodded, willing away the unpleasant memory of Robert coming in and upending her very first seascape. *"Ridiculous,"* he'd said. *"Where do you think you'll get with that? You sure as hell can't sing. What makes you think you can paint?"*

Gwen blinked, briefly turning away. When she turned back to Dan, she found herself caught up in his sky-blue gaze. The way he looked at her was soothing, as if he had all the time in the world to listen to what she had to say, and like none of it was ridiculous.

"I did start painting more then, yes. It was easier without the resistance."

"Resistance?"

"That doesn't really matter anymore," she said, forcing a smile. "I found a way to move beyond it."

"And the clients at Holbrook and Holstein will be glad. I assure you."

"I'm glad you brought that up so I didn't have to."

343

He looked at her earnestly. "Gwen, I've had a great time at lunch with you, really I have. But I have no illusions about why a beautiful young woman like you would spend time with a washed-up old bachelor like me."

Gwen blushed at the compliment but wasn't about to let herself get derailed by his manly attentions. As long as he'd started the ball rolling, she needed to push it along. "You underestimate yourself, Dan. But it's good to know you've reconsidered underestimating my work."

His gaze filled with admiration. She was being a little saucy, and he apparently liked it. "I spoke with Nancy like I promised. Holbrook and Holstein is prepared to set a fair price for your art. We can't quite go up to four thousand, but if you're willing to agree to three-five, we think we can cut a deal."

The way he'd said that made it almost seem real, as if this was actually going to happen for her. Gwen tried to contain her excitement. "Excellent," she said, giving him what she hoped was a warm, even smile. "I'm open to discussing that."

"Of course, I'm sure you're familiar with how things work," he continued. "Gallery sales are commission based, so whatever price we arrive at is provisional."

The corners of Gwen's mouth took a downturn. The fact was, she didn't know this at all. "I'm sorry. I'm not sure what you're saying."

Dan set his empty coffee cup aside and laced his fingers together in a sincere fashion. "I'm saying the gallery takes a commission. That's how it stays in business. Your work for sale there is basically on consignment."

344

The shock and horror hit her in the stomach like a sucker punch. "Consignment? But nothing in Ms. Holstein's email said anything about—"

His gaze softened, genuinely apologetic. "I'm sorry, Gwen. She probably thought you knew. Most of the artists we deal with are...experienced."

Gwen felt a flash of anger, but she quelled it, realizing nobody had intentionally tried to mislead her. "Are you saying I won't be getting any money now?" she asked, trying to mask the desperation in her voice.

"Now?" he asked, as if he'd never considered the possibility. "You mean, like during your ten-day trip to Santa Fe?

"Gwen, we're dealing with a process, here. We agree on what we think a reasonable buyer might pay in this market. That is the sale price. The two of us sign a contract, and then you ship the canvases. Once they're here, we hang them up for sale. As money comes in, it's funneled directly to you, less the gallery's twenty-percent commission."

Gwen felt her entire world crumbling in on her. Maybe it was her fault, hoping for too much in just one visit. But what if things didn't sell? What if enough money didn't come on time? What if the bank failed to extend its credit?

Gwen thought of Marian and her kids, of lives pulling apart... Of Robert's repeated infidelities... Her art box being tossed into the ocean... Something cut loose inside, and she felt like she might lose it at any second, break down sobbing on this already soppy napkin. She opened her purse and pulled out a tissue.

Dan reached a steadying hand across the table and laid it on hers. "Gwen? Are you all right?"

"Excuse me," she said, dabbing the corner of her eye. "I'll be right back."

Dan sat there for the longest time, wondering what he'd done wrong. Could Gwen truly have thought she'd fly out of here in just over a week with wads of cash lining her pockets? Were her circumstances really that bad? She'd seemed so fragile when she'd rushed out of here, as if she might break apart at any minute. Dan had no idea what sort of situation she was in, but he did know one thing. If he could, he wanted to help.

After what seemed like an eternity, Gwen resurfaced, all fresh-faced with newly applied lipstick and powder. Dan was finally starting to understand why women kept so much nonsense in their purses. It was for emergency situations like this.

"Any better?" he asked with concern.

She gave a sniff and lifted her chin.

"Allergies. Never know when they're going to hit me."

"Glad you're okay."

"Yes," she said, taking her seat. "Just fine, thanks." She noted the credit card receipt on the table. "Oh, you've already paid the bill. I'm sorry. I didn't mean for you to—"

"My pleasure," he said, meaning it. He hadn't had a lunch this interesting with a woman in a decade. Everything he'd learned about Gwen had been fascinating. But what intrigued him most was all that he didn't know. "Gwen," he began, hoping to broach the subject lightly. "I couldn't help but notice you were a little…thrown by our arrangement."

"The consignment, you mean?" she asked proudly. "Oh no, I knew all about it. I suspected that's how things went." It was a brave cover, but Dan saw straight through it. Didn't help her that her chin still trembled slightly.

"That's how it normally goes," he answered. "But there's really no need for us to go getting all bogged down in normalcy, wouldn't you say?"

She knitted her delicately sculpted brow. "I'm sorry? I'm not sure I follow."

A few gold tendrils broke free from their pins and spilled forward. Dan had an idiotic impulse to reach out and sweep them back, chancing a touch of her alabaster skin. He stopped himself just in time, tucking away the bill receipt in his pocket instead. "How soon can you get your canvases out here?"

"To Santa Fe? Why, in just a few days. They're all packaged and ready to ship."

"That settles it, then," he said with a wide, easy grin.

"Settles what? I haven't signed any contract."

"No, but if you will, I have an idea," he said slyly.

"What sort of idea is that?" she whispered, angling forward.

Dan looked straight in her eyes with calm reassurance. "We don't normally operate this fast, but I do have a list of potential buyers I can contact."

Her face lit up like the most stunning sunrise. "Are you saying what I think you are?"

"If fortune smiles on us, we might be able to sell a canvas or two before you leave."

"All five?" she asked with a hopeful glow.

Dan feared he'd done the wrong thing, caused her to think it was a certainty that this would go off. But when she'd gone all weepy on him, it had been impossible for Dan to stop himself. The truth was he had the means to buy all five of Gwen's canvases himself without even making a dent in his money-market account. But that would make the dealings between them personal, and Dan had vowed to keep things on a professional level.

Dan returned her gaze with cautious determination. "Let's not go pushing our luck," he said, sensing he'd gotten in over his head. He envisioned a huge, raw T-bone getting tossed onto a grill. Perspiration built at his brow, and he lifted Gwen's soggy napkin from the table to dab it.

"I need to get back to work," he said, standing and helping Gwen with her chair. "Think you might stop by later to sign the papers? The gallery closes at eight. That would be a good time."

"Eight o'clock it is," she said with a smile that knocked his socks off and held potential to knock other items of clothing off too.

Dan said a polite good-bye, then hustled out of there like a rabbit being hunted by a pack of wild coyotes. He needed to get his head together and figure his way through these next few days. Not that this should be a problem for a take-charge guy like him who knew how and where to draw the line.

Dan knew it was for the best, and really in Gwen's interest, for him to back off from any sort of romantic notions now, while the backing was good. No matter what *Santa Fean* magazine said about Dan being the "Best Billionaire Bachelor Catch in the West," privately he knew his shortcomings would give even the most understanding woman pause. Dan had been down that dusty trail once and was determined never to go there again. Didn't matter what sort of attractive filly came out of the gate. The fact of the matter was Dan wasn't riding.

Chapter Three

Gwen left the restaurant by exiting onto the main plaza, an oasis of green in the earth-toned adobe town. Huge shade trees lined its crisscrossing sidewalks, dotted with wrought-iron benches and lampposts. Bordered by the nation's oldest public building, the Palace of Governors, on one side and an array of upscale shops on the others, it was the city's central gathering spot and playground, complete with a bandstand in which an impromptu flautist played. Gwen strode past a snow-cone vendor and a couple of quesadilla carts on her way to explore the smattering of handmade goods the locals had spread on the ground atop woven blankets. She surveyed the assorted silver jewelry, accented with turquoise, and small trinkets for sale with an appreciative eye, and made complimentary small talk with the Native American and Mexican peoples proudly showcasing their wares.

A warm breeze blew as the sun angled high, bathing Santa Fe in its rosy glow, the impressive Sangre de Cristo Mountains just visible in the distance, their highest peaks capped with snow, even in summertime. Gwen made her way up a side street to visit Saint Francis Cathedral, a stunning Romanesque Revival structure challenging the surrounding adobe architecture with its sweeping arches and brightly hued stained-glass windows.

Perspiration dampened her hairline as she climbed the steps to the building's entrance. It was warmer in the sunlight, the scarcely filtered ultraviolet rays bearing down on her, causing her feet and hands to swell. At once, the thin gold band on her left ring finger felt too tight. She twisted it slightly as she continued her ascent toward the cathedral's front door. Gwen hadn't prayed for anything in a long time. In fact, she hadn't been to church since Robert left. Maybe she should have. Thinking it over, she understood she had much to be thankful for. Not least among her blessings was her opportunity to come here.

Gwen passed through the enormous wooden door, her senses immediately engulfed by burning incense. Though she wasn't Catholic, she didn't believe God would mind if she took a spot on a pew for a few moments to mull through her life. What an event it had been. There'd been so much to it she'd never seen coming. When she met Robert in college, he'd appeared so promising. He was ambitious and fun and seemed poised to carve out a good life for himself and any lady lucky enough to join him. When he'd asked Gwen to marry him just before graduation, she'd been over the moon. He had a good job offer in Wilmington, and they could settle in the nearby town where Gwen had grown up and her family still lived. It had all seemed so idyllic at first.

Gwen glanced down at the completely ineffectual wedding ring as her hand rested in her lap. It hadn't taken long for Robert to find someone he thought more intelligent and interesting than her. She bored him to tears with her tales of kids in school and had no real talents as far as he could gather. The people he worked with were insightful, intuitive, interesting… Maybe if Gwen looked more at the papers or followed the news, she'd be interesting too, though he kind of doubted it.

Gwen heaved a sigh, knowing she couldn't continue to beat herself up over Robert's shortcomings. When she was thinking clearly, as Marian often encouraged her to do, she understood that her marriage falling apart had more to do with him than her. Or perhaps it was due to them both and the fact that, once they'd escaped from the cocoonlike sanctuary of the university, neither of them truly fit together. Gwen wondered sadly if she was destined to fit together with any man. Perhaps that wasn't in the cards for her, and maybe that was okay. If her art took off and she built herself a career, something that she adored and was really proud of, that might be enough.

She considered her meeting this evening with Dan, realizing she'd been acting like a silly schoolgirl. It wasn't his fault she hadn't dated since her divorce, so why should she hold him accountable for her surging hormones? Any nice-looking man who'd paid her attention would likely have made her feel the same. As an elementary schoolteacher, she simply hadn't had much opportunity for that. All the men she met were either married or formerly married and quickly reattached. It seemed the decent ones didn't last long on the market. From what she'd gathered from her quick perusals of Internet dating sites, the perpetual bachelors all seemed to have something wrong with them. Then again, Dan appeared normal. Exceedingly normal, healthy, and sexually enticing as well. So why hadn't a tamale-hot catch like him been snapped up already?

Gwen decided to head back to the inn to cool off for a few hours before her gallery appointment. This praying business didn't seem to be going too well. She thought she'd probably done it wrong. It had been such a while, she couldn't tell. In any case, she was grateful to Dan for granting her this chance. At the heart of it, Gwen understood that was all this really was, a chance to sell some of her art to a very fine place and hopefully help turn her sister's life around. That was worth a few amens, no doubt. She dipped her head, offering them quickly, and bowed out of the cathedral before anyone could stop her and ask her for money. That was one part of going to church she hadn't forgotten. There was a lady near the door collecting donations for the restoration fund. Gwen slipped silently past her and out into the sunshine before the woman could hold up a brochure. Maybe once Gwen was rich and famous she'd feel a bit more philanthropic. At the moment, she scarcely had cash for dinner. She'd have to hurry to catch the wine-and-cheese hour before the other guests cleaned out the Havarti.

Dan paced the redwood-pine floors, double-checking the time on his BlackBerry. The afternoon couldn't have dragged out more if he'd planned it. It all seemed to go in slow motion, as if he were deep-sea diving, arms and legs battling against ocean pressure.

The occasional browsers stopped by, and there was the shipment to get out to Los Angeles, but Nancy's assistant Megan had come in to see to that. She wore a nose piercing and a puckish haircut that added to her image of a small sprite sprinting around the gallery. Dan had never seen a twenty-three-year-old with so much energy. She was very astute though, her nimble mind eager to acquire anything and everything about gallery running. She hoped to manage a place of her own one day and apparently did some sort of printmaking on the side.

"That's it, then," Megan said, peering up at him through heavily mascaraed eyes. "Think that I might sneak out early? I've got a date for drinks at Nines." Nines was the hipster bar on an adobe rooftop overlooking the mountains.

"Don't let me hold you back," Dan said.

"Are you all right?" Megan asked. "You've seemed a little...off this afternoon. Maybe you should head out early too."

Dan was more than a little off; he was distractingly discombobulated. He'd spent over three hours poring through Nancy's customary client list, trying to discern those who might be interested in Gwen's work. If he'd had his head on straight, the task might have taken him forty-five minutes. Instead, he'd caught himself daydreaming at every turn, reliving his lively lunch with Ms. Gwendolyn Marsh. Just as in the gallery the day before, he'd been sucked in by the feminine scent of her. Didn't help one iota that she obviously perfumed her legs, legs that were attached to one knock-out of a womanly body, teamed with a damnably adorable and kissable, he couldn't help but reason, face. And, when her eyes sparked with delight at the thought that he might help her, could actually sell her canvases in this absurd ten-day timeframe, Dan's heart had done an unexpected flip-flop.

"I'm fine," he lied to Megan. "Why don't you go on ahead? I've got an artist stopping by at closing. I'll lock up."

Megan grabbed her colorful straw bag that looked large enough to hold a weekend wardrobe and pranced out the door.

Dan strode to the desk and withdrew Gwen's contract from the nearby filing cabinet. He glanced through the folder for maybe the tenth time today, ensuring everything was in order. The paperwork was all lined up. Now all Dan had to do was steel his heart. He was getting far too carried away with this. Just because Gwen looked like an angel and spoke in a sweet Southern twang that was sexy as sin, that didn't mean he'd have to give in to her. He was a rational man, by all accounts, savvy at business dealings and skilled at keeping his emotions in check.

Okay, he'd made that one mistake. But it wasn't like it was going to come back to haunt him. It had been more than a month now, and he'd heard nothing further about it. It had been a harsh lesson in letting sleeping dogs lie. Once you make a pact to move on, there should be no looking back. Looking ahead wasn't sounding so safe at the moment either. Gwen was scheduled to be in town only ten days. She had her life back East to lead, and Dan had his own ghosts to contend with here. He shook off a gloomy feel, determined to make the best of their meeting. Dan was sensible enough to know he could assist a damsel in distress without falling into bed with her. And just to make certain he hadn't forgotten, the fates had pressed a branding iron to his chest a mere six weeks ago to drive that message home.

Gwen tugged at the zipper of her skirt, sliding it up her ample hip. She'd put on a few pounds since her divorce but still looked okay, she supposed. She'd never been accused of being overly thin. Marian was the slight one in the family, while Gwen fought the perpetual battle of the booty. Breasts, hips, and thighs had a will of their own. No matter how she tried, they relished maintaining their prefab form. After a while, Gwen had just given up and decided to enjoy life. As long as she operated within reason, didn't diet or exercise too much, she could stay within the same five-pound range that she'd grown accustomed to and certain men seemed to appreciate.

Gwen flushed at the memory of Dan's sky-blue gaze. At first she'd thought he'd just been flattering her, trying to put a gallery contact at ease. But the more she pondered it, the less she thought so. As they'd sat there discussing canvas pricing, his heated perusal had washed all over her like the clearest Caribbean wave. Gwen imagined the two of them on a distant beach, Dan bare-chested in the sun. He'd tell her once more how beautiful she was, and, half-naked in her tummy-control swimsuit, she'd feel forced to believe it. He'd take her by the waist then, pull her soft body to his, taut stomach muscles tensing as he wrapped his arms around her... Gwen heard the surf crash, water swirling furiously at their feet, as he brought his glorious mouth to hers.

Suddenly, she realized she'd stalled in applying her lipstick and was standing there all puckered up like a ridiculous guppy. "That's the price I pay for that second Shiraz," she scolded herself, vowing to make coffee. She was glad the suite's miniature kitchen supplied what she needed for that. Now where was the sugar cube she could find to quell her outlandish fantasies?

Gwen had considered putting on a flirty dress for her meeting with Dan tonight but now worried that might send the wrong message. She wasn't seeing him for any sort of social reasons, she reminded herself. They were convening to sign a contract, for heaven's sake. Gwen lifted her perfume bottle and spritzed her neck, wrists, and the backs of her knees with its fine aroma.

Gwen's belly warmed as she recalled how Dan had hesitated by her foot just an instant too long in retrieving her dropped napkin. If he'd touched her then, even by accidentally brushing her calf, she would have fainted. They would have had to call in the rescue squad to scoop her limp form off the New Mexican tile. It didn't take an expert to see the super-studly Dan Holbrook held more masculinity in one pinkie than the pallid and self-possessed Robert contained from head to toe.

Coffee, Gwen reminded herself, noting by the clock on the nightstand it was almost time. The sooner she got this over and done with, the better. If she could negotiate the paperwork without chancing to shake Dan's hand, all the better. Even after the coffee, Gwen didn't trust herself to touch him. This was what Marian called an unwelcome consequence of celibacy.

Gwen adjusted her bra, shifting her bosom into its proper place, then, quite as an afterthought, she was sure, gave her cleavage the tiniest little burst of Midnight Jasmine perfume.

Dan looked up as the door chime sounded. There she stood, looking as gorgeous as a desert sunset, the colors of her sexy, short dress swirling about her in mauve, gold, and russet browns. "Are you ready for me?" she asked, dark eyes sparkling with anticipation.

Dan thought he was, in fact had prepared for her all afternoon, but now he felt as awkward and uncertain as a teenager. "Of course," he said, working to get the words out in a businesslike manner. "Come on in." Her womanly scent overtook him as his eyes trailed from her ankles to her cleavage to her faintly colored cheekbones. "Please, have a seat." He indicated a spot, nearly missing his own chair. Dan scooted onto it as she pulled hers in toward the desk just a tad too close. The sweet angles of her knees pressed into his ever so slightly.

A crimson blush warmed her shoulders and swept up her delicate throat. "Oh! Oh my goodness. I'm so sorry!" she cried, backing up.

"No worries! Really," he protested.

Gwen sat up a little straighter in her chair and crossed her legs as Dan opened the file in front of him. He passed her the paperwork with an appreciative gaze.

"You look lovely tonight," he said, unable to stop himself.

Gwen met his eyes, her cheeks still aglow. "Thank you. You look...really super too."

Dan reined himself in, applying his best businesslike tone. "I believe everything's in order there," he said as she fanned through the pages. "If you'd like to look it over, I can answer any questions."

The sun dipped low outside, casting a tangerine hue throughout the wide-open spaces of the gallery as Gwen sorted through the agreement. After a few moments of studied concentration, she addressed Dan with a relieved smile. "It all seems straightforward." She'd worried it might be complicated, filled with legalese and fine-print sections. On the contrary, it basically laid out what they had discussed at lunch, with a few boilerplate clauses she supposed were included in most contracts of this kind. "Where do I sign?"

Dan indicated the line, then added his own signature to the page.

357

"Have you come up with any contacts? I mean, people who might buy my art?"

Dan smiled indulgently. "Don't you think we ought to get it here first?"

"Right! I'll have Marian send it out tomorrow. Like I said, it's all boxed and ready to go. All she has to do is call for shipping."

Dan wrote some numbers on a small notepad on the desk. "This is our account number for Southwest Express. Have your sister call this phone number and bill it to us. She can let them know where and when to pick up the packages."

"Well, thanks, that's very gracious. That will help a lot." Gwen couldn't let him know that her wallet was paper-thin or that her sister was destitute.

"I've actually already sent out a couple of emails, feelers, if you will, to gallery contacts who might have an interest in an East Coast ocean scene or two."

Gwen felt her face warm with excitement. "That's wonderful!" She fought an urge to race around the desk and hug him.

"As soon as the pieces arrive," he continued, "I'll start making follow-up calls. I'm hoping to have some serious buyers in looking by the end of the week. Assuming the shipment goes as planned."

Gwen sprang from her seat and lunged for his hand. "I don't know how to thank you," she said, taking his hand in hers and holding it firmly.

His gaze wrapped around her, trapping her in his heat. "It's my pleasure, really," he said, exerting delicate pressure against her palm. Little tingles raced up Gwen's arm, and instantly she knew she'd made a mistake. She'd told herself to keep her distance. Now, all she wanted to do was get closer still. Gwen released his grip, attempting to steady herself on wobbly knees. If merely shaking hands had this much effect, she'd hate to see the pool of putty she'd be in if he'd dared to kiss her.

"Have you eaten anything since lunch?" he asked with concern.

Gwen pulled herself together, realizing she must have suddenly paled. "I had some wine and cheese back at the inn."

"Havarti?" he asked, with uncanny insight.

"How did you...?"

He repressed a grin, pointing to the back of her head. Gwen ran panicked fingers through her hair, finding a nice little chunk of cheese caught up in her curls.

She stared at him, mortified. "I'm so embarrassed," she began.

"Don't be," he offered kindly. "I get Camembert in mine all the time."

She scanned his face for the hint of a smile but couldn't detect one beneath his deadpan.

"This time, I know you're teasing," she said, and the moment between them lightened.

Small lines tugged at the corners of his mouth as blue eyes crinkled. "Something tells me you're getting to know me too well." His gaze held a hint of longing mixed with caution. "Wine and cheese isn't much of a dinner. I know a place with great steaks, if you'd like to join me?"

Gwen knew she was wrong to say yes. Everything inside her screamed *caution, slippery roads ahead*. But all Gwen wanted to do was get in that spectacular sports car and drive.

"I'd love to," she said, accepting his invitation.

Dan led them down a side street to an elegant outdoor restaurant set a few blocks from the plaza. The shaded pathway to its entrance bypassed the abutting Loretto Chapel, a notable nineteenth-century structure in Gothic Revival style, complete with buttresses and spires.

"Have you been in there?" Dan asked as they strolled by the wind art adorning the chapel's lawn.

Gwen admired the huge hands of the whimsical brass structures cupping and turning in the breeze as the sun sank low. "Not yet."

Her view panned to a fanciful wood carving of a man guarding the chapel door.

"Saint Joseph," Dan said, indicating the statue. "I'll tell you the story over dinner. You do believe in miracles?" He was smiling at her in a playful way.

A shiver shimmied down Gwen's spine, as she thought it was nothing short of miraculous that she was here, right now, with him. Dan Holbrook was not just a feast for the eyes, he was funny and kind and apparently enjoying her company. Plus, he made her feel beautiful. Not just because he'd said it. It was in the way he looked at her, all the time.

"I'll keep an open mind," she said, smiling back at him.

Dan shoved his hand in his pocket to prevent himself from reaching out and taking hers. In some ways, it would have seemed natural as he led her toward the maître d. In others, it was completely absurd! Dan heaved a sigh, grateful good sense had prevailed.

"Are you all right?" she asked, chocolate-brown eyes imploring.

"Just taking in the evening," he said, thankful there was no wait for a table.

He ordered them filet mignon with a mushroom, red pepper, and sherry reduction, Caesar salads to start, and a choice bottle of Chilean red wine. Dan didn't want to mess this up. Gwen's dinner had to be perfect. He'd slipped the maître d an unseen tip to ensure it. He'd also told Gwen upfront that the meal was on him. He'd seen the way her brow had knitted slightly as she'd surveyed the menu prices. Dan wasn't sure what sort of money trouble she was in, but he could bet her budget didn't include places like this one.

"The service is fabulous here," Gwen said as her water glass magically refilled.

Dan had the impression Gwen wasn't used to men treating her right. He was glad to be able to change that, to show her that not all men were schmucks, maybe just the ones she'd previously run into. "Wait until you taste the food."

She smiled sweetly over the rim of her wineglass. "This carménère is delicious. I'm so glad I got to try it."

"Should go well with the steak," Dan said, hoping he'd scored a point. For the life of him, he wanted to impress this woman. She looked prettier than ever, sitting there relaxed in the candle's glow. He compared her now to how she'd appeared yesterday afternoon in the gallery, anxiously combative, like if he didn't see things her way, there'd be hell to pay. He probably liked this Gwen better. Though the truth of the matter was Dan didn't really mind

361

the other one much at all. He could see a man getting used to a balanced measure of them both.

Dan took a sip of wine, knowing he was letting his emotions get the best of him. That was a dangerous mountain to climb when he understood what was on the other side: a clean downhill slide where his heart would take a tumble. Elena had been quite detailed in enumerating his faults.

A crescent moon rose as a smattering of stars poured onto the canvas of the night sky above them. Their salads arrived, artfully served and in a timely fashion.

"So, are you going to tell me the story?" she asked eagerly.

Dan was happy for the chance to take his mind off his gloomy thoughts. "Ah yes, the story of Loretto Chapel," he said, setting down his glass. He leaned forward on his elbows and lowered his voice. "And its mysterious spiral staircase."

"Staircase?" she asked with surprise.

"Legend has it the staircase in Loretto Chapel arrived as a miracle. Some to this day may dispute it, but many others do not."

"Go on," she pressed, intrigued.

"Rumor holds that when the chapel was completed in the eighteen hundreds, the dear nuns who lived there noted there was no staircase to get them to the choir loft on the upper level."

"Oh my!"

"So they prayed for nine days for a miracle. On the tenth day, an unknown carpenter appeared and offered to complete the task. He built the freestanding staircase all by himself without using glue, nails, or any central support.

Then, as soon as he was done, the stranger disappeared just as mysteriously as he'd arrived, without ever having identified himself or demanding any payment. The good sisters of Loretto naturally took this as a miracle, and the man to have been Saint Joseph himself. The proof I believe lies in the number of steps of the freestanding structure, made of a wood not even found in this region."

"Well?" she asked, her eyes twinkling.

"Thirty-three. The age of Jesus Christ."

Gwen leaned back in her chair with a delighted laugh. "That's wonderful! What a fantastic story."

"It's not a story," he said with mock defensiveness. "It's a miracle." The corners of his mouth twitched slightly, and Gwen could tell he was repressing a smile. She was finally starting to read him, and for a girl who didn't like to read, that said a lot.

Gwen cocked an eyebrow and shot him an impish smile. "Do you believe in miracles, Dan?"

He captured her with his gaze, stilling her heart for a fraction of a second. "Let's just say I believe most things in life can be rationally explained."

"Most things don't mean all," she bantered lightly.

He raised his glass to hers as their salad plates were cleared and the entrées arrived. "You've got me there." Everything smelled delicious. Gwen couldn't wait to dig in. She hadn't realized how hungry she'd gotten subsisting on complimentary inn food these past few days.

"How's your filet?" he asked as she took a heavenly bite that literally melted in her mouth. "Cooked all right?"

He was incredibly handsome in the soft light, flames from the outdoor fire caressing the solid lines of his face.

"Perfect. Everything's just perfect. I couldn't have had a better night."

"I'm glad," he said with a grin. "That just leaves tomorrow."

"What do you mean?"

"You've got a bit of time to kill while the shipment comes in. Got any plans?"

"I thought I'd take in an art museum or two."

"That sounds great. I've been considering taking the day off myself."

Gwen set down her fork. "Are you…asking me on a date?"

"You mean unlike this one," he deadpanned.

She gasped with surprise. "This was a date?"

"It could be if you wanted it to."

Gwen's heart went fluttering in all sorts of wild directions. Why on earth was he doing this? Surely there was no sense in it. She'd be gone by the week's end. "I'm not so sure that's a good idea."

"Which one?"

"This a date… Tomorrow. I…I don't know." And she didn't, she really didn't. She was feeling all jumbled up inside, like she'd desperately wanted something and now didn't know what to do once she'd gotten it.

"How about if we just call it an appointment, then? An arrangement between associates to go and see some art. Besides," he added temptingly, "I know who serves the best chile rellenos in town."

It was patently unfair of him to play the food card. Gwen absolutely adored chile rellenos, almost as much as she was starting to adore this man. "It's a deal," she said, smiling broadly.

364

Dan walked Gwen back to the inn, night sounds singing around them. He'd really jumped in headlong with this one, but Dan couldn't completely blame himself. With her lovely looks and warm and charming personality, Gwen had led him right to it. He'd been having such a good time with her at dinner, he couldn't bear having the evening end. The only remedy for that was to suggest seeing her tomorrow. He didn't have much going on at the gallery, and what was left to do Megan could take care of.

Dan stole a glimpse of Gwen strolling beside him in the moonlight and wished for a moment that things weren't transitory. But they were, and he'd need to remain aware of that. Just because they'd planned to spend the day together didn't mean they'd have to become any more involved than they already were. He liked Gwen, dammit. She was sensitive and sweet, and he felt good when he was around her. Dan hadn't felt this good about himself in a very long while. He decided it was time.

They got to the exterior patio door of Gwen's private suite, and she opened her purse to withdraw the key, her cheeks still aflame.

"I had a really great time tonight," she said, beaming up at him and feeling very much as if it had been a date.

"Me too," he said, stepping a fraction of an inch closer. Sea-blue eyes washed over her, threatening to pull her under. And boy, did she want to get swept away. "I'm glad you agreed to see me tomorrow, even if it's just an arrangement."

Gwen sensed Dan could rearrange her heart every which way, if she wasn't careful. "I'm glad I'm seeing you too," she said, feeling the warmth in her cheeks.

"Ten o'clock work for you?" he asked, his tone growing gravelly.

"Uh-huh," she uttered, mesmerized by his gaze.

He moved nearer now, his mouth just inches away. "I'll be damned if I don't want to kiss you," he said, his voice a husky rasp.

And she'd be damned if she didn't want him to. "Dan…" she said, tilting up her chin and closing her eyes.

"But I won't," he said, snapping her back to attention, eyes open. "Not now. Not here. Not like this…"

She started to speak as he brought his fingers to her lips. "If ever I've seen a woman who deserves to be kissed well, it's you. But the timing has got to be right. You have to be sure." He cast a cursory glance at her wedding band and backed away. "I need to be sure. Something tells me we've both gone down a path neither of us wants to travel again."

Gwen's heart sank as her face burned hot. He was right, and she knew it. Neither of them could risk foolishly giving themselves away. It was only a kiss, but a kiss was often the beginning. She was old enough to know that, and Dan clearly was too.

Gwen couldn't guess who'd broken Dan's heart, but he'd obviously been hurt just as much as she had.

"Good night, Gwen," he said, shadows haunting his face.

She watched him turn and walk away, loneliness settling inside her like a large, heavy weight Gwen feared she'd never shake.

366

She let herself into her empty room and cried softly in the darkness, moonlight weeping in through slanted blinds. If only she'd found a man like Dan ten years ago, maybe neither of them would have had to live through these vestiges of pain. But the past was long ago and should be forgotten, Gwen thought, twisting the ring on her finger.

Perhaps meeting Dan now was a good thing, the right thing for them both. Maybe they were meant to be stepping stones, each of them strategically placed to help the other on to a better life. They could be friends, confidants even, during her short stay in Santa Fe. Maybe they'd each give the other someone to lean on, somebody who really understood, for the first time in a long time. That didn't mean they'd have to start falling in love.

Gwen sucked in a breath, praying it wasn't already too late. By the way her heart hammered against her chest, she wasn't sure.

****

End of excerpt from *Santa Fe Fortune.*

Ginny Baird thanks you for reading her work and hopes to hear from you soon.